JOCK WANTED

A ROOKIE REBELS NOVEL

KATE MEADER

1

———

Hale Fitzpatrick had a problem.

This wasn't unusual—as the newly-minted general manager of the Chicago Rebels, problems were to be expected. He'd been brought on to "manage" and part of that was fixing pesky issues as they arose. A team of people existed to help him with this. The resources of a multi-million dollar sports franchise were at his disposal. Plus Hale, or Fitz as he was generally known to friends and enemies alike, could usually fix six impossible problems before he'd drunk his second cup of morning coffee.

So why was today's problem such a pain in his ass?

He looked up from the video detailing this problem into the bloodshot eyes of the man responsible for it. Fitz had dealt with skater punks like Dex O'Malley before. A player at the last franchise Fitz managed had crashed into a police car while driving drunk and Fitz got him off with a suspended sentence and a 90-day stint in rehab. Six months later, that player lifted the Stanley Cup.

This new problem should be well within Fitz's skillset. Dex, a newer forward with the Rebels, currently on injured reserve, had been a naughty boy, and naughty boys were Fitz's specialty.

But the naughty boy had to want to cooperate.

"I'm not dating that." Reinforcing his bad boy/annoying little punk attitude, Dex slumped in his seat, crossed his arms, and screwed up his mouth. "I date models, man. Women with legs for miles and amazing bodies. You want me to go against my nature? No one will believe that."

Fitz slid a look at Sophie, the Rebels newly-promoted PR manager. She was young, possibly a little too young for this job, but she looked unperturbed, which was good because at least one of them should be less inclined to punch a team asset in the mouth.

In the two months since he'd been acquired from Nashville, Dex had spent less time rehabbing his shoulder and more time hitting clubs and making headlines. Hockey wasn't usually the kind of sport that tickled the tabloids, but Dex was making sure everyone knew he was the NHL poster boy for bad behavior. And as most of his on-camera shenanigans were sexual—never a good look in public and especially not in this millennium—the Rebels management had decided to take action. The team was in the final weeks of the regular season, the time to make a push to the play-offs. Dex O'Malley needed to focus.

Forcing him to go without sex for a couple of months was probably too much to expect. So PR had hatched a plan: public Dex would be seen with a more suitable partner and private Dex could do whatever he wanted as long as it wasn't caught on camera.

Sophie had a stable of women on tap—actresses, Fitz assumed—who could be hired for this sort of thing. She had chosen women with wholesome looks who wouldn't have looked out of place on an Amish farm and had offered them to Dex like a restaurant menu.

A chain establishment, where the menus had pictures of plastic versions of the food.

Fitz picked up one of the photos, an apple-cheeked blonde who looked like she regularly skied cross-country to her voluntary gig at the puppy shelter. Probably in Wisconsin. "So she doesn't look like the clubbing type. Which is rather the point."

Sophie took up the thread. "We need someone who will temper some of your, uh, less desirable traits."

Dex sniffed. "I don't see what the big deal is about that last batch of photos from TMZ. You can barely see her pu—"

Fitz held up a hand. "You can see enough. They put a blob over it."

"That blob is there to make it seem like she wasn't wearing panties." Dex sounded almost disillusioned at the lengths an online tabloid would go to get clicks. "She was wearing, like flesh color ones. That rag makes its money on pretending there's shit to see here."

"Sure. But the video is a bit more problematic, isn't it? You're having sex with two women in public."

"It was the VIP part of the club, man! It's supposed to be private. No phones allowed."

"Surprise, surprise, someone broke the phone rule and filmed you getting your rocks off. And more."

"Well, yeah, it's a good thing they showed more. Otherwise I'd have come off as, I dunno, ungenerous or something." He raised his gaze to Sophie, adding a devilish grin. "And I'm not, as you can see *and* hear. That redhead was screaming when my tongue—"

"We all saw and heard," Fitz bit out. "No need to sell your skills here."

Sophie pressed her lips tightly, barely fighting a smile. The last thing Fitz needed was for Dex's charms to start working on the front office staff. One targeted look from Fitz, and she wilted under his scrutiny.

"What it comes down to is this: you will be staying away from clubs and will be attending a schedule of events that we approve. As no one will believe you can actually go for a week without getting busy, we will introduce you to a nice, sweet woman who will keep your public profile on the straight and narrow." Dex opened his mouth but Fitz raised a hand. "Details forthcoming. As you're still on IR for the foreseeable future, your movements are restricted to the physio, the practice rink, and home. Now, get going. You're late for morning skate."

A mutinous-looking O'Malley left Fitz's office grumbling under his breath. Fitz didn't care. He'd promised the team owner, Harper Chase, that he'd take care of this. That he was the man for the job.

Fitz had to get this situation under control so he could return to the item on the top of his to-do list: poaching Bastian Durand from Chicago's other hockey franchise, the Hawks.

Left alone with Sophie, he took another hard look at the gallery of goodness, each so wholesome his teeth hurt. "He's got a point. No one would believe he'd date anyone with a modicum of class. Any chance we could hire a woman who's a little more O'Malley's speed?"

Sophie grinned. "He's kind of charming in a trashy kind of way."

"Do not be taken in. We need to find someone we can control, who will respect the NDA, and can keep his attention until we make the playoffs. By then, if he's made an impact, the other players will keep him in line. Peer pressure is a wonderful thing, but right now, he's too new to be susceptible to that."

Fitz strummed the desk with his fingers. This shouldn't be so hard.

Three days later ...

"Oh, God, there's a new shot of Dex."

Tara Becker looked up from her macchiato to cast a quick glance at the phone screen of her friend, Mia Wallace.

"Yeah, saw it this morning." That saucy devil had been caught with his hand in the cookie jar again, where "cookie jar" meant patting the ass of his latest date, a wide-eyed blonde who wouldn't have looked out of place in the front pew of a church on Sunday. "Some idiot thought 'let's fix Dex up with his complete opposite.'"

"Like some sweet young innocent. An elementary school teacher type or a—"

"A veterinary assistant."

Mia nodded enthusiastically. "Right, some chick who looks after puppies or kids. That's what the PR people think would work."

"What do they know?" Tara spent a lot of time with the Rebels wives and girlfriends, who were the best focus group possible. None of them believed this latest pairing for a hot second. "Bet he sabotaged it, the handsy mutt."

Mia murmured sagely, "He's too hard-headed."

"And we're talking both heads. That boy has a lot of

energy." Tara tapped a nail on the table. "Probably actresses, right?"

"That's what Iz said." Isobel Chase, team co-owner and skating coach, was married to Mia's brother Vadim Petrov, the Rebels captain. "It's not like PR can trawl actual vets' offices and puppy shelters looking for the perfect fake girlfriend for a pro-athlete with an overabundance of sexual energy."

Tara chuckled. "They could start in coffee shops. I'm right here!"

Mia laughed with her, then turned serious. "That's not actually a bad idea. He needs someone he can't treat as a doormat, who knows the culture. But ..."

"But ..."

Her friend looked thoughtful. "I'm just not sure Dex would be a good option because what if you fell for him?"

Tara had made no secret of her desire to land a player. She had good reasons, but she wasn't sure this was the way to go about it. "Not likely, he's so immature. But I could totally help him work off some of that energy!"

"I bet he's a handful."

"At least a two-hander, which I can tell from my careful frame-by-frame examination of that video."

"Tara!" Mia snorted and devolved into a fit of giggles. Tara loved that funny little sound her friend made when she laughed, a kind of whispering wheeze. It was so damn wholesome, kind of like Mia herself.

People thought it strange they were close. After all, Mia was now engaged, as of six whole days, to Cal Foreman, Tara's ex. In the eyes of the world, Tara was hovering like an emotional vulture, waiting for a fissure in the relationship, one she could widen and use to her advantage.

Not her agenda at all.

Tara just liked Mia. Since they had met in this very coffee shop eight months ago—though they'd met unofficially during an unfortunate bouquet-catching incident at Levi Hunt's wedding a few days before that—Tara and Mia had been inseparable, veering on bestie territory. So Tara didn't tell her everything and Mia kept some of the juicier details about her relationship with Cal close to her chest out of misplaced delicacy for Tara's feelings. But they were tight in all the ways that mattered.

After the laughter died down, Tara asked, "So what do the players think of Dex's wandering dick? Has Cal said anything? Or your brother?"

Mia sighed. "Cal's not interested in playing mentor, but Vad tried talking to him."

"Well, the Czar of Pleasure used to rule the nightclubs back in the day. If anyone could understand Dex's attraction to the VIP lounges, it's Vadim Petrov. No offense to your brother, babe."

Mia held up a hand. "None taken. Vad was indeed Manwhore Prime in his misspent youth, but Dex just waved him off when he tried to offer advice. Might have even called him 'old man,' so now my brother has washed his hands of it."

"Tip of the yikesberg!" Tara sat back in her chair and folded her arms. "If it's at the point where the captain is out … Makes you wonder what this new GM is even doing to fix it. Wouldn't have happened on Dante Moretti's watch, that's for sure."

A shadow fell across her sight line, and she looked up. Damn.

Hale Fitzpatrick, the Rebels' new-ish general manager loomed over her. Because of course he was here.

He had a large cup in his hand and Tara could just make

out the code for Americano on the label, which meant he had been waiting on the other side of the bar—out of view, the big sneak—and probably overheard everything.

This had to be at least the third time she'd been caught flapping her gums about him behind his back.

"Hey, Fitz," Mia said cheerfully, smoothing over the awkward pause. "Can't get a decent cup of joe at the compound?"

"Something like that. I hear congratulations are in order. Gold *and* diamonds."

She held up her left hand, flashing the sparkly gem given to her by Cal in Beijing, the day she won Olympic gold with Team USA. "I don't wear the medal as it clashes."

His lips curled ever-so-slightly before returning to the grim seal of before as he turned his gaze on Tara. Gone was the easy manner, in its place a harder, disapproving edge.

A native of Georgia and a former hockey player with a couple of decent runs to the Finals a decade and a half ago, he had taken over as manager at the beginning of the year when Dante Moretti retired to become a stay-at-home dad. Six weeks in and the pressures were already evident.

Or maybe he always looked like Tara was stepping on his last nerve.

Not conventionally handsome, the new GM wore the guise of a street fighter, inhabiting a face with character and experience. A couple of small scars didn't even manage to mar it, just made him look more interesting. His was the kind of face you could explore forever.

His hair was too long, though, and hued a mahogany that should have been boring but wasn't. Natural copper streaks gave it a pop it didn't deserve and made his blue eyes burn a distinct shade of cobalt. As if he needed any more assistance to attract women, with that square jaw, strong brow, and aquiline nose.

Not Tara, however. His charisma and rough-hewn good looks pinged her radar from an objective standpoint, but that was it. He was older than her usual demo, for a start. She'd made a few comments about his age before, purely to earn a quick laugh from her girlfriends, and he'd overheard and called her on it. She'd felt foolish, but then that wasn't unusual. In company, she was often the too-loud, too-brash, too-shallow one. People enjoyed that about her—Tara with her goofy outbursts and silly ways.

But with Hale Fitzpatrick staring at her now, she felt more than foolish.

She felt judged.

"Well, I'll leave you to it," he finally said after an age of withering-on-the-vine scrutiny. "Have a good afternoon."

Tara watched him walk away, that confident swagger, those broad shoulders. Mr. Stealth Attack himself.

"Do you think he heard us talking about Dex?"

Mia shrugged. "Probably. Doesn't hurt for him to get another opinion."

"I always feel like a ..."

"Like a what?"

"An idiot around him. He's one of those uber confident guys who looks at you like you're a bug in a glass."

Mia brushed it off. "Don't let him intimidate you, but maybe in the future, attach a mirror to the back of your head so you know where he is at all times!"

2

———

Located deep in the Chicago suburbs, Misty Pines may as well have been Outer Mongolia as far as Tara was concerned. She had tried to find a home for Chloe in the city, but residential places for adults like her were so hard to come by, and now that her sister had settled, it would be madness to make her move.

Despite the fact it sounded like a porn star's name, Misty Pines was a lovely place with gorgeous grounds, great facilities, and a highly trained staff that could meet all of Chloe's needs.

Tara had tried to take care of Chloe herself, but her sister's profound intellectual disability was just one of her myriad issues. She also had severe motor skill deficits and respiratory problems that required constant attention. Living with Tara, Chloe was basically shut in with no rehabilitation or efforts to bring her out of her shell. She needed professional help.

And that help cost money. Tara had spent all her savings on Chloe's care over the last two years. Before that, the home in St. Louis wasn't good enough—staff barely qualified, no water therapy, like something out of *American Horror Story*. She needed a better residential facility and while a grant helped with the fees, it still cost a pretty penny.

Tara pulled into the graveled lot and checked her make-up. There was a cute doctor on staff who liked to make eyes at her when she visited. If it could get Chloe a little extra attention, Tara would flirt and bat and simper.

"Hi, Rosa!" Tara waved at the reception nurse and kept walking even though Rosa called out her name. Tara knew why, and she'd rather spend a few moments with her sister before she had to chill the good vibe with a discussion of money.

She put her head around the door of the common room. "Are there any princesses here? Looking for a princess!"

Chloe laughed, the sound like a happy gurgle. *Princess* was one of the words that she understood, even if she couldn't say it. She somehow managed to feel it and all the happiness it conjured.

Tara hugged her sister, the purest soul she'd ever known. "Hey, lovely girl, how are you?"

Chloe smiled and patted Tara's hair. Dolling up wasn't all for the cute doctor—Chloe enjoyed it when Tara made the effort.

"What do you think? I went with a more golden highlight."

"It's such a lovely color," an aide Tara didn't recognize said.

"Hi, there, I'm Tara, Chloe's sis."

The young woman, who looked like Snow White with shoulder length dark hair, rosy cheeks, and lovely blue eyes, shook Tara's hand. "I'm May. I've been hanging with Chloe since I started last week."

Tara pinned on her smile. She'd been here before with

trainees doing the work that should be done by more experienced caregivers.

"New here? Well, welcome! Where do you hail from? How long have you been in the biz?"

May's smile seemed genuine in the face of Tara's barrage. "Two years at a residential home in Minnesota, then three years before that at a psychiatric nursing facility. I changed my track to work with gentle souls like Chloe." She touched Chloe's arm lightly, letting her know she wasn't forgotten. "It's great to meet you. Everyone's told me how glamorous you are."

Ah, ye olde flattery. "Listen, I'm sorry if I'm coming off as snippy. I know this work is hard and there's usually a high turnover, which means that Chloe loses friends quicker than she can make them."

May waved it off, obviously used to imperious relatives. "You're fine! Chloe and I were just drawing. I think this is you."

Sure enough, Chloe had sketched two girls holding hands, one of them with dark hair like Chloe, the other with hair as yellow as the sun. Tara's heart melted into gloop. She loved this girl so much.

"That's amazing, Clo-Bear! You're so good at that." Tara sat down beside her and looked at May, who was smiling fondly at her sister. "How has she been this week? I called, but sometimes it's hard to know if people are just ..."

"Placating you?"

Tara nodded. She usually made it out here twice a week, but she checked in daily, which probably annoyed the fuck out of the staff. She'd told them they could shoot her a text or email, but that wasn't in the cards—no one felt obliged to give her daily updates. So Tara called each day at 4 p.m.

before the dinner rush started. By then they should have a good estimate of how Chloe's day had gone.

"She's been great today," May said as she handed Chloe a blue crayon to work on the sky. Tara passed over a green one because her sister liked to go against the grain with her art. "Although, we did have a musical singalong the other night and she wouldn't join in. I'm not sure why. Maybe she's shy?"

"Oh, this girl is not shy. We are twinsies there, for sure! To be honest, she usually likes to sing with me. We did that a lot when we were younger. She knows every song on the *Mamma Mia* soundtrack."

Chloe was nonverbal and couldn't sing, but she loved music. Tara looked around. There were several other residents there, some of them sensitive to noise, so she wouldn't be starting up a singalong right now. She dug around in her purse. "I brought her this old iPod, only with her motor skills, she might not be able to play it. It has ABBA on there because they're her favorite, and I added the Spice Girls, Britney, and a few other classics."

May took it from Tara's hands, her expression one of amusement. "Do they make these anymore?"

"Doubt it, it's even got a dial on it." Tara chuckled. "But I was cleaning out a drawer and it still works. I'm not sure if she'll be okay with the earbuds in—she doesn't usually like anything in her ears—but I found these headphones as well." Tara took out an old headset with big earmuffs. Chloe immediately gravitated to it.

"Oh, you like the look of those," May said to her sister.

"Yeah, you do. Here, Clo-Bear, give these a go." She helped her sister put them on, which took a while because Chloe was alternately scared and fascinated by them. After a few minutes, she settled.

"Now, the big reveal," Tara murmured as she chose one of Chloe's favorites, *Fernando*. With the opening bars, her sister's eyes went wide with delight.

"We have a winner." May stood. "I'll let you two have some quality time together."

Tara smiled her thanks. "Sorry about before. Sometimes, the filter between my brain and mouth is broken. I just need to be sure she's got people in her corner." For so long, Chloe had been abandoned, especially by her own family. Tara was trying to make up for that and sometimes went overboard with her Mama Bear act.

"No problem. Come find me before you leave and we can talk about how to keep you up to date with Chloe's progress."

In other words, let's work out a plan that doesn't drive the nurses crazy. "Will do."

Forty minutes later, Chloe was worn out but knew how to work the dial on the iPod. Tara left the charger with May and they chatted about the sweet nurse texting at the end of her shifts to give Tara an update. She couldn't promise every day, but it would be more of the personal touch that Tara craved where her sister was concerned.

Feeling more lighthearted than when she arrived, Tara headed out only to run into a hovering Caroline Cheney, the Director at Misty Pines. Or the warden, as Tara liked to think of her, which was probably a little harsh. The woman had a facility filled with intellectually and physically disabled people to run.

"Ms. Becker? I hoped we could talk."

"Would love to but—"

"It'll take a few minutes. My office is this way."

Tara followed, each step reminiscent of her frequent visits to the principal's office in high school. She took a seat in the uncomfortable chair on the other side of Mrs. Cheney's desk.

Best to strike first. "I know you want to talk about the fees. I'm a little behind but I should have them to you in a week." As soon as her YouTube payment was deposited to her account. She prayed it was enough.

"Yes, there's that. But I also wanted to let you know that the Kearns Foundation cut its funding."

Tara's gut chilled, already knowing where this was going. "So there won't be a grant this year?"

"We can always seek other avenues, other charities, but there's no guarantee that it would happen. Between the state support, the private foundation funding, and your own contribution"— Which was usually late, was the unspoken editorial—"we've managed to ensure that your sister is taken care of. But it would be better if the source of her fees was a little more ... secure."

Tell me about it!

"I agree. Actually you'll be thrilled to hear that my business is starting to take off, so I'm in a better position these days to contribute more." At Mrs. Cheney's sour look, Tara grabbed her purse. "How about I write a check now for half of what I owe you? And next month, I'll include the arrears and the following month." She had just remembered that one of her plastic friends, the one she kept at the bottom of her lingerie drawer for emergencies, might have some juice on it.

Tara quickly wrote the check, keeping her eyes wide so she didn't cry at the amount of money she was forking over. She handed it off, then snatched her hand back so Mrs. Cheney wouldn't see her shaking. Mustn't show a jot of weakness.

"You know there are other facilities—"

"No!" She smiled to temper her abrupt response. "Chloe loves it here and I've already seen the marvelous progress she's made under your care." At the last home, Chloe had little interaction with others and few opportunities for joy. It wasn't the facility's fault; some places were simply better resourced than others. "Misty Pines is the best place for her. Nowhere else will do."

Mrs. Cheney preened a little while looking sympathetic. She probably had to deal with whining, poverty-stricken relatives all the time and had an expression for every occasion.

"Thanks for the payment. I'll look for the next one at the beginning of March."

"I'll have it to you long before then!" Tara stood, almost stumbling over her purse to get out the door.

She'd bought herself some time. She would need every spare second.

3

————

THE DOOR to Chase Manor opened and Fitz lowered his gaze. A three-foot tall blonde Disney princess stood before him, with her father's blue eyes and a stubborn tilt to her chin that signaled she could only be a descendant of Harper Chase, the Rebel Queen herself.

"Hello there, your majesty."

"I'm a fairy." She produced a wand from behind her back and pointed it at him threateningly. "You're big. Not as big as my daddy. He's a big loaf. That's what Aunt Vi says."

Sounded about right. "Your momma or papa around these parts?"

Former Rebels center, Remy DuPre, appeared with a ready smile and the look of a man thoroughly satisfied with the hand he'd been dealt. After several heartbreaking years coming within kissing distance of the hardware, he'd finally landed the Cup, a wife who rocked his world, and three daughters he adored more than anything.

"You here for me or the boss?"

"I've got a meeting with your better half. Running a few minutes early."

Fitz was generally too busy to make lasting friendships at his age, but one that had stood the test of time was his tie to Remy. They'd first clicked after spending two years on the same team in Atlanta more than a decade ago. That connection had pushed Fitz over the line for the Chicago GM job, and now that Remy was no longer an active player, hanging with him wasn't considered a conflict of interest. They usually met for breakfast once a week, but not today.

Remy placed a hand on his little girl's shoulder. "Maddy, can you let this guy in? He's approved. Fitz, this is my youngest, Madeline, who is all of two years old."

"No, Daddy, I'm three! It was my birthday last week!"

"Oh, yeah? I forgot about that." He winked at Fitz while Madeline blessed his entrance with a flourish of her wand.

"Thanks, Maddy. Appreciate it."

With a proud eye, Remy watched his youngest skip off to a large room just off the main corridor. "Harper's just finishin' up her hair appointment. You want some coffee?"

"Is Gretzky the greatest?"

Fitz followed Remy through the house, a beautifully appointed mansion in Lake Forest on Chicago's North Shore. Everywhere existed signs of their family life from tiny shoes to princess dolls to the energy you felt in a place that knew love and laughter. Fitz had grown up in a house with a similar vibe and periodically, he had a chance to embed himself in it when he spent time with his brother, his sister-in-law, and his nieces, who weren't much older than Remy's brood.

In the large country-style kitchen, he removed a chewed-up dog toy shaped like a hedgehog from a chair and sipped on the coffee given to him by Remy.

Remy filled a dog bowl and set it down in a corner. "Now, where's that damn mutt?" Shrugging, he turned and settled against the counter. "So how's your new forward doin'?"

Good vibes, bye bye. This was why Fitz was here, summoned by Harper to discuss what was now termed "The O'Malley Situation." Fitz knew he needed to speak with the little prick but at the moment, he was pretty steamed, and O'Malley might not survive Fitz in the first flush of anger. Better to talk it out with the boss first.

Last night, the Amish Farm Girl's agent had called to withdraw his client from consideration. Apparently, O'Malley had been rude to her on their second "date"— read: provocative as all get out—and scared her off. So now, they were back to square one.

"Were we assholes like this when we were that age?"

Remy grinned. "Can't remember. I've probably blocked it out. But funnily enough I do recall you gettin' into a spot of bother with a redhead in a hot tub that had Coach on your ass."

That rang a bell. Fitz rubbed his mouth as memories formed like fluffy little clouds across his consciousness. "But I didn't flaunt my bad behavior in public. I don't know what this kid's problem is—and I can't believe I called him a kid —but it's a pain in the ass for this team. This kind of distraction makes us look like we can't control our players." With the trade deadline approaching, negotiations for certain deals were at a delicate stage. One agent had already pushed back on letting his player go to the Rebels under a free agency agreement.

O'Malley's problems were starting to become the team's problems.

"Might be time to invoke the morality clause," Remy mused. Short of an arrest, it was rare as fuck for any team to go to the nuclear option.

"He needs another talking to—maybe there's something botherin' him that's causin' him to act out." He shook his head, irked that he had to deal with this.

And then because his day wasn't going badly enough, in walked the last person he expected to see.

Tara Becker.

They'd had a couple of run-ins at parties during the holiday season, and run-in was as adversarial as it sounded. Each time, he'd overheard her comment on his geriatric nature, all forty-two years of it. He'd always thought of himself as being in decent shape for a man his age, but apparently women of Tara's generation were ready to put him out to pasture.

"Gentlemen, do I smell coffee?"

"Sure do." Remy grabbed a cup from a tree mug that was shaped like a ... dildo?

"Oh, I've got it. Don't trouble yourself." She placed what looked like an inverted umbrella on the floor beside the kitchen's trash can. Helping herself to a pour of coffee, she moved about, getting sugar from the cupboard and creamer from the fridge, with an ease that said she'd been here before.

Harper's appointment. "You cut hair?"

"Have shears, will travel." She eyed him critically. "You could do with a trim. Getting a little shaggy there."

"I'll keep it in mind," he muttered.

A Valkyrie shriek went up from somewhere in the house. Remy placed his mug down and was already halfway to the source when he called back, "That's my cue. I'll tell Harper you're here."

And then there were two.

Tara blinked big green eyes at him, framed by sparkly silver make-up that made her look a touch otherworldly.

Like a siren of old, the kind that drew innocent men to rocks. Her lips were plush, matted with a dark pink lipstick that matched her sleeveless pink blouse. Heaps of blonde hair cascaded in waves over her bare shoulders.

From office gossip, he'd learned that she'd dated Cal Foreman for a few weeks last year before the power forward fell for Petrov's sister. That those two women were friends seemed odd. Next to Mia, who had sporty, all-American, girl-next-door looks, Tara looked like a porcelain doll that needed to be hand-painted and dressed every morning.

"Tara Becker." She thrust out her hand. "Pleased to meet you. Officially."

His hand moved to grasp hers, which was bordering on ridiculous because they had already met. Three times. "Hale Fitzpatrick. People call me Fitz."

"Why? I prefer Hale." No one called him Hale except his mother. "Here to figure out the O'Malley conundrum?"

"Just a check-in with the boss."

Her lips curved, and she employed a knowing tilt to her head that told him he needn't be coy. Everyone knew about this problem.

"So I think you and I got off on the wrong foot," she said.

"Did we?"

"Yeah, I made a couple of off-hand comments and it was thoughtless of me. Actually, I think you look great."

For your age, was the unspoken addendum. Rarely did he worry about his advancing years, but the longer he worked with young players and by extension, their WAGs, who seemed to get younger every year, the more aware he was of the gap between himself and the men he was charged with mentoring.

"Thanks?"

Oblivious to his sarcasm, she went on. "You obviously

work out, dress sharply, and I know the front office staff and a few of the WAGs are all laying bets on when you're going to start dating. But I expect you want to settle in with the team first before it's full-steam ahead with the F-plan."

"The F-plan?" Now he was intrigued.

"The Fitz plan," she said with a sly grin that stirred something that should not be stirring. Was he so hard-up for hard-on fodder that the attentions of a pretty, vapid woman were sending blood south?

"At the moment I'm focused on my career. I'm kind of too busy for dating."

"With this Dex business. Good Lord, he's a rogue, isn't he? And that woman the PR people set him up with ... who thought that was a good idea? She's all wrong for him. Like anyone would believe Dex and Ms. Goody-Two-Shoes-Hallmark-Channel as a couple." She bit down on her lip, awareness sparking her astonishing green eyes, rimmed with flecks of hazel-gold. "That was you, wasn't it?"

"Might've been."

"You overheard me and Mia talking about it in the coffee shop as well."

"You weren't exactly discreet."

She curled a strand of blonde hair around her forefinger. "So you got a chance to learn what the inner circle is thinking. Free market research."

What one puck bunny on the make was thinking. Gold dust!

"Not sure how unbiased that segment of the fanbase is."

"Unbiased? There's no such thing as objectivity when it comes to down 'n dirty gossip featuring horny young bucks with too much in the way of cash, free time, and hormones," she said with an air of authority. "People tend to have 'feelings' about their celebrities, not all of it rational or logical.

You might think that fixing Dex up with some sweet-as-pie innocent is the way to rein him in. In reality, you're setting him up to fail. One, people can see right through it, and two, he needs a stronger hand. Someone who can stand up to him."

Like you, perhaps? In that coffee shop, she had joked about being the one to tame him.

Okay, he'd play along. "So what do you think we should be doing, Ms. Becker?"

She moved across the kitchen to where she'd left the umbrella thing. Placing a foot on the trash can pedal, she overturned it, tipping blonde hair into the trash from what he realized was a portable cape.

"The fake relationship ruse is tricky as hell. You have a player who likes to play. Who's been a naughty boy. Who has the tabloids in a tizzy. And you have a female-owned team that doesn't like that. Not at all."

"Maybe *I* don't like it."

"So you're an ally for the ladies. Good for you! Of course, these days, people are much fussier about the sex lives of their players. You've come up with a plan to keep Sexy Dexy on the straight and narrow until the playoffs, but he probably hates that he's been told what to do and who to do it with. Am I warm?"

"-ish."

She grinned like she'd won a prize, and there it was again, that flicker of interest in his cock. "So, how's it going with the Amish Farm Girl?"

That was *his* exact phrasing. At his grim look, she whispered, "Word gets around."

Probably Casey Higgins, Harper's assistant, who was dating Erik Jorgenson, the Rebels goalkeeper. This organization was incredibly incestuous, not to mention indiscreet.

"It's … going."

"Ooh, cagey." She waited, probably expecting he'd spill all the juicy details. When he remained silent, she added, "That's it? It's … going."

"What do you expect me to say?"

"That this Dex situation is under control." Spoken by Harper Chase, who had just walked in, and was now opening the fridge to retrieve a water bottle. In profile there was no missing the baby bump, all five months of it.

A petite blonde with the biggest, brassiest balls of anyone he'd ever met, man or woman, Harper had turned this franchise around five years ago, sending the team from zeros to heroes. Lately she'd been taking more of a back seat and had tasked him with sorting out the O'Malley issue because she was tired of mothering them. Fitz understood—the team were mostly youngsters who needed a lot of hand-holding, and that could wear on a woman who had her own family of three with another on the way.

"We're gettin' there," Fitz said casually, not enjoying that Tara was looking at him like she only had to crook her finger to get him to fess up to a bunch of secrets. Such as that time he stole a Snickers bar from Mr. Corkhill's corner store when he was ten. Or when he told Jenny Struthers that he couldn't go to junior prom with her because Lara Johansson had already asked him (when in fact he was angling to go with Mira Patel).

"Nice cut," he said to Harper. "And color?"

"You noticed? It's a shade lighter than my usual." She smiled at him, then spoke to Tara, "I shot you the payment and tip on Venmo. Put me in for eight weeks from today."

"Will do!" Tara took another sip of her coffee, rinsed the mug, and placed it on the top rack of the dishwasher.

Just then Madeline walked in and pointed her wand at Tara. "I want hair like Mommy!"

Harper placed a hand on her daughter's head. "Tara has to go, honey."

"Oh, I have a few moments to spare. You know I think you could do with something different than your mom. Something special. How about ... princess hair?" She held out her hand for the wand. "May I?"

Maddy passed it over with great reverence.

"Make this golden-haired child a princess!" Tara tapped the wand gently against Maddy's forehead and made a comical face when nothing happened. "Oh dear. Looks like I used up all the magic on your mom."

"That's me," Harper said with an indulgent smile. "Greedy."

"No worries! I can do it the old-school, non-magical way while your mom takes care of business."

Harper sent Tara a look of immense gratitude. "No need to spend too long on it. I have to talk to Fitz in the study so if you could—"

"Make sure Daddy has her in his sights before I leave. Gotcha."

"Thanks so much. Fitz, let's chat."

His last image of Tara was her sitting in the kitchen with a sprite in her lap while she worked on twisting the little girl's hair with a gentleness that made him feel ... something.

This time, not below the waist.

He'd much prefer that any urges about Tara Becker remained in the realm of lust.

In Harper's study, the boss took a seat on a comfortable-looking sofa near the window and gestured for him to sit. In a couple of minutes, he had her up to speed on the latest.

"So this is now affecting business," she said gravely. "Luckily the trade deadline is later this year and some of those trades will still go through, of course. But we should really have our ducks in a row by now for draft agreements and free agents. If agents are warning their players against us ..." She shook her head. "Any progress with Bastian Durand?"

"He's hard to pin down, but I think he might be open to a meeting. However, we need to be careful about the potential to change the team dynamic." Bastian's older brother, Reid, was already playing center with the Rebels, a position switch that reaped dividends before Reid suffered an adductor muscle strain and had to go on IR. "Two brothers with a history of not getting along on the ice? That might be trouble. Never mind that he could wipe out the budget."

"Let's move talking to him up the list, but this Dex business must be resolved. What's the next step?"

"Other than invoking the morality clause—which is a precedent we don't want to set when the behavior isn't illegal—we need to find someone who looks like she belongs. He doesn't want to be told who to date, but he especially doesn't want to be told to date someone sweet."

Tara had nailed that one on the head.

Harper opened her hands. "So don't go with sweet. Go with someone who would at least look like they match Dex's interests."

Tara again. She might indeed be good for this, but then he saw her with Maddy and it ... confused him. He didn't enjoy the mixed messages his body was getting from her.

"Are you thinking what I'm thinking?" Harper asked with a glint in her eye and a head tilt toward the door, which he assumed was code for "perfection exists on the premises."

"Ms. Becker is ... unique, to say the least."

"She's already been a player girlfriend. Dated Cal for a while."

He inhaled deeply. "From what I've heard, she has her sights set on becoming a WAG. In a deliberate fashion."

Harper looked amused. "And?"

"You don't see a problem with that?"

Her smile was tungsten, warning him to be careful. "With what exactly?"

"Placing a woman with such mercenary ambitions in the path of one of our players?"

"Oh, please. Like these grown men can't defend themselves from the hot, personable woman who already fits in. Let the players worry about their love lives. This is business. I think we should offer it to Tara, and if she makes something out of it, good for her." She picked up her phone. "Let me see if she's still here."

Annoyance flared. They had barely discussed it.

"Harper, you asked me to take charge of this and now you want to unilaterally hire someone who might not be suitable?"

"Not unilaterally. We're discussing it, aren't we? Let's see if she would even be interested." There was a knock on the door to which Harper said, "Come in."

"Hey, there!" Tara bounced in, Maddy on her heels. The little girl's hair was in funny little twists, like mini-cinnamon roll explosions on her head. She beelined for Fitz and climbed into his lap.

"I'm a princess now."

"You sure are, button."

"Just a couple of minutes to run something by you, Tara," Harper said. "We've been discussing the Dex situation and frankly we're having a hard time finding a good fit for our PR plan."

"The fake girlfriend deal?"

"Right." Harper didn't sound surprised that Tara was already up to speed but again, no secrets in this org. "Now this isn't set in stone but we're wondering what you might think."

Tara blinked as if this was news, the manipulative little phony.

"Generally or specifically?"

"Would it interest you? As a job for a few weeks just to keep Dex distracted on the drive to the playoffs?"

"Maybe," she said, her gaze flicking to Maddy as she made twists in his hair to match her own. The little one was murmuring a babble of approval.

Fitz needed to assume some measure of control here, but it was mighty hard to play the hard ass when you had a toddler styling your hair and telling you how pretty you looked.

"What makes you think you'd be a good fit? Any acting experience?" He tried to sound disinterested.

"Sure. Improv classes with The Second City, which are better than acting classes, because I can yes-and the heck out of any situation. But more important, I have already been a player girlfriend. With Cal."

"So a short stint dating—"

"Uh, three months."

"In public?"

"Yes, in public!" She rolled her eyes in Harper's direction, as if to say, *is this guy for real*? "Do you think he wouldn't want to be seen with me?"

"Not at all. I'm sure any man would be proud to have you on his arm, Ms. Becker."

Tara narrowed her eyes in evident suspicion. "Well, we weren't compatible. He and Mia are perfect for each other, and while I'm not claiming perfect compatibility with Dex O'Malley, I will say that I'm most definitely in his league. Maybe slightly above it."

"Too true," Harper murmured.

Fitz had already lost this battle, yet he felt obliged to continue with his due diligence. "So you're a good match for O'Malley. Or think you are."

"A good match! You heard it here first, Harper." To Fitz, she added, "Look at me. I'm exactly what a guy like Dex O'Malley would go for."

Her self-confidence made him want to challenge her ego.

Catch her out.

Bring her low.

An image of Tara on her knees before him, her beautiful lips in a sexy pout tried to take hold. He shook it off.

"If you're so sure he'd go for it, why aren't you making a play right now?"

"And have Dex dump me a couple of days later? We both know he's not ready to settle, which is fine. So few of us are. Dex needs a firm hand, someone to keep him in line, but who also looks like she should be on his arm. Who can talk the talk and walk the walk in five inch heels. A few visits to the WAG box, some photo ops at trendy restaurants, maybe a couple of appearances doing good works at the dog shelter —we can talk to Kennedy about that, she's dating Reid Durand—or at the soup kitchen in Uptown where Levi Hunt volunteers. And I'm already friends with most of the girls, so there won't be any drama there. One big, happy family."

Fitz slid a glance to Harper. She was usually hard to read

but he recognized immediately that she liked Tara's take on the situation. Here was an attractive, outgoing woman on the spot with a ready-made PR plan.

How convenient.

"You'd have to sign an NDA," Harper said. "Maybe even lie to your friends. The fewer people who know how the sausage is made, the better."

"Sausages!" Maddy screamed.

"She's hungry," Harper said, standing and lifting Maddy off his lap. He had enjoyed the comfort of her little girl warmth and scent, which reminded him of his nieces. "Tara, we're going to discuss it some more, but what I'm hearing is that you might be up for it if we can negotiate the right compensation. I know you have a business to run, so I'm hoping we can work around your schedule."

"Oh, I can figure that out." Tara grinned at them both, throwing out over her shoulder, "You know where to find me."

Wherever that was, it wasn't far enough.

4

———

Fitz didn't like this set-up, not one bit.

This was the supposed pinnacle of his (second) career, a new challenge. For the last eight years, he'd bounced about from team to team, city to city, and while he'd usually left most teams in better shape than he'd found them, it was hard for him to settle. Rarely had he been forced out, but once he'd made an impact, he was usually ready to move on. That restlessness extended to his relationships with women —since his divorce ten years ago, he held the women he dated at a distance, much to his mother's chagrin. She wanted to see him hitched and happy with a passel of grandbabies.

He was happy to tell her he was getting all his broody needs covered with his hockey players behaving like horny teens and Fitz on hand to offer paternal slaps on their wrists.

This team was the ultimate challenge. A scrappy underdog outfit with a lot of talent, they did well but could do better. It was imperative that every piece on the board pull its weight, and a player like Dex had the potential to contribute big time to the team's success.

If they could keep him out of trouble long enough.

Fitz liked clean solutions.

Using Tara Becker was not a clean solution.

She had already dated a player, so how sensible was it to have her date another, even if it was fake? Would it create a ruckus in the locker room? Fights in the WAG box? A different kind of negative publicity?

"Why so sad?" Sophie asked him as he opened the folder she'd delivered to his desk.

"I have a bad feeling about this."

"Every effort to manage damage comes with a risk," Sophie said, like she was reciting from a PR manual. "All we can do is make the decisions we think will minimize it the most. And once you sign off on it, you don't have to be involved. All out of your hands."

Good. He could get back to running the franchise—making trades, forecasting revenues, building the team to win, if not this year, in the years to come.

But first he had to bring these two bubbleheads together and give it some sort of team blessing, assuming they both showed to today's scheduled meeting. Irritated to be kept waiting, he looked down at the background check Sophie had provided.

"Anything we should be concerned about?"

"Nothing really. Even her side hustle is almost too good to be true."

Fitz turned the page on the report. "YouTuber? Doing what? Lessons on being annoying?"

"She has a channel where she makes ASMR videos."

"I don't know what that means."

"Autonomous Sensory Meridian Response," a voice called out.

Tara stood at the entrance to his office in what could best be described as a cocktail-slash-ballet dress. A shiny neon pink, its ruffled skirt stopped six inches above her knees while the neckline plunged to show the kind of cleavage that should not be visible in a corporate environment. Her blonde hair was teased to full volume and waved over her shoulders.

Bare again. In February.

"Ms. Becker, you're late."

"I'm guessing I'm here before Dexter, though?" She tottered in on four-inch heels—silver with pink jewels studded along the sides—threw a wrap down on one chair and took a seat in the other. She placed a tiny matching pink purse on his desk.

An insult, though he couldn't be sure why. He just sensed a dig.

"I'm reviewing your background now," Fitz said.

He wanted to put his jacket around her shoulders.

Nope.

Back to the report. Born in Missouri twenty-eight years ago. Mother living in Florida with a husband of four years, so probably not Tara's father. No mention of him, but she did have a sister living in the Chicago suburbs.

Credit terrible. Debt considerable. She owed over twenty thousand dollars on her cards. Tutus and bejeweled shoes will do that.

She'd had several jobs in the Chicago area over the last ten years, most of them at hair salons. Now she appeared to be an independent contractor.

An independent scam artist, more like.

"I have about forty bucks in my checking account until

my next payment drops from YouTube," Tara said. "In case that's not in there."

"What exactly are you selling, Ms. Becker?" He couldn't help it; the words just slipped from his mouth.

Her lips curved, as if she understood that he wasn't merely asking about her blogger channel or whatever it was.

Tara Becker was a woman on the make.

"Pleasure, Hale. I'm selling pleasure."

He narrowed his eyes. "I thought that happened over on OnlyFans, not family-friendly platforms like YouTube."

"Oh, this isn't X-rated. My videos are just for fun. You know that pleasant thrill you get when someone whispers in your ear or you hear a cat scratching the side of the bed? Well, people like to watch videos of that and I give the people what they want."

Fitz cast a glance at Sophie, who shrugged. "My sister watches videos of a guy rustling fabric. It relaxes her."

Tara was checking out her nails while Fitz checked her out. Her eyelids shimmered with blue and green make-up, like a tropical bird.

"And people pay you to do this?"

"I've monetized the traffic, so if people watch most of the video, YouTube gives me a cut of the ad revenue. A girl's gotta make a living!"

"And this isn't considered antithetical to the values of this organization?"

He posed this question to Sophie, but Tara answered.

"The values of *this* organization? You currently have a guy caught getting a blow job and more on camera, and you're worried if me reciting Avengers fan fic in a husky voice is controversial? Let me tell you, my side-gig is the least of your worries."

Sophie chuckled. "She's not wrong."

So some internet weirdos had found each other. Good for them.

"Are you going to have time for this? Dex O'Malley is a full-time job."

"I sure am."

O'Malley stood at the door, arms crossed, looking half-amused, half-annoyed to be here.

Tara checked her phone. "You're ten minutes late, lover."

O'Malley's brow wrinkled as he walked in and placed a hand on the back of the chair where Tara had thrown her wrap. "I've seen you around. With Petrov's sister?"

"That's right, I'm Tara Becker. Mia Wallace is a friend of mine." Remaining seated, she offered her hand like a queen expecting a curtsy. "And if your bosses agree, you and I are going to be good friends as well, but that's all. You're a job to me. Nothing more."

Tara may as well have placed a puck at the center of the playoff circle and told O'Malley he wasn't allowed to touch it first. The spark lighting in his eyes was almost predatory. Whether Tara knew it or not, she had made herself the one thing that O'Malley wanted and guaranteed he would be saying yes to the plan PR was cooking up.

Clever? Perhaps.

O'Malley took her hand and rubbed a thumb over her wrist. Something in Fitz's chest shifted, a knot of discomfort behind his breastbone.

Tara might be claiming O'Malley was a job, but that wasn't her game, not at all. This woman was looking to land a big hockey-playing fish.

She released O'Malley's hand, gestured for him to sit, and looked Fitz squarely in the eye.

"Let's talk about the terms, shall we?" As if she was in charge.

"Today, we'll outline the broad strokes of the plan and get the paperwork squared away," he said. "Ms. Becker, we have an NDA for you to sign and a separate contract covering your compensation."

O'Malley laughed. "You're paying her?" He turned to Tara. "Babe, you should be paying me. Any chick would be dying to be in your position."

"I think that's your problem." Tara gave a serene smile. "'Any chick' makes it sound like you're not very choosy. You don't want to sound like you'd bang anything that moves, do you?"

O'Malley blinked, evidently surprised that Tara had opinions on this. "I like the way you move."

"All right, all right." Hale sent a sharp look of rebuke O'Malley's way. He might not approve of her mercenary motivations, but he wouldn't tolerate a hostile work environment. "Ms. Becker is being hired to do a job here, so maybe less leering and more respect."

"Thanks, White Knight. I can handle it."

"You shouldn't have to."

After another speared gaze at O'Malley, Hale carried on. "Sophie, maybe give us an idea of what the next few weeks will look like."

Sophie smiled. "We've just passed Valentine's Day, so that's an opportunity we've missed—"

"Aw!" Tara said with a flicker of a glance Fitz's way, perhaps checking in to see if he cared. He did not. "We could have done some great photo ops for that. Ice skating in the park, romantic dinner at a French bistro."

Sophie nodded enthusiastically. "But that's okay! We can do all those things and get out from under the crush of the Valentine's Day feed overload."

"Yeah, personalize it to me and Dex. We're so crazy

about each other we don't need a Hallmark holiday to dictate the terms. I've been thinking we could take a few good photos down at the animal shelter, then back at the practice rink with Dex teaching me to skate, though I already know how. Maybe a cute 'good morning, honey' video on Insta. See if we can get it going viral."

"I don't have any of that," O'Malley grumbled. "Instagram or whatever."

Sophie smiled patiently. "I'll take care of that. You can log into the accounts we set up or let us keep an eye on it."

"In fact," Fitz said, "it might be better if Sophie created the content for all of it. That way, we can maintain tighter control."

Tara muttered something inaudible.

"Sorry, I missed that. Usually your critiques are loud enough for us all to hear."

"I was merely commenting that you've got to let us play to our strengths. I'm sure Sophie knows her stuff but if it's too scripted, it looks forced. We need to let the real personalities shine through."

Fitz stared her down. "Really? You mumbled all of that?"

Her eyebrow raise was imperious. "I'm doing you a favor here, mister, so maybe less of the 'tude. Now, what's our origin story? I have ideas ..."

TEN MINUTES LATER, Dex left with a plan in motion for them to meet for coffee tomorrow where a "fan"—aka Sophie— would snap a photo and post it with appropriate hashtags. Tara remained to read the NDA. It was important that she didn't look like a complete pushover who would sign anything put in front of her.

When Harper had offered her the job, Tara had almost done a jig on the spot. The universe had answered her prayer and come up with a solution to her immediate money troubles—and potentially a shot at wiping them out for good. She needed to play this carefully.

A minute later, Sophie left Hale's office to take a call, leaving Tara alone with the Rebels' GM. Which was fine because she was busy reading.

Or would have been if she didn't feel like she was being watched. She looked up, and sure enough, he was staring at her with no shame whatsoever. At least try to be coy!

"Yes?"

"Any questions?"

"I've only got as far as the first paragraph. Third grade reading level, y'know."

His mouth quirked. Perhaps the man had a sense of humor after all.

"Maybe we should have just drawn a picture of you and O'Malley holding a puppy with a big dollar sign on your shirt."

Tara grinned. "Yup, think I'd understand that just fine."

"Funny, because I'm not sure I understand this at all."

Tara shifted in her seat, uncrossed her legs—which were looking tan, toned, and tip-top—and recrossed them. Hale kept his gaze locked on her face, not even a flicker down south.

"What's to understand? I'm offering my very valuable services in the hopes of increasing my brand awareness."

"Your brand? This whisper video stuff?"

"That's part of it, but also my stylist business. There are lots of routes to success these days, and latching onto another well-known brand, such as a professional sports franchise, is one that could be very beneficial. I'm friendly with some of the WAGs and team members, I know how this world works, and I'm a very good actress. You should be paying me a fortune!"

He snorted. "We are."

"Well, more." Tara looked at the contract again, her gaze skimming to the numbers. "A thousand a week is kind of on the low side."

"It's Actor's Equity rates, as if you were in a Broadway show. Think an over-the-top musical and everyone doing jazz hands."

"Right, but this is going to take up a lot of my time. I have to rearrange some of my clients' appointments and I'll probably miss the chance to create my channel content this week *and* the next because the team is on that away bender."

He grimaced. "You don't have to come on the road, Ms. Becker."

Deny her the chance to jet set and cement the bonds of early days bliss? Not likely. "I really should. A slow burn doesn't work for damage control. We need to compress an entire relationship build into a couple of weeks. I should be on that plane."

He sighed. "So you'll be getting travel perks and expenses paid while you're with us. The salary you're earning is on top of that."

Tara touched the pen in her hand to her lips, dialed up her sexiest pout, and fluttered her eyelashes. "How about $1500 a week? It's really a drop in the bucket for you guys. Also a complete tax write-off."

"Let me think about it while you read the rest of the big words."

Hiding her smile of victory, Tara looked down at the contract again. All the multi-syllabic words were blurring, given her mild dyslexia and the fact it was a complex legal document. Really, she should ask someone else to read it but she couldn't afford a lawyer and the only person she'd trust would be Mia, who was currently visiting her mom in New York. Tara got the impression that she needed to close this deal today before Hale changed his mind.

A sentence jumped out at her.

"What does this mean?"

About to point out the offending language, she was forced to wait until he unfolded his big frame from his seat and came around to her side of the desk. He placed a hand on the back of her chair and leaned over. "What are we looking at?"

She swallowed, a touch overwhelmed by his proximity. Whatever aftershave he was using—something woodsy and citrus, though weren't they always woodsy and citrus—had her feeling fluttery. His hand was close to her bare shoulder.

If he moved his thumb a smidge, it would brush her skin and ...

Back to business. "This line: Neither party is obliged to engage in intimate or sexual activity for the purposes of this contract."

"Which part do you not understand?"

Tara twisted to meet his searing gaze. "You're telling me I can't—y'know—with Dex?"

"I'm telling you that there's no expectation for the purposes of this agreement that you—y'know—with Dex." He switched his position to lean on the desk right in front of her, a move that pulled the fine gray wool of his suit pants taut against his thighs. If he leaned back a little more, she was sure she'd know which way he skewed.

Or if she put as much effort into figuring it out as she was reading this damn contract, she could take a guess. *Definitely to the left ...*

Her mouth felt dry as he continued. "In case you feel pressured to make it look more real than it should. You don't have to accept O'Malley's advances or anything of that nature. It's for your protection."

A contract clause that was the equivalent of a condom.

"Of course, that doesn't mean you can't—"

"Y'know," she filled in.

"Right. You're consenting adults, but I guess that's the point. Consent is key here and I don't want O'Malley thinking he's got an easy score."

There it was, that sweet streak again with the man playing at gentleman bodyguard. He'd done that before when Dex got a little saucy.

"Oh, there's nothing easy about me." It was a thing to say though she wondered if he thought exactly that. Easy, up-for-anything Tara.

He remained silent, just looked at her for so long that she returned to the contract and the blur of black and white.

"So tell me something," he finally said.

"About?" *Don't look up. Eyes on the prize.*

"Why are you doing this? Really."

It made sense that this man would be the one to ask her straight out. Imagined bodyguard or not, he had the organization's rep to protect and interlopers like Tara needed to be handled appropriately.

She could tell him about Chloe, how she was her sister's guardian, and that her well-being meant more to her than anything in the world.

That all her life she'd been told it was a good thing she was pretty and that she'd better use what she had before it was too late.

That she would like to meet someone who connected with her on a soul-deep level, but she'd settle for security for the people—or person—she loved any day of the week.

But Hale Fitzpatrick was spearing her a look of such disdain that she knew she'd get no sympathy from that corner. That expression was as well-known to Tara as the flecks of amber in her green eyes. She was fully cognizant of the impression she made on people.

Women were usually threatened by her, except for a select few she clutched close to her heart, such as Mia.

Men were usually interested in her, or at the least, aware of her sex appeal. *Bimbo*, they thought. *Blonde. Ditz. Airhead.* She'd heard it all, and to a certain extent, she cultivated that image.

Maybe she wasn't the sharpest knife, but she had a good heart. She also had street smarts. When you left home at sixteen, you developed coping mechanisms. Ways to survive.

Surviving was Tara's brand—at least her internal one. She didn't let people know that, not even Mia.

No, Tara's perceived brand was fun. Glamour. Boys. That's how she viewed most of the male species. Boy-children with oversized egos and an overweening attachment to their dicks. They could be led so very easily by those appendages.

Even Hale Fitzpatrick, though not in the traditional way. Flirting and cooing wouldn't work on him, he was far too sharp for that—and the way things were going, he would never be susceptible to Tara's charms.

"My motives are my own," she finally said, feeling a pang of something. A missed opportunity to find common ground? Surely not with a man like this.

He gripped the desk to the right of his thighs, as if bracing to give a lecture. Her walls rose brick by brick to withstand the onslaught.

"Let me tell you what I see here. A woman with history with one of my players, maybe others, who has managed to carve a space out for herself in the Rebels inner circle. Who has positioned herself as a girlfriend-for-hire with what looks like a well-thought-out strategy. You might have Harper Chase thinking you're an entrepreneur or a savvy business woman, and I've no doubt you are. But that's not all, is it? It's as if you've been planning for this eventuality all along. Am I close?"

Tara took a good long look. So, like all men in his position, he was a judgmental ass and already didn't approve of her. Why not be up front with him? See if he could handle her truth. To paraphrase the inimitable Nora Ephron, be the heroine of your life, not the victim.

"Well, I've been waiting for this day for what seems like forever, Hale."

"Because?"

"I plan to marry a hockey player."

5

———

FITZ WASN'T sure what he expected Tara to say, but certainly not that. No prevarication, no hesitation. She just came right out and announced that she was a gold digger.

Pretty fucking ballsy.

"You plan to marry a hockey player?"

She pulled a finger trigger at him and winked. "And they say men don't listen to women."

"Any hockey player?"

"Not any hockey player. I'm not going to break up a marriage or try to convert Cade Burnett from his love of penis. But there are several eligible men out there and I see no reason why I can't land one of them."

Honest to a fault. "You don't want to find someone in a more ... traditional manner?"

"Like online dating?"

Sure. "Or in a bar or your place of employment?"

"Well, my choices are the comments section of my YouTube channel or the guys whose hair I cut. Not really the most likely pool. And I've had plenty of other jobs where I could've met someone. Where I have met someone. Bars, dog groomers, florists. I just haven't been lucky enough to go the distance." She touched the pen to her lips, a trick she probably used to draw the male gaze there. He resisted like a champ. "To be honest, I have certain attributes that might be wasted on a man who is not a professional athlete."

This was bordering on ridiculous, but he was weirdly compelled to analyze the train wreck before him. "Which are?"

"In case you haven't noticed, I'm not bad to look at. In fact, I'd say I'm a nine, so I'm open to seven or above in the hockey world. I'm also good at social media, throwing parties, holding puppies and small adult dogs that fit in Prada purses, and basically making a big, burly guy look even bigger and burlier. Is that a word?" She didn't wait for a response. "I'm also a great listener and make a killer mac-and-cheese. The secret is Worcestershire sauce. I am bringing quality to the table."

"I see."

Her look was the definition of unimpressed. "Do you? Because I think you see a woman with grabby hands who's looking for a ticket to Easy Street. That's not me. I've been working since I was ten years old and I plan to work my way into a great relationship that will benefit both parties. You might think I'm a gold digger, but the truth is I'm a realist. I want a guy who works hard, looks after his body and mind, and accepts that I'm an equal partner. And I don't want to wait for this Prince Charming to find me."

Was it possible he felt some measure of admiration for Tara Becker? A woman so candid about her naked ambition, who didn't care what anyone thought, had to have some quality worth admiring. But while honesty might be worthy of appreciation, it didn't change the fact her goals were decidedly mercenary.

"You're not worried you might be cutting yourself off from other possibilities in this drive to get a rich pro-athlete?"

"Which possibilities?" She waved around. "Show me these amazing opportunities I'm missing! I sincerely hope you're not telling me I should stay in my lane or some such nonsense."

"No. I'm saying that a healthy bank balance doesn't always amount to a healthy relationship. There's more to it than who pays for what."

She blinked those gorgeous green eyes, all pity. "Well, I know that! But I also know that I won't be happy with the guy who drives the Zamboni. I'm sure he's very nice—"

"And happily married."

"There you go. Missed my shot!" She let loose a husky giggle that made his cock stir. *Down, boy.* "I see where you're going and it's kind of sweet that you're trying to look after your players' well-being. You're a leader of men-children and they should be guarded against greedy crones who'll make them look amazing and improve their reputations."

"Ms. Becker, that's not—"

"Tara. Call me Tara. We're in business together."

Not the kind of business he liked to do. "I leave it to agents and lawyers to protect the players' wallets." Only half the truth. "I'm thinking more of you. I wouldn't want you to get hurt."

What possessed him to say that? This woman clearly knew what she was doing and who was he to say her goals were out of left field? She appeared to be of sound-*ish* mind and had decided that money, fame, and a pro-athlete would make her happy. As Harper said, let the players worry about their love lives.

"That's ... kind of you." She sounded as surprised as he

felt. "But you don't need to have a care for my heart. I'm realistic about what I'm getting into here."

It sounded like she didn't care if this turned into something meaningful—and while he might be able to credit that to her moneygrubbing tendencies, there was something almost melancholy about the way she said it.

Like she had low expectations for any relationship.

Christ, was he supposed to feel sorry for the poor little gold digger who couldn't find love?

He refused to fall for it. Any of it.

Right this minute, he was tempted to rip that contract out of her hands, go back to Harper and tell her this was a terrible idea. Instead he continued the interrogation, trying to get to the root of her motivations.

The root of her.

"What if O'Malley doesn't fall for your considerable charms?" He didn't think he had ever sounded so sardonic. His Southern politeness was straining at the bounds. This woman clearly brought out the worst in him.

She saw it, too. Saw right through his effort to maintain a veneer of civility around her.

"If Dex doesn't respond appropriately, I'm sure I'll survive."

By working her way down the roster. "Perhaps you'll use this time getting close to other team assets."

Contemplatively, she touched a finger to her lush painted lips. "Y'know, that's very possible. The next Mr. Tara Becker could be waiting in the locker room as we speak!"

Don't take the bait. Don't take the bait.

"I need a guarantee from you that while you're working with O'Malley, you won't fool around with any of the other players. I can't risk turning this into the equivalent of *Real Housewives.* Are we clear?"

"I think a Real Housewives of Chicago centered on the Rebels WAGs could be a real boost to—"

"Are we clear?"

Her green eyes glittered. "Crystal." She turned to the last page of the contract and scribbled her signature on the line.

"Thought you were going to hold out for more money."

"Oh, you'll be giving me a bonus before the next few weeks are up."

TARA MIGHT HAVE SCARED the bejesus out of Hale when she told him she had Dex O'Malley in her sights. (And maybe a few of the other players, too—naughty, naughty!) But first, the boy had to play along, which meant he'd need to show for their "coffee date" the next day.

"Any thoughts, Cal?"

Cal Foreman, ex-boyfriend and current fiancé of her bestie, Mia, sighed, the Most Put Upon Man in the World.

"I'm not his keeper. I'm not even sure why I'm here."

Mia grinned and grasped his hand. "Because we're supporting our friends as they embark on this wonderful adventure."

Cal rolled his eyes. "I barely know O'Malley. This morning he rolled in ten minutes late for morning skate, got torn a new one by Coach, made about one in five passes, then headed out before we hit the showers. He's probably sleeping off an all-nighter and forgot all about your meeting."

"It's not a meeting. It's a date." She didn't even need to put imaginary quotes around that word. Everyone knew, or at least everyone she cared about.

"Still not sure why you're doing this, T," Cal said, his tone soft with concern. "If you really need the money—"

"That's not what this is about. Sure, I could always do with the extra cash ..." The cash advance she'd withdrawn to cover the latest Misty Pines payment had maxed out the last of her credit cards. She'd have to talk to the Rebels' front office about getting an advance on the compensation for this deal. "But it's definitely an investment in my future."

"With a player," Mia said, frowning.

"Don't pout, babe. You'll get weird lines around your mouth." Tara cupped her friend's jaw, giving it a light brush with her thumb. "So fresh and pretty. Isn't she a peach, Cal?"

"She sure is."

Easily distracted, Cal gazed lovingly at his fiancée, and Tara didn't even feel a pang of envy. She used to after these two hooked up a few months ago, but now it had developed into a fondness for them both, individually and as a pair. They suited each other so well, both prime athletes who loved animals and movies and pizza. They had more than that in common, of course.

They just got each other. Clicked.

Tara had never encountered that with anyone and doubted she ever would. Men rarely chose to dig deeper with her, but then she had the depth of a puddle as one of her exes once said. (He was drunk, and it was "a dirty puddle," but she got the message.) She'd tried to open up with guys after a few dates, but it never came out right. She always sounded spoiled or whiny or forced.

These days, she focused on what she could control: her appearance, her flair, and her flirt.

Mia finally pulled herself out of the Cal Foreman tractor beam and turned back to Tara.

"I don't know if this is such a good plan. What if you get too … invested?"

"In Dex? Oh, that boy can't hurt me. I am impervious!" Mia still looked concerned, so Tara added, "You sound like Hale."

"Hale?" Cal put his coffee cup down. "You're on first names with Fitzpatrick?"

"It annoys him when I call him that. Probably reminds him of his crusty old granddad who taught at West Point, made him gut the fish they caught together, and never allowed him to have a hamster."

"Wait, is that true?" Mia shot a quick glance at Cal who shrugged.

"It could be," Tara said blithely. "It's the vibe I'm getting."

Her phone buzzed with a text from PR maven Sophie.

Five minutes out.

Which meant twenty.

"Any minute now," she said to the happy couple.

Cal pushed his chair back and stood. "I'm going to hit the head and if he's not here when I come back, I'm out."

Such drama. Tara gave him a salute. "Yes, sir!"

Another eye roll and he moved off, which left Mia looking—*oh my God, quit it with the sad eyes!*

"You know this is purely a professional thing," Tara said, pre-empting her friend's speech.

"I know you say it is, but I also know that you have hashtag-goals. Relationship goals. This marry-a-player scheme."

Growing up, Mia hadn't known her father, a Russian billionaire, who died before she had a chance to meet him. When she connected with her older brother Vadim after their mother had kept them apart for the first sixteen years of Mia's life, he split the family inheritance with his sister. Except for her brother, Mia Wallace was wealthier than the entire Rebels put together, and that included players and owners.

Determined that Mia's riches would not be an issue in their friendship, Tara had made a point to never discuss money with her. Billionaire heiresses should stay on their side of the divide. If she was to tell Mia about Chloe, her friend would want to help and this was the one relationship where there was no quid pro quo, nothing transactional between them.

But that didn't mean Tara couldn't ask for moral support for her goals. She'd thought that putting her snag-a-hockey-hunk plan out there into the world would ensure there was no confusion. People wouldn't try to matchmake her with inappropriate targets.

So what if it came off as mercenary. It was! She had dollar signs in her eyes and a safe deposit box where her heart was, and she wanted a hot athlete with a big bank account.

She had plenty to offer in return. A great body, a killer smile, and an unerring love of hockey. She would make a wonderful companion and was prepared to devote herself full-time to being the best trophy a man could ask for. Looking great on any guy's arm was coded in her DNA, but she also knew the culture.

Hanging with the girls while their men were off in battle.

Commiserating with her hockey husband after a hard loss.

Drinking champagne from the Stanley Cup after a Game Seven win in double overtime.

She could do that. She was meant to live that life.

"Listen, babe, remember about eight months ago, you had a goal of your own to win a certain dreamboat in a suit."

"Sure, but—"

"Sure, but nothing! You had your heart set on your brother's agent, one Tommy Gordon, and while you can admit now you were *completely and utterly* in the wrong, which I could have told you from the second I heard you bitching and moaning about Cal, did I encourage you to give up your dream?"

"No—"

"No, I didn't! I knew it was crazy, not because you couldn't get that guy, because you could, but because as soon as you and Cal started playing hide the puck, no one else was even in the running."

Mia pointed with her index finger. "Which goes to prove that I was going for the wrong thing. Latching onto something that made no sense, a guy I hardly knew, all because I thought I wanted a mature, sophisticated guy who was unlike any of the jocks I knew."

"When really you were destined for a hockey player lummox who treats you like a queen."

Mia's face crumpled as it always did at the mention of her man. "He does, doesn't he?"

"Yes, he does. You're very lucky. You've found your soulmate."

"And you're not going to find yours if you stay on this narrow path with such a singular focus. It took me a while to figure that out."

Tara shrugged. "I'm not as wise as you. I need to make all the mistakes before I find that perfect guy."

Her friend eyed her suspiciously. "You say this, but you don't believe it."

"Oh, I believe it. I haven't screwed up nearly enough yet. No lessons have been learned. No bottom has been rocked."

Mia looked over Tara's shoulder toward the coffee shop entrance. "Here they are."

Tara turned, expecting Dex and Sophie. Instead, a different pair graced the environs of this coffee establishment: Dex and Hale Fitzpatrick.

Why was he here? She had thought that once she signed the contract, he'd be well out of it.

Dex went to the counter without even acknowledging her while Hale came over.

"Mornin'."

"Hey, Fitz," Mia said. "You here to pull the strings?"

"Sure am." His midnight gaze lingered a charged beat on Tara, making her stomach flip.

Hell. She didn't want to feel anything interesting for this guy.

He spoke to Mia. "I like to keep an eye on my pet projects."

Tara's are-you-patronizing-me radar pinged. "Would've thought this was well below your pay grade."

"Where this team is concerned, nothing is beneath my notice."

At that rumbly tone, Tara shivered, not unpleasantly. "Where's Sophie?"

"She'll be along. Maybe you and Dex should try talking for a while so those photos look nice and natural."

Cal and Dex appeared, and Dex put a coffee cup down on the table. "I hear you like caramel macchiatos."

Blinking in surprise, Tara looked at the cup, the man, and the cup again. The label had her very specific instructions: half oat-half skim caramel macchiato with a quarter shot of vanilla syrup.

She'd always thought Dex attractive and had followed his career with interest. In Hale's office, he had looked weary, as if the pressures of hockey superstardom were grinding him down. Or maybe he was just hungover. Today, he looked more bad-tempered than tired.

"That's so sweet of you. Have a seat." Dex maneuvered around Hale who was still standing there like a fifth wheel. "How was practice?"

Dex shot a quick glance at Cal. "Okay. I—well, I didn't get a lot of sleep last night. My neighbor likes to throw parties."

"Would've thought that was up your alley," Cal commented, dry as dust.

"I've been told to reel it in." He peered up at Hale, who was scrolling through his phone, the faker. "I should have joined the fun because I didn't get any sleep anyway. Usually, I can relax better after a night at the club."

So the improved appearance didn't quite stretch to his mood. He sounded like a sullen teen who'd been grounded and couldn't play his video games. Solo joystick activities—heh—from here on out.

Tara snuck a look at Hale, who she could've sworn was smiling at something on his screen. Was he laughing at Dex? No, that couldn't be right. But then he caught her peek and gave a subtle raise of his eyebrow, sharing ... a moment of recognition.

There her body went again, shivering in a nice way.

In a hot way.

She did not want to be sharing secret smiles and eyebrow lifts and hot shivers with this man about how ridiculous Dexter O'Malley was.

Picking up her fresh beverage—Dex had bought it for her after all, which was very promising—Tara smiled at the small gathering.

Except for Hale. He was not included.

Yet he was still here, hovering.

Very few people had this nerve-wracking effect on her. The last person was her stepfather, and that was close to thirteen years ago when he spent hours cataloging her undesirable traits and drawing up plans to fix her. Drugs, therapy, and when that didn't work, sending her away to have her personality ironed out to something more palatable.

She bet Hale would prefer she wasn't so extra.

"Thanks for delivering Dex," she said to him. "We can probably manage the next part ourselves."

Hale didn't even look at her. Just kept his VIP gaze trained on his phone and walked away to another table. *Oh, God, just leave!*

Just then, Sophie appeared. "Hey, team! How's it going?"

Everyone murmured the usual noises and then it was full steam ahead with Sophie taking photos of "natural" poses. Cal made some faces about the absurdity of it all, Mia kicked him under the table, then Tara forged a nice foot-shin connection that made him yelp again. Dex looked bored but perked up enough to manage a few smiles.

And we're off.

6

———

As Tara had so cheerfully pointed out, this was definitely below Fitz's pay grade.

He had offered to do Sophie a favor and deliver O'Malley to his "coffee date" while she put out a fire at Rebels HQ. Apparently, the double date idea would get more traction—people already loved Foreman and Mia together—so Sophie was anxious not to miss the opportunity. Foreman had practically rolled his eyes into the back of his skull, so it was imperative they get Dex into position before the Bostonian decided this was beneath his interest.

Hale knew the feeling.

The plan was to drop O'Malley off and go about his business. He'd already instructed the guy on Tara's drink, because he wasn't sure he'd go to the trouble of finding out for himself. (The things Hale did for his job.) Chatting with the barista about the blonde's coffee preferences yesterday had been instructive—it was a fussy drink for a fussy woman—and told him all he needed to know about Tara Becker.

The woman was high maintenance.

She hopped up to grab a sugar packet—the barista had been no help there—and Fitz let his eyes indulge and run over the curve of her ass in dark jeans, tucked into fur-lined boots. An up-tempo number came on and she wiggled that heart-shaped ass as she stirred her coffee and hummed along.

Christ, she looked good.

Previously he'd thought her pretty in a put-on kind of way. Perfect make-up, sexily-teased hair, the frou-frou clothes. Today, she wore what could best be described as suburban mom winter wear: a teal puffer vest over a cream wool sweater. Much more appropriate than her usual, and as a group, they looked like they were sitting around at a ski lodge in a "Visit Vail" commercial.

Sophie was giving instructions to capture the perfect couple poses. O'Malley placed his arm around Tara's shoulder, and Fitz got the fleeting impression that this made her uneasy. She should be more relaxed; after all, this was everything she wanted.

He caught her eye and she stared right back. None of your business, that look said. While she might be wrong-headed about a million things, Tara Becker was right about this.

Beneath your pay grade.

Only when his phone rang with a call from his brother did he manage to rip his gaze away.

"Hey."

"Uncle Fitz?"

His heart warmed at the sound of Joni, his six-year-old niece. "Now what in the heck are you doin' with your dad's phone, button?"

Joni giggled. "He doesn't know."

"Well, I won't tell him if you don't. What've you been up to?"

The little charmer proceeded to tell him a long story that sounded suspiciously like the plot of *Encanto*, which he knew all about because they'd made him watch it only thirty-three times this past holiday.

"I don't think there's anyone livin' in the walls. I'll tell your daddy to check before you go to bed tonight."

The next voice was his brother, Bode's. "Don't encourage her, she's a menace with my phone."

"She likes shiny things." Not unlike a certain magpie in this coffee shop. He snuck a peek, oddly irked to see she was doing exactly what she was being paid to do: throwing herself into her new role as player girlfriend, which apparently required gazing at O'Malley like he was reciting poetry.

"She likes bankrupting her parents," Bode was saying. "She ordered ten thousand dollars' worth of furniture using Ava's iPad last week."

Fitz chuckled. "Born digital and with the shopping gene. Watch out."

"I know, I know. Anyway, how's your sex life?"

"Jump right in, why don't you?"

Bode laughed. "Ava will demand details the minute I get off the phone. She says I never ask the right questions. I'm supposed to enquire after who you're bangin' and what her chest measurements are."

"Somehow I doubt my sister-in-law put it in those terms."

"I'm paraphrasin'. And Mom's worried about you."

"Oh, did she ask about chest measurements as well?"

Bode chuckled. "She may as well have. She's co-opted my wife to find you someone special."

"I don't have time for that right now." He lowered his voice. "There are a lot of problems to resolve with the team before I can even go down that road."

"Your contract's for three years, right?"

"Might take that long to fix it."

"By which time you'll be too old to find a woman or father children."

With each call to his family, they ratcheted up the pressure. His mom was lonely after the death of Fitz's beloved father four years ago and had thrown herself whole hog into enlarging the clan.

"Didn't expect to hear Mom's talking points repeated back verbatim. If it's meant to be, it'll happen."

It wasn't as if he didn't know what marriage was like. After all, he'd been hitched for six years to his ex, Peyton, only parting ways when it became clear that they had little in common. Peyton was a party girl who loved the perks of being married to a hockey player and didn't get that all he wanted to do was crash and chill when he wasn't playing. He had craved a settled life with someone to keep the home fires burning. Their surface attraction never developed into anything deeper.

Since their split, he had moved around too much for anyone else to make an impression. His career, especially with his first GM position, had to take precedence.

Tell that to his family.

"Time to get on the dating apps," Bode was saying.

"Seems kind of deliberate." As much as he liked the logic of laying out your wants and needs, an app was almost too structured for Fitz. But maybe it was no different than Tara Becker's strategy to land a mate.

If she appeared in his list on a dating app, would he jump at the chance?

She was certainly attractive.

More than that. She was gorgeous.

But their values weren't even close.

If anything, Tara was a little too like Peyton: blonde, perky, a good-time gal. Maybe that was why she put his back up.

Bode brought him back to the conversation. "Well, Ava and Mom will probably have a list of eligible women for when you visit next month."

The Rebels were playing Atlanta in March. In spite of the relentless matchmaking, Fitz was looking forward to visiting, which reminded him that he needed to get gifts for the girls.

"Other than magical houses and expensive furniture, what are my beautiful nieces into these days?"

SINCE HIS ARRIVAL in Chicago in January, Fitz had been meeting once a week for breakfast with Remy, Remy's brother-in-law and former player Bren St. James, and Dante Moretti, Fitz's predecessor as GM. Bren was retired but was kept active by his teenage daughters while Dante was rocking it as a stay-at-home dad to a six-month-old.

At their usual table at Riverbrook Diner, Remy tapped his empty coffee cup. "I call this meeting of the Rebels Brain Trust to order."

Remy had been labeling their breakfasts as such, even though they'd promised not to give him unsolicited advice about the team. They spent a few minutes getting their orders in and chatting about their families, though Fitz couldn't really contribute there. Using his brother's children as proxies didn't sit well, and when you're not even close to settling down, it was hard not to feel envy at the personal lives these men had mastered.

"So my wife has a friend," Remy said with a sly look at Fitz.

"Here we go," Bren muttered.

Remy frowned. "Are you doubting my wife's ability to make matches?"

Dante gave a soft chuckle. "She tried to set me up so many times—badly—I lost count." He turned to Fitz. "I'd just moved to Chicago as well and wasn't looking for anyone. Didn't stop her."

Remy pointed with his fork. "So it was wasted on you because you were already slipping away for secret hook-ups with Burnett. Fitz here is different. He hasn't had time to meet anyone."

No, he hadn't. An introduction from someone he knew wasn't a terrible idea. It seemed less forced than using an app, or existing on the periphery hoping to pick up scraps, like Tara.

Was that what she was doing? A woman with a plan, she made no bones about her motivation.

"Milk curdled in your coffee?" Bren asked in that low Scottish burr, evidently picking up on Fitz's annoyance. He needed to stop dwelling on the dating dilemmas of his play-ers. Let the PR people do their thing.

"Just thinking about the team. Got a lot of work to do before I can worry about anything personal."

"Well, if you were lookin' for someone, what would you want?" Remy asked, a dog with a bone, before answering his own question with a finger count. "Female. Fertile. Okay with you bein' on the road. Doesn't think that Georgia accent makes you sound like a rube."

"From the man who sounds like he has a mouth permanently full of crawfish," Fitz shot back.

The others laughed as Remy shook his head, grinning.

Dante held up his phone. "Sounds like your O'Malley problem is on its way to being solved. These photos on the Rebels Instagram account are getting good traction, but it's the rest of it that's social media gold."

"Rest of it?"

He took the phone from Dante and was immediately confronted with an image of Tara. Or rather, a video. She was blowing kisses at the camera while a bubble appeared above her head with Dex's photo in it. Pink hearts were exploding, raining on the screen and his peace of mind.

Resisting the urge to unmute and hear whatever nonsense she was spouting, he passed the phone back to Dante.

Dante raised an eyebrow. "A lot of likes and comments here. And the follower numbers for the team's account have gone up."

"You keep track of that?"

"I notice when it jumps considerably. Tara and Dex have social influencer mojo, but in truth, it's Tara. She's the X-factor."

She clearly had an awareness of what worked to promote a brand, in this case her own. For now it had a positive spillover effect on the team, yet her motivations still pissed him off.

"She wants to marry a hockey player."

Bren's coffee cup stopped midway to his mouth. "She said that?"

"Yep. Blurted it out like it was no big deal. Thinks she's gonna have Dex down the aisle before she can click her heels three times."

"Pretty bold," Remy said. "But y'know somethin', I've always liked a bold woman. And Tara's a nice girl as well. Maddy adores her."

"A nice girl?" Fitz failed to see how these different parts of her personality could possibly mesh. "She's a gold digger."

"Maybe she's just honest," Bren muttered.

Remy smiled up at the server who had delivered a hot, gooey cinnamon roll to him. When she left, he spoke. "Lots of people have ambitions like that, fewer people are brave enough to admit it. As for Tara, she might be the kind of calming influence O'Malley needs."

Or he would break her heart. But she didn't have a heart to break—isn't that what she hinted at in his office? And why the hell did Fitz care if she was hurt after walking into this situation with her eyes wide open?

"I don't like to see people being taken advantage of."

"Who's getting the raw end of the deal here?" Dante asked, verbalizing Fitz's thoughts aloud. "The woman who wants a rich husband or the guy who's getting his rocks off regularly with a willing and beautiful partner? If Tara's ambitions are out there plain as day, then O'Malley can make up his own mind about whether that's a problem."

"Yeah, let the kids have their fun," Remy said. "Unless you have some other objection?"

Fitz shook his head. "No, just don't want it to blow up in our faces."

Tara was supposed to make things better, yet Fitz suspected she was only going to make things worse. A woman like that would always be bad news.

The food arrived and the conversation moved on to hockey, the kind of gamesmanship that Fitz understood.

7

HARPER TOOK a seat beside Fitz in the executive box and sighed. The first period of the game against the Detroit Motors was not going well, and the Rebels were two goals in the hole.

"I think we're officially in a funk," she said.

"Perhaps," Fitz said cautiously. He'd been brought on to take the pressure off her, especially given her pregnancy, and he hated that he might not be getting the results she expected. The team had two wins in their last six games and were having a hard time gelling, especially with current injuries and other distractions. "If we can get O'Malley and Grey up to speed, we could still make the playoffs, at which point momentum would likely take over."

"How's the Dex situation?"

"He's staying out of clubs. No headlines."

"The Instagram photos went down well. Pretty cute, actually."

So everyone kept telling him. After his brief look on Dante's phone, he hadn't paid attention, assuming the spin was either positive or neutral, and that Sophie would have told him if it wasn't. He was trying not to micro-manage, but the bottom line was that he didn't want to get caught up in *her*.

"Tara's really thrown herself into this a hundred percent," Harper said, with no irony whatsoever.

"You were right. She's perfect for O'Malley." There it was again, that frisson of annoyance when he thought about this woman, but especially when he thought about her with his player. Was he really going to begrudge two pretty airheads whatever pleasure they could derive from this?

The buzzer signaled the end of the period and the players skated off.

Fitz stood and stretched, musing on whether a visit to the locker room for a chat with the guys was in order. "Can I get you anything?"

"Ginger ale would be—wait, what's going on here?" Harper's gaze was trained on the rink where the clean-up guys were busy clearing the ice before the next period. "Who the hell is that?"

Someone was on the ice with a shovel.

A pink shovel.

Fitz's heart sank.

Like something out of a shampoo commercial, the skater's flowing blonde hair bounced in thick curls down her back. Wearing a wispy tutu over knee-length leggings and a pink jacket, she looked like Tinkerbell on blades.

Did people still think this woman's affiliation with the team was a good idea?

On her back was a photo of a face. Was that—fuck, was that O'Malley? The Jumbotron hadn't picked it up yet but the broadcast feed on one of the mute screens in the box was all over it. He raised the volume.

"Looks like we have an O'Malley fan in the house," Chuck Carter, one of the CSN commentators, was saying.

"She's got a pretty smooth motion." Jenna McDonald, Chip's co-host, sounded impressed. "Maybe the Rebels should put her on a shift. She could only improve their fortunes."

An ABBA song played while Tara cleared the ice, the one about a woman looking for a man after midnight. The perfect tune for a predator on the hunt. He wouldn't be surprised if she'd chosen it, thinking it the height of hilarity.

"Did you sign off on this?" Harper asked.

"No, I did not." It might seem like a harmless stunt but there were liability issues to consider. Not officially an employee, Tara was not insured to skate on the rink, never mind the fact Fitz should be in the loop about anything that deviated from the routine.

He dialed Sophie. "Whose idea was this?"

"Oh, I thought—"

"No. Get her off the ice now." He turned to Harper. "It's being taken care of."

Harper's lips were slightly curved. "The crowd likes her, but that doesn't surprise me. And at least she's not half-naked like those freakin' cheer squads."

Some of the league's teams used scantily-clad "ice girls" to clear the ice and do PR duties. As soon as Harper and her sisters took over, the Rebel Ice Girls were decommissioned, but it looked like they had a new one in the house.

Tara Becker: setting feminism back by fifty years.

The crowd sang along as she completed one more circuit of the ice. She stopped and did a sassy pose with the shovel, one that got her on the Jumbotron—her ultimate goal, no doubt—and raised even louder cheers.

Fitz growled. "I'm heading down."

Two minutes later he found the latest addition to the ice-sweepers leaning against the wall outside the locker room, casually balancing on guard-wrapped blades while she chatted with the Rebels mascot.

"Ms. Becker!"

Tara jumped at his roar which had echoed much louder than he expected in the back-of-rink space. The Rebels mascot—a weird cross between a cat and a duck—made to move away. They had just hired a new person to wear the costume, as the last one had been caught stealing merch, and Fitz had yet to meet him.

"Hold up. Was this your idea?"

The mascot shook its cat-duck head.

Tara moved in front of it. "Don't you dare shout at Ronnie Reb. She had nothing to do with it."

She? Ignoring that, he focused on his true mission. "We're not covered for you to be on the ice. You're not even wearing a helmet!"

"And ruin this hair? I've been skating since I was four years old. Have a little faith!" She turned to the mascot. "You'd best get along now, Pep. Mr. Fitzpatrick is probably going to say a bunch of mean things and you'll want to defend me with your duck claws. I give you leave to exit this situation with as much grace as someone of your mysterious species can muster."

The mascot might have shrugged? Fitz had no idea and he didn't care. Still, given Tara's farewell speech, he felt obliged to wait for it—or her—to move off and out of the path of his wrath.

"This is not okay," he gritted out.

"When you see the exposure, you'll sing a different tune.

Lots of clickety-clicks and shares across the Interwebs." She turned to show him her back and he was forced to stare at Dex O'Malley's stupid face printed on pink satin. "Isn't this cool? I asked Aurora to make it for me."

"Who?"

"Theo Kershaw's gran. She runs the Theo's Tarts fan group which are currently in a turf war with Reid's Rebelles —that's Kennedy's grandmother's fan group for Reid. Reid Durand? One of your players?" Her tone was one of censure for not keeping up on the various fan clubs and their petty squabbles. "Those grannies are vicious, Golden Girls on crack. Anyway, I thought it would be fun to get a jacket for Dex, like I'm his Number One fan, with less ankle hobbling, of course. But sitting in his section would be kind of lonely, especially as there's only one of me and tons of fans for Theo and Reid. Dex is too new, you see? So I had a chat with Mia and she scored me a pass and we bedazzled this shovel. It has a double-meaning, because of the gold digger thing." She grabbed the shovel which had been leaning against the wall, its handle covered in pink wrapping paper, rhinestones dotting the shaft. "So surprise, surprise, you don't approve, but well-behaved women don't make history, or that's what they say. You know what I prefer?"

No fucking idea.

She took his seething silence as encouragement to share.

"'If you want something said, ask a man. If you want something done, ask a woman.'" Imparted somberly like she was freakin' Gandhi. "Margaret Thatcher. Now I don't agree with her politics, but she got that right. Or at least Meryl did when she played her in the movie. Oh, here they come!"

The door to the locker room opened and the team started trickling out.

"Hey, guys! Good luck out there. So close in that first

period!" Her green eyes gleamed on seeing O'Malley exit. She passed her phone to Fitz, covered in a Little Mermaid-themed case. "Do you mind? Dex, let's get a pic. Just a quick one."

Dazed from the Tara onslaught, Fitz had no choice but to do as he was told. It was probably the quickest way to wrap this up.

Or not.

Tinkerbell-Tara appeared to be going nowhere as she had more wisdom to vomit.

"Now Dex, focus on that puck in the next period! Imagine it's one of the exec's heads."

There was no missing her sly, cat's eye of a glance in Fitz's direction. Dex looked a little shell-shocked—who wouldn't?—but soon he was getting into the spirit with his arm around Tara's waist and his hand splayed on her hip.

The lurch in Fitz's chest roared his disapproval.

Dex asked, "You put my face on a jacket?"

"Of course I did! I'm your best girl, aren't I?" She gave an exaggerated wink which made Dex laugh—a genuine sound, the first time Fitz had ever heard anything remotely authentic coming out of his mouth.

She didn't stop there.

"Cade, you can do this! And I know little Rosie is so proud of you!"

"Thanks, Tara," Burnett mumbled, his mouth kicking up at the corners as he walked by.

"Mr. Kershaw, as always, having a great hair day."

How she could tell this when the man was wearing a lid, Fitz had no idea. Kershaw saluted her with his stick.

"Cal, babe, you missed that goal in the tenth minute by a smidge. It's on your blade in this period, I can feel it!"

And so on, with each player getting a personalized pep

rally until Vadim Petrov, the captain, appeared at the rear. She said something that sounded like Russian—Russian!—to which Petrov gave a curt nod, an eyebrow raise to Fitz, and carried on down to the tunnel.

"I hope they do okay," Tara mused as her gaze followed the players, like a momma duck watching the babies strike out on their own. She took her phone back and checked the photo, her eyebrows drawn together. "Hmm, not bad. Next time, you might want to take more than one so we have choices."

Next time? No fucking way. "You and I need to have a chat about what just happened here."

"You mean me encouraging the boys to be the best they can be?"

"That's not your job. Neither is it your job to clear the ice or skate around in a tutu like a demented Tinkerbell. You have one task—to stop O'Malley from making a spectacle of himself. That's it."

"Sure, sure." Thunderous applause echoed through the tunnel. "Oh, sounds like the guys scored a quick one. Awesome!"

He should be thrilled but this Tara business was muting the pleasure. Every action she took made his job more difficult, and did she have to look so damn good in those leggings? As for that stretchy top which had slipped to reveal pink lace barely keeping her plump breasts in check, was that necessary? Compounding the insult, a fucking freckle winked at him like a beacon from the soft, pale flesh of her cleavage.

"Well, as always, Hale, it's been a pleasure." Grinning, she daintily walked away into the locker room, leaving him looking like a slack-jawed yokel.

He was still standing there, stunned into speechlessness,

when approximately thirty seconds later, a text came in from Harper.

> Figure out the liability thing. I want Tara on the ice at all the home games until the playoffs.

8

———

Tara stepped off the elevator onto the fifth floor of the Castle Apartments and headed toward the hulking statue standing in the corridor.

"A little help, Dexter?"

"Oh, right." He rushed forward and took the heaviest shopping bag from her hand. "I didn't expect you to be doing this."

"I help out Kennedy sometimes with the deliveries." Kennedy Clark, Reid Durand's girlfriend, was building a concierge and personal assistant business that included grocery deliveries for the Rebels. Tara could always do with the extra cash and when Kennedy told her Dex was one of her newer clients, she asked to be given this job. He had yet to invite her over, so she needed to move this along.

"I hope you don't think it's too intrusive of me."

"No, not at all," he said as he brought all the bags but one into his apartment.

She followed him, noting that it was the typical bachelor pad with not much personality. He still had stuff in boxes, though of course the TV and video game console was set up. Priorities.

"Now, they didn't have any mangoes at Mariano's, but they have really nice ones at the Rogers Park Fruit Market so I grabbed some there. And they always have better grapes—lovely Concord ones. Look at how purple they are!" She started to unpack the bags and transfer the produce to the counter. "I usually like to wash and bag these immediately into snack-sized servings. I bought some extra sandwich bags which are the perfect size. That okay with you?"

Dex leaned on the counter. "Yeah, but you don't have to do all this."

"I am being paid. By you, actually, so I don't mind." She grinned at him. "How did you sleep?"

"Sleep?"

"Yeah, you have circles under your eyes. And I know you said before that you have trouble sleeping, something about a noisy neighbor."

He frowned. "Yeah, she's a party girl. But that's not it, not really. I've never slept well, to be honest, and I hate taking anything for it."

He probably should talk to the team doc about that, but she wouldn't push just yet.

"Despite your sleep deprivation, you played well the other night. That goal was amazing."

He preened a little. "Think I got a boost seeing my face on your jacket. It's kind of nice to have someone in my corner. I don't really know anyone yet."

The Rebels were a tight group, so it was always hard to be the new guy. She got the impression that Cal didn't think much of him, probably because Dex was a different person when he hung out with his teammates. One on one like this, she was seeing that he wasn't a complete tool after all.

"Well, you know me. Sure, it's a strange situation with the whole contracted girlfriend thing, but it doesn't mean we can't be friends." It would be so easy to throw herself at Dex—she doubted he'd refuse—but she'd rather get to know him a little first.

After all, if this was to be the next Mr. Tara Becker, then she should be sure they wouldn't kill each other before the honeymoon was over.

"How about I make you a sandwich and tell you all about my strategies for getting a good night's sleep?"

SINCE FORMER YOGA instructor Kennedy had decided that the lure of the open road couldn't compete with a hot NHL player in her bed—along with the adoration of a cute, bedraggled puppy—she now offered a weekly session for her friends. It wasn't a complete health fest; nothing labeled Downward Dog and Daiquiris could ever claim that. But it was a chance for Tara to hang with a bunch of awesome women, who had achieved the ultimate goal.

Happiness with a pro-athlete.

Harper Chase had offered the use of the players' yoga room, an open and airy space at the Rebels practice facility, when the team didn't need it. Tara had also brought her scissors so she could give a couple of trims to those who wanted it—namely Mia and Isobel Chase, who needed an inch or two off to remove the split ends. Despite Tara's protests that using elastic bands and washing every day were bad for their hair, these girls were too damn sporty to heed her advice.

Finished with forty minutes of body-bending poses, they all gathered around for the main event: dishing and drinking their choice of daiquiri, pineapple-coconut or strawberry-basil. (Youngest Chase sister, Violet, married to retired captain Bren St. James, was an avid experimenter with the flavors.) They also had a virgin version for Sadie who was four months pregnant with Gunnar Bond's child.

"Take a seat," Tara ordered Isobel, wife of the team captain, the hot, tatted Russian, Vadim Petrov. She placed her stylist's travel cape, which looked like an inverted umbrella, over Isobel's shoulders, and ran a hand over the ends of her client's hair. "Have you been using the conditioner I recommended?"

"I have! But my hair doesn't seem to want to absorb anything."

"Hmm. I'll give you the name of something else."

"Bull semen," Violet said with an air of authority. "I heard it strengthens the hair shaft. Pun very much intended."

"Or we could try a regenerating mask from Sephora first?" Tara offered. "Maybe go the trusted route before whacking off a bull's ding dong."

That launched a spirited conversation about the consistency of you-know-what and other uses for it apart from hair treatments.

Yoga, so educational.

Elle Butler, Theo Kershaw's wife and baby mama, cut in. "Speaking of managing the spunkier elements of the group, Tara, how goes it with Rebels Club Kid Dex O'Malley?"

Tara shot a glance at Mia who was the only one who knew it wasn't for real with Dex. Or maybe not. One look at Mia's sisters-in-law, Violet and Isobel, told her that secret might not remain so for much longer.

"It's early days," Tara said diplomatically.

Isobel eyed Tara in the mirror. "Instagram official, though?"

"Yeah, but ..." Sadie said. "Is he the one?"

The one? Tara's ambitions were well-known and garnered her notes of concern—and criticism—from the other women in her immediate circle. Everyone was so hung up on finding the perfect match. This OTP business was so overrated.

"We're still getting to know each other, so it's a little soon to say if he is or isn't. Anyway, I'm not sure I believe in all this fated mates stuff. It seems so random. I've no doubt you guys are happy, but look at the hoops you had to jump through to get there."

She pointed at Violet. "You had to inherit one third of a sports franchise, live with sisters you barely knew, then become a nanny to a hockey player." She turned to Elle. "You had to get knocked up after a one-night stand. And don't get me started on Sadie." That poor woman had been assigned the recycled number of a broken man's dead wife! Those were some freaky circumstances. "All of you had to pretzel your lives to put yourselves into contention. Maybe that could happen for me and maybe it could be Dex, so we'll see if it develops into something."

Instead of worrying if it could be perfect, she could look at it as a business arrangement and see if it panned out to something ... good.

She could live with good if it meant Chloe was looked after.

"Sounds like there's not much of a spark," Kennedy said.

Not like with Hale.

Oh dear, here come those strange thoughts again.

She had to admit that he'd weighed on her peace of mind a little too much in the last few days. Just before today's yoga, she'd spotted him in the Rebels gym, working out on the weights. Mesmerized, she had allowed herself a moment to enjoy the sight of massive shoulders, oak-trunk thighs, and a very attractive butt. Excellent musculature that had her fingers itching to grab, claw, and claim. In profile, he had looked incredibly focused, a man who wouldn't let anything—or anyone—steer him off track.

Being the subject of that focus had felt amazing. The memory of him thundering toward her after her rink shenanigans, like a grouchy ogre, still gave her a forbidden thrill. Not only did he look good in a sweat-dampened tee and shorts, but he could also rock a suit like no one's business.

Mr. Control Freak had not liked her rink-clearing impro-visation. Oh no. When he'd bellowed at her in that hallway, she had felt an irresistible urge to poke at him. Provoke a reaction.

Make him sweat.

Which made her sweat.

Seeing those gorgeous blue eyes burst like supernovas as she stood up to him sure got her engine cranked. His face when she encouraged the boys! Which was fun or maybe not fun because it was dangerous, and she didn't have time in her life right now for dangerous.

Back to the mission: Dex O'Malley.

Tara snipped an inch off Isobel's length and ignored her wince. Those ends had to go.

"I don't need sparks. Dexter is very handsome and finan-cially secure—check and check. Sometimes, that's enough." Had she not been telling herself that for years?

Or rather her mother had intoned it as she dragged on a cigarette. *You're not going to have much to offer beyond that pretty face of yours, Tara, so get yourself a trade you can carry anywhere and grab the first decent husband prospect that comes along.*

The operative word being "decent." Tara might have two arms, two legs, and the ability to turn the worst hair into a masterpiece, but it would never give her the security she needed for Chloe. Sparks were for people who could afford the consequences.

Casey Higgins, Harper's assistant, popped her head around the door. "Hey, did I miss it?"

"Yeah, we finished up about fifteen minutes ago," Mia said.

Casey beelined for the blender jug. "I mean the adult beverages. I couldn't get away for Corpse pose but I'm here for the liquid lunch. Harper sent me, told me to drink enough for her seeing as she can't. What's the goss?"

"We're trying to figure out if Dex is the one for Tara," Elle said matter-of-factly.

"Of course he's not," Casey said.

"Explain," Kennedy said, pointing her glass at Casey who poured from the pineapple-coconut pitcher, the star of today's lineup.

"Dex is kind of young and can barely look after himself," Casey said with an air of authority. "And he comes off as kind of a dick. You deserve better, Tara."

That was nice, but these women barely knew Dex. Or her, for that matter. As well as rehabilitating his reputation with the public, it looked like she might have to make him look better in the eyes of the org.

Time to move this relationship into the next gear.

                                  9
                          ——————————

TARA HAD ALWAYS THOUGHT it a little strange that the players
hung out at a regular bar near the Rebels arena where they
were at risk of being mobbed. Oddly, there seemed to be an
unspoken rule that they shouldn't be bothered—too much
—by the civilian population.

So here they were at the Empty Net for a "Welcome to
the Team" gathering, organized by Tara. They had a couple
of new players, but really, this was so Dex could get to know
his teammates in a more convivial setting.

On the way in, Tara ran into Mia with Cal. Her friend
wore a cute Marc Jacobs dress that Tara had found in a
consignment store. It had never suited Tara but looked so
good on Mia.

"You wore it! Doesn't she look amazing, Cal?"

Cal put his arm around his fiancée. "She always looks
amazing, but in that dress, gorgeous girl, you are wicked
fine." He gave her a kiss and soon they were making out as if
they were the only people here.

When they finally came up for air, Tara commented

wryly, "Just try to keep it PG when we have obvious photo-hounds in the vicinity."

While this wasn't the kind of place where tabloids hung out looking for risqué skin shots, there was always the chance a regular fan might take a photo. Tara had promised Sophie—and by extension, Hale—that she would keep Dex's focus on her alone. That way, he wouldn't be tempted to spread himself around so much like the man whore he was.

"There he is," Mia said, pointing over Tara's shoulder in the direction of the bar. "And he's with Reid. Not sure who I feel sorrier for."

Dex stood at the corner of the L-shaped bar, talking animatedly to Rebels center Reid Durand. The same grumpy Reid who would rather cut off his right hand than give anyone but his girlfriend, Kennedy, and his cute pupper, Bucky, the time of day.

Reid was looking straight ahead, his focus on some point on the floor like a puck was about to appear there any second (or he prayed it would). In for the save, Kennedy appeared beside him with a beer in her hand and waved them over. Tara would have a word with her about getting Reid to be nicer to Dex.

Though she suspected it'd be easier to convince Reid to climb up on the bar and sing the soundtrack from *The Lion King*.

"You all look gorgeous," Kennedy said, hugging Tara, then Mia, and finally a kiss on the cheek for Cal. Kennedy, her blonde hair streaked with pink, had a pixie punk vibe. She leaned in toward Tara. "Just so you know, Dex has turned a few women away. Said he was waiting on his girlfriend."

Surprising. Other than the grocery delivery a couple of days ago, Tara hadn't had much one-on-one time with him yet. She took a few steps closer, and the surprises kept on coming: Dex's expression brightened and he took her hand in his. "Hey, beautiful."

"Hi! Sorry we're late. Cal took a little persuading."

"Yeah, you should have just brought the girls." He shot a rueful glance at Reid who was talking intimately with Kennedy, probably letting her know he hated this socializing business with the heat of a thousand suns. "It looks better when there are more girls. We should have gone to a club."

"That's the kind of image we're trying to rehabilitate, Dexter. You surrounded with a harem of pretty young things is a little too much MTV rap video, circa 2003. These days, it's about connections, friendships, teammates, your crew." She looked around, wondering how to get Cal on board. "We have to minimize the risks to the team's rep."

Dex scowled. "You sound like them."

"Who? The people who pay your huge salary?" Good Lord, she was going to have to lead him by the hand. "Babe, let's try to have a nice time, get a few photos, and have you tucked up in bed for a good eight hours before morning skate. 'Kay? Now, I'd love an adult beverage."

Looking a touch dazed by her command of the situation, he guided her to the seat beside him at the bar. "I already ordered pitchers for the guys. Or you could have something else."

Beer wasn't really her thing but she'd make an effort. "A beer would be great."

While he poured, he kept his gaze a foot above her marvelous cleavage. Good boy!

"So, how are things going with the team? Made any friends yet?"

"These guys aren't really the buddy-buddy type." Quick dagger of a look at Reid. "Kaz came out to the club the last time, but I think he's trying to stay on the down low so he can get back with his wife." Tate Kazminski was in the middle of a contentious divorce; that he was trying to reconcile with his almost-ex was news.

"Well, a lot of the guys have settled down over the last couple of years and aren't really into the club scene anymore. There comes a time when you have to clear out your contact list, hang up your leather pants, and throw out the family-size box of condoms." At his look of confusion, she added, "Because you're a one-woman man."

He scoffed and eyed up her legs. "Why would I do that? I mean, yeah, it's better without the latex but ..."

Tuning out, she looked around, seeking out new team members. She raised her hand in a friendly wave to Jace Henderson, the new D-man, which seemed to confuse the hell out of him, the poor love.

Dex was still talking. "*Sexually-transmitted diseases are so rare these days ...*"

Still not getting in my panties without a rubber, buddy.

Thankfully, her clutch danced to save her, probably Cal or Mia checking in. However, her phone displayed a text from an unknown number.

You look bored.

Uh, creepy! She cast her gaze around—Mia waved at her from near the juke box but this text wasn't from her. Tara expanded her scrutiny to the far corners of the bar before shooting back a reply.

Who is this?

"... most women like it that way as well," Dex was saying, still harping on about the superiority of condom-free sex.

She stood on the foot-rail at the bar, even covered her eyes, practicing for when she would be standing on the deck of a Mediterranean super yacht.

Nothing ... not a face she recognized ...

Another text came in:

The man who pulls the strings.

Then she saw it. Or rather, them.

Broad shoulders, the kind she could climb aboard, topped by a strong head with mahogany hair and glinting copper highlights.

Hale was here, standing on the other side of the L-shaped bar.

She shouldn't be surprised. The invitation had been extended generally and there were front office staff here, but she hadn't expected to have to run interference with the management.

"Back in a sec," she murmured to Dex as she rounded the corner, exchanging pleasantries with the people she knew all while her pulse ratcheted up in unexplained irritation.

Tap tap on his multi-muscled back. When he turned, he smiled and damn, it was so unexpected her heart tripped suddenly.

Annoyed at her reaction, she barked out an abrupt greeting. "What the hell are you doing here?"

"Hello, Ms. Becker, nice to see you as well. Can I get—"

"None of the soft soap, Hale. I want to know why you're here."

"It's a free country." There was that smile again, like it was all a joke. She felt like the butt of it, but then she often did around men like him.

Smart men. Powerful men. Older men.

He moved aside a few inches. "Have you met Bastian Durand?"

The Hawks forward was standing behind Hale, a beer in his hand. She'd run into the younger Durand brother at a couple of parties and he'd always been perfectly pleasant to her.

"Hi, there," she said with a smile that she changed to over-the-top flirtatious as she watched Hale's expression turn grim.

He moved his body just enough to block Bastian. Interesting.

"How are things with O'Malley?" Hale asked.

"Perfectly fine until you texted me."

"You looked bored."

Had she? She might not have been a hundred percent involved in the conversation, but that didn't really explain why she had jumped at the chance to get away from Dex.

Or maybe she'd jumped at the chance to talk to Hale?

Oh, she didn't like that.

She leaned in and lowered her voice, loving and hating how close she stood to him. "I'm supposed to be sitting with Dex, playing the devoted date." She felt rather foolish now that she had marched over here in some sort of hissy fit. But Hale had actively sought her out with that text, which was confusing, to say the least. "I'll let you get back to it," she said, waving between Hale and Bastian.

Before she could back away, someone nudged her elbow

and she turned to find Pepper Calhoun. Pep was currently temping as the Rebels' mascot, which was kind of weird because she also happened to be Coach Calhoun's daughter. Tara had yet to get the whole story.

"Hey, Pep! You want a drink? The boss is buying."

Pepper grinned to reveal a gorgeous smile that extended to her hazel eyes. Tara's gaze was immediately drawn to her dark hair—stylist eyes always went north. Could do with some shaping, for sure. That mascot head couldn't be helping.

"No, I've already ordered a—" She stopped speaking, her eyes widening at something over Tara's shoulder.

"You okay?" Tara turned and found Bastian Durand in a similar state of astonishment.

"Pepper? What are you doing here?"

And then Pepper Calhoun did the last thing anyone would expect in the presence of a superstar like Bastian Durand: she turned up her nose, like she'd encountered a particularly noxious smell.

"My father *is* the Rebels' coach, but then you wouldn't have forgotten that, would you?"

Bastian reddened. "No, of course not. That's not what I meant."

But he was speaking to the void because Pepper had already left before she had a chance to pick up the beer she'd just ordered.

Tara exchanged a questioning glance with Fitz and got an eyebrow shrug of ignorance in return.

"Uh, I need to see Reid and Ken. Later, Fitz." Bastian placed a twenty down on the bar, grabbed Pepper's beer, and headed off in hot pursuit, clearly a man on a mission.

"What's going on there?" Tara asked.

"No idea. But I sure as hell don't need another complication."

"Right. Because all that matters is how it affects you and your beloved team."

"Exactly." He ignored her sarcasm. "I'll catch him later and do some diggin'."

"Contract negotiations at the urinals?"

He laughed and for once, she felt it was with her instead of at her. "Something like that. What are you drinking?"

"I *was* drinking a beer before I was rudely summoned."

"You mean 'saved from a fate worse than death'? And I wouldn't have pegged you for a beer-drinker."

She rolled in her lips, hating that he was right. "I'd love a French martini, please, heavy on the Chambord."

Hale leaned over the bar, the action straining his suit jacket against those powerful shoulder muscles. Her fingers itched to smooth over his back and she had to dig her nails into her palms to keep her composure.

Once the order was in, he faced her again.

"So how come you're mad at me?"

"I'm not." She was; she just didn't know why.

"You were pretty fired up when you arrived. Seemed kind of hostile."

She murmured something, hoping he wouldn't pursue it.

"What's that? My hearing's going, with age and all."

She may as well be honest. "I thought you were spying on me because you don't trust me to do a good job."

He gave her a searching look. Sometimes, his regard was so intense she felt every one of her faults laid bare. Just like Dr. Bill and the many talk therapy sessions he'd forced on her as a teen.

The world does not revolve around you, Tara.

If you continue to take, your selfishness will be detrimental to this family.

"Sounds like I managed to ruffle some feathers."

"I get the impression, oh, I don't know why, that you don't approve of me, so I guess I internalized that and then—"

"Externalized it when you saw me."

Subject change needed. "So you're trying to get Bastian onto the Rebels roster?"

"Just feelin' him out." He handed the martini glass to her, then raised his own glass of bourbon to her.

She gestured her thanks. "His shots on goal and PPG are excellent. A little too excellent."

His eyes narrowed, and this close she could see feathery laugh lines around them. For all his grumpiness with her, Hale Fitzpatrick came across as the kind of guy who enjoyed life. There was a sensualist buried behind that bruiser exterior, yet she clearly brought out a different side. The hard-assed, bossy, dominant side. "Are you sayin' Durand the Younger is too good for this team?"

"Oh, most definitely. Sure, you have a few good players, but Bast is in a league of his own and ..." Her grin wouldn't stay away. He looked so shocked that she might know what she was talking about and that she was using that knowledge to imply the Rebels hadn't a snowball's chance in this too-toasty bar of getting Bastian on board.

Catching on, he shook his head. "You might be right. Bastian would wipe out the budget but we need to make a bold move."

She knew the feeling. "Here's to bold moves." She raised her glass, gratified when he clinked his against hers. "Have you talked to Reid about bringing on his brother?"

"No comment." But amused. Oh so amused.

As Tara was never afraid to share an opinion, she offered hers freely.

"You should run it by Kennedy. She knows them both well and would probably have a better read on the situation than talking to either of them alone."

"I should base a decision to acquire a player on a conversation with his brother's girlfriend?"

"Behind every great man is a woman who knows more about team dynamics than you think." She shrugged. "But don't ask me. I'm just a casual observer."

He viewed her with interest and after a long pause, said, "You really think I don't trust you to babysit O'Malley?"

"I think you don't trust me to do anything." Tara took a sip of her martini, realizing that she sounded like she cared for Hale's opinion.

She did not.

Except ... she might crave his approval just a teensy-weensy bit.

And it pissed her off.

"You're wrong. I've checked the social media stuff—"

"Sophie told you where to click, I suppose."

"Uh huh. Step-by-step on downloading the mobile application and everything," he murmured, so accepting of his role in their psychodrama.

There was that smile again.

So, so bad for her.

This is about money. Keep it transactional. "So, I've been meaning to talk to you about that raise."

"Raise? You haven't done anything yet."

"Are you kidding? Dex's and the team's Insta accounts are already seeing a big increase in followers and the photo of us at the coffee shop is getting great traction. Not to mention my circuit around the rink and the fact that the boys won their game after I intervened. You can't put a price on that kind of brand awareness."

But she was happy to try.

"Intervened? One photo, a Tinkerbell-on-ice impression and some ra-ra-go-get-'em-boys, and you think you should be gettin' a raise?"

Ignoring his snark, she plowed on. "How about an advance on the payment for this first month? Like a signing bonus?"

"You mean an advance against the salary we'll be paying you? So not a bonus at all?"

Such a stickler. "Yes, if you want to quibble about terminology. I'm a little behind on ... something, and this cash would be a life saver."

"Sure, take it up with Sophie." His look said: *Why the hell are you asking me?*

"Okay. Just thought I should clear it with you first. With you being the General."

"What's that about? Because I'm the GM?"

"Sure, but it's more like you're a control freak, must have your finger on the pulse, need to know who's doing what at all times. Marshaling the troops. Directing the plays."

"Right now, I don't feel like a general of anything."

That sounded suspiciously like a confidence. Was Hale telling her something personal?

Instantly, she felt panicky, itchy, and very, very hot. *Don't fuck this up, Tara. Don't make it weird.*

She nudged him with her elbow. "Things will improve. New blood, new approaches, new everything—that often gets a man and a team out of their ruts."

He looked at her curiously. "A man?"

"Sure. Sometimes you have to throw out the playbook to effect real change."

"Is that what you're doing? Throwing out the playbook?"

Maybe. She'd been trying the same thing for a while with little success. This deal with the Rebels to fake it with Dex might be her best shot at finally moving ahead of her problems instead of existing permanently behind the eight ball.

Which meant she really should be on the other side of the bar listening to Dex espouse his theories on rubber-free fucking.

Yet why did this feel like the place to be?

Rather than fight it, she answered his question as honestly as she could. "I'm trying to dig myself out of a hole and carve out a new path." For her and for Chloe.

He nodded, with something like understanding in his eyes, and that reaction made her feel warm. She edged closer, feeling excited.

Connected.

He looked at her for what felt like an eternity. Stripped her to the marrow in the process.

"The social media stuff is all exactly where it should be. Dex seems to be behaving himself, the two of you look like an 'It' couple, and the press about O'Malley's activities has died down. You're doing a great job, Tara. Keep it up."

So it was abrupt, or maybe not. Likely it was a reminder that she was an employee and these heart-to-hearts were off the menu.

Still, her throat felt tight. No one thought she was good at anything, so to hear that she was good at this—faking it— was gratifying.

Wasn't it?

She needed to get out of here before she ... she didn't know what. But it would involve feeling flush with pride because Hale Fitzpatrick gave her a kind word while glaring at her like she was no better than something stuck to the soles of his Ferragamos.

"Thanks, General." She gave him a cheeky salute. "I probably should get back to my charge before his eyes wander."

10

———

Fitz watched Tara walk away for a little too long.

Hell, even a second was too much because it had him thinking dangerous thoughts.

Like how that silver dress made her ass look like a Georgia peach he wanted to take a bite out of.

And how she had seemed so damn wounded when she thought he might disapprove of her handling of this assignment.

Not to mention how she knew her shit about hockey.

That turned him on most of all.

No, it was her ass. He didn't have a hard-on for a woman who could talk the talk. He had a hard-on for a pretty little trophy wannabe with a body made for sin.

He shouldn't even be here, but Bastian had said he could only meet at the Empty Net—sure—and Fitz needed some alone time with the guy without his agent butting in. Not exactly kosher but sometimes the rules had to be bent to get results.

Bold moves.

Whatever had possessed him to shoot off that text to

her? He'd spotted her the moment he entered the bar and while waiting for Bastian, he had felt this strange need to reach out to her when he should be leaving her the fuck alone.

He drained his glass of bourbon and steeled himself for the night ahead. Maybe it wouldn't be so bad if he could talk to ...

Tara.

That's whose name entered his head. Not one of the Rebels Brain Trust or a player. Not even Bastian. He had to admit he got a certain kick out of this woman.

A kick to his libido. That and ... nothing.

He wouldn't be anywhere near her; instead he would gaze at her body parts from a distance: those long legs, perfect ass, great tits. That cascade of hair he could already feel draped over his chest. Those lush lips he could almost taste.

He wouldn't look into her gemstone eyes or enjoy that subtle eyebrow lift that told him she was poking fun.

That maybe they were in on the joke together.

Because they weren't. He had nothing in common with Tara and if he did, he wouldn't be talking to her long enough to find out.

Yet he couldn't take his eyes off her. She had christened this gathering as some sort of welcome event for the new players, and now she was playing at party host, placing Dex into a grouping here, chattering away with Jace, their new AHL acquisition there. Everyone seemed to be having a good time, and Sophie was doing the rounds, taking photos and uploading to the various channels to prove the fun times were happening.

When did this public relations stuff get so complicated? Before social media, teams relied on friendly sports journos to smooth over any bumps in the road. There would be no need to bring on a "civilian" to fix a team's reputation problem.

Not that Tara was a true innocent in all this. If anything, she was an instigator, a firebrand, a complete mindfuck.

And more.

Standing beside her, inhaling her scent, he'd had an almost unbearable urge to touch her, taste her, drag her to a private corner and do unspeakably depraved things to her. In other words, act like one of the horny young bucks in his care. Was there something in the air?

As if summoned, the horniest of the bucks appeared at her side. O'Malley placed a hand on her waist and whispered in her ear. She smiled, a touch practiced, and that cheered Fitz for the first time this evening.

Tara Becker had O'Malley's number.

Or Fitz liked to think she wouldn't be taken in by whatever he was offering. But wasn't that exactly what she wanted? A not-too-bright jock who could give her everything she needed?

Sophie appeared in his sight line, smiling as she approached. "Hey, I'm surprised to see you here. Checking up on Tara?" She tilted her head. "Or maybe on me?"

"No, other team business brought me here. Everything seems to be going just as you planned. Good job."

Sophie glanced at her phone, then back at him. "Tara's super savvy about this kind of thing, has tons of great ideas. A dream to work with."

So everyone kept telling him, and he could see with his own two eyes what an asset she was.

Pity he couldn't remove those same eyes from her assets.

He turned back to the bar and raised his hand for

another drink. "How's the calendar shoot set-up coming along?"

"Pretty good. You know, we have it all under control, Fitz. You really don't need to worry."

In other words, *butt out.*

Despite his Southern background, he found it difficult to approach his life and career with a laissez-faire attitude. Letting things ride or take their course wasn't his style. If he could press a button to make it happen, he would. He just wished that the path of one of his players—and by extension the team—wasn't so wrapped up in the hands of a self-serving moneygrubber.

"Oh, that should make a good one," Sophie murmured, her photographer focus on the perfect tableau.

Tara was the center of attention, surrounded by several players as she regaled them with a story that had them hanging on every word. Sophie moved off to take photos while Fitz turned his back, striving for some measure of control.

Work. Think about what needed to happen with the Bastian Durand situation.

Even if they could afford him—and it would be a squeeze—was it a good idea to bring him onto the same team as his brother? There had been some bad blood between them on the ice during a crosstown classic in December. The two of them went at it and Bastian ended up with a broken wrist, a concussion, and an exit from Team USA for the Olympics. That can't have sat well.

If he talked to either of them, would they tell him the truth about the current status of their relationship? Or would it be in his interest to gather intel from the girlfriend of one of his current players? He shook his head, not quite believing that he was considering taking Tara's advice.

Just the thought of her had him turning, seeking her out. His gaze scanned the bar, though he didn't have far to wander. Tara had her arm linked with Jace Henderson, who frankly, looked terrified as she introduced him to a trio of women seated at a corner table. The kid was green, barely of legal age, and far too young for ... anyone. Like he needed help getting laid!

A song he didn't recognize came on, and Tara squeezed Jace's shoulder—as if signing off on her matchmaking or whatever—and jumped in mid-conversation with Kennedy and Mia. She raised her hands in the air and waved them, then hugged both of her friends. All three of them were laughing, and Fitz was struck by Tara's joy, an undeniable sweetness about her.

He blinked away the thought. She wasn't sweet. She was a sexpot.

Ignore her.

Yet his gaze inexorably found its way back, metal to her magnet. He allowed himself a stolen moment to enjoy the sway of her hips and the back-and-forth of that beautiful ass as she danced away. Thinking of her in those terms was much safer. It was a damn pleasure to feast his gaze on Tara Becker.

Fuck, he wanted her.

He shouldn't. She was technically an employee in an albeit fake relationship with an asset to the organization. Fitz didn't need this sort of complication.

He sensed a movement at his shoulder. O'Malley stood beside him, leaning his elbow on the bar.

"Fucking hell, she's hot, isn't she?"

Possessiveness fisted his lungs. "She works for the team and she was hired for a job, so don't let your crayon stray outside the lines."

"Are you kidding? She's looking to bag a player. Has been for months, I heard."

A red mist danced before Fitz's eyes. "You will treat her with respect, do you hear me?"

"Sure, I'll respect her with my coc—"

"O'Malley, I'm serious. She's signed a contract. We're not your pimp, so hands off."

He raised both hands in a surrender that Fitz didn't believe for a second. His next words confirmed that his concession was one big joke.

"Okay, okay. But if the mood takes us, then that contract is worth shit."

11

―――――

Fitz disliked plane travel intensely.

He didn't hate it—he didn't hate anything but knew that while on a plane, he was not at his best. It made him nervous, which had the domino effect of making him irritable.

This trip to New York was one of two they would make during the regular season. There and back, they were looking at four plane rides. And that was just one city. He used to take Xanax to calm him down, but he didn't like how it made him feel. The drugs made him loopy and chatty, which was completely the wrong way to be when on a plane with the men you led. To his knowledge, he hadn't made any mistakes or revealed too much, but it could happen. So he made do with a stiff drink at the start of the trip and a fierce concentration on work.

Usually Harper would sit with him and they'd talk business, the perfect distraction. But she'd decided not to take any chances with her pregnancy. "Geriatric" they called it because she was over thirty-five. Medicine sure had a way of kicking you in the teeth.

O'Malley walked past him with a nod, headed toward the back of the plane to play cards with a few of the guys. Had he spent more time with Tara, made good on that leering promise to get to know her better?

Since the club a couple of nights ago, images of her on the dance floor, swaying her hips and wiggling her ass, had haunted his dreams. Even now he could almost hear her laugh caressing his ear. Well, not caressing. More like grating.

He opened Instagram and checked Tara's feed.

Sophie had told him O'Malley's metrics were up, but Tara's were the real revelation. Her feed was filled with reels —short videos set to music—of her wishing her "boyfriend" a good morning. Each day for the last week, she had done this, usually with cute commentary.

Tara looking at her watch and wagging her finger.

Tara holding up a Starbucks cup with O'Malley's name on it ("Sexy Dexy").

Tara yawning as if she had just awoken, her hair tumbled and tousled against her pillow, cartoon birds flying around like something out of a fairytale.

He couldn't turn on the sound, but even on silent it was clear that Tara had screen presence. Her public agreed. The likes were in the thousands, comments in the hundreds, saying she was cute or gorgeous or so lucky to have O'Malley.

He replayed the one with her in bed. Unless she went to sleep in full make-up with perfectly-painted lips, then this wasn't a real shot of Tara waking up. But if it was ... some lucky fucker would see that in the morning.

It was ten minutes past the time they should have taken off. A flight attendant walked by and Fitz grabbed her attention.

"Is there a reason we haven't left yet?"

"We're still waiting on another passenger."

Everyone on the team had traveled here directly from the pick-up at the arena. Before he had a chance to ask who was holding up the flight, Tara's laugh sounded again, insinuating itself like a forest vine around his brain stem. Only it was no longer in his imagination.

She was here.

She stood near the plane's entrance, her blonde ponytail swishing as she spoke with the other flight attendant. They seemed to be in a deep conversation which stopped when the attendant took a large garment bag from her and hung it in the plane's coat closet. Then they hugged.

Fitz would bet they had met less than two minutes ago. But that was Tara. Friends with all.

She proceeded to make her way down the aisle with her suitcase in tow, stopping at each row, saying a few words to anyone who would listen. Flight attendant Barbie. She even paused to greet Hudson Grey, their recent acquisition from New Jersey. Hudson was gay, a fact that was common knowledge, so Tara wouldn't get any juice from that lemon.

Didn't stop her. Next she turned to the player across from Grey, Jace Henderson.

Every player was likely fair game, everyone a potential mark if O'Malley didn't work out. Fitz had warned her off, which was probably like throwing chum in shark-infested waters.

Where Tara was the shark.

A couple of the players looked over their shoulders or around their seats as she passed by. Her smile was wide, her breasts were pert, and her ponytail bounced. A blast of sunshine in a frigid Chicago winter.

All Fitz saw was the potential for chaos, especially when no fewer than three players jumped up to help her stow her luggage, a pink suitcase covered in images of Disney princesses.

He returned to his phone. When he looked up again, Tara was standing with her head cocked, her elbow on the seat in front of him. Somehow, he had known she would stop by.

"Working hard or hardly working, Hale?"

The pilot announced the flight's imminent departure and Fitz checked his seatbelt for the third time.

"Probably should take your seat," he said because she didn't appear to be in a hurry to do so.

"Can I have the window?"

Before he could respond, she was climbing over him into the window seat, her ass mere millimeters from his mouth. Unlike the newer team planes with single captain seats, this plane was an older model refitted with roomy pairs. More than enough seats existed so everyone could sit solo. Evidently, his position on the aisle wasn't quite enough to convey the message that he wanted to sit alone.

She made a fuss settling in, placing a large purse at her feet, but not under the seat where it should be stowed during take-off. Phone in the seat pocket, then a change of plan as she pulled it out and answered a text, then started scrolling. But not for long. Yanking the window shutter down was the next thing to attract her attention—and distract his.

"Shouldn't you be sitting with O'Malley?"

She leaned in, her shoulder touching his. "So we can fool this lot into thinking we're love's young dream?"

"That *is* why you're here."

She picked up her purse and rooted around. Out came a

copy of *Marie Claire*, a bag of gummy bears, and an eye mask. For a two hour flight.

She ripped open the candy. "Gummy?"

He shook his head. He might choke on it during take-off.

She popped one in her mouth and said around her chewing, "They're just regular ones, not edibles or anything like that."

"We're about to take off, so you should probably put your purse under the seat."

"Sure, sure." She didn't, instead leaned in once more, this time getting her scent right into his nostrils, now mixed with the sweetness of the candy. "You're awfully by the book. Though I see you still have your phone on. Big no-no during take-off and landing, except we all know it's BS."

It was in his hand, practically dented from how tight he was holding it. He turned it over to switch it off.

"Checking out my feed?"

"Just making sure you're not doing anything that might damage the team."

She snorted, as if to say, *I'm not the problem here*, and he had to say she wasn't wholly wrong. Tara was actually solving the team's problem, and any issue Fitz had was all on him.

The airplane started its taxi down the runway.

"Seatbelt," he ground out.

"So have you checked out my TikTok yet?"

"Nope."

"Well, it's mostly cross-posted from there to Insta so lots of repurposed content. I had a chat with Sadie about it because she used to work for a big influencer type who hawked vaginal wellness products. Punani Power? You've probably heard of it."

That would be a negative. "Who's Sadie?"

"Sadie Yates, the dress designer? She's engaged to Gunnar Bond, one of your first line centers?" He'd met Sadie and her sister Lauren, had just forgotten her name. "Anyway, Sadie gave me some ideas for how to recycle content, best times to post, that kind of thing. Sophie knows that, too, but I like to get more than one opinion. Trust, but verify, y'know."

"We're about to take off, so you probably should—"

"Right, seatbelt." She popped another gummy bear. "Sure you don't want one?"

"Tara, you'll need to put that purse under your seat and fasten your seatbelt." The flight attendant smiled at Tara but gave him the beady eye, as if he was responsible or had any say in how Tara Becker behaved. *Officer, she just sat here without a word of invitation!* "And you'll have to put your phone in airplane mode, sir."

"On it, Brooke," Tara said cheerfully.

With his phone in airplane mode and pocketed inside his jacket, Fitz gripped the seat's arm rest and watched as Tara made her pre-flight preparations. Cutting it fine, though. The plane was picking up speed, the engines loud (louder than usual perhaps?), that familiar lurch in his stomach signifying abject fear.

He could admit it to himself. He was terrified of flying.

But he was usually able to ignore it, distract himself with work. Only now he had her, making it worse.

"God, flying's so ridiculous, isn't it?"

Not just flying. "It's fairly dull, actually."

"Yeah, dull. That's it. Though, I suppose you can get work done or catch up on your reading ... or your social media monitoring."

The plane gathered speed, the engines almost whining with the effort. Each time he wondered if this was the day the plane made it mere feet off the ground then gave up because it was all too much for a hunk of steel that really shouldn't be airborne.

Speaking of monitoring ... "I noticed you're friendly with some of the players, Henderson in particular. What's going on there?"

Her mouth quirked, that same tease to her lips that signaled she understood how much she got under his skin.

"Oh, Jace is such a sweetie. He's kind of homesick since he got called up to the big leagues from Rockford, so I've been introducing him around."

"I noticed. To women in bars. We're trying to stop another O'Malley situation, not create new opportunities for inexperienced players to be led down crooked paths."

"Is that what you think I am? A bad influence?"

The worst. "You have one job, yet you seem to think the rest of the team is your business. Maybe focus on what we're paying you for."

She shrugged. "I'm a multitasker. And when I see someone in need of a friend, I won't sit idly by. It's called empathy and pro-sports could do with more of it."

Oh, sure, she was doing all this out of the goodness of her heart.

"How's the 'marry a hockey player' plan going? O'Malley coming around to your charms yet?"

She stared at him, again with that glint of amusement.

"We're getting to know each other. Early days."

"So not love at first sight, then?" What was wrong with him? He didn't care about any of this, yet some part of him needed to know if they were forging a connection.

"Oh, God, no. That doesn't interest me at all."

"Why not? Doesn't everyone want to meet someone with similar goals and values?"

"Sure. But that's not quite the same thing as falling in love, is it? You can be simpatico with someone, on the same wavelength, know exactly what the expectations are, but love doesn't have to enter the equation. For some of us, Hale, love will never be on the menu."

This woman wanted to marry a pro-athlete, had been completely up front about it, but didn't think love was part of the package? Perhaps he shouldn't have been surprised that her transactional view of relationships would be free of the most important component.

Shut up about it. Don't even ask.

"What happened to turn you off romance?"

"Oh, I'm all about romance. But those are merely the trappings, the moments that make you feel special, and I suppose for a fleeting nanosecond, you can pretend that romance is the same as love. Romantic dates, chocolates, flowers. I love a good bouquet—ask anyone here." She winked, an acknowledgment of her bouquet catch melt-down at Levi Hunt's wedding last summer. He'd overheard some of the front office staff gossiping about it, making fun of Tara, yet here she was, projecting her usual amused self-deprecation. "But I'm not mistaking that for love."

"Let me rephrase. What's turned you off love?"

"Oh, the usual. Bad role models. A mother who married several times, all in the name of L-O-V-E, who was prepared to sacrifice the people she should have loved with all her heart while she gave everything to the next guy on the docket. I know that makes me sound like a sad sack and you'll say that I just have to meet the right person to show me different. I'm very self-aware about my shortcomings in this area, so don't you worry about me." She patted his hand, the one still wrapped like a boa constrictor around the arm rest.

"I'm not worried."

Her look said, *sure, Hale.* "What about you? Met anyone since you moved to Chicago?"

Yes, but she's with someone else.

Well, if that wasn't the most absurd thought to ever enter his brain. "I'm not in a hurry, though my family thinks I shouldn't be wasting any time. Given my age, y'know."

She chuckled. "Your momma wants grandbabies?"

"She already has two—my younger brother, Bode, got the jump on me. But she's a Georgia woman and there can never be enough kids to spoil. She misses my dad. He died four years ago."

"Sorry about that. That must be tough on her."

He nodded. "It was. Is. They were a great match. I miss him, too."

She waited a beat, let him indulge in the fondness of his father's memory.

"And now she wants to see you settled, make a good life like she did with your dad. Doesn't that interest you?"

It did, but he needed to settle with a team first. "I've moved around a lot so it can be hard to commit when you don't know if you'll be around through the end of a contract."

"Sounds like an excuse."

"That's what my mother says. But I've been married before and it didn't work out."

"Why not?" She sounded amazed that anyone would dare leave him in the dust.

"We had different notions of what marriage looked like. I wanted a quiet life, she preferred living loud. Not a criticism but we were too different and the cracks started showing during the off season. Marriage to a hockey player isn't all hearts-and-flowers. The world revolves around him for at least six months solid, probably longer because hockey players are selfish fuckers at best."

He paused, expecting some inane commentary that never came. Instead she was listening, her pretty brows furrowed in focus, as if he was the most important person in the world.

He coughed slightly. "I guess I'm looking for somewhere to lay my hat before I unpack the suitcase. Once I get that right—the job, the team—I can focus on the rest. Give it a hundred percent. Kids, picket fence, the lot."

"I imagine you don't do anything by half. You were like that on the ice."

That she remembered—or claimed to—made his chest warm. "During my peak years, you were in what? Junior high?"

"More like middle school."

"Damn, that's cold."

She grasped his arm. "It's not a dig! Just the facts. You had that great game during the Finals against Boston, the one where you scored the Gordie Howe hat trick."

"I can still feel that hit. Saw double for days."

"Lifting the Cup a week later helped clear your vision, I bet."

He laughed, surprised to realize he was enjoying himself. But the moment he acknowledged it, the suspicions took hold. Was Tara a true hockey fan or just well-researched in service to her great plan?

The flight attendant made an announcement. "The seatbelt signs are now off so you're free to use your electronic devices."

They were in the air. Several minutes had passed and he hadn't even realized they'd taken off and reached cruising altitude.

Tara popped another gummy bear. He leaned in and helped himself. "Thanks."

"Sure, any time." They held each other's gaze for a smidge too long before Tara cleared her throat and broke it, reaching for her purse. "I'd better go find Dex and make sure he hasn't blown all my shoe money in a poker game."

He stood to let her out—no way was he allowing her to brush that lush, curvy body anywhere near his dry mouth or grasping hands.

"See you later," she said, sounding almost shy and not like Tara at all as she maneuvered by him in the aisle.

"Later," he muttered, then sank back into his seat with his seatbelt on once more.

12

———

Tara might have insisted to Hale that she would not be denied the perks of travel for this job, but she didn't enjoy being so far away from Chicago and Chloe.

In truth, she hated it.

However, this was Dex's first away game since coming off the injured list, and PR insisted she represent. Her skate around the Rebels rink had been a hit on socials, and while she wouldn't be doing anything like that on this trip, Sophie had encouraged her to make a record of the journey in her own inimitable way.

Last night, she'd had a lovely dinner with Cal, Mia, Reid, and Dex—fab social media op!—where her "boyfriend" had been attentive and a little flirtatious. He didn't try anything on, which meant he was either warned off or was playing the long game. (That he might not be interested in her sexually never occurred to her.) As she didn't think Dex subtle enough to not go the full-court press, she had to assume the General had laid down the law.

Silly man.

She shouldn't have talked to him on the plane. One

minute she was poking fun at his work habits, trying to get a rise out of him, the next she was in the window seat soothing his nerves. She had recognized the signs immediately: the white-knuckling of his phone, the barely-discernible sheen of sweat at his hairline, the fact he didn't even blink when she sat down beside him.

Though that might be because he was starting to accept that as typical Tara behavior.

She knew that talking to him, even if it was just nonsense, would get his mind off the fear. Only it wasn't nonsense—well, it might have been from her, she could hardly remember a word out of her mouth. But from Hale, she learned that he was searching for a connection: with a team first before he took his personal needs seriously. He wanted to belong.

Then he would give his family life the full effort. He would apply himself to that the way he did his career because he was looking for the real deal, not some easy-bake oven relationship like Tara was seeking from Dex. Something that might not even last.

No guy would look at her and think: *I hope to hold hands with you in our rocking chairs.* Not for Tara a man who would adore the ground her walker walked on. She had to get in, make her mark, and get out.

It wasn't just that conversation with Hale that had thrown her. Her mother usually checked in once a month on her daughters' well-being, a scheduled call that covered the necessary obligations. This morning she'd deigned to get in touch outside the regular time, and it was easy to see why.

Tara was lately running in more prominent circles. Of course Monica Becker, now Galliano, was going to be interested.

> Can't wait to meet Dex, baby! Tell him I'm
> a fan!

Ugh.

A quick run in Central Park might shake off the malaise that'd come over her. Tara adored New York's energy, a city of scrappers and scramblers, a bit like her. About halfway through her run, she spotted someone she recognized ahead of her: Hudson Grey, the new Rebels forward recently traded in from Jersey. Such a cutie! Far too young and well, gay, for her but there was no harm in being friendly.

She caught up and pulled alongside. "Hey there!"

Frowning, he removed his right earbud, likely thinking she was a deranged fan instead of an integral part of the team. "Uh, hey."

"I'm Tara. We were on the plane ride out together from Chicago? I said hello before but you were in another world entirely. I'm dating Dex O'Malley."

Awareness dawned, along with relief. "Right. How's it going?"

"Good, good." She continued to jog with him, thankful he'd slowed a little to accommodate the conversation and her aching thighs. "So first time on the roster tonight. How do you feel?"

"A bit nervous. My parents are coming in from Connecticut."

"Oh, I wouldn't worry. I'm guessing they probably saw you in the Frozen Four final two years ago when you scored that game winner. As far as they're concerned, you've already peaked."

His reaction was a half-smile, probably a combination of surprise and terror that she had the information at her fingertips. So she was a fan—sue her! "That's one way to look at it. But I want to make them proud."

"I kid! You have your best years ahead of you and they will be with you all the way. They must be thrilled. And you've landed in a great place with the Rebels. Very progressive, close-knit, a real family atmosphere. I think you're going to shine here." She amended, "Or there. Meaning back in Chicago."

Rumor had it that Hudson's previous team were jerks when he came out, so things could only get better for him. While every crew had their share of small-brained Neanderthals and most had management who claimed to be LGBTQ-friendly, the Rebels actually did the work.

Hudson smiled, and boy did that transform him. "Want to run with me? I've got about fifteen minutes left before my ball sac freezes."

During their run, Tara learned that Hudson loved true crime podcasts and Indian food, and they had a great chat about *Only Murders in the Building*, that funny Steve Martin and Martin Short show which must have filmed close to here. Tara could totally see herself as the Selena Gomez character. That chick had an amazing fashion sense.

That was this morning and she'd spent the rest of the day making a video for her YouTube channel, one where she whispered while she brushed Mia's hair and gave it a trim. (She had to keep re-doing it because Mia couldn't stop laughing about her "whisper porn side hustle.") Funnily enough, that was how she'd discovered it, while looking for haircutting videos to polish her skills—apparently some people's ASMR response was triggered by the sound of cutting hair. The more she researched it, the more she realized there was a whole subset of people out there who were soothed by normal sounds presented in a pleasing fashion.

It would never make her a millionaire but it was fun to combine two things she liked to reach people and make them happy.

Now it was game time. Just outside the executive box in the Spartans' arena, Tara's phone buzzed with a call from Misty Pines.

She ushered Mia on ahead. "Hey, I'll meet you in there. Gotta take this." Once Mia was out of earshot, she answered.

"Hi, Tara, it's May."

"Hi!" Nurse May had been amazing about calling in whenever she was on shift. Tara had missed her call earlier while she was in the shower and had been forced to leave a message in return. "Is everything okay?"

"Yes, I know I said everything was fine earlier, but I wanted to let you know that Chloe has a slight case of bronchitis."

Tara's heart plummeted. "Serious enough to call about?"

"Not really. I didn't want you to find out about it from another nurse the next time you're in and then wonder why I didn't say anything."

She had a point. Tara had taken Chloe's care team to task before about not keeping her more informed. She wanted to know if her sister had so much as a sniffle, even if she couldn't do a thing about it.

"But you don't think it's worrisome?"

"The doctor is monitoring her—"

"The doctor's been in?" She'd raised her voice, just as Hale walked by. Damn. She turned away for privacy and lowered her tone. "It was bad enough for a doctor's visit?"

"He's here every day anyway, Tara. We asked him to take a look and he said we just need to keep an eye on her. Perhaps I shouldn't have called you."

"No, no, you did the right thing. I'm not in Chicago right now so it makes me nervous to be so far away."

Which is what she would be if she landed herself a hockey player husband. He could get traded to anywhere—but she'd always assumed she would be within a plane ride of her sister and that funds wouldn't be an issue. She could get back to see her as often as she needed.

But now, she felt off-kilter, stuck in this limbo where she couldn't just leave because she had a job to do and was as poor as a church mouse.

"I'll be back in town tomorrow and I'll check in then, see if I should come visit." No should about it but phrasing it that way kept this all in the realm of *no problemo*!

"That sounds like a plan. But don't worry. She's had colds and respiratory infections before and she's always come through. She couldn't be under better care."

Tara knew this. She closed her eyes and took a breath. "Thanks, May. I appreciate it. Truly."

Blinking herself back to business, Tara headed into the visitors' box. She had spent time in Mia's box at Rebels Arena but had never visited the owners' suite, or the equivalent for visitors, at an away game. There was an advantage to hanging with her girl crew back in Chicago—men were not usually invited. No need to worry about how you looked or if your cleavage was too in-your-face or if your laugh was too high-pitched. But here, she didn't have a choice.

Here she had to be in performance mode.

The hockey suite in New York was pretty fancy: big screens, leather seats, a great spread.

And him.

He stood at the bar, talking to Sophie, looking like the alpha beast that he was. That suit on him was just yum, and she was struck by how he always seemed so in charge. Even on the plane ride out when he wasn't 100% at ease, he still projected an image of a man who could deal with anything thrown at him. And foolish girl that she was, Tara had thought she was actually helping by jabbering on and on to distract him. As if a man like Hale needed comfort from the likes of her.

He caught her eye, and there was no mistaking his appraisal of her body, a heated censure that made Tara feel both under and overdressed. Appropriately, Mia was wearing cute leggings, booties, and a chunky sweater. Tara had chosen a short tulip skirt with a revealing slit and a V-necked silk shell that did great things for her tits. She was a bit chilly, but she expected she'd warm up fairly quickly because …

Hale.

If spending a few minutes in his presence got her a little heated, then so be it.

"Need a drink?" she asked Mia, who was currently texting Cal before the game. Should Tara be doing that with Dex?

Probably not. Texting was personal, real-couple stuff, not for sharing on her Instagram.

"Please. An IPA or whatever they have."

"Will do."

She had just put their orders in when she sensed a presence to her left.

"You okay?" Hale asked before she had a chance to ask him.

"Fine, thanks."

"You looked like you were in the middle of something intense on the phone outside."

She made a point not to involve other people in her

drama. Men, especially, didn't enjoy a girl who came off as issue-ridden unless it somehow made the sex better.

She affixed her best nothing-to-see-here smile. "Oh, just my shopper at Macy's telling me they didn't have my size in the latest Manolos. They're all out so boo hoo, right?"

Brow in lines, he stared at her for a heartbeat that sent her own pulse into a riot.

Say something. "So how was your day?"

"Good. Got a few laps in at the pool, made a few calls." He moved in a little closer, and again she was struck by his solid presence—and how warm she felt this close to him. "I never thanked you for what you did earlier on the plane ride out to calm my nerves. That was kind of you."

Oh. Maybe she had helped after all. He sounded genuinely grateful, so she needed to accept his praise with grace.

Or babble like there was a sale on words in the word store.

"It's not a big deal. People are afraid of all sorts of things. I have a thing about steam trains going into tunnels. Every time I see that on screen, I get this weird, cringy feeling because it's so obviously a metaphor, y'know." God, she needed to shut up before she told him what it was a metaphor for.

"Sex," she said, though he hadn't asked. Just saying the word moved the thought from the background of her brain to the blinking-neon foreground.

Sex, it seemed, was uppermost in her mind whenever she saw Hale.

When had she made the switch from "you irritate the fuck out of me" to "please fuck the irritation out of me"?

"Trains entering tunnels are all about sex," she continued because apparently she needed to finish this very important TED talk. "That's how they would code it in old movies, like the end of *North by Northwest*. It's obvious that Cary Grant and Eve Marie Saint are getting it on in the train bunkbeds. They're even married! But they couldn't show anything so Hitch"—*don't say cock*—"Well, the director had this train going into the tunnel."

She took a breath, and Hale took the opportunity to offer his important thoughts on this important topic.

"Because it's a metaphor for sex."

"Correct."

And then there was silence, a long, awkward crapola of silence. Except maybe not that awkward because Hale was half-smiling at her, undoubtedly laughing at her absurdity which was understandable. She was suddenly very, very chatty.

"Saw you with Hudson Grey this morning in the hotel lobby. What's that about?"

Well, not about sex. Could we stick to the fantasy portion of the conversation, please?

"We ran into each other on our morning runs. It was nice to jog with someone."

He sighed heavily. "I've already indicated how I feel about this. You with other men doesn't work with the optics we're going for."

Her with other men? Sheesh, did Hale come straight from an eighties rom-com where the male dummy thought the woman dummy couldn't be friends with a guy?

"You do know that Hudson is not interested in me in that way nor I in him? And you don't have to worry about me shooting my shot with any of the other eligible marks." She almost howled with laughter at the look on his face when she said "marks." "I'm a one player woman at the moment. Also, it's your lucky day because I'm determined to ignore your bad humor and help you out. Been thinking about your problem."

"My problem?"

"Pleasing that momma of yours. I can help."

Something flashed in his eyes. Something predatory and ... God help her, sexy. "Help how?"

Annoyed but intrigued: the Hale Fitzpatrick story.

"I'm pretty good at social media stuff so I could help you set up a dating profile. Get your mother off your back."

"I never said I had a problem. In fact, I said I didn't have time to date. Too much work."

"Makes Hale a dull boy. If you wait until this team wins a Cup, you could be waiting forever." She leaned in, noting his aftershave was woodsy with a hint of citrus. Like a lemon tree forest. "You're going to have to start putting yourself out there. Flood the apps with all things Hale."

She wasn't sure why she was offering her services. All she knew was that this man threatened her equilibrium in a way she didn't quite understand. It seemed safer to remove him from the field of play, so she wouldn't have to consider his impact on the game.

And he would be happier if he found someone. It might make him less grumpy.

"I'm not sure a dating app is for me. It sounds like effort."

"Happiness takes effort," she said. "You think it just falls into your lap with a snap of your fingers? Sure, some people meet in fortuitous circumstances but most of us have to put the work in."

"Is that what you're doing? Hustling to make your happily-ever-after?"

They exchanged disapproving stares, meaning Hale disapproved of her and she disapproved of his disapproval.

Yet she still wanted to help because it was ingrained in her DNA.

"You used to be a scouting manager in Vancouver, right?"

"I was."

"And even now you're always in scouting mode. You look at the stats, the numbers, the history, the form for every player you're considering taking on or ditching by the trade deadline. The NHL draft is nothing more than a dating app for teams and players."

His eyes dipped to her lips. She'd gone with Lisa Eldridge's Velvet Petal today, a little less bold than her usual Taylor Swift red. Nice to see it getting some male eyeball action.

Though when Hale looked at her, he seemed to use his entire body, like all his cells became active for this one activity. For her.

She felt a little toasty. Where was she again? Oh, right. Explaining how the world works.

"For me, a guy can look good on paper and those stats are all I have to go on to start. That's how he's presenting himself—his socials, news pieces, how he carries himself in interviews, did he buy his parents' a house with his signing bonus. They're all clues to the package I'm getting. Now, all that might look good but sometimes the click isn't there IRL —that stands for 'in real life.' You've got to put yourself out there, seeking the click. No dates, no chance of clicking! Analyze the player stats—meaning dating profiles—and then put your foot onto the ice. Get your hands dirty. Are you a warrior or an actor-whatsit?"

"Actor-whatsit?" A half-hook of his lips, like he was finally starting to understand that resistance was futile when it came to Tara.

God, he was attractive.

And double God, Tara was babbling again.

"Who's the guy who decides if the risk of insuring something is worth it?"

"An actuary?"

"Right, an actuary. Be a warrior, not an actuary." She picked up her drinks. "If you need a woman's opinion, I'm happy to help. Check in with me at the first break."

She didn't wait for a response, just left him standing there, a touch dazed. She liked to think she had that effect on people.

Better to be polarizing than not considered at all.

13

———

Tara Becker kept surprising him.

Fitz usually didn't do well with surprises. He liked knowing what he was getting into, calculating the over/under and figuring out the cost/benefit. He applied that strategy to his work and to a certain extent, his dating life. With most women, he enjoyed short-term flings, knowing it would go nowhere. Just a way to let off steam.

It had been three months since he'd had sex.

Three months focusing on his job and his players' problems. Now that things were settling and this O'Malley situation was somewhat under control, he could indulge. Have some fun.

Which brought him back to Tara.

No doubt about it, Tara was fun, the kind of woman you took to bed and enjoyed the hell out of before you got serious.

Not that he would even go there. It would be far too complicated with this O'Malley set-up. He had insisted she keep away from anyone else on the team, and that included executives. There was always the chance that she would end up sleeping with his player and that would be very untidy indeed.

Were they together already? O'Malley had expressed interest back at the Empty Net and he was right when he said Tara wanted to bag a player. Would she sleep with O'Malley to further her chances? Or would she hold out because it would be more beneficial in the long run? Like Anne Boleyn leading Henry VIII on a merry dance while she waited for the tyrant to put a ring on it.

Did he just compare Tara to Anne Boleyn?

Though things didn't work out so well for her. Anne Boleyn, that is.

Christ, he needed to exit this line of thinking. Tara was a grown woman and could sleep with whomever she wanted. If that was part of her plan to score an NHL husband, it was none of Fitz's business.

Except he wanted it to be his business, or at least he didn't want it to be O'Malley's business. Not quite the same thing, but a little too close for comfort.

He walked to the bar along the box window and put his drink down. He needed to focus on the team, think about the little improvements—or bold moves—he could make to get them on the right track. They had all the right ingredients, a great roster of players, but something was holding them back.

Just as something was holding him back.

That conversation he'd witnessed outside the box was not about shoes. Tara had said something about a doctor before frowning at him and turning away. Was she ill or did she know someone who was? Rather than let him see that side of her, she had elected to put up a front. Show him the fun and fluffy side.

Hale didn't like that she'd done that with him. True, she

didn't owe him a peek into her real self, but that didn't mean he didn't want to see it.

To understand what made her tick.

Five minutes in, O'Malley had made an appearance on the second line with little impact. He'd played okay in his first Rebels game at home, especially after Tara's encouragement. Not much should be expected after such a long layoff, but Fitz couldn't help thinking this PR business was distracting him.

That Tara was distracting him.

She and Mia were seated in the box's front row, chattering away in low voices, coming alive as soon as the puck was in New York's blue zone, which wasn't often enough.

At the break, they were one-zero in the hole and Mia had stepped out, leaving Tara alone. He wandered over and gestured at the seat beside her.

"May I?"

She looked surprised. Good. "Of course."

He sat and after a moment, asked, "What do you think of the game?"

"The boys have their work cut out for them. New York's defense is solid, Mulvaney is a beast out there, best on even strength points so far this season. It's easy to see why the Rebels can't penetrate."

"You know your hockey."

"Oh, a little. My stepfather was a big fan and it was pretty much the only thing we had in common." Her expression clouded and he saw the effort she made to pull out of some dark recess. "But our Dexy is back! That's something."

"For all the good it did."

"Now, it's his first turn on away ice after injury." She touched his arm, gave it a gentle squeeze. "Have a little faith."

A little faith. Is that what was needed? Maybe instead of a little, he should take a leap.

Her hand on his arm burned through to his marrow. He looked down to see it was no longer there, though some phantom sensation remained.

He should look at this problem like that. This was merely a transitory attraction, nothing more. He could acknowledge that Tara was a beautiful woman; he didn't have to do anything with that information.

"What you said before about helping me set up a dating profile, were you serious?"

Her expression was unusually passive but he suspected something moved below the surface. "Of course! And I have a ton of matchmaking success."

"Cal and Mia. Anyone else?"

She touched a finger to her lips.

He wished she wouldn't.

"I was instrumental in telling Kennedy that she should be making the most of her roommate situation with Reid. Forced proximity is very conducive to intimacy. And look how that worked out."

"So you have a good track record."

Was he going to regret asking for her scattershot thoughts on his dating options? Some part of him wanted her opinion—or maybe his dick was talking and just wanted to be near her. That lush body, her mind-scrambling smile, the quick way she matched everything he threw at her ...

Which meant he either needed another drink or he craved the attention. With his sex lull, there was always a chance a little flirting with a beautiful woman was lowering his defenses.

"Where do we start?" he asked, his voice low, conscious that the next period would start up any minute.

She took out her phone. "Let's start with you. Tell me what you like."

"Work. Hockey. Coffee. My nieces. My dog. Not necessarily in that order."

She liked that mention of his nieces.

He had known she would.

"How old are they?"

"Joni's six, a little scientist in the making. Loves flowers and animals and fire. Then there's Gracie, who's four, and loves princesses. Both as adorable as they sound."

"I know all about little girls and the love of princesses." She appeared a touch wistful, her mind elsewhere for a brief second. "And what are you looking for?"

A moment of madness.

He swallowed that instinct down. "I travel a lot so I need someone who's not too clingy, who doesn't mind long periods of being alone, who's adventurous but not rash. Who's looking for a connection. Something real."

"So a Ms. Perfect who doesn't make too many demands of you, especially as you're off doing Very Important Things."

"My job is what it is. I can't change that right now, so that's what's on offer."

The moment he said it, the air became charged, an unmistakable energy zinging between them.

That's what's on offer.

A pretty blush tagged her cheekbones. She understood what he had said even if he didn't understand it himself, or how they had landed here. Somehow, this exercise in what he wanted and what he could give had become a testing of the waters.

But he wasn't looking for a connection with Tara, was he? Nothing real was on the table.

Just sex.

That's what he wanted from her.

The skaters were coming back on the ice and this conversation had already strayed into uncharted territory. He spotted Mia at the entrance, on her way back in.

He unfolded from the seat, not missing Tara's subtle appraisal of him as he stretched upright. The seed had been planted.

"I'll leave it with you," he said.

She nodded, her straight white teeth dragging along her lush lower lip.

That seed was already blooming.

"I'll get back to you."

14

———

ON THE FLIGHT BACK, the atmosphere was muted, understandable after a loss. Tara tried talking to Dex, who had not played to his potential.

"Hey, babe, how are we doing?"

Dex leaned back against the head rest. "Fucking terrible. I thought I'd be closer to good form by now."

"These things take time. You know you have the skills, it's just a matter of putting it all together."

He peered at her from beneath his ball cap and took her hand in his, locking their fingers together. He had touched her before—a hand on her waist, a peck on the cheek—but this felt more personal. Like he wanted something from her, and it wasn't just the usual horny boy behavior.

"You think so?"

"I know so. Just close your eyes and try to get some rest. It'll look better in the morning."

Her eyes flickered across the aisle. Hale's gaze was fixed on her hand in Dex's. Before she could smile at him, he turned away.

Her heart did not enjoy that little exchange. "I'm going to get some water. Need anything?"

"A beer."

"I'll get one for you. Just relax." She'd get him a ginger ale but she'd take her time, hoping he might just fall asleep. He looked wrecked.

Most everyone else was out for the count, even Cal and Mia who were wrapped up in each other like cute little kittens. Walking back toward the galley, the loss wasn't uppermost in her mind. Neither was Dex's sour mood.

No, all she could think about was that conversation in the box with Hale.

Why had she offered to help him with his dating profile? Supposedly she had good reasons but for the life of her she couldn't think of a single one. Something about getting him out of her hair, off the market, removing him from the game …

So much for that. Instead she'd learned about his cute nieces and his desire for a connection and that he might want to fuck her.

That was the vibe he gave off back in the box. One second she was teasing him about demanding a woman who won't cling and will put up with his travel, the next she was wading through the sexual tension, trying to gain a handhold on the rocky shore.

Should she have been that surprised? After all, she had looked good tonight and most men responded to her when everything was on point. Hale was no different. She might enjoy talking to him more than the average male, but the bottom line was that this was an attraction that existed on the surface.

Nothing deep. Nothing real. Just sex.

Why did that seem so … disappointing?

In the galley, she ran into Hudson Grey with Tate Kazminski, aka Kaz. Hudson had one earbud in and had probably taken out the other because Tate was a bit of a chatterbox. Also, a notorious gossip.

"Hey, did you have fun?" she asked Hudson. "I know you didn't win but you got to play a few shifts. And you rocked!"

"Thanks." He gave her a bright smile. "Coach said he liked what he saw."

"Yeah, he did. You were putting the veterans to shame."

Tate snorted. "Hey, veteran in the room."

"Tate, you played well, too! You came so close to scoring in the second period. I loved that little toe drag move you did."

He looked appropriately mollified. "You saw that, huh?"

"The whole world saw it! Could I get by you? Need to grab a ginger ale for Dex."

As they moved aside, she asked Hudson, "So what are you listening to?"

"*Murder in Midhaven*—the world of accountants in Iowa is freakier than you'd think."

"Oh, I loved that one. I won't spoil it for you."

"Speaking of spoilers," Tate said, "I heard you and O'Malley are just playing nice for the cameras."

So much for discretion. "It's early days. We're taking it slow."

"O'Malley wouldn't know slow if it hit him in the head with a puck. I guess what I'm getting at is: what's your actual dating situation?"

"Occupied. I can only handle one of you at a time!" Best to keep it light, though she couldn't help her curiosity. "Thought you were trying to get back with your ex?"

He gave a miserable shrug. "It's not going so well, but I

thought that maybe you might be in the market. To make her jealous."

She slid a look at Hudson who was eyeing Tate like he hadn't a clue.

She touched his arm. "You know, women don't really enjoy gamesmanship like that. Be honest and if it's meant to be, it'll happen."

"Sounds like good advice," Hudson said sincerely. So young, but she appreciated the back-up.

"That's right, listen to your auntie Tara. She knows of what she speaks!"

"Does she now?"

Hale stood at the entrance to the galley, taking up the narrow space and sucking all the air out of it. And Lord knew they needed all the air they could get.

He was scowling—general managers didn't like to lose either—and yet she was glad to see him. His dark gaze flickered to Tara's hand on Tate's arm, then back to her face. Yet again, she felt like she'd been caught in a cookie jar sitch.

"Gentlemen, do you mind giving me a moment with Ms. Becker?"

Murmurs of *sure, sure* accompanied them on their way out, though Hudson did send a sympathetic glance before he left her to be mauled.

Because that's what it felt like: an imminent attack from all-points Hale.

"Tough luck tonight. I really thought they'd pull it out."

He ignored that. "I thought I was clear about you targeting other players. Your remit is O'Malley alone. That's what you were hired for."

"I'm just being friendly. It's my personality."

"Well, change it."

She felt her eyes widen. "Change my personality?"

"No flirting with the players." He stepped closer, his voice almost a hiss. "If you're going to be holding hands with your boyfriend and acting like you two are an item, then try not to look like you're ready to jump the bones of the next guy who pays you the slightest bit of attention."

What was this guy's problem? She had been nothing but kind to him between her comfort during the flight out to her advice on setting up his dating profile. Had she completely mistaken the tremor of lust between them back in the box, what sounded like an offer to indulge in something more than flirting?

Now he wanted her to dim her natural ebullience because he assumed she was out to score?

Pick a lane, Mr. Grump.

"How about you mind your own business?" She moved to walk by him, which meant she brushed her arm against his. Only an arm, but it was more than enough. Her entire body thrummed with awareness and yet again, despite the condemnation reeking from his pores, she felt a danger-ously overwhelming attraction to him.

She hadn't got more than a couple of feet before she heard, "Tara, come here."

Not much mustard on it, but she felt the heat of his command anyway. Whipping around, she bit out, "I'm not a dog."

He closed the gap between them and placed his hand on the galley wall, which gave her an eyeful of bulging bicep. "I know you're not a dog. I'm just not finished with this conversation."

"No, this conversation ended when I told you I can speak to whoever I want." Or was it whomever?

Whatever, she was done with this.

But the rom-com gods weren't done with her: the plane

lurched and pushed him toward her. She raised her hand just in time to stop him from crashing into her.

And got the full force of his hard pec against her palm.

Wow.

He didn't move away. "What's going on between you and O'Malley?"

"Why?"

His expression darkened. "Because I already told you that you didn't have to do anything with him. Remember?"

"I remember. You also said that we're consenting adults, so what Dex and I do is none of your damn business."

His eyes narrowed. "What happens to every man on this team is most definitely my business. And as you've signed a contract with this org, then what you do is also my business."

Her hand was still on his chest. It felt far too intimate for the conversation they were having, though they were actually talking about sex. Only her sexual—or nonsexual—habits with another man.

The nerve.

She pushed him back a couple of inches and dropped her hand.

He noticed. Frowned. Didn't seem to like it, but then Hale didn't like much about her right now.

"I'm an independent contractor and my sex life is completely off limits in any discussion. I'll sleep with whoever I want whenever I want and I won't be running it by you." Pretty proud of that exit line, she pivoted and walked a couple of feet toward the bathroom. She needed to splash cold water on her face.

On her breasts.

Everywhere.

As she pushed on the concertina door, the weight of a

splayed hand warmed her back. A couple of seconds later, she was in the bathroom, but she wasn't alone.

The click of the lock brought the bathroom light on. From experience she knew this kind of illumination washed her out completely, so best not to renew her acquaintance with the mirror.

Which left only one place to look. Of course, the light hadn't made *him* any less attractive.

"What the hell are you doing?"

"We're not finished." He looked furious, and that self-righteous indignation seemed to make him larger, pumping his muscles with anger juice. Or maybe it was the size of the space, barely bigger than a postage stamp, that contributed to this impression.

She crossed her hands over her breasts but because of the tight confines, they landed under her rack, which had the effect of plumping them up.

"Say what you need to say."

"O'Malley is bad news."

Getting B-movie villain vibes. "Bad news?"

"Don't get your hopes set on him because he'll just break your heart."

The foolish man assumed she had a heart to break. She'd fortified that useless lump a long time ago so no man could penetrate. The only person who could touch it was Chloe.

The only person who mattered was Chloe. That was why she was here.

"Aw! You're worried about little ole me?"

He didn't appreciate her sarcasm. "O'Malley won't be settlin' down anytime soon. I think you know that, so you're hedgin' your bets with Kazminski. Get him while he's raw from his separation. Always good to have a Plan B, right?"

"Ah, so you're *not* worried about me? My heart's not in danger, but your boys' wallets are? Is that what you're trying to say?"

He moved in, placing his hand at the side of the mirror, effectively caging her in. "You were hired to do a job. Make O'Malley look good. No need to use this as a testing ground for your husband hunt."

"Who said anything about testing? I'm playing for keeps here."

His blue eyes flashed a lightning storm and for a moment, she thought he might want to kill her.

Or kiss her.

And the second that thought entered her mind, she was willing it to happen. Cheering it on. She wanted his lips on hers—even if they were angry or annoyed or disapproving —more than she wanted anything.

Hale Fitzpatrick couldn't fulfill any of her Maslow hierarchy needs, but he could give her a distraction. The sensation of being desired, even if that was fleeting.

To be wanted in this moment was a powerful thing.

However, the man was not making a move. He might look like he wanted to kiss her but he sure as hell was putting up a good fight to ensure that didn't happen.

Maybe he needed a push. "What's wrong? Feeling protective over your men? Whatcha gonna do to keep those poor babies safe?"

Yes, she was in control here. She would goad him into kissing her because he sure as hell wouldn't be able to get there by himself. The man was trying to scare her off while protecting "his boys." Hale the White Knight. Hale the Team Bodyguard.

Hale the Furious.

He inched closer. She parted her lips, ready for him. Dying for him.

A throb started up low in her belly. Lower, still, and so urgent she needed hands between her legs. Her hand. His hand. She didn't care.

But first, his lips on hers.

Do it. Just do it! "What are you waiting for? An invitation? I thought men like you just took—"

His lips touched hers, though touch was too tame. More like consumed. The anger on both sides leeched out, leaving passion and hunger in its wake.

And yes, she was a hungry girl.

His tongue tangled with hers, ratcheting up the need to another level. She clutched at his arms, those beefy biceps that felt so good against her palms. Gripping tight, she let herself be transported to a pleasure palace inside her head, one where she was petted and touched and adored to the point of madness.

He pushed her back against the sink—or maybe she pulled him back. It felt like they were in this together. It wasn't some one-sided deal where she wanted it more or he was slobbering all over her.

This was equal.

She had never felt that. There was always one person with the advantage.

She had hoped it would be her when it came to Hale. That she could control him like any other man, but Hale wasn't one to be manipulated. She might think she had goaded him into a kiss but he was here because he wanted it.

Wanted her.

Oh, Tara. She let herself believe this. Sank into the moment of pure bliss.

Bliss included grabbing his ass, mostly because she was concerned about the kiss being the limit of what was possible. A healthy ass grab should signify her intentions.

She wanted Hale to fuck her in this airplane bathroom.

Now that the word was out there, pulsing in the space between them, her kisses turned desperate. There was moaning and clutching and greed, and she might die if it ever stopped.

He pulled back, his face harsh with lust. Bafflement was mixed in there, too, like he couldn't understand what was happening.

But he figured it out quickly. His hand cupped her ass and seated her over the sink, so now she had no choice but to part her thighs and let him in.

Oh, God. Cruel fingertips coasted along her inner thighs, lighting up all the nerve endings on the way.

"You wet for me?"

Yes. A thousand times, yes. "Find out for yourself." She might be easy but she refused to make it easy for *him*.

He moved her thong aside. His eyes shuttered briefly, like he couldn't believe it, or it brought him so much pleasure he had to take a moment's respite to deal. Either option worked for her.

Hale's fingertips pushing aside her panties worked for her.

His hot breaths panting against her lips worked for her.

His eyes hazed over with desire—for her, only her—hell, that worked most of all.

"Jesus, Tara. What the fuck are you doing to me?"

What was she doing to him? About to protest his read of the situation, she was stymied by a quick, testing stroke of his index finger along her folds. She bucked, greedy, needing to be filled. Surely he was the one driving her to the brink?

That testing stroke became a slow, sultry tease as he added another finger to the first. Two were better than one, both of them covering more ground, creating pulsing, sensuous circles through her soft, willing flesh. She rolled her hips, anxious to get closer, to pull those fingers inside her. To get one or both of them on her clit.

"Hale," she gasped. "Please."

Attuned to her need, he turned his finger and rubbed it against her clit which throbbed a hard heartbeat in response, then pushed a finger inside her pussy.

"Oh, *ohhh*." She clamped down hard, loving the sensation of being filled. His lips touched hers, his breath came in hot, jagged pulls. His tongue stroked inside her mouth, matching the finger-thrusts. Realizing she was taking, she moved her hand to the front of his pants and stroked the massive bulge she found there.

Suddenly the fingers were not enough.

She needed the power she felt beneath her fingertips. She needed it all.

"Let me—"

"No, honey." He pushed her hand away and plunged a second finger in with the first. Stretching her. Pumping inside her. Stars popped behind her eyelids. His thumb rubbed her clit and she burst apart, a shower of sparks raining down.

When she opened her eyes, she met his storm-struck gaze, the blue turned to midnight.

Hale the Furious had returned from battle.

He remained silent, staring at her for an age. She was supposed to react, she supposed, maybe thank him?

But she didn't feel grateful. She felt shipwrecked, like

she might break out in tears at any moment. They pressed against her eyelids, thickened her throat, and she fought them off because no way was she going to let him see what he'd done to her.

"That shouldn't have happened," he said, low and dangerous like this was her fault.

And she supposed it was. She was the one in control, the one who goaded and pushed.

Keep telling yourself that.

"Well, you had to test the goods, right? See if I make the grade for your precious players." She pushed at his chest and slid rather ignominiously off the sink. So there was barely room to swing a dick, but Hale Fitzpatrick didn't even have the decency to give a couple of inches of space. Instead he continued to crowd her, so she turned to face the mirror and checked her reflection—and his with it.

Gone was her lipstick, left were her lips puffy with Hale's all-consuming kisses. Her eyes sparked with the green of a nocturnal animal's—a hunter seeking prey, she liked to think, instead of a fearful little kitty cat hiding in the bushes. She widened them, as if that could make them shine brighter, but really to stave off those imminent tears.

Her hair was a mess. He'd done a number on it there, so she teased it with her fingers for something to do with her hands.

How had they gone from that teasing vibe in the box back in New York to this?

"Tara, I'm sorry, I should—"

"Oh, don't apologize for showing a girl a good time in an airplane bathroom. Five stars. Would recommend! A memory I'll treasure, and I'm only sorry you wouldn't let me return the favor." He still stood close, barely an inch between them, so she pushed out her bottom and brushed his erection.

Oh, God. With that teasing touch, she wanted him to think he'd missed out. Instead she was left feeling like a huge void had opened up inside her.

She almost buckled at the thought of him still hard and pulsing and furious, and all she had to do was give a lascivious rub against him. Driven wild, he would lift her skirt, tear off her thong, and drive deep inside her.

She deserved it, but he didn't.

"I'll give you a moment to take care of business, though I'm guessing you'll only need a few seconds." She grabbed a couple of tissues from the dispenser—for any pesky tears that might spring up later—and put her hand on the door's lock. "Plenty left for you to clean up."

He gave her The Look, hard and flinty. Apparently, he thought he had a right to be annoyed here—and as he wasn't getting any handy assistance from her, perhaps he was right.

She threw back the lock and stumbled out with about as much dignity as a woman could muster in such a situation, which is to say, not very much.

15

Hockey players didn't quite rise to the diva levels of football or baseball, but like all pro-athletes, they could whine with the best of them. Having to get half-naked in the middle of winter was as good a reason as any for them to grumble.

Welcome to Rebels Calendar Photo Shoot Day.

Sophie had the idea to kill two birds by sharing behind-the-scenes of the shoot on the team's social media while also focusing on the growing romance between Dex and Tara. And while Fitz wouldn't usually feel a need to hang around during a photo shoot, Harper had made it clear he should stay on top of this, i.e. ensure Dex O'Malley showed his face … then showed every other part of him.

Fitz hadn't seen Tara in a couple of days, not since the plane ride home from New York when he had acted like a randy—and jealous—teen. He shut his eyes, embarrassed at his behavior. But hell if those closed eyes didn't help conjure up the memory of her raspy moans, greedy grasp, and hot, slick pussy. In the two nights since, when he wasn't berating himself for being a jerk, he was beating off to the memory.

The taste of her still lingered on his lips. The scent of her was lodged in his lungs. The memory was something different, something embedded deep. Those little sounds she made when his mouth first touched hers—Jesus, it would stay with him as long as he lived.

Today he would have to see her. He wasn't looking forward to it. He'd behaved rudely and now he would have to apologize.

"It's really fucking cold," Cal Foreman muttered. "Why the hell are we doing this in February?"

"Because if we leave it to after the playoffs, we'll never get you lot in the same space until the season starts up, by which time it would be too late to send to the printers." Fitz grinned at his star right-winger. "You're doing us a huge favor."

"Worried about shrinkage, Foreskin?" Theo Kershaw dropped his pants though Fitz was fairly sure no one had asked him. "I could see why that might be a concern."

"Clearly not a concern for you, what with your huge ass and all, Superglutes. No chance of that shrinking."

"You're both pretty!" Mia patted them on their shoulders. "Hey, the photog wants the two of you over there under the bright lights. Off you pop and get warm, fellas."

Kershaw and Foreman swaggered off to discuss poses with the photographer.

"This doesn't seem like your scene, Mia."

She grinned. "Hot pro-athletes getting naked for a good cause? I think that's everyone's scene."

"I stand corrected."

"To be honest, I should be watching tapes for Athenas recruitment." Mia, along with Isobel Chase, were both instrumental in bringing one of the new expansion teams for the Women's Hockey League to Chicago. It would kick-start in the fall with a plan to share the Rebels Arena complex. "I said I'd hang around for Tara. She has an idea—oh, here she is."

Tara had just walked into the studio with Kennedy and a couple of women Fitz didn't recognize, all in possession of animal carriers. Within seconds, the screech and whines of their charges rivaled those of the players.

One grabby tabby clung to Fitz's leg. Another, an adorable black kitten, was wandering around looking for trouble, but was quickly scooped up by Tara.

"We thought it would be good to include some animal shots with the players," Tara said to him without preamble. "And then Dex and I can say we're thinking of adopting one. Animal pics have amazing social media value." She looked down at Fitz's leg. "He likes you. You should pick him up."

Fitz wasn't sure that *like* was the operative word. Latched onto seemed more appropriate. What was more surprising was that Tara was talking to him like nothing had happened. No sad-eyed stares or passive-aggressive comments.

He picked up the tabby and looked into his eyes. "What's your name, little guy?"

"That's Marmalade. And this rogue is Pickle."

"Poor Pickle. What a terrible name."

Tara nudged his arm with hers. It was almost friendly. "Don't let him hear you say that! He'll get a complex."

"No, he won't. Cats think they are the shit, so this cat thinks he has the best name even if he doesn't. Nothing I say or do will convince him otherwise."

Tara smiled, and fuck, but Fitz had the strangest urge to lean into that smile. Instead he settled Marmalade in his arms, if only for something to do.

"You're probably right," Tara said. "Cats are the cockiest

son-of-a-guns. Or is it sons-of-guns?" She stepped in closer, close enough that the kittens' heads touched. Marmalade gave Pickle a lick on the forehead. Pickle swatted him back because he was a little asshole who didn't care what he was called.

For the briefest moment, Fitz felt at peace.

Kennedy walked over and held her hands out. "I'm going to need Marmalade. I think he and Theo are going to get along great."

He handed the cat over and feeling somewhat at a loss, placed both free hands in his pockets. Kennedy divided a look between them, mouthed huh, and walked away.

"What was that for?" he muttered to Tara.

"Oh, she's probably wondering about the vibe between us." She lowered her voice to a stagey whisper. "Wait 'til I tell her what happened on that plane!"

He slid a glance at her, wondering what her game was and how she was able to see the humor in it when all he could see was a man losing control.

"Any chance we could talk in private?"

"Ooh, is that a euphemism? Looking for a repeat performance of our Fly the Randy Skies experience?"

This woman. "I'd just like a word alone."

He had barely finished the request when she spun on the extremely high and spiky heels of her knee-length boots and walked outside. She leaned against the wall in the studio's corridor and went eye-to-eye with Pickle.

On his approach, she put on her fakest smile.

Since when was he able to tell the difference?

"How can I help?"

"I need to apologize for what happened the other night. I don't know what came over me."

"I think that would be me. On your hand!" At his wince,

she went on. "It's fine. If anything, I should apologize to you for leaving you hanging." She patted his arm, all condescension. "How did it go? Get the job done?"

Because he was all class, he'd waited until he got home, but she didn't need to know that. "I shouldn't have barged into the bathroom like that. Made you feel uncomfortable."

"Before you made me feel very comfortable indeed." She winked and he could feel his blood pressure shooting up. Why couldn't she be mad at him like a normal woman?

"Tara. I'm trying to say I was a jerk and I regret it. I shouldn't have lost control like that."

Dipping her chin, she stroked Pickle's head. "Well, I did sort of goad you into it. You were feeling protective of your boys. Completely understandable."

If only it was that easy. "That wasn't it."

"No?" Ultra casual, but he detected a quiver of uncertainty. Enough doubt about her self-worth to make every protective instinct in him rear up and crave the feel of her in his arms.

He needed to be an adult and come clean.

"I was jealous."

THANK God for Pickle because Tara was having a hard time holding her shit together. She'd been trying her best to act like she didn't give a flying fuck what Hale thought of her. She had strutted into that studio with her friends, both human and furry, in her best boots like she owned the place, head and boobs held high. Knowing that Hale would be on site, she had gone in with humor as her shield and sass-talk as her sword.

And it would have worked, too, if Hale hadn't pulled her aside to apologize.

Just when she thought she had an out, where he set them back on their unequal footing—him the Cock of the Walk, her the scrambling social climber—he threw her another curve ball.

I was jealous.

"Of Dex?"

"O'Malley, Grey, Kazminski, anyone on the team you paid the slightest bit of attention to."

Okay. She took a look at Pickle; he was no help whatsoever.

"So you were kind of mad at me for doing my job and being friendly."

"Bingo."

"I'm not sure what to do with this information, Hale."

"Just wanted you to have the facts. I behaved in an ungentlemanly fashion and made it sound like it was your fault I turned into a caveman. That wasn't fair or right. You don't have to accept my apology, but I'd be mighty grateful if you did."

How could she refuse? It sounded heartfelt. Mature. The world would be a much better place if people stood up when they realized they'd been jerks.

"Of course I accept it. Or Pickle accepts it on my behalf." She kissed the little kitten's head, purely for something to do because Hale was staring at her, a burner of a look. She peeked up, feeling a flush through her body at his intense regard.

"Thanks, Pickle," he murmured, which made her giggle like an idiot.

He moved closer, ostensibly to rub Pickle's head. His

fingers brushed against hers and sent a thrill of sensation through her. Was she really letting him off this easily?

"Of course, gentlemanly behavior can be vastly overrated," she murmured, as it seemed she was. "If you'd remained a gentleman, I wouldn't have renewed my membership to the Mile High Club."

He raised an eyebrow. "Renewed?"

"You think that's the first time I've indulged in some hanky-panky in an airplane bathroom?"

"No. But I'm not sure it counts without hitting a home run."

She pressed her lips against a grin. "Pretty sure orgasms are the finish line. I guess your membership is still pending."

He chuckled just as Pickle made a break for it. Hale scooped him up and settled him against his shoulder. "What are you up to, little guy? Need a change of scenery?"

"He likes you." *I like you.*

"He likes whoever's got the best petting technique, Tarabell."

Tarabell? *Swoon.* "Well, I can vouch for yours."

His eyes turned almost black, and hoo boy, was that something. Lusty and sexy-with-intent Hale was a sight to behold. "You liked my petting technique?"

"I did."

She could keep it flirty, though God knew why she even wanted to venture down this rocky path. A man like Hale Fitzpatrick wasn't interested in a woman like her—not in the truest sense. And the more time she spent with him, the more she realized she truly did like him.

So dangerous, but perhaps worth the risk? She had a plan and it was okay to take a few sexy side trips on the way.

He moved a smidge closer. "Enough for a repeat?"

There it was, out in the open. Of course, when a man expertly penetrates with two amazing fingers, that would usually be a hint that he desires you. But that time in the airplane bathroom had been almost against his will—not that consent was an issue. Only that Hale was clearly letting his dick call the shots and he hated himself a little for it.

Now he seemed to have made peace with the attraction between them, if only for a while.

Tara understood well enough that she wasn't the kind of woman who figured in the long-term plans of men like Hale. But that was fine, wasn't it? If he was looking for a trophy, maybe she'd fit the bill. But she suspected he wanted someone educated, the kind of woman who could throw a dinner party, converse on politics or social issues without sounding like a nincompoop, whip up a four-course meal, and put the kids to bed—likely without a nanny.

"Tara?" Sophie put her head out the door, frowning on seeing them close together. "There you are! Let's get some shots of you and Dex together."

"Be right there!"

Once she was gone, Tara muttered, "Now everyone will know."

His brow rumpled. "Know what?"

"That there's something going on between us."

"There *is* something going on between us." He cupped her jaw and her knees buckled. Pickle made a mewling sound, or maybe that was Tara. "I think there's a very strong attraction here and I'm hopin' you might want to act on it."

"We did."

"Properly. In a room that's not thirty thousand feet in the air. In a big bed where I can worship you to the point of madness."

Holy Pickle.

"But I would never want you to feel pressured or in any way uncomfortable."

Dropping his hand, he stepped back and her entire body shrieked at the wrongness of it.

She needed him close. His name emerged from her mouth as a graveled whisper. It didn't even sound like her.

She placed a hand on his chest, right above his heart and next to Pickle's warm body. The *th-thunk* she felt under her fingertips gave her goosebumps.

Those lips want to taste you.

This man wants to bed you.

That heart is beating for you.

And when he cupped her jaw, she let herself believe that this was a good idea.

This kiss started sweet but it didn't stay that way, probably because Tara wasn't feeling sweet. More like ravenous. She made some weird sound in her throat, not a whimper, more of a grunt. Not very ladylike, but she didn't care. Hale's mouth on hers was amazing.

His tongue touched hers and sparks exploded behind her eyes and in her chest and low in her belly. His hand stretched behind her head, holding her in place, a possessive grip she loved. His thumb stroked her cheek, a strangely soothing gesture in the middle of the madness.

It was an exchange of gifts, a recognition that only these two people could kiss like this. Exactly what she'd imagined a kiss with your soulmate would feel like.

Soulmate? Tara, you silly girl.

He tore his mouth away, but his forehead stayed against hers. Thank God she'd worn these heels today so she could meet him at his level.

"You're makin' me crazy, honey." He swiped a thumb along her lip. "Come over to my place tonight."

She nodded her assent, powerless to resist him. Desperate to hold onto this feeling of falling into a new, limitless world.

"I should ..." She thumbed over her shoulder. Back to work. "Will I take Pickle?"

"Nah, I think he's good right here."

Lucky Pickle.

"So, you'll call me?" Did Hale really ask her to spend the night with him? And did she really agree?

"I will."

Any more conversation would ruin this perfect moment when she was heady from the perfect kiss and anticipation fluttered in her belly. Anxious to escape these strange, confusing sensations, she walked away, returning to the world she understood: hot, shirtless pro-athletes playing with kittens and puppies.

16

───────

Tara was trying to look at this from a feminist perspective.

She needed sex. Hale had already demonstrated he was good at orgasms, so why not return to that well? While they clearly weren't each other's type, they had chemistry up the yin-yang.

Hale was probably the sexiest guy she'd ever been with. Even when he was a jerk.

Or maybe that's why she found him sexy. She was fairly self-aware about her patterns. She had a thing for bad boys who treated her a little cruelly and kept her on edge. Was that why she was so attracted to Hale? Because she knew that he knew she was not in his league, completely unworthy of a real relationship with someone so smart, fine, and sexy?

But Hale wasn't a complete jerk. He had acted like one—there was a difference, we all have our less-than-stellar moments—and then fessed up in a very mature manner that he was jealous. Tara had been with jealous guys before, and in her youth, had even gone to some effort to make them so, but she'd never encountered a man who admitted the little green monster was responsible for his bad behavior and apologized for how it had shaped events.

Hale was an adult—and Tara hadn't dated an adult before.

Except this wasn't a date.

He didn't want her for that. He might act like a real man with his straight talk and apologizing ways, but he had made no promises and likely never would.

She would do well to remember that. This was transitory, a way to relieve the pressure of being around him so much. (And why was he around so much? He didn't have to be!)

Now she was parked outside his house a mere five hours after the photo shoot—three of which she'd spent getting ready—as nervous as a virginal bride on her wedding day.

What if she wasn't any good?

She enjoyed sex and had always thought of herself as generous and up for pretty much anything (except anal), but did that mean she had any skills? It was easy enough to please someone who was young, dumb, and full of come. The guys she usually slept with were happy with a nice pair of tits and some quality hair flouncing.

Hale had been around the block, so he might have higher expectations in the form of intelligent conversation. Such as how to fix climate change or solve the Middle East crisis.

She should turn the car around and just head home to a binge watch of *Breaking Bad*. The world of meth dealers seemed safer right now. Or she could pull up her Big Girl Thong and get this show on the road.

The passenger door opened, making her jump. Hale clambered inside, a gorgeous frown shaping the downturn of his lips.

"Tara."

"Hey."

"You've been out here for ten minutes."

"More like seven."

Sardonic eyebrow raise. "Psyching yourself up? That doesn't sound too promising."

He wore a charcoal grey half-zip sweater over dark wash jeans, and he looked like he might have just shaved. He smelled amazing and the urge to place her cheek against his chest raged through her like an imminent volcanic eruption.

"I was on the phone," she lied, taking a guess that he couldn't see that level of detail from the window of his house.

"But you're not now. And you're still here. Not in there." He took her hand, locked his fingers in hers. It was a little too perfect. "What's on your mind, Tarabell?"

I'm not good enough, not even for a fling, but I so, so want to be.

"Just a case of the jitters. You ever get like that? Second-guess every decision? Well, of course you don't. You've probably never had a sliver of self-doubt in your life."

"Hey, hey." He raised their joined hands to his lips and brushed soft kisses over her knuckles. "Only psychopaths go through life with that level of confidence. I've doubted plenty—choices about my marriage, my career, gas station sushi."

"Living on the edge, I see."

His lips curved against the backs of her fingers. "But I don't have a single doubt about my attraction to you. It's as real as it can get. So tell me what's got you jittery."

"I just don't want people thinking I can be passed around like some NHL version of spin-the-bottle." It was her own fault. She'd dated Cal, now she was fake dating Dex with the intention of turning it into something more, and maybe she had been too friendly with some of the others.

Instead of seeing her as genuine WAG material, she may have positioned herself in the stocks so people could throw rotten vegetables at her.

"I don't think that. No one does. And frankly it's no one's business what we do."

Ah, of course. A secret fling, which made sense given her employment situation vis-à-vis the Rebels org. It wouldn't look good for the GM to be seen with the supposed girl-friend of one of his players. Talk about a PR nightmare.

"I'd like to keep gossip to a minimum but I know what people think of me." Tara tended to evoke strong reactions from people. She would never forget the silence when she stopped by Rebels HQ to discuss the contract, then the echo of titters had followed her all the way to the elevator.

"What's that, then?"

"That I'm a ditz. An airhead. Sure, I come off as kind of silly and inconsequential, but I'll have you know I got this morning's Wordle in three tries, though usually my average is four, and while my goals might seem ridiculous to you, it doesn't make me a bad person. Or a fool. Or ..." She trailed off, having no idea of the point she was trying to make.

What's another five-letter word for *idiot*?

"Hey." He cupped her jaw with his free hand and drew her mere millimeters from his mouth (see, she could even work in metric!). "I don't think you're a ditz. Or silly. Or inconsequential. Not only are you beautiful, you are also smart and funny and charming."

"Okay, stop right there." What he'd said was perfect—smart, funny, those were some five-letter words she could get on board with. Any more would ruin it. She leaned in to kiss him, hoping that would be enough to disintegrate the silly string tangling up her brain.

Success! His mouth on hers felt like the best idea—how had she thought this bad?

They weren't each other's futures, but the present was very much in play. His responding groan sent a bolt of lust through her. Holding her jaw, kissing her deeply, he wiped away all the fears.

Desire. That's what this is about. *And Tara Becker, you are worth it.*

"Come on." His breath on her lips was divine. "Let me show you this is the best place to be right now."

"Lead the way," she whispered.

Heat blasted her as they stepped inside the front door and then something else. A small, waddling beast rushed her, like he was trying to tackle her during the Puppy Superbowl. But because he was a pug, he didn't have quite enough heft to do any damage.

"Oh, who's this?"

"Down, Goober. Don't go slobberin' all over our guest."

She hunkered down and gave him a thorough petting. She would have thought Hale a golden retriever or Irish setter kind of guy. "You call your puppy Goober?"

"Sure, he's a son of the Peanut state, but Peanut was too cute. He's more of a goober." He knelt and rubbed his head. "Aren't you, boy? You're just a big ole dummy."

Goober's wrinkly face implied he'd heard this manner of insult before and was yet again, drawing on deep reserves of grace.

"And I've also got another visitor who you might know."

He gestured to a spot further along the hall where a tiny ball of jet-black fur with big green eyes stared at her.

"Pickle!"

"Uh huh. When I tried to return him to the shelter people, the little guy dug his claws in. I'm giving him a shot to see if he and Goober get along."

On hearing his name, Goober trotted along to Pickle and sniffed, then gave the new arrival a gentle shove that moved the furry blob several inches. So cute!

"Jury's still out," Hale said.

She hauled herself upright and took a quick look around. It was a nice place, almost like a show house— probably a lease because he'd only been with the team for a couple of months. She placed her purse on a bench near the door.

"Let me take your coat." He slipped it off her and hung it up in the coat closet.

"Something smells good. Are you cooking?" No response. "What's wrong?"

"You are fucking gorgeous."

Oh. She looked down at her dress, a teal-taupe striped wrap that accentuated every curve and went great with her Balenciaga boots, one of her amazing thrift store finds. "I wasn't sure what to wear given the weather and the fact I was driving. And how once I got here, I might not need to be wearing anything for long. Did you cook?"

"I did. I thought you might be hungry."

Like a date. No, she couldn't devote even 1% of her brain power to that notion. This was just something that mature, adult, real men did for their hook-ups. Feed the booty call.

"Not really," she said though her stomach was hollow because she'd been too nervous to eat. "Not for food, anyway."

She stepped forward, anxious to get the night started. She had never felt so tentative, so unsure of her charms. She placed a hand on his chest and pressed. Perfect.

"Where's the bedroom?"

"Upstairs with all the other bedrooms." He tilted his head and took her measure, seeing right through her take-the-lead flirtatiousness. But she was too far gone now to change up the message of maneater siren.

Taking his hand, she led the way though she had no idea where she was going—in all the ways that could be taken.

At the top of the stairs, he switched places with her and guided her into the master bedroom where two bedside lamps and a gas-powered fire provided a subtle, romantic glow. Here the decor was more personal with a few framed photos on the dresser. A couple of guys who might be brothers or college buddies, a team shot of the LA Quake—Hale's last team—lifting the Cup, even a pic of Goober.

The fire's flames danced, burnishing his hair with copper. She reached for him, stroking her fingertips through the strands.

His hands found her hips and pulled her close, and for a moment they stared at each other, caught up in something different than all that had gone before. She didn't want different because that would bring on more jitters. This was a fun, sexy detour and Hale's intensity was not going to change it.

"Could you remove your sweater, please?"

His eyes gleamed, amused at her politeness. He may as well enjoy it; it wouldn't last once she got a look at the goods.

He did as she asked, rumpling his hair in the process, and glory be, come to mama! *Look at that chest.* Massive and smooth and so damn perfect she almost wept.

Running her hands along his pecs, she luxuriated in the feeling of ownership, if only for tonight.

"You're perfect."

"A bourbon a day for muscle tone."

His humor settled her some. "I know you exercise. I saw you in the gym one day before my yoga class." Ogled, to be exact.

"My secret's out. Perfection takes effort, especially at my age."

She coasted her hands down the blocks of muscle that were commonly called abs on other mortals; she'd never felt any as amazing as these under her fingertips. "You know I don't think you're old. It was just a silly joke to get a quick laugh."

"That's okay. I've still got what you need."

He meant sex, she supposed. But she needed more. She needed his care, though she could never reveal that. She would have to steal it in kisses when he wasn't looking.

Starting now.

She pushed him back, watching as desire flickered across his face. Taking control seemed as good a way as any to ensure she understood the parameters and didn't allow herself to get caught up in silly dreams.

He stopped at the bed and grasped her wrists, turning her away from him so she faced a full-length mirror on the closet door. With a care that made her shiver, he pushed back her hair to reveal her neck. When his lips brushed her ear, then traveled below it to apply a devastating suction, she lost her balance, falling against his chest.

Falling deep ...

He placed an arm around her waist, continuing to kiss, lick, suck and drive her insane. Wetness pooled between her legs and she had to work to stay upright, which might be a problem.

Hale Fitzpatrick was taking his time.

FITZ HAD NEVER SEEN any sight more beautiful than Tara Becker standing in his hallway.

The woman had spent a good ten minutes sitting in her car trying to convince herself this was a good idea. He'd like to say he knew the feeling but he didn't.

Fitz thought this was an excellent idea. At least he had while he waited for Tara to arrive, his ear alert to every sound, worried she would text or call to cancel. Seeing her unable to take the step to his door, hearing her doubts, made his heart keen for her.

I just don't want people thinking I can be passed around like some NHL version of spin-the-bottle.

In that moment he hated every single person who had ever trashed her, and that included himself. He had formed an opinion about her whip-quick, and while his views hadn't completely changed—mainly because her goals to snag a hockey husband remained and he fucking hated that idea—that glimpse of a different, softer Tara had grabbed hold and pulled him in.

In the hallway of his home, when she bent down to

huddle with Goober, Fitz had the oddest sense of the rightness of it.

Tara here. Tara with his growing family of pets. Just Tara.

And when she took off her coat, he was blinded by her beauty and he let her know, partly because he had to and partly because she needed it. To be propped up.

In that moment, she realized her power. Gone was nervous Tara, back was the flirty tease, the snappy wit. He'd let her have it but he wouldn't let her hurry him.

Her neck tasted too damn good.

Her ear was a sweet little morsel he could nibble on all day.

Her perfect heart-shaped ass against his erection—and hell if he hadn't dreamed of that since the moment she rubbed against his cock on the plane to let him know who was boss—was the best of it all. He planned to kiss that gorgeous ass, lick between the cleft, taste her everywhere.

But all in good time.

He pulled at the tie wrapping her dress, watching in the mirror as it fell open to reveal a lilac bra and matching panties. Her full breasts heaved at the sight of herself and of him watching like a ravenous beast. He placed an open palm over her stomach and trailed up her rib cage. So soft and smooth.

Shivering, she fell against his chest and rested there.

"You doin' okay?"

Asked mostly to cover the fact he was *not* doing okay.

"Fine." A breathy little sigh. "I'm guessing you like to take it slow?"

He rubbed his knuckles over a stiff and responsive nipple, then along the plump swell spilling over one of the cups. "I like to savor."

Coasting a hand down her body, he cupped between her

legs. Held there for a few seconds while her damp heat filled his palm.

"Part your legs, honey. Gimme some room to work."

Another shiver from her that he felt all the way to his balls. He tightened his body against hers so there was no doubt of his aching desire for her. Skimming the border of her panties, he dipped a finger inside through a narrow strip of curls. She wiggled, her pert ass rubbing against him—the little tease— then she raised her hand and cupped the back of his neck.

"Good girl. You hold on tight now." Slowly, he moved his fingers inside all that soft, slick flesh. Jesus, she was soaked, so slippery, so hot, and he exhaled heavily against her ear. "You feel so good."

Her grip tightened on his neck. "Please, Hale. Faster."

"That's it. Tell me what you need."

His cock was as rigid as a railroad spike, and the thought of driving deep inside her made him groan and fueled a biological imperative.

Make her come.

Make her scream.

Make her *mine*.

His fingers picked up the pace, stroking and slipping and thrusting, taking her higher with each pass. A soft glance against her clit was all it took. She fell apart in his arms, her fingers on his nape hard enough to bruise.

Her eyes fluttered open and met his in the mirror. There was no hiding the vulnerability he saw there and part of him wanted to wrap her up and hide her away, keep her for himself. A conflicting part of him needed to bring back the strong woman who led him by the hand to his bedroom.

Because if Tara had hidden depths, then he was in big fucking trouble.

Smiling, she turned in his arms. "I'll see myself out, shall I?"

Saucy Tara was back, raising her shield. No chance. He intended to blast right through it.

Holding her face in his hands, he kissed her, drawing her moan. "We're just getting started."

He slipped her dress off her shoulders and threw it over a chair. Guiding her to the bed, he sat her on the edge, then knelt to unzip her boots. He looked up as he removed them to find her watching him, those green cat's eyes glowing in the firelight.

"I had planned to take it slow—" He kissed the inside of her knee. "And figure out what you like—" Another kiss, another knee. "But I'm not sure I have the patience."

She leaned down and cupped his jaw. "Thank God, because if you don't get inside me in the next sixty seconds, I'm going to scream." And then she kissed him so deep and dirty he almost came right there.

Thirty of the allotted sixty seconds were spent in a mad, undignified scramble—on his side, anyway—to undress. Within twenty seconds and with Tara's help, he was suited up with a condom, which left ten seconds to meet her demand. Still he couldn't resist taking a moment to glory in the gift on his bed: this beautiful, captivating woman who made him a little bit crazy. With his cock notched at her entrance, he kissed her again, needing to connect with her in every way he could.

"Ready?"

With eyes glazed, she nodded.

"Say it, Tarabell."

"Yes."

Cupping her sweet ass, he pushed inside, loving the

competing tension of tightness and slickness as she eased his way home.

"Oh, oh, ohhhhh!" She arched into him as he rocked into her, each stroke bringing him deeper inside. "Hale, oh, God, that's—that's so good."

So chatty, but he loved the honesty she exhibited in this moment.

In all their moments.

He loved her moans, her clasps, her need manifested in every gesture, from how her body strained to pull him close to how her eyes glowed with power. Because there was no doubt that she was queen of this kingdom, and he was merely a lowly subject.

"You okay?" she asked because he had stilled, needing a moment to take it all in. It had been a while for him and every ounce of focus was being spent not blowing the second he slipped inside that velvet glove.

"Just tryin' to keep up."

She dug her heel into his ass and shifted slightly to take him deeper. He should continue to thrust, stroke through to another climax for her and a much-needed release for him, but he couldn't stop looking at her.

And she was returning the favor, staring at him with those gorgeous jeweled eyes. Time slowed as he moved inside her, every tiny nudge bringing him closer to a place he'd never visited.

Had a woman ever felt so good? Not just the physical sensation of being milked by this perfect clasp, but the closeness and connection it fueled. He was old enough not to confuse emotion for sensation, but with Tara, so many feelings were running amok. Annoyance and jealousy and even affection all had a part to play.

With each passing second, her power over him increased. He needed to earn some of it back.

He withdrew a couple of painful inches and pushed deep again, watching as her beautiful lips stretched to a cat's smile. Nothing coy about her, just pure acknowledgment that this was absolutely amazing.

Another squeeze from her almost sent him over.

"Don't you dare," he murmured.

"Why not? Stamina problems?" She did it again, milking his cock, and he retaliated by pulling out—sheer hell—then pushing in, deeper still, seeking heaven, all while they watched each other. She closed her eyes and he gave her sweet ass a light pinch.

"Stay with me."

He moved again inside her, reaching for some closer connection, some way to bring down the walls she had lifted. Gripping her tight, he pumped hard, pistoning his hips ...

Waiting, waiting, waiting ...

She opened her eyes, and what he saw there flipped a switch. He stroked harder, deeper, then realizing how close she was, he rubbed between their bodies until she tightened around him, clutching him so hard he had no choice but to let go. Shooting hot pulses of need into her that matched each groan that erupted from his throat.

The butterfly flutters of her pussy around his cock continued, yielding throbs of pleasure long after he'd come.

It had been a while—that was the only reason why it was so good.

It couldn't possibly be anything else.

18

IF HALE WANTED to go for Round 2, Tara probably wouldn't say no.

Okay, she would be so up for that. Yet she found it hard to believe anything could top it.

"How we doin'?" he murmured.

She blinked at him, wondering if she looked a fright. Deciding it didn't matter.

"That was ... wow." Of course, she wouldn't have anything intelligent to say after he'd fucked her brains out.

"Wow it was. Back in a sec," he said, getting up to take care of the condom. The sight of that amazing ass attached to that even more amazing body, all power-laden muscle, made her sigh. But not for long. She needed to get her brain working.

Think, Tara. What kind of pillow talk does a man like Hale Fitzpatrick expect?

He returned and of course, the front view was just as impressive as the back. Grinning, he slipped back under the covers and leaned up on an elbow. Most guys would usually be out for the count now, needing the Z's to replenish their bodily fluids.

Not this one.

She said the first thing to come into her head. "That Boris Johnson's a bit of a muppet, isn't he?"

"Boris Johnson?"

"Yeah, I mean, all those lockdown parties and filling suitcases with wine coolers. That's crazy, isn't it?"

He regarded her quizzically. "Absolutely."

In for a quid. "I don't know how the Queen puts up with him. She has to meet him once a week and that must be so tricky for her. You saw how those meetings went in *The Crown.* If I was her age, I'd be saying, nope, it's time for a nap."

"Fan of the British royals, then?"

"Not particularly, just making conversation. Current events, the news of the day. I figured you wouldn't really be up on the Kardashians and this might be more—" *Retreat, retreat!* "How are things coming along with Bastian?"

"He's kind of cagey, which is to be expected. Tara, are you okay?"

"Of course I am! I just had a lovely orgasm. Two lovely orgasms, actually—wouldn't want to sell your skills short, and now I'm just—I dunno, talking." She moved a hand to his chest. "But I don't have to if that's not what you want."

"No, talking's fine. I like talking." In her heart she added, *to you,* to the end of that sentence. He smiled and her heart sped up dangerously, then her stomach got in on the action with the rumble to end all rumbles.

"Hungry?"

Food! She could talk about that until the cows came home. "I could eat. What did you cook earlier?"

"Beef bourguignon. I actually made it this morning in

the slow cooker and it's probably reached peak gravy levels. Interested?"

"Hell, yeah." Though she'd have to dig deep into her topic list to keep the conversation going. "I'm just going to head to the bathroom first to freshen up."

He leaned back against the pillow, hands behind his head. The position showcased his arms spectacularly.

Pulling the quilt with her, she sat up, realizing this sheet business never quite worked the way it did in the movies. Her dress was over the back of the chair—that was considerate of him—but she'd have to leave the bed to get it.

He would see her naked.

Which was silly to be worried about after what they'd just done. She had a great ass and nice legs. Any man would be lucky to witness them walking away from him.

Which was usually how they were seen. She didn't get a lot of invitations to stay.

"You're thinkin' awful hard over there."

"Could you maybe turn away when I get up?"

"Nope. Consider it a male perk. And you already saw me." He had her there, but he was perfect with not a glob of fat. He looked so gorgeously smug. "Wouldn't have pegged you for the shy and retirin' type."

"There's lots you don't know about me."

He ran a finger along her arm, sending shivers to every extremity. "No, but I want to."

"Really?" It came out barely above a whisper.

"Really."

Before she could react, he took pity and hopped up to open a dresser drawer. "How about you wear something more comfortable? That way I can undress you more easily after dinner."

Standing before her gloriously naked, he laid out clothes suitable for a post-shag interlude: Sweatpants, a Georgia Bulldogs shirt with a cute pug, and a pair of thick Rebels socks.

"Aw, it looks like Goober!"

"Haven't heard my dick called that before, but there's a first time for everything."

She giggled. "Hale."

Leaning down, he brushed his lips softly over hers, like he wanted to capture a sliver of her joy.

She wanted to share it.

As easy as can be, he pulled on another pair of sweats—no shrinkage, no awkwardness, no nothing—and an LA Quake T-shirt and kissed her on the top of her head. "Come down to the kitchen when you're ready."

She swallowed against the sweetness of it.

Five minutes later, she walked into the kitchen, conscious that her nerves were building again at the prospect of one-on-one time with, okay, a guy she liked a little too much. For the pants, she had to fold over a couple of times at the waist and ankles. The shirt swam on her, the socks were perfect.

She'd sneaked down the stairs a couple of minutes ago to grab her purse with her travel make-up bag. Hale had done a number on her lipstick—kissed it right off, which was dreamy—but now she had to restore the glamour.

He smiled at her when she walked into the kitchen and there went her heart again. Kaboom.

"Red or white wine? Or I could make one of those martinis you like."

"I shouldn't if I'm driving. Maybe water?"

"Do you have somewhere to be tonight?"

She wandered over to the fridge and focused on a photo

of Hale with two striking dark-eyed little girls who looked a little like him. Must be the nieces.

"I—I'm not sure." *Be brave.* "Do I?"

"I'd like you to stay but I understand if you need to go. Get your photo taken with O'Malley or whatever."

Was that a strain in his tone? Even for the short-term, a man like Hale wouldn't like to share.

"He's hanging with the boys tonight. Poker night at Levi's." And then she wished she hadn't said that because it sounded like she was here only because Dex was busy.

Anxious to make up for that, she moved forward and placed a hand on Hale's chest, which was fast becoming her favorite position with this man. Or a close second to him being inside her. "I'd love a glass of red. And I'd love to stay if that's what you want."

"That's what I want." He practically growled it and then his mouth was on hers and there went the lipstick again. She may as well not bother.

They sat at the counter with glasses of fruity Shiraz and the hearty stew over pasta. So, so good! Her nerves dissipated after a few sips and she didn't feel the need to babble and keep his interest with inane conversation topics.

"Are those your nieces on the fridge?"

"Sure are." The softness in his voice told her everything and was another threat to her equilibrium. "Any niblings of your own?" he asked. "I know you have a sister."

How much had the background check revealed? "None yet."

She had the strangest feeling that Hale would understand if she told him about Chloe. That he might even think more highly of her.

But she didn't want to use her sister to make herself look like a saint, forced to sacrifice her body on the altar of

WAGdom. Chloe wasn't her only reason for setting matrimonial goals that included a pro-athlete. Tara also happened to like nice things.

Anyway, her chance to spill passed when Hale asked, "And your mom? Are you guys close?"

"Not terribly. She thinks I'm too flighty." Though Tara had enough gravitas to take over Chloe's guardianship when it mattered. "I need to pick something and stick to it. That's her opinion."

"Plenty of time. You're young and you've obviously developed skills along the way."

"Sure have. No one makes a prettier corpse."

His wine glass stopped halfway to his mouth. "Excuse me?"

"Didn't you see that on the background check? I thought I wanted to be an actress and about ten years ago, I was living in New York and got a gig as a corpse on *Law & Order: SVU*. I was found in an alleyway and I'll tell you, I froze my excellent butt off while they kept re-setting. Christopher Meloni was so sweet, though. He brought me coffee in between takes."

"Caramel macchiatos with half-skim and half-oat milk."

"Not back then, though, oat milk wasn't a thing." Hale knew her drink? "Anyway, I didn't have much luck in the acting biz outside of that one job. I was destined to play dead sorority girls or Slasher Horror Victim No. 5. So I returned to my roots and started styling hair to pay the bills." She gave a small wave. "That's a hair biz joke."

He smiled. "Good stylists do well, don't they?"

"Sure they do, and it's great to have a trade to fall back on, but I have some debt as I'm sure you saw and I always seem to be playing catch-up." She wanted more security, more home-cooked meals, more of this. "I know you don't approve."

"You care what I think now?"

Yes. "Just making an observation."

His phone pinged and he flicked a glance to it.

"Team trouble?"

"Momma trouble." He tapped the screen. "Damn, she's relentless. Wants to set me up with a beauty queen."

Her heart checked. "Really?"

"We're playin' in Atlanta in a couple of weeks and even though she's currently on a cruise with her pals, somehow she's able to find time in between spa treatments and swimming with dolphins to get me a date. A former Miss Georgia."

"Sounds ideal."

"Some long-distance thing? Hard pass."

"Right, you'd want your needs sated locally. Sex on tap, Chicago-style."

That drew his laugh and crinkly eyes. *Gorgeous.* "FaceTime hook-ups might not work for a tech-challenged oldie like me."

Uh huh. Step aside, Ms. Georgia.

"But your momma's right. You probably should be getting your feet wet in the dating pool."

"Not sure that's the part of my anatomy that needs to take a dip."

Sexy devil. "Oh, that reminds me. Hold on a sex. Uh, I mean, sec." With a cheeky grin, she headed to the foyer to grab her phone. On her return, she said, "I came up with a dating profile for you."

Surprise lit up his eyes. "When did you do this? Before or after we had our fun?"

"Uh, right after our cozy chat in New York. Not that you

deserve it after you were such a bad-tempered beast. But it's some of my best work, so I'd hate for it to go to waste."

Was she mad, encouraging him to get his hot ass out there on the scene?

No, not mad. Perfectly reasonable. How else could she ensure these lines between them didn't blur into hope?

She passed over her phone, ignoring the shiver-shock when their fingers touched.

"Let's see what you think of me." He cleared his throat and read aloud, "*I'm a driven guy who loves hockey, family, travel, and my dog. My life is crazy, noisy, and busy, but I'm hoping to find someone to enjoy coffee and the quiet times with me.*"

Before he could critique it, she jumped in. "Now, I know it's short, but all the profiles are these days. In our image-obsessed world, a good photo and a pithy soundbite gets much more traction than a book of prose or a laundry list."

He met her gaze. "Pithy?"

"Blame Wordle."

He returned to the screen, looking to pick it apart, no doubt.

"We can change it. Talk more about your career or your stew-making skills or—"

"It's perfect." He smiled at her, that gorgeous grin she was starting to crave like a drug. "Mighty generous of you to take me on as your project, though kind of strange, given what we just did."

She swallowed, fully aware of the irony of setting each other up to be with different people. Him because his job required that he fix the Dex problem, her because she was fucking insane.

"I hate to see a good guy go to waste. And it doesn't matter what you say in your profile, really. You're a total babe magnet." She touched a hand to his arm and held it there comically, as if it was stuck by whatever made things magnetized. Science, she supposed.

He took her hand in his and squeezed it. "Like I've said before, I don't really have time to date right now. The prospect exhausts me, to be honest. All the small talk while you try to get to the real talk, holding back your weird until you feel they're ready to see it. My current focus is on getting the Rebels to the playoffs."

Any woman would feel blessed to make small talk with this man. Talking to him, even when she was spouting nonsense, was the most connected she had ever felt to anyone. There was a generosity to him that really resonated with her.

"Then get your profile in order, so you're ready to go."

"And in the meantime, find someone to enjoy coffee and quiet times with, who also happens to be in tune with my schedule?" He made a gesture to his head like he'd had a lightbulb moment. "Or maybe I've already found this perfect distraction."

That was Tara, the perfect distraction. She refused to be hurt; after all, she'd offered to help him with his stupid dating profile.

Instead, she played along. "I do like coffee." *And hockey and family and travel and your dog.*

His fingertips caressed her palm, and she let herself absorb the pleasure of Hale's attention. "But you're not all that quiet. In fact, you're a bit of a scream queen."

"The humblebrag? Would've thought that was beneath you."

"Know what I'd rather have beneath me." He slid off the stool and swiveled hers until he was positioned between her knees. With a touch so gentle it melted her heart, he cupped her face with both hands and kissed her. "Think I need to hear more about the Queen's weekly hook-ups with the British prime-minister."

Mortified, she shut her eyes briefly. "You must think I'm insane. I didn't want to bore you."

"Like that could ever happen." Stepping back, he held out his hand to her. "Come on, Tarabell, let's go upstairs and talk politics."

19

———

"Just a trim," Hudson said, running a hand through his sable hair. "Don't go too mad."

"Oh, I know how you boys love your flow! I won't interfere with the process."

Hudson sat in the chair in the yoga room while Tara put her magic cape around him. She ran a bacterial wipe over her scissors and held up a strand of his hair. A little dry but could be worse.

"So how do you feel about the last game?" Two days ago, the night before the photo shoot, the Rebels had won at home against Atlanta.

"Had a few good shifts. Almost scored. Can't complain."

"I'll say!" She snipped a lock. "And are you settling in okay? Where are you living?"

"At the corporate apartments place on Madison. They put people up there until they find a place."

"Have you started looking?"

"Trying to find the time."

"You need to talk to Kennedy, Reid Durand's girlfriend."

He frowned. "The dog walker?"

"She's not just a dog walker, Hud. She does personal concierge services for busy professionals such as yourself. I sometimes help her with grocery deliveries to the players." She trimmed a little more. "I'll recommend a conditioner for you. Don't worry, it won't be too smelly. So have you hung out with the boys yet?"

"A little."

"You should talk to Cade about the best gay bars. Though maybe he's out of the loop now that he's hitched to Dante and saddled with a kid. Know any other people in Chicago?"

He looked uncomfortable. "One guy. But we haven't talked in a while."

"Complicated?"

"Like you wouldn't believe."

Sounded like a bad break-up. Hudson was a sensitive jock, which made her wonder what this mystery guy had done to hurt him.

"What's that look for?"

"Oh, just thinking about you and your guy."

His brow lined.

"Hud, I've been in this business long enough to read between the snips. What did he do to ruin things?"

"How do you know it wasn't me?"

She held up her hands. "Because you're too sweet to have done anything purposeful to hurt someone else."

He waited a beat before replying. "It wasn't anyone's fault, just two people at different places in their lives. That's all."

She understood that kind of disconnect even if she didn't quite believe it was Hudson's reason for that glum expression. It sounded like people got hurt.

After a pause, he spoke again. "So, on the plane the

other night, Kaz said you and O'Malley were together for the cameras. Is that true?"

"Yes."

"But you want more?" He blushed. "Kaz said something."

"I suppose I wouldn't mind if it turned into something more." Weirdly, that tasted like ash in her mouth. "For now, we're getting to know each other. What did Kaz say?"

He shrugged, torn between team loyalty and wishing he'd kept his mouth shut. She let him off the hook.

"You know, Hud. You're going to hear a lot of crap about people in this org because as well as being a tight-knit, family atmosphere, it's also a hotbed of gossip and dirty little secrets. Just remember to listen to all sides and make up your own mind, 'kay?"

He smiled up at her. "So what's going on with you and Fitz?"

Her eyes widened in the mirror, instantly betraying her thoughts. Had Hudson Grey just played her?

"Where's that coming from?"

"He demanded to see you alone on the plane. And he couldn't take his eyes off you at the calendar shoot. I think the big bad boss has a thing for you."

Before she could let her heart revel in that statement, she put on the brakes.

"The big bad boss has other things to worry about."

"Like you?" Cocky grin.

"No, not like me! Believe it or not, I'm here to make his life easier." Repairing players' reps, creating dating profiles, giving the GM several orgasms. She was a regular fixer. She gestured at her client's head. "Do you want more off?"

"That looks good."

"Yeah it does! Theo's up next—he's more high maintenance than you, but today you gave him a run for his money with your insolence, you cheeky monkey." She shot off a text to the Rebels D-man. Kershaw had great hair, full and thick like Hale's, but darker. Tara was dying to get her hands on it.

While she waited, she was tempted to send a text to Hale. Or another one, to apologize for leaving at the ass crack of dawn. So maybe she had awoken an hour before that and spent a good fifty minutes watching his stubble-rough jaw and perfect cheekbones and strong lips. The other ten minutes were reserved for Pickle play. (The cat, so not as much fun as it sounded.)

Rather than think about how wonderful it would be to spend a lazy morning in the gorgeous man's bed, she had focused on all the other reasons not to be Hale-adjacent when he awoke.

Her breath probably smelled.

Her make-up had smudged.

Her hair was a bedraggled mess.

Basically, she was not at her most desirable after a night of being fucked stupid by a man who knew what he was doing, and that was not what Hale had signed up for, was it? He wanted the Barbie fantasy, the ready-for-action fembot, and she had provided. Then she'd removed herself from the morning-after equation and slipped out like Cinderella.

Being the gentleman he was, he'd texted to make sure she got home safely, but since then—six hours and forty-three minutes ago—nothing.

Which was fine.

The double-team of heart and hormones insisted that additional steamy trysts with Hale would be very nice, but her brain knew the score:

Run. As fast as her heels could carry her.

It would be too easy to fall for Hale, the same Hale who

would eventually be on the dating market. Beauty queens and ambitious mamas were in the mix! If she let herself enjoy any more coffee and quiet times with him—in between the orgasmic screams—she would lose that heart she claimed was a fortress.

"Heard you're chopping hair."

Dex stood at the entrance to the yoga room. "Hey, you! Need a trim?"

Coming across as more subdued than usual, he walked in, hands in his sweats, and looked around.

"Grey said you were being super cool and friendly."

She pushed him gently to the seat and ran fingers through his hair. "He's new in town, so he could do with a friend. You remember what that was like."

"Yeah, but you're supposed to be nicer to me. Because we're dating."

All these silly, attention-hogging boys! "What can I do here? I think you'd be better with shorter hair. You have a great jawline and it gets hidden by this."

He squinted in the mirror, perhaps imagining himself with less baggage of the hair variety. "Maybe a bit of a clean-up."

"Excellent!" Tara got busy snipping.

After a couple of minutes, he spoke. "The other night on the plane ..."

Had he seen something between her and Hale? Hudson the Observant had picked up on something, but had anyone else? She and Dex had interacted since at the photo shoot but hadn't been alone.

"Oh, yeah?"

"I was a bit off with you because of the loss."

You were rude.

"Totally understandable." Patience was key because a

true hockey WAG would need that in spades. Hale had pointed out how self-absorbed hockey players were, even him when he was married. Best to keep things drama-free and maintain a rep as a cool chick. "You'd had a rocky night and you needed time without me twittering on at you. I completely get it."

"But I feel better when you're around. At the games. Traveling. I know I didn't do well that night but I think, on the whole, you bring me luck."

That was sweet, if somewhat misguided. "You make your own luck, Dex. Now what do you think of the length?"

"Did you want to grab dinner tonight?"

She almost dropped the scissors. "With you?"

"Hey, sorry I'm late," Theo said, swaggering in and immediately scowling at Dex, or as much as good-natured Theo Kershaw was capable of scowling. "O'Malley, you stole my spot."

"I'm spending time with my girl."

My girl. Where was this coming from?

Theo narrowed his eyes and leaned against the window, arms folded to show off his amazing guns. "Thought this was a set-up to make you look like a good guy."

"I am a good guy!" Dex shot a sneaky glance at Tara in the mirror. "So it started that way, but Tara and I are getting to know each other better."

Were they? She knew his hair better than him. But she also needed to move forward with her plan to lock a player down.

It sounded like Dex had come to play.

All the more reason why she needed to call a halt to any fling with Hale. Dex was the endgame here.

"We were just discussing dinner plans before you came in," Dex said.

"You headed over to Erik's later?" Theo asked. "He's doing the housewarming thing now that Casey has moved in officially. Everyone will be there: Goodie, Calia, Jorvi, Rennedy. Might even be a few OG supercouples."

Dex looked baffled. "Goodie? Jorvi?"

"Gunnar and Sadie's couple name. And Levi and Jordan's." Theo shot him a look of disgust, then one of commiseration with Tara for having to put up with such dim-wittedness. "What should we call you guys? Tarex? Sounds like boner medication. What about Dexara?"

Tara didn't like the sound of that either but Dex was smiling at her, so she smiled back, feeling a little foolish.

Keep it to small talk. Too soon to show your weird.

"Have you come up with Dex's nickname yet?" Theo was known for taking considerable care with inventing a nickname for each new acquisition.

He grinned. "That's easy. It's OMGeeeee because that's what the chick on the video was screaming—"

"Yeah, she gets it." Dex flushed, which was quite a surprise for a man usually incapable of shame. He shot a glare at his teammate. "Sorry about him. He never knows when to shut up."

Who was this guy? She placed her hands on his shoulders and spoke to him in the mirror. "What do you think?"

"Looks good. What do I owe you?"

"I'm charging a flat fifty for everyone. Just Venmo me." She gestured at the QR code she'd laminated and fixed to the mirror.

"Could I have a word ..." He tilted his head toward the door.

"Sure. Theo, take a seat. I'll be with you in a sec."

"Will do. I'll try not to use my super hearing to listen in but I can't guarantee it. I have a responsibility to the team."

Dirty gossip mongers, the lot of 'em.

Dex frowned at him and took her hand. Once out of range of Theo's super hearing, he said, "I know this seems weird because I haven't been as ... attentive as a boyfriend should be. I'd just like to get to know you better and maybe Jorgenson's party would be a good way to do that. Less pressure in a group setting."

This side of Dex was fascinating. She wondered what she'd done to bring it out, or if she really wanted to see it.

Yes, you do! Think of Chloe. Stick with the plan.

"This is just a players' thing, right?" In other words, no chance of running into Hale.

"Far as I know."

"Okay, then I'm in."

20

___

WALKING INTO JORGENSON'S HOME, Fitz steeled himself to see Tara. This morning, she had skipped out of his bed and only when he got a text a half hour after he'd awoken, did he stop being as cranky as a man without his morning coffee and the hot woman he'd expected to wake up to.

Her message was peak Tara.

> Had soooo much fun! I'll spare you my morning-after discussion of the Congressional filibuster! (Spoiler: I don't know what the filibuster is.) Kiss Goober and Pickle for me.

He'd laughed his head off, then descended into a funk again when he realized the day stretched out before him Tara-free. He wanted more, for them to continue as long as they both found it useful or desirable or ... necessary.

Necessary? In the sense of physical release being necessary, perhaps, but that didn't have to be with Tara. Any woman could fill that role. Any woman could moan and whimper and sigh when he ran his hands over her lush curves and found the spots to light her up.

Of course, he wouldn't mind if that was Tara. He would like very much if it was Tara because he liked her. This shouldn't have come as a surprise—he didn't fuck women he didn't like or respect—but acknowledging that thought sent a pulse of excitement through him. So Tara had her faults, not least among them this wrong-headed notion of how to land a husband. But she was also sweet and sexy and so damn funny.

And in an awful hurry to get him dating. He hadn't missed that. While he appreciated her help in that arena, he was beginning to think his needs could be serviced closer to home.

"Fitz, you're here!" Erik Jorgenson, the Rebels goalie, pumped his hand. "Are you hungry?"

Within a minute he had a plate piled high with Swedish delicacies, so he stashed himself in a corner and did a spot of people-watching. Or Tara-watching, if he was being honest. She had yet to show. O'Malley was here and Fitz felt some small measure of relief that they weren't together.

Belly full of meatballs and aquavit, he mingled for a few minutes until he happened on a spirited discussion between Foreman and Remy DuPre.

"Here, Fitz can help us decide." Foreman held up a picture of a cute terrier with tons of personality. "What do you think of Bobby O as the Rebels mascot?"

"Don't think so." Remy was quick to elbow him out of the way and show another puppy, a funny-looking thing of indeterminate breed. "Kreuger is a better candidate."

"These are the choices? Nah, nah, gentlemen. I think we need to take this up a notch." He showed them his lock screen, already displaying Goober at his Gooberest. "No contest."

"A pug?" Foreman sounded disgusted. "Pugs can't represent. They're too lazy, waddling around. Would never work as a mascot."

"You're all wrong." The deep voice of Bren St. James entered the conversation. "Gretzky is the original team pupper and no one can top him." A big black lab, with a big grin to match, greeted them from St. James' phone.

"But his owner is no longer on the team." Reid Durand offered his own puppy, Bucky, up for consideration, a rescue where Durand had done the actual rescuing from frigid Lake Michigan in rather spectacular fashion. "Foreman, your dog isn't even in this state. As for you old timers—"

"Watch it," Remy drawled.

"We can't consider a dog belonging to former players. This isn't some legacy thing."

"Legacy? Whose legacy?" Kershaw appeared out of nowhere as if he was waiting to be summoned to the perfect entry point.

"No one's," Foreman said. "You don't have a dog so you're not part of the conversation."

"Think again. We just picked this little guy up from the shelter." His phone displayed a picture of a cat. "Meet Marmalade, the star of the Rebels calendar photo shoot."

Foreman sniffed derisively. "Still not a dog."

"Only dogs can be mascots," Durand said, in a rare moment of agreement with Foreman. These two usually sniped like the proverbial. "Cats are too selfish."

"But they're so funny," Jorgenson chimed in. "Look at Kevin being an asshole." He showed a quick video of his cat pouncing on Jorgenson's head ninja-style from the top of a kitchen cupboard. "I taught him how to do that."

"You didn't teach him anything because cats cannot be taught," Remy observed. "Little fucker learned that all by himself. And he's not even your cat. He's Casey's."

Fitz said, "Well, if the contest includes cats and dogs—"

"It doesn't," Durand said.

"Then I think we have a winner." He scrolled to his photo albums and found one he'd taken yesterday evening of Pickle and Goober getting snuggly on the sofa.

Everyone liquified into puddles at the sight. Game over.

"Wait a sec." Kershaw took Fitz's phone and started pawing at it, trying to enlarge the image. "Is that a woman's foot in there?"

Shit. Hastily, he took the phone back, realizing now that it was indeed a woman's foot and that he might have captured Tara's face in another photo later in the roll. She'd looked so adorable in his sweats, post-dinner, post-orgasm, surrounded by critters and cushions.

"No comment."

"No comment?" Foreman said with a smirk. "No comment that it's a woman's foot or no comment in general?"

"You can see it's a woman's foot," Jorgenson said. "There's nail polish."

"Men wear nail polish," St. James said. "But that's not a man's foot. Far too dainty."

"All these assumptions about feet and nail polish and gender," Remy said, rubbing his chin, "when Fitz could just put our concerns to rest and tell us if he had a barefoot woman lounging on his sofa recently."

"Unlike you lot, I like to keep my personal business personal."

"Good luck with that." Durand eyed the plate in Kershaw's hand. "There are mini quiches here?"

"Ready to drop off the diet wagon?" Jorgenson asked. Durand was well-known for being a rabid adherent to his diet and exercise regimen.

"No, Kennedy likes them."

Kershaw thumbed over his shoulder. "Pretty good spread as usual, Jorgenson." He pointed a mini-quiche at Foreman. "Hey, have you heard the latest about O'Malley and your ex?" This was typical of Kershaw who liked to leapfrog indiscriminately from topic to topic.

"Tara?"

"Yeah, she and O'Malley are apparently giving it the old college try."

"No, it's all fake to make him look like less of a ho," Durand said.

Kershaw shook his head. "Not from the way they were earlier when I stopped by to get my hair cut. She did a good job, didn't she?"

Fitz's body tightened. What did Kershaw mean by "the way they were earlier"? Before he could ask for more information without asking for more information, Jorgenson added, "Yeah, O'Malley doesn't look like he's faking anything."

With no subtlety whatsoever, all eyes turned to an almost hidden recess of the room where O'Malley was standing and talking to Tara, who must have arrived in the last couple of minutes. Though standing was more like "looming" and "talking" was closer to leering. Tara wore a low-cut top and Hale could see her damn cleavage from twenty feet away, which meant O'Malley had a front row seat for the best show in town.

That. Fucker.

She threw her head back, laughing at something he said,

revealing her slender throat. O'Malley took it as an opportunity to lower his gaze to her breasts.

She had to have noticed, but she kept her smile in place. An act, perhaps?

She hadn't been acting with Fitz. He was sure that he saw something of the real woman and not just in his bed.

Who now had her sights locked on the original target ... and then he spotted Sophie doing the rounds, taking pictures for the team's social media. The white-knuckled grip on his glass relaxed a touch. Tara always knew where the cameras were. That's what she was doing: making it look good for the public.

So he suppressed his growl when she leaned in to hear something O'Malley said.

And he didn't kick the wall behind him—or anyone standing close by—when she gave O'Malley a huge smile that the asshole did not in any way deserve.

And he "managed" his feelings when she patted his chest and moved away a few steps, only for O'Malley to catch her hand and pull her back to bring her lips mere inches from his.

Tara's relationships—fake or otherwise—were none of his business.

Yet he couldn't help feeling that this woman was entirely his business. A sexual obsession, perhaps, but one he needed to shake so he could move on. Apparently taking that step was harder than he thought.

"You okay?"

He turned to St. James who had just uttered the most ridiculous query ever.

Of course I'm okay.

In a rare moment of reflection, he refocused on St. James' words, surprising himself when he came up with another answer: Fifty-fifty, with a lean toward an over-whelming desire to crush the face of one of his team's superstars.

So, not okay.

"O'Malley's been told he needs to be respectful toward Ms. Becker."

"He doesn't have a hand up her skirt," Kershaw commented, always saying what everyone was thinking. "Probably counts as the height of gallantry where Dex is concerned."

"He'd better not make her his plus one at any upcoming weddings or he'll never hear the end of it," Kazminski muttered, newly arrived to the conversation. A couple of the others chuckled.

Fitz turned to Kaz. "That respect for Ms. Becker extends to the rest of the team."

A bristling Kaz went on the defensive. "You weren't there. She threw a tantrum when she didn't get that bouquet at Hunt's wedding and Foreman had to practically stop a cat fight."

"It wasn't that bad," Foreman said. "And there was no risk of a cat fight. This is Mia and Tara we're talking about."

"Sure, they're friends now," Kaz said. "But everyone knows her deal. She's a gold digger."

Seething, Fitz cut in before Foreman could. "I can't pretend to know her motives and you certainly don't, but I do know that Tara is currently employed by this organiza-tion in a public relations capacity which makes her part of the Rebels team. So fewer snide jokes, if you don't mind."

"Sure," Kaz bit out, but he was clearly fuming at being admonished. Fitz didn't care. He wouldn't stand by and listen to anyone insulting ... another employee.

His gaze returned to the couple, only Tara was no longer

beside O'Malley, which was probably best for Fitz's blood pressure.

Did he really need to take the side of an independent contractor over one of his assets? Fitz had not attended Levi Hunt's wedding, which happened long before he was on board. He didn't know what went down and frankly it was none of his business.

But neither would he stand by and listen to her being insulted.

She deserved respect—and Fitz would ensure she got it.

Tara's heart was beating much too fast.

Hale had just defended her against an insult, something about her being a gold digger.

He really shouldn't have done that. His relationship with the players was sacrosanct and no way would she ever want to get in the middle of that. But to hear him shutting down a nasty jibe did strange things to her.

On the topic of strange—or stranger—things, Dex was paying her a boatload of attention. The man was flirting with her, and not in a leering, or completely leering, manner. He had complimented her on her outfit and spent only seven point five seconds on her boobs.

They happened to look spectacular tonight so she'd allowed Dex's dipped gaze south for a moment. Tonight's version of Dex was a touch more sensitive than usual, and she would normally be all over it, except for one startling fact.

She had imprinted on someone else.

"Hey, lady!" Mia came over and hugged her, swaying a

little which meant she was already tipsy. "Having fun with Dex?"

"Tons."

"Liar," she hissed. "Casey's right. He's not the one."

Tara had never said he was, but all her friends seemed to be one-track when it came to this kind of thing. Not every relationship had to be hearts-and-flowers-love-you-forever. Some could be pragmatic.

Tara was a very pragmatic woman. She needed to remember that.

Eyes on the prize.

"He thinks I bring him luck on the ice."

"Players are very superstitious."

True. She moved to change the subject to something more pleasant. "So I was thinking that I'd like to throw a little shindig for you and Cal, just something small. To celebrate your medal and your engagement."

Mia threw her arms around her. "You're such a sweetheart, you know that? Any guy would be so lucky to have you."

This was standard Mia after a glass of wine. For all that muscle mass, she was surprisingly lightweight in the alcohol absorption stakes.

"One day I'll bless someone with my favor. So you're okay with a party?"

"Of course, but Cal and I will cover the costs."

"No, it's my treat. I won't be getting you a wedding gift though, this is it." She was sure she could find a way to do the party on the cheap.

"No, no. It's too much and you know I can afford it." She moved in closer, tilted her head. "So we don't talk about money much but this whole thing with Dex, I'm guessing that's about the dinero. You know you only have to ask if you need anything."

Tara felt a pressure in her chest, the weight of secrets and the burden of a life kept small. She refused to taint what she had with Mia with the tawdry scent of cash.

"Doing just fine, thanks."

"But the marriage-to-a-hunk scheme, that's—uh, what is that?"

Well, either you need money or you don't. "It's not just money, Wallace. I want to be a little bit famous and I want a stud in the sheets. Snagging a player kills three birds with one bang. So don't worry about your millions—"

"Billions," Mia said somewhat morosely before Cal put an arm around her and whisked her away, leaving Tara alone.

Over at the snack table, she turned her nose up at the numerous herring dishes before helping herself to a Swedish meatball. She snuck a glance over to the hallway where Hale was standing with—huh—Sophie and some-one's baby. She recognized the Rebels onesie as belonging to Rosie, Cade and Dante's little girl. He was patting her back —Rosie's, not Sophie's—and showing off his uncle creden-tials in a way that made her weak.

Jealousy comingled with broodiness, but before she had a chance to analyze it, Dex appeared at her side.

"Hey, beautiful." To her shock, he brushed his lips over hers. In a case of classic bad timing, someone knocked against her from behind and she ended up pressing the kiss back— and getting a preview of coming attractions against her belly.

She stepped away. "What are you doing?"

"Kissing my girlfriend. We're hot, we're single, we're Instagram official. Don't you even like me a little?"

She couldn't get into this now. The sheets were still warm in Hale's bed, and while she had no intention of going back there, she wasn't ready to take this next step with Dex in front of everyone.

It felt all wrong.

Need to think. "Listen, I have to use the little girls' room. How about you holster your pistol and we can discuss later, okay?"

Before he could respond, she backed away. Of course Dex was hot, and they would be amazing together—at least, on paper—but it all felt like it was moving too fast. She had hoped there would be more … chemistry?

This marriage idea was supposed to be a business decision yet here she was rejecting the advances of a man who would meet all her requirements. Damn Hale Fitzpatrick for making her question everything!

The restroom on the first floor had a line, so when she ran into Casey, she asked if it was okay to go upstairs—she didn't want to assume—and Casey assured her it was. Passing Tate Kazminski in the hallway, she winced at the funny look he bestowed on her. As she walked away, she heard him humming.

Kanye's *Gold Digger*. So original.

Tears pressed against her eyelids. Ridiculous, considering how she was closer to the prize than ever.

At the top of the stairs, she ran into Hale. Perhaps some part of her knew he'd be here.

"Hi!" Too cheerful.

"Hello," he drawled, and she felt it everywhere that sexy rumble could penetrate.

"Having fun?" *Next, ask him about the weather and the traffic on his car ride over.*

"I've had better."

Had he seen Dex laying that kiss on her? And so what if he had? They had made no promises, yet he had defended her against Kaz's jibes.

They stood there staring, waiting for the other to take the conversation in a direction that would dictate the story going forward.

He was better at this game of chicken.

"Something wrong, Hale?"

He moved closer. She stood her ground. Her pulse rate —which was usually high around him—went bananas.

"Is O'Malley bothering you?" He sounded more concerned than jealous.

"I can handle him."

"You shouldn't have to." A muscle throbbed in his jaw. Their toes touched and even that was enough to get her all hot and bothered.

A voice sounded on the stair, and the next thing she knew Hale had taken her by the hand and led her into the nearest room—a bedroom.

Before he could say anything that ratcheted up the sexual tension to even higher levels, she jumped in. "I heard you chiding Kaz for something he said about me. You didn't have to do that."

"Didn't I?"

"I don't want to make trouble between you and your players." So she'd brought it on herself, but it still rankled.

Hurt.

Of course, a secure future could smooth away a lot of that hurt. Not all of it; she didn't expect to get out of this journey unscathed.

Crackin' eggs and makin' omelets, baby.

"No one is going to trash talk you in my presence."

That was in no way deserved, but she let herself savor the care.

"That's sweet of you."

"Nothin' sweet about it. Still mad as all hell at you since you snuck out of my bed this morning."

"Oh, you don't want to see me first thing. Not a pretty sight."

He shook his head, like he couldn't believe this front she insisted on showing. Like he expected her to let her guard down a little when they were alone.

Because sex had given him the right to access some private place inside her.

Worse, she wanted to take the risk. Open her heart.

"Goober should have woken me up. Damn dog is useless."

"And what would you have done? One for the road?" At the thought of it, of being in Hale's bed, wrapped in his strong arms, her knees turned to jelly.

"Made sure you couldn't walk for a week, honey."

"Oh, that good, huh?" She fluttered her eyelashes. "But I'm walking just fine now and we'd already done it so I guess you didn't bring your A-game last night?"

His hands fell to her hips and yanked her right into his A-game. "Cheeky wench."

"Wench?" A helpless giggle escaped her lips. Relationships should be fun—she'd seen it with others—but she'd never expected it for her own.

Not a relationship. Just a chance to let off steam.

"I have to go." Before she did something stupid on the bed behind them.

He searched her face. "Come home with me."

Home. He was killing her. "That's probably not the best idea."

"Because you didn't have fun yesterday evening or after dinner or at least two more times in the early hours of this morning ..."

"You're counting?"

"Always. I'm a stats guy to the bone. Or boner." He moved closer and she felt something statistically significant against her hip. "I need to see you again."

To what end? It was supposed to be a fun detour. She didn't have the bandwidth for a fling and a fake relationship, one that she was trying to turn into something real. She was barely treading water here.

"This isn't part of the plan."

His brow darkened. "Like O'Malley is?"

She couldn't deny it. Her goal was to create something lasting with a guy who wouldn't challenge her, spark any fires, or hurt her. Dex checked all the boxes so she needed to be making nice with him instead of making eyes at the man who got her engine—and heart—cranked in a dangerous way.

When she didn't respond—when she couldn't—he stood back, putting space between them that wasn't just physical.

"Best get on with it, then."

She had gotten what she wanted—a moment to indulge in the heady air that surrounded Hale. Now she would put away that needy part of herself and return to the mission.

21

———

FITZ STRODE toward the concierge in the team hotel in Atlanta. He should have bought presents in Chicago but he'd had other things on his mind and now here he was: giftless with small female children ready to tear him to shreds if he showed up empty-handed.

Tara hadn't spoken to him on the plane ride out for a two-game series against the Atlanta Rockets, not even to distract him from his nerves, instead giving all her attention to O'Malley. Fitz had tried his best, but he'd found his gaze wandering and inevitably settling on the most interesting person on the plane. Whenever she glanced his way he averted his eyes, suddenly finding the back of the seat fascinating, acting like a kid caught spying on the girl he liked in the eighth grade.

The woman was an infuriating constant in his thoughts and he longed for the day when they could wrap up this O'Malley business and he wouldn't have to see her any more.

But first, presents. Just as he reached the concierge, Tara walked into the hotel lobby with Hudson Grey, both flushed from their run and breathing heavily. Grey nodded at Fitz, murmured something to Tara, and went on his way.

"Good run?" Fitz said to Tara as she approached.

"Great run! That boy has legs. You should let him use them more on the ice."

Fitz had been thinking something similar and was planning to talk to Coach Calhoun about it, but he certainly wouldn't be acknowledging to Tara that it was a good idea.

"So how was the flight out?" she asked.

"You were on it. How did you think it was?"

She held his gaze, that hook of her plush lips a silent admonishment for being irritable.

"Off somewhere?"

"I am," he conceded, regretting his testiness. It wasn't Tara's fault that he had a problem with rejection. "Know anything about what women want?"

"Gold, diamonds, fast cars."

"Even the littlest ones?"

"Oh, the desire for trinkets imprints *pret*-ty early." At his laugh, she went on. "Shopping for your nieces?"

"Yeah, I meant to do it yesterday but now I have some time before the team meeting." He really shouldn't but what the hell. She could only say no. "I don't suppose you'd be interested in helping me get the perfect gift?"

She blinked, clearly surprised that he would want her company after their less than amicable run-in at Jorgenson's party. He wasn't going to apologize for wanting her in his bed, and neither was he going to pretend that spending time with her wasn't high on his list.

"I need to shower, so how long are you willing to wait?"

"For expert help, I can wait for however long it takes."

She was back in fifteen minutes, wrapped in a winter coat and a fuzzy hat and scarf. So damn cute.

"Tell me more about your nieces."

"Well, Joni's into animals and is super chatty. Grace seems more of a princess fan and is a bit quieter. She also likes to shop. Actually they both do." He told her the story about Joni's iPad furniture order, which had Tara laughing as they exited the hotel.

She held up her phone. "There's a toy store in Buckhead that looks like it would have a good selection. It's a twenty minute cab ride, if you can bear it."

"Think I can manage."

Once settled in a cab, he took another look. The chilly March air—not as chilly as Chicago but cool all the same—had given her cheeks a rosy glow and her eyes a glittering sparkle.

She caught him. "Hale."

"Can't I look?"

"It's what follows the look that's the problem. Haven't you heard I'm dating one of your players?"

He scoffed. "Fake dating. And here you are."

"You asked for my help. Didn't know it constituted a binding agreement." Her lips curled. "You just don't enjoy sharing."

"Who does?"

Her smile was all-knowing and incredibly infuriating. "Admit it, Hale. If Dex wasn't in the picture, would you even be interested?"

He turned to her sharply. "You think my interest in you stems from a desire to stick it to O'Malley? As you're so fond of saying, have a little faith."

She looked a touch baffled. "No, I know there's attraction there but you could ... well, you could have anyone. This is more of a proximity thing. I'm here and technically available and that's nice when you're feeling frisky. But we both know that this isn't what you really want. What either of us do."

Why not? a small voice said.

So he wasn't what Tara had in mind for her future—when it came to young, dumb, and hung, he could manage one of them and it wasn't related to age or intelligence—and Tara certainly didn't fit Fitz's usual mold.

So that was that.

Yet it didn't stop him from wanting her with an intensity that shocked him.

"Other than wanting more ice time, what else does Grey have to say?"

"You could ask him yourself. Take a walk in the trenches with the troops."

Fitz had bi-weekly meetings with each team member, but there was a scripted quality to them that didn't really encourage confidences.

"He might be more forthcoming with you."

"I think he's lonely." She turned to him. "But he's settling in, game-wise."

He nodded and moved on. "I hear you're now the unofficial team hair stylist."

"None of them want to actually make appointments so it works and they like having someone to whine to." She smiled at him wryly. "Several of them are so young. They come to these new teams, knowing hardly anyone, expected to make friends at the drop of a puck. I know you set them up with places to stay and the team fills in the rest, but they could really do with more emotional support." She shrugged, took a quick glance out the window, then back to him. "Sorry, I don't mean to tell you how to do your job."

"Don't you? You haven't held back so far."

"I have opinions!" Her laugh was dirty and sweet and

sent a shot of lust to his groin. "But seriously, I like talking to them, listening to them, recommending a course of action. Like I'm the Rebels den mom, though I wouldn't want to step on Harper's size fives."

"You're not. She's got so much going on with her pregnancy and she'd rather I step up to the support plate, only I'm not sure I have the temperament to listen to the problems of a bunch of very well-paid frat boys. I don't remember being this whiny when I started out."

"Hmm, back when dinosaurs ruled the rinks, a player was probably expected to rub some dirt on it and carry on. These days demand greater sensitivity. No one's expecting you to hold every hand, but it's probably good to keep your door open so the boys know you're available. That care is a hallmark of this team. One of the reasons why they gel so well is because the openness and honesty is in full force." She smiled. "Blame the female leadership. Women make everything better."

This woman certainly did. It had been a long time since he felt this excitement with anyone, and then he recalled that she wanted someone else.

Or something else.

Yet he had to wonder. At Jorgenson's party, she had made all the right moves in response to O'Malley's plays—the coquettish laugh, the wide-eyed admiration, even allowing a stolen kiss. On paper, it looked like the relationship was moving along and Tara was edging closer to the blue zone: a proposal from a hockey himbo.

Who probably didn't know a single thing about her. The guy didn't even have the benefit of a background check!

"It was Harper's idea to hire you for this job," he said, determined to remind her that it was exactly that: a job. "If

I'd had my way, we would have gone with Amish Farm Girl #2."

"Oh, yeah, you did not look pleased when she dropped me in your lap. In a manner of speaking." Another grin that had his heart leaping dangerously in response.

"I can admit when I'm wrong. You've obviously made an impact."

And positioned herself for a big score.

"That was the goal."

"The team's goal. The question is whether yours is still in play." Could Tara admit she might be completely off-base and that O'Malley could never make her happy?

Her look was sheer pity at his obviousness. So he was jealous. This was no secret.

"I'm not easily deterred," she said, all challenge.

Which meant he needed to gear up to a new level if he was to come out on top.

They arrived at their destination, a store called Toy Box in the upscale neighborhood of Buckhead, a few miles north of downtown Atlanta. Ten minutes later, he had a grow-and-glow terrarium for Joni and a princess-themed dreamcatcher kit for Grace. Tara had weighed the pros and cons of each gift and put considerable thought into what she thought the girls would like.

While his purchases were being wrapped, he spotted her in one of the aisles near the cash desk, examining a colorful box.

"What've you got there?"

"This looks like a fun gift for someone I know." It was a light-up aquarium, like a lava lamp with plastic fish floating in it.

"Just add it to mine," he told the cashier.

"No, thanks, I've got it." She whipped out her wallet and

took a moment to choose a credit card. As she passed it over, she slid a glance at him. "I can manage eighteen bucks."

After a few seconds, the cashier winced. "I'm afraid this card has been declined."

"Oh, that's the wrong one. Sorry!" Tara squinted at another card. "This one should be fine. Well, maybe." Frowning, she worried her lip before pulling out a different card altogether.

"Tara, I've got it."

She touched his arm, her eyes shiny. "Thanks. I promise I'll pay you back."

"Not a big deal." He grimaced at how he'd phrased it. Obviously it was a big deal for Tara, who lived her financial life close to the edge. "How about lunch? My treat because you helped me out."

"I told you the name of a store that you probably could have figured out for yourself. And you don't need to buy me lunch. Or anything."

He curled his fingers around her lapel and lowered his lips to her ear. "I'd rather be eating you in your hotel room but as that's not on the menu, then I'll have to make do with watching your pretty little mouth while you slip morsels of food past those gorgeous lips."

"Hale." His name came out in a breathless puff. "You're impossible."

"Am I? Or am I just appreciative of the company of a beautiful woman? Besides I wanted to get your opinion on Angela Merkel's successor."

"Who?"

"The new German chancellor. I figure if anyone can give me a breakdown of the various power players and factions in the mix when it comes to the EU, it would be you."

"Oh shut it. I was trying to keep you entertained during the afterglow."

Mission accomplished. "Nothing makes me hotter than a woman with the inside track on geopolitical events."

She picked up her package. "I should have known all you needed was me to say, 'Oh what an amazing lov-ah you are. Do me again, big boy, and don't go easy!'" To the cashier who was watching the byplay avidly, she said, "Men, right?"

Fitz had never wanted to kiss someone so badly. If she wasn't so sure she needed a man who was the complete opposite to Fitz, he would be going the full-court press here. Every moment with Tara revealed layers that surprised and fucking delighted him.

The woman was all wrong for him so why did it feel so damn right?

The cashier shot a glance at Hale then back at Tara. "Talking's overrated."

"More like completely wasted on this knuckle-dragger." She flicked her hair and gave a mock flounce. "Okay, feed me, General."

22

"Wow!"

Fitz laughed at his sister-in-law's expression when she entered the visitors' box at the Atlanta Rockets arena. Unfortunately the effect was ruined by his family's sartorial choices: Rockets gear from head to toe.

"Guess those Rebels jerseys I got you are a waste," he said to Bode.

"Always looking for rags to clean my car." Chuckling, Bode gave Fitz a hug. "Thanks for doing this. The girls have been bouncing up and down all day."

"My pleasure." Fitz leaned in to kiss Ava on the cheek. She looked great, but then she always did. "Found the place okay?"

"Uh, we had a personal escort from the entrance, Mr. Showoff," Ava said before letting out a squeal. "Oh my God, there are macarons here!"

Dante was a fan when he was GM, so it was a tradition to always include them on the snack table, even for away games. At this point, it was considered bad luck if the box didn't have them.

"Let me get you a glass of wine." He'd also sent a car to pick them up so they could let their hair down. Parenting—even when the progeny were little angels like his nieces—was hard work.

Joni and Grace loved their gifts, so much so that they had set up shop on a patch of floor space in the box to play with them. To be honest, he wouldn't mind getting down there and helping them out. That glowing terrarium, in particular, looked like a lot of fun.

"Great choices, Fitz," Ava murmured.

"I had help."

"Oh?"

"Yeah, a friend of mine knew exactly what they'd want."

She raised her eyebrow at the mention of "a friend," but didn't get a chance to push it because Joni had spilled some clay from the terrarium and needed Mom to figure it out.

"Who's that?" Bode asked. While Fitz had been busy schmoozing with a couple of high-profile visitors from the League brass, Tara had arrived and was already talking to Ava. This shouldn't have surprised him. What was curious was how it pleased the hell out of him.

He sure liked the idea of these people he enjoyed meeting each other.

"Tara Becker. She's dating O'Malley."

"Oh, yeah. She's the alt-mascot, doing the ice-clearing. And she hangs in the box?"

"The player partners don't usually travel that much—a lot of them have kids—but Tara's different." He looked away to the bar and picked up a glass of bourbon, but soon his gaze was seeking out the woman he was fast becoming obsessed with.

Somehow, she had zeroed in on his people without introductions. Joni sat on one side and Tara on the other, while she braided Joni's hair. She wore a short leather mini skirt, a deep-V sky-blue blouse, and fur-edged ankle boots that showcased her shapely legs.

"She's a hair stylist by trade," he said to Bode, as an explanation for why she was fiddling with his oldest daughter's hair.

"She's gorgeous. Great legs and … the rest."

Fitz winced, not liking to hear Tara being spoken of in such reductive terms. The rest had lately become far more interesting.

Bode slid a glance to him. "Okay?"

"Why wouldn't I be?"

"I dunno. You're looking at O'Malley's girlfriend like she's done something to piss you off. Or is that mood for me?"

"Just pre-game jitters."

"Yeah, you were like this when you played. Glad to see nothing's changed." He sipped his beer. "Mom's been sending me photos. You'd think that cruise Wi-Fi would cramp her style."

"So endeth the pleasant conversation."

Bode rolled on. "Apparently I'm the soundboard for your dating prospects, like I don't have enough to do."

"Well, after she realized I won't do anything long-distance, she started sendin' me pics of women from Chicago dating sites. Meaning she joined them, Bo."

Bode shuddered. "Catfishing in your name?"

"Jesus, I don't know. I've already got a profile ready to go, anyway. Tara helped."

Fitz would have shut his eyes at his stupidity if he wasn't so sure it would make him look even more of an idiot.

"Tara?"

"She's not ..." He course-corrected. "She's good at that sort of thing."

"At what sort of thing?" Bode squinted, took a beat to work it out, then unloaded with all barrels blazing. "Are you telling me that you're screwing around with the girlfriend of one of your players?"

He raised a hand to shush him. "No, I am not. One, she's not actually his girlfriend because it's a PR move to make him look good after his recent brush with the tabloids." He hoped. "And two, screwing around implies present tense and there's nothing happening. In the present tense."

"Should've been a fuckin' lawyer."

"My MBA not impressive enough?"

His brother sighed. "Why'd you want to complicate it? Just do what Momma says and choose a nice girl to give her more grandbabies. Though, maybe ..." Cue the most annoying eyebrow raise ever and an unsubtle nod to where Tara was smoothing Joni's braid. "This woman looks like she has the maternal instinct that Celeste would approve of."

"She reserves it for the players. Agony aunt while she cuts their hair." Listening to Tara talk with such pride about her conversations with the guys made his heart swell.

Don't look at her. She's not for you.

Joni ambled over. "Uncle Fitz, look what Tara did! Do you like it?"

"Sure do, petal. Hey, you want a bite to eat? We have your favorite."

"SpaghettiOs?"

"Nah, the budget couldn't swing it." He grinned at a chuckling Bode. "But we have cheese and crackers."

"I love cheese and crackers!"

"Yeah, you do," Bode said, before adding to Fitz, "Here, bring this over to Ava while I hunt and gather for the kiddo."

He passed a glass of white wine to Fitz, which he delivered to his sister-in-law.

"I've been told to ply you with alcohol," he said to Ava as he sat beside her. "I think your husband is hoping it makes you easy later."

Ava chuckled. "It will! An easy sleeper, that is. One of these and I'll be out."

"Oh, God, I know what you mean," Tara said as she rolled Grace's hair into twists then created mad spirals on the side of her head. "I used to have much higher tolerance, but as I near the big 3-0, I'm a total lightweight."

"Embrace it. My thirties are almost behind me and I don't think I'll miss it," Ava said. "But we should ask someone who has those days long in his rear view. Fitz, how does it feel?"

Mouthing *ha ha*, he caught Tara's eye. "Why do I get the impression y'all are ganging up on me?"

Ava grinned, then gave him a sympathetic look. "Just kidding. You've got to get a move on, though."

"I've been telling him," Tara said, her green eyes sparkling with humor. "By the time he gets his act together, he'll be too old to pick his kids up." This very personal observation had Ava staring at him. Oblivious to the undercurrent, Tara turned Grace around, took out a compact, and held the mirror open. "Here, sweetie, take a look. Do you like it?"

With an enthusiastic nod, she turned and snuggled in against Tara.

Something in Fitz's chest lurched. Fucking Bode.

"Ava, you should load up a plate before the game starts," Tara said. "I'll keep an eye on this cutie."

"I can get it for you," Fitz said, suddenly eager to be away from Tara.

Ava jumped up with a crafty smile at Fitz. "No, stay, stay!"

"Funny how you immediately gravitate to the people who know me," Fitz muttered as he took Ava's seat and rubbed Grace's arm. "All so you can talk about me behind my back."

"Not my fault you were late to the party. And I'm happy to talk about you to your face." She smiled over Grace's head. "These girls are the cutest."

"Comes from havin' the best uncle in the world. They loved their gifts, by the way."

"Knew they would. I have excellent taste." A moment later, she murmured, "They're a lovely family." There was something wistful about the way she said it.

"Yeah, I'm more than a little envious."

"You want this, don't you?"

"I do. How about you?"

She looked surprised at his directness. "I suppose. If that's what whoever I end up with wants."

"But what about you? What do you want, Tara?"

Her lips parted; she appeared uncomfortable with the line of questioning.

But he refused to let up. Something told him it was important he challenge her. "I don't mean children specifically, but more what would make you happy. You've said you have a hockey player husband in mind but beyond that, what's the plan? Are you just going to spend your life taking care of his needs while ignoring your own?"

"Who says the two can't be compatible? Some people have an innate need to take care of others. And it's not like I won't be getting something out of the bargain. Security, well-being, time to catch my breath."

Why would she need that? What kind of pressure was she under to make this happen?

Don't push. It was none of his business but ... also, it was. Tara had edged under his skin and made herself vital.

"You think you'll find meaning in that kind of relationship? Looking after a man-child who doesn't understand the first thing about what makes you scream in pleasure, what makes you tick up here." He touched a finger gently to her forehead. "What—"

"What, Hale?" Her bottom lip trembled.

"What lights you up. I think you'd be bored stupid in a lackluster marriage with someone like O'Malley. The guy can barely lace his own skates." She parted her lips but he wasn't finished. "And before you think that's my jealousy talking, I'll have you know that yes, it is—partly—but mostly I believe you're selling yourself short. This thing with O'Malley might look good on paper, but surely you see that the lived experience can never match your expectation."

His candor surprised even him, or maybe the source of it. Some deep well of feeling that arose instinctively. Fitz enjoyed analyzing situations, problems, and people, and using facts to inform his decisions. He wasn't much for a reflexive approach as it rarely led him down the right path.

Take this situation with Tara. Against all common sense, he had let his desire for this woman override how it looked on paper. She had been hired to date a player and sanitize that same player's rep, and here was Fitz endangering that campaign. Sneaking around. Risking a PR disaster.

Because the lived experience was so much better than what his brain insisted was good for him.

He chanced a glance at Tara, who was looking at him intensely.

Look at me like that forever. Like I would hang the moon for you.

Because I just fucking might.

"I appreciate the vote of confidence," she said quietly over Grace's head. "I didn't get much of that growing up so it always surprises me when I hear someone telling me I might have more to offer than what people see."

People had likely underestimated Tara all her life. Placed her in the pretty box and told her that was all she needed—or was all she was good for. Hell, Fitz had been there, thinking she was no different than his ex or any other woman who married a guy for fame and riches.

Bode and Ava stood at the box window with Joni, surveying the warm-up. His sister-in-law chose that moment to give him another knowing look over her shoulder. He couldn't help his smug glance in return.

He felt good around Tara, for all the good it would actually do him.

He took a sip of his drink. "They think something's going on between us."

"Well, whose fault is that? Try being less charming and flirtatious in my presence. In fact, you should be staying away from me altogether."

That she didn't deny the hum of energy between them gave him a thrill that bubbled in his veins. He swirled his drink in the glass, watching the amber liquid like it could offer up the answers.

"Maybe I don't want to." He turned his head, knowing she would be seeking him out for connection just like he was. The chemistry was too combustible between them.

"Stop. It."

He grunted his non-agreement and waited for her to

smile. Oh, she fought it, but with a cute little girl in her arms and his unyielding attention, she couldn't win that battle.

"Impossible," she murmured on a smile that lifted him through the arena's roof. Would a win tonight feel better than this? He didn't think so.

Tara's phone buzzed. Without waking Grace, she deftly extracted it from the purse at her feet and looked at the number. "I have to get this. Could you ...?"

He took Grace from her as the phone buzzed to silence, meaning she missed the call because she hadn't wanted to disturb his dozing niece. She left the box, returning five minutes later, her face a mask of worry. "I need to return to Chicago. Family emergency."

He recalled a sister in the suburbs. "You're leaving? Now?"

"I managed to get confirmed for a flight out in a couple of hours, but if I get there sooner, I might land an earlier one."

"Let me get a town car for you—"

"I don't have time. I'll just take a cab." She twisted away, then turned back, evidently trying to ward off tears. "I'm sorry. I don't mean to be rude. I just ..."

"Honey, it's okay. Do you have time to go back to the hotel?"

"I do. I-I really should go now. I'm sorry."

"No need to apologize. Let me walk you down to the exit."

"God, no! The puck's about to drop. I'll be fine." She ran a hand over Grace's hair, her expression soft and helpless. "Could you say goodbye to your family for me?"

He nodded, wishing he could do more. Before he could verbalize that or hand off Grace to her parents, Tara had squeezed his arm and was out the door.

Screw this, Hale thought.

Twenty minutes later, he entered the hotel lobby and met Tara on her way out with her Disney suitcase in tow.

"Hale! You should be at the game."

"They'll survive without me." Grabbing her luggage, he rolled it to the entrance, where a cab was waiting. He dropped the case in the trunk, ushered her into the back seat, and followed her.

"What are you doing?"

"Making sure you get there okay."

She opened her mouth. Closed it. Sank back against the seat, defeated.

He dialed up Scottie, the team's travel director. "I have a favor to ask. Tara Becker needs a seat on the next available flight out of Atlanta to Chicago. She's currently on flight ..." She showed the confirmation on her phone screen. "AA234 at 9:23pm but we're hoping to get her out sooner. We're headed to Hartsfield-Jackson now—could you work on it and call me back?"

"Will do." He rang off.

"Must be nice to have people at your beck and call."

"It has its benefits." He took her hand and squeezed it. "You don't have to tell me what's going on but I'm happy to listen."

She swallowed and looked out the rain-flecked window. Took another shallow breath, then shook her head. Several taut moments passed before she spoke.

"My sister, Chloe, is ill. She's in a care home and the nurse called to tell me her respiratory infection is worse. I thought it was a mild case of bronchitis but it's more serious."

He let that sink in a second. "What kind of care home?"

"One for developmentally and intellectually disabled adults. She's been there for just over two years but in official care for the last eleven. Since ..." She took another breath. "My mom couldn't look after her and I can't either, so this is the best we can do. Luckily, she loves it there. The staff is so kind and she's been making great progress." Her voice was pitching higher with each new peel of the onion, as if she was trying to excuse a wealth of past decisions.

"I'm sure she's in the best place she can be. I'm guessing she needs someone watching her pretty close. Bit of a troublemaker like her sister, perhaps?"

That teased a watery smile. "She's a little prankster and quite the handful. Loves to play games and sing her favorite songs from Disney. Well, she can't sing—or not aloud, she's nonverbal—but I sing for her and she dances along with her hands and eyes. It makes her so happy." Her eyes misted over. "And I've been here, enjoying myself, while she's been falling ill. I should have been there."

"Hey, you can't be everywhere at once. You're working ... to help pay for her care, right?"

"Yes, but I should be staying closer. Only—" She shook her head. "She's my responsibility. She's so vulnerable and I'm her person. The only one in her corner. I haven't always been there for her but now I am. Or I'm supposed to be." She swiped at the leaking moisture and widened her eyes, as if she was telling those tears, *Not today, fuckers!*

"We're gonna get you there. How old is she?"

"Thirty-five. My big sister, though she's always been more of a little one."

He nodded, realization dawning. "You looked out for her when you were younger."

"Sort of. We couldn't afford specialized care so she lived at home."

That must have been tough on the family. On Tara, especially, who might have had to forego a lot of the usual childhood experiences because her sister took precedence.

I've been working since I was ten years old ...

"Your mom's still around, isn't she?"

"She remarried and moved to Florida. I'm Chloe's guardian now."

Said with a determination that spoke to a fractured history on this topic. As her sister's guardian, Tara was likely on the hook for her care, financially and otherwise. The conundrum that was this woman was starting to resolve, the pieces swimming together to form a clearer picture.

Gold digger ... with a heart.

His phone rang with an incoming call from Scottie. "Go."

"We have a seat for her on the United 8:30pm flight. Boarding starts in ten minutes. Ticket's under her last name. I've emailed the details to you."

"Thanks, Scottie. I owe you one." He squeezed her hand when he ended the call. "Flight's at 8:30pm."

"I don't know what to say. I'll pay you back."

He smiled. "It'll be deducted from your next paycheck, Ms. Becker." It wouldn't, but letting her think so was one less thing for her to worry about.

Hartsfield-Jackson airport was relatively close to the city's downtown and within minutes, they were pulling up to the terminal. Fitz paid the cab and grabbed Tara's case. Within a minute, he had her boarding pass from one of the self-service machines.

He gave it to her. "Got your ID?"

She nodded, her eyes big and expressive. Then she

threw her arms around him and hugged him tight, her lips brushing his neck. "Thank you."

He closed his eyes, not wanting to release her. If he could go with her, he would have, but that seemed intrusive. This wasn't what either Tara or he had signed on for.

But he could still be her friend.

"Will you call me later and let me know how Chloe is?"

Quick nod. "Could you apologize to your family for my leaving so abruptly?" She shook her head. "Sorry, I said that already. I didn't even get a chance to tell Dex. He'll expect me to be there after the game."

"I'll let him know. I'll tell him you had to leave but everything's okay."

"Thanks. I'd better go." Trembling, she kissed his cheek and it was so damn sweet he almost knifed in half. "Bye, General."

23

TARA OPENED HER EYES, feeling a stiffness in her neck and a lethargy in her muscles. Watery sunlight filtered through the blinds of the hospital room where Chloe had been moved because she wasn't breathing easily. This room was outfitted with a humidifier, and Tara could hear Chloe's wheezes over the hum of the machine. On her nightstand stood the aquarium lava lamp she'd bought in Atlanta, a gift that she hoped her sister would soon appreciate.

A nurse came in—different from the one who told Tara last night that her sister was resting comfortably. That maybe Tara didn't need to come home at all.

But Nurse May had sounded concerned. And Tara would never forgive herself if something happened while she was off gallivanting with her fake boyfriend.

With Hale.

Hanging with him for toy-shopping and lunch had been so much fun. As for his nieces, how adorable were they? He had looked at them with such pride and longing and clearly wanted that for his future.

Of course, the man seemed to think his opinions about

her future were worth sharing. *I think you'd be bored stupid in a lackluster marriage with someone like O'Malley.*

Maybe he was right. But she wasn't looking for a love match. Who cared if Dex or any other player didn't understand what lit her up? She had a responsibility to Chloe; her own needs were secondary.

Unburdening to Hale had felt good, though. She hadn't told a soul about Chloe, and now that someone else knew, she felt ... lighter? To have someone else listen and better still, act on her behalf, filled Tara with a strange hope that maybe she wasn't completely alone in all this.

A drop of kindness is a dangerous thing. She would do well not to mistake Hale's for anything more.

"Hi," Tara whispered to the nurse. "How's she doing?"

"She slept well and her vitals are stable. The doctor will be in soon." She smiled at Tara. "Maybe grab some coffee."

"Okay, thanks." Tara stroked Chloe's apple-red flushed cheek and tried not to wince at the rasp she heard when her sister inhaled.

On her way to find a caffeine IV, she took out her phone. It was just after eight—how had she slept so long slumped in that uncomfortable chair? She'd left a message for her mother last night, telling her about Chloe's condition, but nada from that quarter.

However, there were several texts from Hale.

> Everything okay?

> Just checking in.

> Let me know how you're doing.

She had sent him a message when she arrived at the hospital, but now she saw it was showing as undelivered. He'd also left a voice mail.

"Tara, this is Hale." As if it could be anyone else! And he identified as Hale, not Fitz, which meant ... nothing. "You said you'd let me know you landed safely, and while there are no reports of any commercial flights crashing, I'd still like a confirmation from you directly. Also, how's Chloe?"

He remembered her sister's name. Well, that was his job, wasn't it? To be detail-oriented and recall people and stats and contract clauses.

But still. He had asked after her directly.

Just standard kindness. Don't read into it.

She should return his call. It was the polite thing to do and right now, she would love nothing more than to hear his voice. She could admit that much. Coffee forgotten, she sat down on a bench in the corridor and called him.

"Tara?"

"Hi. I'm sorry, the message I sent didn't go through. I should have paid more attention and—"

"It's okay, honey. How's your sister doin'?"

"Better, I think. Or maybe the same, but not worse? I'm waiting to talk to the doctor, but the nurse said she slept well."

"Good. Get any sleep yourself?"

"Fits and starts."

"Maybe you should try to get home for a couple of hours."

She looked up because there was a weird echo on that last sentence. Hale stood before her, in the glorious present-in-Chicago flesh, his phone to his ear.

She jumped to her feet.

"What are you doing here?" *Just being kind. Just being kind.*

"When you didn't text back, I got worried that somethin' was happening and you were trying to manage it by yourself." He stroked a thumb along her cheek and she fought not to lean into that warm touch. "I'm guessin' that the DIY strategy is typical for you seein' as this is the first I'm hearin' about your sister."

The thrill of seeing him was dimmed by his veiled criticism. Was she supposed to be sharing stuff with the man she had screwed once? She'd been managing just fine for years and she had a plan—an excellent plan—to manage fine for the years to come.

Now Hale was riding in with his kind eyes and know-it-all attitude telling her how she should be doing things. Yes, her DIY strategy was typical because if Tara didn't do it, who would?

"We're not really that kind of fuck buddies."

He quirked his lips. "I guess not. Just curious about who you're telling your deep, dark secrets to."

"Oh, any player who'll listen while I tidy up that flow. Those are the true targets, don't you know?"

Storm clouds formed in those usually clear blue eyes. "You tryin' to make me mad at you, Tara? Because I got up at four in the a.m. *and* white-knuckled a flight here in coach *and* the coffee sucked on the plane, so you keep pokin' and we'll see how mad I can get."

This guy was driving her nuts! He was afraid to fly and yet he'd done this for her?

Walls crumbling from a kindness attack ...

"Coach? The humanity."

"Right?" He grinned and their little spat of a moment ago was forgotten. When had it become so easy?

Recalling where he had been this morning and why, she grabbed his lapel. "How did the game go?"

"Three-one to us. Your boyfriend scored one, assist on another."

"Good for him."

"Yeah, good for him." Taking a hold of her hand and lacing his fingers through hers, he looked around. "So you still need to talk to a doctor? How do we make this happen?"

Usually she'd be going full-scale "can I see your manager" to get a result here, but she also recognized that it was early. Plus the warmth of Hale's hand around hers was a little too perfect to give up just yet.

"Let's go find some decent coffee."

CAFFEINATION COMPLETE, ten minutes later, Hale sat with Tara while the doctor explained her sister's condition. His gaze strayed through the open door to where a dark-haired woman was sitting up in bed, wide awake, playing with a Disney princess doll, likely a Belle. Hale knew all the princesses.

Tara asked, "So she can return to Misty Pines today?"

"Definitely," the doctor said. "We kept her overnight as a precaution. The nurses at Misty Pines were a little concerned about her cough but she's breathing easier now."

And hospital beds cost a lot more than nursing home beds. Though a nursing home can't have been cheap, either.

The doctor took his leave and Tara turned to Hale. "I think I'm supposed to feel comforted by that. Who's to say that won't happen again?"

"You've got to trust the experts but also keep an eye on things."

"I know. It's just that she's so vulnerable. Of course, she can communicate in her own way, but I worry that she might not be able to tell us everything she's feeling." She shook her head, seemed to realize that she might be sharing more than she normally would. Christ, Hale liked this brand new Tarabell, or at least the layer it added to the other one. "It was really sweet of you to come, but I know you have work to do."

The team had won last night, so all was right with the world for now. "Nothing I can't delegate."

Her eyes went wide. "There's a game tomorrow night in Atlanta. You have to get back for it."

"To do what? My input is at a higher level than game play."

"You don't want to fly back, do you?"

He smiled. "Not in a hurry to. I'll square it with Harper. Right now, I'm here for whatever you need. Coffee runs, chauffeuring, orgasms."

"How generous."

"Right? Seriously, though, I'm at your disposal."

"Well, um, would you like to meet my sister?"

He should have expected that—after all, Chloe was the reason they were both here—yet he somehow knew this was momentous for Tara. She didn't share her private life with just anyone.

"I'd love to."

"You would? I mean, she's a sweetheart to me, but she's not great with strangers. Just giving you a heads-up in case ..." She trailed off, looking lost. Had this happened before? Tara letting someone get close only to be disappointed by their reaction?

"She hasn't met me yet. Women adore me."

She rolled her eyes and stood, smoothing out her skirt, that sexy leather one that didn't need smoothing. Even after an overnight stay in an armchair, she looked spectacular. Her edges were softened, though maybe that was Hale's changed perception now that he knew what she was fighting for.

And he had no doubt that Tara was in the fight of her life, for her sister's future and security. There might be a smidge of concern for herself in there but it was purely survivor's instinct.

"Come on, then. Time to meet the princess."

Tara went ahead and Hale followed. Chloe looked up, a smile on her face that immediately vanished as her cough took hold for a few worrying seconds. Hale's chest tightened at her distress.

"Is the princess ready to receive visitors?" Tara called out in a gentle sing-song as she sat on the bed and rubbed her sister's back gently.

Chloe grinned again and held up the doll in her hand, then her gaze moved to him. Her eyes—green like her sister's—darted back to Tara, then to Hale, the beginnings of panic.

"Howdy, Miss Chloe," he said in a soft tone. "How you doin' this fine mornin'?"

"Clo-Bear, this is Hale. He's a friend of mine and he's been dyin' to meet you." She threw up a hand dramatically. "Now you have me dropping my g's, Hale Fitzpatrick!"

Chuckling, he moved closer and placed his hand at Tara's back, letting her know he was here for her. Then because he liked how that felt and it had been an eternity since he was this close, he gently knuckled a few inches up her spine. She shivered but didn't pull away.

"Well, Miss Chloe, it looks like princesses are your favorite. Is that Belle?"

Chloe looked down at her doll and clutched it a little tighter.

"I like Belle, too. She's a great princess, real smart,

coming to the rescue of her dad, making the Beast seem like a regular dude. I think my favorite is Snow White, though."

"Oh, Chloe loves Snow White as well. She has one back in her bedroom at Misty Pines."

"Yeah, my nieces love the dwarves, though I'm guessing we can't call them that anymore." He sent a questioning look at Tara who was smiling like he'd just said the funniest thing. "What?"

"Oh, nothing. I think 'dwarves' is still okay because they're fairytale dwarves, not representative of people in the real world. But who knows? I might have that all wrong."

"Gotcha. Just wanna be sure I'm keeping it woke."

She burst out laughing. "Keeping it woke? Yeah, gotta be sure you're doing that."

Damn, to make her laugh like this felt like a fairytale sprinkled with Disney magic. Sure she was laughing at him. No matter, he'd take it.

He turned back to Chloe who was watching both of them avidly. "Sorry about that, Miss Chloe. Your sister is hoggin' all my attention as usual."

He wondered how much she understood, but maybe it didn't matter. She understood love and that it was embodied in Tara, who was holding her hand and stroking her palm. Watching them together was like seeing someone open a gift on Christmas morning.

Chloe grasped Tara's arm and, pointing at the phone in her hand, made a noise that Fitz couldn't interpret.

"Okay, just one." Tara opened up the music app on her phone, found a playlist, and clicked a button.

"There's my theme song!" *Money Money Money*, an ABBA tune. She winked at him before hitting the stop button. "Now, wait a second, this is the one you like, Clo-Bear." She clicked another song and a piano intro filled the room along with the sunshine of Chloe's smile. After a few seconds, Fitz recognized it as *S.O.S.*, one of the Swedish group's biggest hits.

"You probably remember this when it was released, right?"

"Sure," Fitz muttered. "Me and my white jumpsuit loved to jam to this at the roller rink back in olden times."

"Figured as much." Grinning, she turned to her sister. "Clo-Bear, this is one of Hale's favorites!" And then she started to sing the chorus.

Chloe's face brightened and she moved her head back and forth as Tara sang the rest, sweet and clear, her voice filling the room with joy.

How could twenty-four hours completely revise your opinion of someone? Though, if Fitz were truly honest, a one-eighty on the subject of Tara Becker had occurred long before that. There'd been hints that she was a whole lot more than the wide-eyed bimbo she presented.

Only now he wasn't sure having this information was a good thing. Knowing Tara had possibly well-intentioned motives for seeking a rich husband should have clarified his thoughts, not left him more agitated than ever.

She smiled up at him, including him in the recital, and Fitz could only gaze at her with a yearning he could barely understand.

Bold, beautiful, big-hearted Tara.

"Do you think we can get him to sing, Chloe? Can Hale hold a tune?"

He couldn't—but right now he didn't care.

Of course if anyone was to ever accuse him of singing ABBA songs before he'd had a second cup of morning coffee, he would deny it to his dying day.

24

———

Tara had never felt so warm and secure in her life. Slowly she came awake, though the knowledge of her surroundings took longer. A large hand was clamped possessively over her upper chest, its arm curled around her body in horseshoe-shaped shelter.

She was in Hale's bed.

She wiggled, checking in on the situation down south. Panties were intact and she knew nothing had happened because this was Hale. The man was an absolute gent, even if wonderful pressure was being exerted from behind and the stirrings of hot, gorgeous man were making themselves known.

He nudged against her neck and snuggled in tighter.

Oh, this was nice.

But it took no more than a few quickened heartbeats for reality to impinge. *Chloe.* As soon as the thought formed, her phone appeared in her sight line on the nightstand. She didn't recall putting it there, so Hale must have, knowing she'd want to inquire about her sister as soon as she woke up.

As if the man needed any more checks in his favor.

Her phone's clock said it was just after two in the afternoon. Still nothing from her mother—no surprise there—but there was a message from Nurse May, letting her know that Chloe was back at Misty Pines and would be ready for a visit tomorrow.

In other words, Tara should keep her nit-picking, worry-wart ass away.

Setting the phone down, she replayed the morning's events, starting with Hale appearing like a golden god before her morning-blurred vision. Though she'd pushed back, checking his kindness, Hale had peeled himself off the plexi and given as good as he got, letting her know that he was here for her.

Seeing him with Chloe, chatting to her gently like she was one of his nieces, had burned into Tara's soul. The man had even sung ABBA! Just having his sheer strength and solidity in her corner was a salve to her battered senses. She had no idea how much she needed that support until he offered it so freely.

She vaguely recalled falling asleep in the car and him half-carrying her inside. Now he was lying on top of the covers with a blanket over his body. Not only that but he had his shirt on. She snuck a peek under the throw to find him frustratingly fully-dressed. But then so was she.

His eyes opened slowly, and something magical changed in them. Tara had seen desire and indifference in the eyes of past lovers, so this was a new one.

Hale looked ... happy.

"Afternoon," he murmured, his voice sleepy and so sexy.

"Afternoon," she managed around the lump in her throat. "Why are you on top of the covers?"

"Because if I was under them, I'd be taking advantage."

"Is that such a bad thing?"

He leaned up on his elbow and regarded her with the usual Hale laser precision. "You've made it clear where this is going. And I don't need a pity fuck."

"Oh." She moved a hand over his shirt buttons, undoing them as she ventured south. "How do we feel about pity hand jobs?"

He grasped her wrist. "Tara, you just had a scare and you're feelin' kind of vulnerable. You don't owe me anything because I gave you a ride home."

It was more than that and he knew it. "What happened to the offer of coffee, rides, and orgasms?"

"You got a ride and I can get the coffee started. The orgasms will have to wait until you're in a better place."

She gestured with her hand, implying what better place than this? He didn't bite. Hale was taking this gentleman business to the max.

Without sex to distract her—to distract them both—she was back in her head where the landscape was tangled and thorny. Hale was watching her, evidently waiting for ... more.

This is it. This is all there is.

"So no to the orgasms. Whatever shall we do?"

"Talk it out." He reached over and pushed a stray strand behind her ear. "How are you doin'?"

His gentle tone almost undid her. "A little tired. A lot emotional. Feeling inadequate, like I've made a mess of things."

He stroked a thumb over her cheekbone. "When you're someone's primary caregiver then it's bound to be overwhelming at times. Tell me more about Chloe. What she's like."

"Where do I start? I mentioned that she loves music and you've seen and heard that."

"Yeah, not sure she was impressed with *my* vocals."

Tara was, though. "Disney is her favorite—she loves all the soundtracks, especially *The Lion King* and now she's nuts for *Encanto*."

"She's got that in common with my nieces. I think I heard that Bruno song a zillion times this last holiday."

As had Tara. Though *Surface Pressure*, the one about the older sister, Luisa, the family's rock, had made Tara feel more seen than ever. Or at least until Hale barged into her life with his kind eyes and bossy manner.

"She loves pretty dresses and getting her hair done. She has the sweetest manner, most of the time, but she can get cranky when she doesn't get her way."

"Sounds like a lot of people I know."

Tara relaxed her head against the pillow. "I missed out on a few years with her while I was off doing other things, so I've been getting to know her again. I thought she would have forgotten me but she didn't."

Chloe had welcomed Tara back into her life like she hadn't upped and abandoned her for almost a third of it.

"You're hard to forget."

"Not so easy to forgive."

He narrowed his gaze. "You think you've done things that are unforgiveable?"

"I know this is the part of the conversation when I'm supposed to acknowledge forgiving myself as the first step toward loving myself, right? Well, this girl has found a loophole and skipped right to the loving myself part. Part narcissist, part histrionic."

"Self-diagnosed? Or was this the stepfather psychiatrist?"

That background check had been thorough. "Dr. Bill said I exhibited worrying traits as a teen." She finger quoted that last phrase, deepening her voice to sound like her stepfather. "Mostly I was selfish and attention-grabbing. With him, all my behavior could be attributed to something in a textbook."

He frowned. "I don't think I've ever met anyone less selfish."

It took a moment to get air into her lungs, as those unfamiliar words—or at least the unfamiliar arrangement of them—knocked the stuffing out of her. "You're basing that on what you've witnessed in the last 24 hours. It's going to take a lot longer than that to make up for my sins."

"Come here." He lifted his arm and gestured for her to move into his embrace. The covers separated them, but it still felt amazing to be held by him. "It's okay to think of yourself for a while. If you were a narcissist, you'd lack empathy or self-awareness. That's not you, Tarabell. You've been listening to the griping of a pro-hockey franchise for weeks now and looking after your sister for years, so how is that selfish? As for being attention-grabbing, you will always have my notice, but that's only because I'm a little bit obsessed with you." He brushed his lips across her forehead, a whisper of a touch.

Tara had never thought of herself as a good person. And certainly not good enough for the standard happiness equation others saw as their due. It was such an abstract concept that she had no idea how to go about attaining it.

But here in Hale's arms, she felt the first inkling in forever of what happiness might be like. And it fucking terrified her how much she wanted it.

A little bit obsessed? Right back atcha, Hale Fitzpatrick.

AFTER ANOTHER POWER NAP, she awoke—alone. Hale had left sweats and socks on top of the dresser, so she dressed, made a quick call to check in on Chloe, then headed downstairs. As she rounded the landing, Hale's voice carried toward her.

"Now why would you assume it's a woman, Harper? I tell you I'm helpin' out a friend and your brain immediately goes there."

She froze, her foot hovering above the first step.

"You know I wouldn't normally do this." Another pause, then a soft, raspy chuckle. "You ain't squeezin' it out of me, boss. Just know that I wouldn't do this unless it was important."

He must have hung up then because he went silent except for walking around. She heard the pitter-patter of Goober alongside him. Man and best friend.

Pickle appeared on the stair, looking curious and maybe a little left out. She picked him up, unashamed to use him as her shield.

"Hi," she said to Hale's back as she walked into the kitchen.

He turned and smiled and damn, it was like being punched. "Hey, you feelin' okay?"

"I think so. I called Misty Pines. Chloe's settling back in."

"Yeah, I checked in with them, too. Probably sick of hearin' from us." He sauntered over and placed hands on her hips, a kiss on her forehead, then another on Pickle's. "You hungry?"

He had checked in as well? That casual reference to us as if it was perfectly natural was terrifying. Swallowing back the lump that little piece of knowledge produced, she responded with, "Starving."

"How about breakfast for a late lunch? I've got fixins for an omelet, some tomatoes and mushrooms."

"I'd love that. I can make coffee if you can stand to imbibe so late in the day."

"I can, but nope, you will sit and watch me juggle all the things."

"All the better to ogle you."

With Pickle in her lap, she ogled like a champ while he made coffee, making him laugh at how leery she got. Goober sat at her feet, flopping away, clearly having a no bones day.

She'd give anything for one of those.

"I overheard you talking to Harper earlier. Are you in trouble because you're not in Atlanta?"

"Trouble?" He started halving cherry tomatoes. "We're not in high school, Tara. She knows I wouldn't be skipping out if it wasn't important."

"You didn't have to do that. It seems so ... over the top."

His look was quizzical. "Helpin' a friend out?"

"No. Sure, lots of people are generous with their money and you were able to use the team's resources to get me on that flight. And I will pay you back, I promise. It's just, taking the time to drop everything and be here—that extra mile was unexpected."

The coffee timer beeped. None of those cute Keurig deals for Hale, this was a real pot of Joe. "Pour me a cup, honey. Creamer's in the fridge, sugar's in the cupboard above the maker."

She did as he asked, getting a strange thrill out of the domesticity. When she passed him the cup, he sipped and smiled his pleasure at her. It was odd to have pleased him with something not related to her looks or the crazy shit she said that made him laugh.

This one small thing.

She loved how he wasn't pushing her to explain her life, was giving her the space to make that call. And she wanted to talk more about the important things. About all the decisions—good and bad—that had brought her to this point.

"You interested in a story with your afternoon coffee?"

"If you're the heroine, I would love nothing more."

25

HOW DID Tara become her sister's guardian?

It was the question that had him itching since he'd found out about Chloe. That background check had told him her mom was still alive, living in Florida, so why the hell was Tara on the hook for her care?

She dropped Pickle to the floor and the little ball of fluff curled up beside Goober, obviously vying for Cutest Cat Ever.

"Going to need more coffee for this. Maybe all the coffee," Tara said, her voice small. She looked so vulnerable in his oversized sweats, and while he hated that she felt exposed, this was too important to let slide.

She stirred her coffee, rinsed the spoon, and dropped it in the dish holder caddy.

"I grew up in a suburb just outside St. Louis. My mom—Monica—and her first husband had Chloe, and then Mom had a one-night stand with someone else, which resulted in me. I've never met him." The words came out in a gush. "Things had already been stressful for my mom and Chloe's dad, and I was the last straw, I suppose, because he left.

Mom managed for a while with my grandparents' help and then when they couldn't, a lot of Chloe's care fell to me."

"At what age?"

"Ten?" She leaned against the counter, her coffee in hand. "She's seven years older than me. The age of ten sticks in my head because I remember for my tenth birthday I had a Disney princess-themed party and I was so happy I got an Ariel doll from *The Little Mermaid*. Anyway, Chloe loved the princesses, too, and she wanted it and got upset when she couldn't have it. Mom gave the doll to Chloe and then I threw a tantrum. I was quite the little madam." She flushed, embarrassed at the behavior of her ten-year-old self. Fitz would hazard a guess the "little madam" moniker was gifted by Tara's mom.

"That was also around the time that Mom met Dr. Bill."

"The psychiatrist."

"Right." She visibly squirmed at the mention of him, this asshole who told a little girl in his care that she had some personality disorder because she was acting her age.

"He said it was good for me to take on more responsibility, so each day when I got home from school I had to look after Chloe. Feed her, bathe her, keep her entertained. My mom and stepdad had certain expectations for me and how I should contribute. Of course, they should. Only I couldn't take part in school trips or sleepovers or hang with my friends because I had to be at home, looking after my sister. I was quite the bitch about it, too. Making a fuss." She looked down at her coffee.

He'd bet the entire Rebels salary budget that she had spent the last few years atoning for the perfectly natural reaction of a child being lumbered with the responsibilities of an adult.

"When you were ten?"

"Yeah, I really resented it." She winced and he wanted to wrap her up and tell her it was okay to have such mixed feelings about her sister. This was her life, too. "Caregiving is hard work, so I know it was tough on my mom. She needed a break."

"Isn't that what social services are for?"

"Dr. Bill didn't like people to interfere. He thought we could handle it all in house. And for a few years, that was how it went. I fell behind in school but it didn't matter because I wasn't all that smart to begin with." She shook her head, looked down. "Anyway, next came the dreaded teen rebellion phase. At fourteen, I was staying out all night, getting into trouble, partying. I looked older—or I made myself look older. Dr. Bill diagnosed me with ADHD and put me on the usual drug cocktail you throw at moody teens, but I hated how they made me feel. Like I wasn't here on this earth and was floating above everything, looking in on my life. Maybe I didn't like what I saw through that window."

She managed a tight smile. "Eventually Mom and Dr. Bill had enough of my shenanigans and sent me to the Cliff in Utah."

"The Cliff?"

"It's a wilderness boot camp for troubled teens."

He'd heard of places like that. Prisons, to be exact. "How long were you there for?"

She ran a nail along the edge of the sink. "Three months. But my abs were amazing when I was done and I could bench press a bison!"

"Tara."

Her head shot up. "No pity, Hale. That's not why I'm telling you this. By the time I got back, Chloe had been put into care. It seemed Dr. Bill and my mom couldn't really manage without the extra pair of hands."

Without the free labor, more like. What assholes.

"Then he got a job at a small college miles away, one of those crappy diploma mills because who else would hire him? And Mom made us move and leave Chloe in some horrible place run by the state. They did their best, I suppose, but they had very few resources beyond the minimum. No grants or private funding. And even though I was back from the Cliff—pun intended—it was too late. Mom and Bill didn't care. They were just glad to be rid of her."

She met his gaze then, strong and direct. "I've been trying to get her to transfer guardianship to me for a while, and about two years ago, she relented. She and Bill divorced and she's on Husband No. 4 now. She didn't care anymore—not sure she ever did but I don't want to waste my energy judging her. We do what we have to do. Sure I went a few years doing my own thing, living what I thought was my best life. Trying new things, spending money, keeping busy." To erase the guilt, he supposed. She took a deep breath, seemed to right herself. "And as soon as I reconnected with Chloe, I got her out of there and into Misty Pines. I'd saved enough and there's Medicaid and they have grants ..."

"But not enough to cover it all, I'm guessin'."

"That's where the plan comes in. Gotta get myself a husband!" She tilted her head. "Do I look better to you now that you see what a genuinely good and sweet person I am?"

All that front. He felt privileged to be allowed a peek under the hood.

"Never thought you weren't good or sweet."

She wagged a finger. "Now, now. We all know your opinion of me when we first met."

"I think we both made snap judgments."

"Guess we did." She smiled, still thin but he could sense her relief at having opened up a little.

"C'mere, Tarabell."

Her breath hitched but she wasted no time doing as he asked and falling into his arms. It felt so damn good to hold her like this, to feel her soften and accept his protection, if only for a short time. After a minute, she inhaled in a way that said she was back to full strength and leaned back to peer up at him.

"Thanks."

"Any time."

She gestured to the eggs he'd cracked into a bowl for the omelets. "Better get going on those eggs, or they'll lose their fluff."

Speaking of losing fluff ... some of it, or the illusion of it, had fallen away where Tara was concerned. Here she was shaping her life around the needs of a vulnerable person. That had to take a toll, but it also showed a woman with incredible strength of character.

He returned to the eggs, finished whisking, and got them in the pan.

While he teased the edges of the omelet with the spatula, he said, "It's not your fault Chloe ended up in that bad institution when you were sent away. It sounds like you were working yourself to the bone, and too much of the burden of her care was on you."

"Oh, I know that. But I did resent her for the longest time and those feelings—well, they're hard to shake off. When I came home from the ranch and saw she wasn't there, my first instinct was relief. That I could become a normal teenager again."

"Nothing wrong with wanting that. You were a kid." And now she carried that guilt around like a deadweight. "And you're making up for it with this get-hitched-to-a-rich-hunk scheme?"

"Yes and no. For the right price, a hockey hunk can have all this!" She jerked thumbs into her face as if she was some sort of hot mess, when really she had never looked more beautiful, inside and out. "Of course I want my sister to be safe and well looked after. But I also want that for myself."

So, sticking with the story and keeping up the gold digger act so he wouldn't feel sorry for her? Got it. "But why a hockey player? Why not shoot for an investment broker or some hot-shot tech CEO?"

"Is it so bad to want some nice eye candy to look at while I spend the green? I don't need to be able to discuss geopolitical events with him, just enjoy what's on offer. The prize for my great sacrifice."

Back to Tara the airhead who didn't think she was smart enough to snag any guy she wanted.

"Plenty of the players are doing okay in the brains department." He split the omelet onto two plates and placed them on the kitchen counter. Tara grabbed flatware and paper towels for napkins. "What if you end up with someone who actually wants to see past that pretty exterior and, I dunno, engage in conversation?"

"I'll worry about that if I get close enough to score a ring. I have tons of talking points to get me through. Climate change, water security, why the Royals hate Meghan. You name it, I have an opinion." She sliced off some of the omelet, popped it between her lips, and swallowed. "Hale, this is amazing!"

"It's eggs, not rocket science."

"Don't sell yourself short. The future Mrs. F will love all these culinary touches. Of course, you don't want to give her ideas that you might have actual skills in the kitchen you're willing to use on the regular. Maybe whip this special out for her birthday and Mother's Day."

She gave him a wicked raise of that eyebrow and he laughed along with her, though he wasn't feeling particularly joyful. He didn't want to think about some imaginary future bride, not when his head was full of Tara.

But he got the message she was sending. This thing with Tara couldn't possibly have legs. She had clear notions about what she wanted and Fitz didn't fit the bill.

That should have been fine, yet his ego didn't enjoy the straight-up dismissal from contention. He had money— maybe not as much as she'd like—and they had amazing chemistry, more than he'd had with any other woman.

Seemed he wanted to have his Tara and eat her, too, which was pretty damn selfish of him.

HALE HAD a few phone calls to make, so Tara cozied up on the sofa under a fleece blanket and flicked through the options on Netflix. The GM liked science fiction shows and sports biographies and was halfway through the third season of *Golden Girls*.

That made her smile.

Goober looked up at her from the fluffy hearth rug, his floppy jowls almost begging her to stroke them. So she did. He made a ruff-ruff of contentment; she picked him up— this puppy was a beast!—and set him on the sofa next to her. Oh, that made the doofus so happy. Sure, his expression hadn't changed beneath all those wrinkles, but his eyes looked a little brighter.

Her phone rang with a call from Mia.

"Hey!"

"Where are you? I heard you had to leave Atlanta in a hurry."

"Oh, one of my clients had a last-minute interview and he needed a haircut."

Tara could fess up about Chloe but then there would be the inevitable questions and the offer of financial help. That wasn't what their relationship was about, and if Mia thought for one second that was why she had befriended her, she'd die. Neither did she want to let on about Hale, not when she was supposed to be making a play for one of Cal's teammates.

"Dex was asking Cal about you, said you haven't returned his texts. Maybe you should call him."

The texts were along the lines of "Where R U?" and "UOK?" (It actually took more energy not to let the words autofill, but whatever.)

"I told him I was in Chicago. He's barely had time to miss me."

"Maybe he's become accustomed to your face."

"Or my ass."

Mia chuckled, but then asked, "T, are you okay? You seem a little subdued."

"Me? I'm fine." She dialed up the cheer. "Looking forward to the game tomorrow."

"Come over to my place to watch. All the gang will be there for daiquiris without the stupid yoga first."

"I'm in!" Making plans with her girl crew would be better than hoping Hale asked her to stay and watch with him.

"Great, see ya later." Mia hung up.

Tara closed her eyes, willing away the guilt at being so cagey with her friend. One day she'd tell her, when she felt the relationship was on a better footing. When it was okay for Cal and, by extension, the rest of the team to know what she was bringing to any relationship.

Not that she was ashamed of Chloe. Not at all. But she had once shared her sister's existence with a guy she was seeing. Very soon, she was seeing the back of him as he walked out of her life.

It's kind of ... a lot, Tara. You're kind of a lot.

All her life she'd been told that she was a handful, so she couldn't risk giving anyone another reason to dismiss her as wife material. Which meant she had to be careful about who knew the details.

But how amazing it had felt to share with Hale. Scary at first, but he had listened with such patience, not trying to hurry her, saying all the right things. She had never confided in anyone to this level.

But then Hale was an analytical guy, the kind of person who needed to understand people puzzles. From the start, he'd been trying to dig into her motives—all with the aim of protecting his players, of course.

Regardless of his own motives, it still felt good to have someone give their perspective. When you've been told you won't amount to much—in the immortal words of her mother, *"it's a good thing you're pretty, Tara"*—it was hard to appreciate that maybe you had more to offer. But Tara knew she did for Chloe. All her decisions these days were made with her sister's welfare in mind—and that would remain—but maybe she could forgive herself for what had happened in the past.

Hale was right: It was a lot to load on a little kid.

For now, though, she had to deal with the present. She shot off a text to her mom, who had still not checked in about Chloe, then another to Dex: ***How's it going?***

Her phone immediately rang with a call from her fake boyfriend.

"Where are you? Fitz said you had to leave Atlanta."

"I had some business to take care of back home."

"But I need you here. I scored last night and that's because you're my good luck charm."

So sweet. Though she could have told him that the increased sleep and less drinking was really where the credit lay. "Eight glasses of water a day, Dexy. Makes all the difference. Remember, I wasn't even in Atlanta last night."

"No, but I thought you were and that's what matters. The placebo effect. But now I know you're not here so that's going to mess me up."

"You don't need luck. You are a goal-scoring machine and you are going to go out there and prove why you should be on the first line. Your plus-minus is top-notch—"

"That was before my injury."

"If you could rack up those numbers before, you can do it again. But it takes work, babe. None of it happens overnight and it certainly doesn't happen at the club or in a bar. Now what did you eat for lunch?"

"Chicken and penne pasta and ..."

He detailed every calorie he'd ingested today and after about five minutes, she decided to call it.

"Now it's time for a nap. No wandering around the city getting into trouble. You need to sleep."

"Yeah, but Grey is probably in the hotel room looking at dudes sucking each other off."

Sweet baby Jesus and all the carpenters. "Have you witnessed this behavior?"

"No, but—"

"No, but nothing. Hudson has sleep needs as well, so stop being such a weirdo and go take a nap. And be nice to your roommate, who is new to the team and the city. You remember what that was like?"

"Yeah. No one was nice to me."

She stifled a growl. "It's a two-way street, Dex. Now you're playing and contributing while not bringing the rep of the team down, you've earned their respect. Text me after lunch tomorrow and we can run through your routine, okay?"

"Okay," he grumbled. "And Tara?"

"Hmm?"

"Thanks for being there for me. You're alright."

She twitched her nose. "This I know, but it's nice to be appreciated. Now go to sleep, Dexter." She hung up. A little tough love, that's what he needed. How did Harper Chase manage all these divas?

"Was that O'Malley?" Hale had just walked in with Pickle perched on his shoulder—too cute!—or maybe he had been eavesdropping the whole time. She had nothing to hide, though she rather enjoyed the idea he might be jealous. The last time, she'd come out of it okay in the orgasm department.

"Yeah, wondering where I am. He's got it into his head I'm his good luck charm."

Hale petted Pickle who was enjoying a little hot-man neck time, the lucky thing. "Players are superstitious, and if it works for him, then who are we to say it's not true?"

"I suspect it's more along the lines of extra sleep and better nutrition."

"That, too. But I remember thinking every little thing made a difference when I played." He frowned. "Goober, did you give Tara the sad eyes so she'd put you on the sofa? Because I know you can't get up there by yourself, you lazy lump."

"Ah, don't be a meanie!" She stroked Goober's soft head. "He deserves to be up here. The little guy's been keeping me company while the Big Man on Campus makes his Very Important Calls."

Hale went to lift Goober with his non-Pickle-holding arm, but Tara grasped the puddle of puppy and pulled him close.

"I see how it is." Switching to her other side, he squeezed into the corner. "Shift up. I'm not a stick insect."

She did, enjoying the close quarters.

"Want to share your blanket—I mean, my blanket—or does only the puppy get the Tara cuddle treatment?"

She rearranged the fleece so both Goober, Pickle, and her man—no, Hale, not her man, never her man—were comfortable, which involved her being snug as a bug between them. Hale placed Pickle in his lap and pulled Tara into his chest, where she happily settled, her head under his chin.

"You sounded pretty cozy with O'Malley."

"Jealous?"

"Yep."

She lifted her head, surprised at his candor. "Really?"

"Would you rather I pretended not to be? You're dating the guy."

"I know, but it's work. Not real." Her heart was beating fast.

"But you have a goal to get yourself an NHL husband. Lots of muscles, short on brain cells, and I'm gonna guess O'Malley fits those parameters perfectly. No one could ever accuse him of Mensa candidacy."

So testy! Dex was kind of needy, though. She was already a caregiver to a vulnerable person, she didn't need

that with a man even if that man met all her (low) expectations.

Hmm. Dex was actually her best bet right now and here
she was thinking he might not be good enough?

"So you're not a fan of Dex," she said neutrally.

"I think you can do a lot better than that."

"Li'l ole me?"

Hale narrowed his gaze. "You can quit the act
around me."

"What act? This is it—the whole package. Frothy, frilly,
whole-lotta-fun Tara."

"Uh huh. Who keeps her secrets close. Who loves her
sister with all her heart. Who will do anything to guarantee
that sister's security and future."

"She's my family." She tightened an arm around his
waist while Pickle eyed her enviously. *You had your shot,
kitty.*

"Right, but this plan to sacrifice yourself to make up for
what you see as transgressions in your past is kind of fucked
up." He moved his lips against her temple. "Surely you see
that."

"It's not as much of a sacrifice as you think. I'll do okay
out of it."

He sighed, evidently not happy with her take. "What
does Mia think about this plan?"

"She thinks it's weird and that I should wait for the one.
You know how all the Rebel WAGs have these amazing
couple origin stories? She wants something like that for me,
but I've told her I don't believe in all that."

"What a cynical little Tarabell you are."

She lifted her head. "This Tarabell is practical."

"Then why don't you tell Mia about Chloe? I thought
you were tight. She could help."

"We are. But you know how certain friendships fulfill certain roles. For some, it's the party-time friendship, for others, it's the swap-your-Hello-Kitty-stuff ship. Then there's let's-watch-a-game-together mates, and the Mile High Club buddies—"

"The Mile High Club buddies? How many people are in that knitting circle?"

"Oh, it's a very exclusive club. Maybe five, ten guys, tops."

"You little—" He started to tickle her and like all things Hale, did it excellently, probing her weak spots with a surgical precision. Disturbed by the motion, poor Goober gave a light growl and Pickle jumped off to wander the hallways of Fitzpatrick Manor.

"Okay, okay, that was the first time!"

"Not a renewal of your membership?"

"No, my inaugural orgasm. On a plane, that is. Happy?"

He looked so damn smug she wanted to throat-punch him.

"So with all these friendship variations, who are you telling about Chloe? About the pressure you're under?" He squinted, took a second to think it through, then declared, "You haven't told Mia because she's wealthy."

She should have known he'd figure it out. "She's my friend. We talk about lots of things but we keep a few things back. Her, because I used to date Cal, me, because ... when I met her, I guess I was lonely. I'd just broken up with Cal and she wasn't his biggest fan either. It was funny, the two of us bitching about him. And then ..."

"She fell for him."

She nodded. "I was surprised at first, a little hurt, even, but then I realized how great they were together. And she never made it weird. She never told me we couldn't be friends because I used to sleep with Cal and she never told

Cal he couldn't talk to me anymore because I was an ex. She treated me like a normal person. A true friend." She shrugged. "I don't want her to think that I'm looking for something from her, which reminds me. Wait here." She shot up from the sofa, which made Goober snuffle in surprise.

When she came back, she handed a twenty dollar bill to Hale, extracted from an ATM at the hospital. "What I owe you. And I know I owe the org for the flight back to Atlanta, but this is what I owe you."

"It's twenty bucks. You helped me with gifts for the girls."

"For which you bought me lunch. I have to separate it out. I will not be paying for orgasms from you."

He looked annoyed, but then he seemed to relent. "You don't need to pay me a dime, Tara Becker. I'm happy to give you all the orgasms you want all day long at no extra charge."

"Oh, really?" She coasted a hand down to his pants, over the zipper and what was behind the zipper, and then back up to pull it down. The scrape was the loveliest sound in the whole wide world.

No slouch, he pulled off her sweats and lowered his hand to skim the waistband of her panties, coasting up to her breast and applying a velvet touch there. More than enough to turn her nipples to hard points and generate wetness between her thighs. But then with Hale, it didn't take much.

She was so gone for him.

His hand splayed against her rib cage felt so warm and rough. Experienced. He cupped one of her breasts and glanced a thumb over a hard nipple, which turned it harder, a result that should have been impossible. "You look gorgeous right now, Tara. Absolutely edible."

"Then devour me."

With a rough sound from his throat, he kissed her and of course, he tasted perfect.

"Open up to me, honey."

Honey. She knew that was one of those all-purpose endearments yet on this man's lips, it felt different just as under his touch, she felt different. Like honey. Slow and languorous.

She parted her lips, let him slip past her defenses for the full Hale kissing experience. Why did his mouth feel better than any other? Why did his touch feel so unique? She needed to shut her brain down because if she continued that self-interrogation, it would lead to a conclusion she wouldn't like.

This is the one.

Slipping a hand inside his pants, she felt his cock pulse and thicken, which only made her wetter.

His kiss grew more sultry, deeper, hotter.

She cupped and rubbed, drawing a guttural moan from him. Feeling him grow harder in her hands thrilled her. This powerful man was putty, all because of her. Yet her control of the situation was illusory. With Hale, she was spiraling, descending into a well of want in which she was doomed to drown.

But what a way to go.

He separated his lips from hers, and what she saw astonished her. Not just desire, but a crazy level of want that matched her own. Something seemed to switch on in his brain. With one hand, he ran his palm over her bra-cupped breasts, her stomach, her mound. He stopped in between her legs, his eyes harsh and assessing, like he had plans and she was going to suffer untold pleasure because of them.

Oh, to be part of this man's plans.

Before that thought hit home, he pushed his heel against the panties' fabric and gave it a wicked rub, enough to make her arch off the sofa.

"Pop out one of those gorgeous tits for me, Tarabell. I need to feed."

Oh God.

She moved a hand over her right breast, amazed how good it felt to touch herself while he rolled her panties down and off. Two strong hands separated her thighs.

"Now, honey. Don't make me wait."

Swallowing, she slipped her breast out of the satin cup and plumped it for him. "Here, it's all yours."

"Damn right it is." His mouth latched on with a lusty suck while she writhed beneath, anything to create more friction. Her mound met his fabric-shielded cock and ground on him like a rutting animal. She needed his mouth, his fingers, his cock—anything to fill the emptiness.

The void she'd felt for years.

"Hale, please. Oh, God, please."

He lifted his head from her breast and applied his lips to hers, twining his tongue, fucking her mouth the way she needed her body to be taken. She reached down to shuck him of his briefs, crazy for skin-on-skin, desperate to get full of him.

Now.

Freeing his cock at last, she took all that strength in her hands—yes, a two-hander—and stroked from root to tip. He pulled back, sat back on his knees, drawing her forward while she continued to move her hands up and down using his pre-come to ease her slide.

He put his hand over hers and stilled the motion. "Not yet."

"Hale," she gasped as he pushed her back and settled in between her legs.

His intense gaze as he stared at that sensitive flesh there, almost undid her.

Inclining his head, he started to lap.

Soft at first, too soft.

She wriggled, needing more, and he heard her silent plea. The tongue became more ardent, his fingers on her thighs more insistent, the throb in her pussy a build she scrabbled to climb. She ran her hand through his hair and encouraged him with soft, filthy words.

Her thighs fell wider, her ass ground against the sofa cushion until finally she spilled over the edge like a pool of jelly.

26

The Rebels were on a good streak, with Ws in four of their last five games, so the Empty Net was the natural choice for a post-game celly. The regulars were loving it, buying drinks for their heroes, clapping them on their backs, and complimenting them on various plays.

"Wait until the next time they lose," Mia said drily.

Tara smiled. "Yeah, the public is a fickle beast, for sure. But then we all love a winner."

Speaking of winners, Dex had scored the game-clinching goal with a minute left on the clock, and the boys had held on for the two points and another inch up the conference standings. Now he was over with the guys replaying one of his finer moments. A couple of pretty women were hanging on his every word, but every now and then he looked her way and smiled.

It was confirmed: Dex O'Malley had a wee crush on her.

This should have thrilled her. After all, Dex was her endgame, wasn't he? Yet all she could think was that she had to be careful about leading him on.

She turned to Mia. "So we need to plan your party! Any preferences?"

"We could do it here," Mia said. "Rent it out so it's invite-only."

That sounded expensive. Much cheaper to hold it at Chase Manor or Vadim and Isobel's, where Mia lived when she wasn't at Cal's. Gearing up to make her case, Tara stuttered and stopped because Hale had just walked in and all rational thought left her brain.

He looked so good, sleekly suited and so handsome her knees melted. He looked around, searching, and when his eyes landed on her, they darkened in approval.

A corresponding reaction occurred deep in her belly. Deeper.

Over the last couple of weeks, they had spent most nights in Chicago together at his place. Just sex, she kept insisting, though he usually fed her as well. And then there was the cuddle time on the sofa with Goober and Pickle as well as the odd TV show (with the White Cheddar popcorn Hale had stocked because Tara said she liked it). The man made a mean French martini, too, just how she liked it with the extra Chambord.

But he also shared things. About his family and how much he had admired his dad, who had passed away a few years ago. About his early days in the NHL and how he missed it. About his goals for the team and his corresponding hopes for his career. Was this what it felt like to click with someone? To exist on the same wavelength and read their expressions and know how they might react in any given situation?

More than that, she was starting to care about Hale on some level beyond general fellowship or well-being for a person in your circle. She wanted what was best for him and a small part of her screamed "me" every time she thought about his future.

I can be what he needs. Someone to keep the home fires burning. Someone with whom to discuss games and trades and team strategy. Someone who understood his drive and need to succeed.

But a bigger part of her—the sensible part—knew that Hale was not right for her. Because while she might understand all those needs of his, a relationship was so much more. A man like Hale needed a smart, no-nonsense, nurturing type, and while the chemistry between them was fire, it couldn't last.

There was only so far she could ride the train of her flirt and flair.

For now, she would enjoy his attention and pray she could extricate herself with grace when the time came.

Chloe was getting stronger each day, but Tara was nervous about leaving her to travel to away games. She had been staying put in Chicago and checking in on Hale's fur babies because his usual dog walker wasn't completely reliable. And if she spent a few extra minutes-slash-hours curled up with them in Hale's bed while inhaling his pillow like a weirdo, no one need ever know.

He was walking over now, and she had to do everything in her power not to admire that loose-limbed swagger as he parted crowds, his gaze locked on her like she was a puck skipping into the blue zone.

Back to Mia. "Here's fine for a party. Or at Chase Manor. Or anywhere that can handle a crowd. And we could do karaoke."

Out of the corner of her eye, Tara could see that Hale had been stopped by Sophie. What was it with that woman? Didn't she see enough of him at work?

She had the temerity to touch a hand to his hair, the same hair Tara had trimmed this morning before his bathroom mirror. Only fair after he awoke her with his gorgeous head between her legs. (Unable to turn off her stylist brain, she'd noticed his hair was ripe for her shears after she gripped it hard during a particularly stimulating point of the proceedings.)

Mia was nodding enthusiastically. "I love that idea!"

"Love what idea?" Cal appeared behind Mia and wrapped himself around her.

"Karaoke," Mia said. "Tara and I are brainstorming engagement party ideas."

"Wicked. So did you ask her, gorgeous girl?"

"Uh, not yet."

Cal kissed Mia's neck. "Mia wants you to be her bridesmaid. Or one of them."

"Cal!" Mia gave him a gentle thump on the shoulder. "I was about to do it."

"And now you have. Or I have because Tara's my friend as well. You in, T?"

Like she would ever say no. She loved these two dummies so much. "Of course I'm in!"

Mia swatted away Cal's hands and hugged Tara close, whispering, "I'm so glad."

"Did you really think I'd say no?"

"No. Well, I wasn't sure. Cal is your ex and I'd hate for it to be awkward for you."

"Are you kidding? I'm so happy for you both."

"I know." She lowered her voice. "But I also know you want that for yourself. Not Cal, but your own happily-ever-after or your version of it."

True, but that didn't mean she would begrudge her friend the dream life she had found with Cal. As for her version of it, it was starting to become harder and harder to envision. This fling with Hale was such a distraction from her goals.

"What have I missed?" The man of the moment appeared, having finally escaped that PR vamp's handsy clutches.

"Tara just agreed to be my bridesmaid along with Isobel and Kennedy."

Space at the bar was tight, and Hale slotted in behind Tara. She could feel the heat of him through her coat and the thought of leaning back against that strong chest made her a touch dizzy.

"When's the happy day?" The breath from Hale's words fluttered against her ear.

"We're thinking July at Chase Manor," Mia said, referring to the home of Harper and Remy, which had become the Rebels' matrimonial chapel. "If the boys make the playoffs—I mean, when they do—we'll want to give them plenty of rest after their Finals run, though I expect some of them will have left town by then."

"Fine by me, keeps out the riff raff," Cal muttered.

"Hey!" Mia protested, only to be quieted with a kiss.

"Better get another round in," Hale said. "All this happiness is thirsty work. French martini, extra Chambord, Ms. Becker?"

Tara felt a small pressure along her spine. Hale's knuckles? Hidden from view, he rubbed gently along her back sending sensuous shivers to all points.

"That would be great, thanks," she managed.

A couple of minutes later, she had a serviceable French martini in her hand and had put a few more inches of safety between her body and Hale's. As much as she loved the closeness, she risked making a fool of herself.

"Not liking that much," he murmured.

"What?"

"You all the way over there."

"It's a foot of space."

"And if you stand too close, you might be overcome by my manly hormones. Gotcha."

She fought a smile. "Yes, please keep your manliness in check. There's only so much we poor females can handle."

Before he could flirt back, Mia pulled her away from the bar and out of earshot.

"What's going on with you and Fitz?"

Assume a vapid blankness. "What are you talking about?"

"He knows your drink."

"Lots of people know my drink."

"Cal, what does Tara drink?"

Cal frowned. "Something fruity."

"See? And he was standing really close to you. Is he bothering you? Because I know he hasn't been very supportive of the whole fake-it-with-Dex thing."

"Oh, I can handle any criticism that comes from that quarter." She looked back to see Hale talking to Levi Hunt and his wife, Jordan, who was a sports reporter with CSN. It was ridiculous how much she wished he was standing behind her, his lips brushing her ear, his knuckles kneading a wicked path down her spine.

"Okay." Mia didn't sound convinced. "I wanted to talk about Dex anyway. Did you know he's telling everyone in the locker room that you two are dating for real?"

That little rascal. "Maybe he's doing a Method acting thing. Embody the hockey hunk boyfriend, to make it seem more real."

"Have you seen how he looks at you? The boy has it bad."

So she wasn't the only one who had noticed. She chanced a look in his direction, and sure enough, Dex was staring at her again. He gifted one of his standard-for-the-masses thong-melting grins, which had her smiling back awkwardly, her thong very much intact.

"I suspect this is just Dex seeing a challenge because I haven't slept with him."

Mia studied her. "If he wanted to date you for real, would you go for it?"

She should be over the moon that he was buying what she was selling. Was that it? Was she feeling guilty because Dex might be into her more than she was him?

Or did it boil down to the fact that Dex wasn't Hale?

Hell. If Hale Fitzpatrick became the standard by which she measured other men, she'd never squeak across the matrimonial finish line.

"I'd have to get to know him a bit better," Tara said carefully, back to Dex's worthiness to be Mr. Tara Becker. "When I started this, I didn't think he could ever be in the running because he's such a player. I like a bad boy as much as the next girl, but I don't want to look stupid when one cheats on me."

"Maybe he's capable of being reformed," Mia said. "And every girl loves a guy who's willing to forsake all others, as the vows say."

Sure, but now that she'd had a peek at the possibilities with a man like Hale, she wasn't sure Dex could ever be good enough.

27

ONE OF THE things Fitz had missed most about being married was waking up wrapped around a warm woman. The comfort in that soft weight, listening to her breathe, thinking about all the things you'd like to do to her ... your professional life might be in the toilet, the world might be exploding, but a woman in your bed made this small corner of the universe a better place.

Or maybe it was just Tara.

"How long have you been staring at me?" Her eyes were still closed.

"Hours. Thinking about sniffing your hair next."

She let loose a giggle. "Creeper."

"I'm not ashamed. You're gorgeous and you smell good. My needs are pretty basic."

Eyes fluttering open, she cupped his jaw, running her soft hand over the scruff on his chin. "Sex, food, hockey. The trifecta."

"You know it, Tarabell." His phone buzzed and he leaned back to the nightstand to check. Ava had sent him a photo of

Joni's terrarium complete with a baby badger figurine hiding among the grasses.

The accompanying text said:

She's calling him Uncle Fitz.

"My niece is trolling me." He showed the screen to Tara and watched her expression soften, then turn curious.

"Do you miss being married?"

"I did for a while. I don't think I'm built to be alone, so I miss the companionship more than anything. But when I think back on it, I see that we weren't really a great fit." He pushed a strand of hair behind her ear.

"How can you be sure? I mean, you connected enough to tie the knot."

"Which we thought was enough. She was a party girl, loved the WAG lifestyle, and wanted to be the center of everything. But then I was traded to another team and she hated it, having to give up all the connections she'd made. Starting over. And stuck together, I realized I didn't enjoy my time with her. I was looking for excuses to be alone. No one's fault, just a drift apart. We didn't really challenge each other—well, yes toward the end, in a negative way. But it was just our way of trying to say goodbye without either of us admitting we'd gotten it wrong."

She sighed. "No one likes to admit that."

"Yeah, when you've invested time and emotional capital into a relationship, giving up on those sunk costs can be a real mindfuck. We want to think it can still be salvaged long after it's healthy."

The spot between her eyebrows crimped in thought. "I've never been with anyone long enough to feel something might be worth saving."

"Not even with Foreman? So what happened there?"

"You mean did I think he was going to propose at Levi Hunt's wedding and did I fight Mia for the bouquet?"

She didn't sound overly upset about it. Yet there was a time when Tara thought Foreman was the one to take her down the aisle and Fitz felt something about that.

"We hadn't been dating that long, a couple of months, and I thought there was a connection. We got along, the sex was good, and he's pretty easygoing, which is good for someone like me who's a lot to handle."

Angler flared. "Who said you're a lot to handle?"

"Guys I've dated have commented on the baggage I bring to the table. I've done some impulsive things. Acted rashly on occasion." She rubbed his chest, almost absently. "I was a train wreck in my teens and early twenties, and some people look at my decisions now and say not much has changed."

"I dunno. What I see is a woman turning her life upside down to care about another human being. So I don't agree with your methods but I understand what's behind them. Maybe you're a handful but so fucking what?"

"I'm trying to be better. Less troublesome, so it'll go smoother."

Did she mean the husband hunt? "Are we talking about Chloe?"

She swallowed. "I don't see her as a burden but some people do. We're a package deal and not everyone's up for that."

"You thought Foreman would be on board? Did you tell him about Chloe?"

"No. But at that time he was a little older than most guys I've dated, so he seemed more mature. More ready for a commitment. Boy did I have that wrong. Turns out he was ready, just not for me."

Her cheeks were flushed. "I'm pretty embarrassed about how I acted, getting all frosty about Mia intercepting the bouquet. Now people look at me and think, there goes that marriage-mad chick. How desperate she must be!" She smiled in that self-deprecating way of hers. "But I made a couple of friends out of it—Cal and Mia. In fact, I've made a lot of friends through the Rebels. The women are awesome and all so talented. The guys are amazing. And I love how supportive everyone is."

Yet she still kept secrets from all of them. All but him.

People might accuse Tara of working people for her own gain, but Fitz saw how she interacted with people. She was genuinely interested in them, whether it was charming the pants off everyone at a party or bar or game or listening to their concerns while she cut their hair.

Her ostensible goal was a husband, but Fitz suspected there was more to it.

Tara was looking to belong.

Fitz understood that. Changing jobs and cities every few years meant it was tough to put down roots. He had hoped a family of his own would give him that grounding he needed. Yet here he was making no progress because this woman had him all tied up in knots. He should be dating with intention, not screwing around for fun.

"I like that you're trouble," he whispered, laying a kiss on her lips. "That you're impulsive and spontaneous and that you know what you want."

"Even though you don't agree with my plan?"

"I don't have to agree with it to recognize that you're big-hearted and kind, a good sister, and a great asset to this team."

Her mouth fell open. "You think I'm an asset? As valuable as one of the players?"

"Now, I wouldn't go that far—"

"Oh, I would!" She pushed him back and straddled him, wearing his Georgia Bulldogs shirt and ... damn, nothing else. "You think I'm a team player!"

She was grinning, so damn proud of herself. To capture this feeling and bottle it, the sheer pleasure that Tara brought him, that would be perfect.

The heat of her bare sex against his stomach branded his skin. Wandering his hands up her thighs, he waited for those shamrock green eyes to haze over, for her to realize what was coming.

Her.

His thumbs found her soft, supple flesh, already damp with need.

"Hale," she whispered as she placed her hands on his chest, moving across his pecs, mapping her way to some tender spot inside of him.

It wouldn't be hard to find. She already had the coordinates.

"Take it off," he said, meaning the T-shirt, and she did, and Christ was she lovely. Perfect teardrop breasts, stiff pink peaks, the flare of her hips creating that bombshell hourglass figure. He pushed his thumbs inside her, drawing her sensual hiss, and all the while she held his gaze.

She'd gotten braver in that area.

Her soft hands found leverage against his chest while she started to move on his thumbs, taking her pleasure, carving her own path.

He'd expect nothing less.

But she didn't have to go it alone. He could be with her all the way.

Gathering her wetness, he circled her clit slowly because that's how she liked it. He loved knowing this about her, these secrets. All her secrets. Undulating her body, she rocked gently at first then a little quicker as she found the rhythm that worked for her.

Against her ass, his cock tapped out a request to get in, but that greedy bastard would have to wait its turn. This was all about her.

"Hale, I need ..."

"What, honey? What do you need?"

She shook her head, arched her back, and ground on his hand. "Not ... enough ..."

His erection was downright painful now as each motion of her body up and down dragged her ass against his shaft, teasing, tormenting, so much so he couldn't wait another second. His need to claim her superseded all other considerations.

He'd flipped her over and was inside her before he realized he'd forgotten the condom.

"Hale, we need to—" She broke off as her pussy pulsed around him, squeezing tight enough to trigger his release. "Ohgodohgodohgod."

Fuck. He pulled out just in time, shooting over her stomach, marking her in ropy streaks. Catching their breaths, they gazed down at the evidence of his brief moment of insanity, then back at each other.

"That was close," she murmured. "I'm on birth control, by the way, but still."

"Shit, honey, I'm sorry. I lost it there for a second."

She cupped his jaw, stroking along the line of bone. "I'm pretty irresistible, so easy to see why!"

He laughed away his discomfort. Damn, she was irresistible. "I promise I'm good to go. Full work-up before I took the job and there hasn't been anyone in a while." Neither had he gone without protection since Peyton ten years ago.

"Me, too. I've never not used a condom." She smiled. "It felt pretty amazing for the three seconds you were in there, but we probably shouldn't risk that."

He should agree, but something inside him was asking, why the fuck not?

Maybe his body knew something his brain had yet to acknowledge. Was it possible some biological imperative was telling him to plant a flag in Tara in a way that would bind her to him completely?

Because that was absolutely, positively absurd.

Wasn't it?

WHEN FITZ ARRIVED at the diner, the Rebels Brain Trust were drinking coffee and checking out highlights from last night's game. He took a seat and nodded his assent at the server who was at the ready with the coffee pot.

"Good work," Remy said to him. "O'Malley's finally proving his value."

"Or Tara is," Dante commented.

Tara and Dex, the super-fucking-couple. That everyone saw them that way was starting to really piss him off.

Starting? It had been like this from the minute Harper suggested it.

Fitz was the one who got to see the real woman, who got to hold her and touch her and hurl her over the edge with pleasure. And yesterday morning he'd been so out of his mind with need for her that he forgot to suit up.

Tara had tapped into one of his fundamental needs: to be a father.

Bren squinted at him from beneath his brows. "What's up?"

"Needs to get that dating business sorted," Remy drawled rather presciently. The guy had always seen too much. "Did Harper give you her friend's number?"

"Yep. And someone in the office thinks his sister or cousin would really suit me. And my mother just got back from a cruise where she met at least three viable candidates. And my brother thinks I have tons of options on the apps and I just need to get my thumb out of my ass and make a move."

Bren chimed in. "They're not wrong. Instead of meeting us to talk shop and how creaky your bones feel once you hit forty, you could be sleeping late and auditioning for the second Mrs. Fitz."

The Scotsman was not usually so chatty, and when he spoke this much, it commanded attention. Everyone absorbed what he said, reading between the lines until the light bulb went off and Dante finally voiced the group's conclusion.

"You already have someone on deck."

Fitz looked around at the guys. "Yes. And no."

Remy grinned. "So you don't need any recommendations from my wife?"

"I don't, but not because I'm all set. I can figure this out for myself."

Dante looked up from his menu, though he got the same thing—the Tex-Mex skillet—every time. "Famous last words."

"It's kind of complicated."

Which set all three of them off into knowing laughter.

Bren leaned back in his chair. "Are you a recovering alcoholic who shouldn't be in a relationship but can't keep his hands off his kids' nanny, who also happens to be his boss?"

"No, I am not." Jesus, had that really happened to Bren

and Violet?

Dante raised an eyebrow. "Lemme guess. You're involved with a player whose career you control and who's still not out to anyone he cares about?"

Hale knew that much about Moretti and Burnett, and he also knew how Remy and Harper had sealed the deal. "It's Tara."

That knocked all the jokes on their heads.

Remy finally spoke up. "Barefoot sofa woman?"

"Yep. It wasn't supposed to happen."

"Been there," Dante said.

"We all have," Remy concurred.

"First off, she's not in an actual relationship with O'Malley. That's purely for show." Most everyone knew this but it bore repeating, even if she was acting as O'Malley's confidante and giving him pep talks to stroke his ego.

Even if there was a chance they might actually go the distance.

The possibility made him ill.

"There was a spark and we both decided to be adults and do something about it. Neither one of us is what the other has in mind for the future." The words sounded rote on his lips, repeated so much now in thought and speech that they retained little meaning.

Bren rubbed a hand across his wry smile. "I could ask what the problem is, but from your grim expression, I'm guessing that the just-a-fling pep talk isn't gaining any traction in your brain."

While Fitz still thought Tara's marriage-for-money scheme was bonkers, he understood her motives. What he was no longer sure of were his own.

"Tara's a lot of fun. She's sexy and sweet and there's a damn sight more to her than she lets on."

"She's also on the make," Dante said cautiously. "Or has something changed?"

"No, she still has goals in the matrimonial arena. I'm not her endgame and ..." He paused, then completed that sentence the way he usually did. "Neither is she mine."

"So, just a short-term thing, then," Remy said. "To tide you over."

"Exactly." Fitz wasn't sure what he expected from this crew, and as long as he was going with the Tara-as-fling story, he wasn't going to get much guidance.

Luckily, Bren was astute enough to poke holes in the narrative.

"Unless," the Scotsman started, "you want there to be more."

Fitz liked to think things through, and he especially liked talking it out with people he could trust. Telling them about Tara's (mostly) altruistic motives to marry a hockey player would be akin to breaking a confidence, but he could try to sort through his feelings about this woman with men who had their fair share of trouble winning the one they wanted above all others.

"It started as attraction and graduated quickly to obsession. On my part, anyway."

Remy nodded. "It can be hard to separate that out from anything else."

"She's a very beautiful woman," Bren muttered. "No shortage of admirers."

Dante's expression was grave. "I've no doubt she fulfills certain needs, Fitz, but there's a difference between what's right for now and what's right for you. Tara has a lot going for her and we can all see why you would be attracted to her, but she's made it clear she's gunning for someone with a fat bank account. Even if you fit the bill, do you want someone with that mindset? What happens if you lose your job or get sick or can't live up to that side of the bargain? Will she stick around, or will she be onto the next sucker?"

"Hey," Bren chided gently. "We don't know that's her game for sure."

"She's said it is," Dante replied.

Fitz blew out a breath. "It's part of it. She's also made it clear she's not looking for"—love—"anything meaningful."

He felt awful, like he was betraying her by being so candid about her intentions. Tara would be the first to agree with him, but she wouldn't like knowing he'd discussed her.

"Yet you still feel there's something there," Bren said. "Otherwise we wouldn't be having this conversation."

"I can't imagine being with anyone else, yet Tara's not what I imagined for the future."

"Because?" Remy prompted. "She acts like an airhead?"

Fitz shot him a look. "That's just it. It's an act. She has her reasons, and while I can't get into them, I understand them. Playing the bimbo is one of her weapons, but underneath she has so much more to offer."

"But you're not getting any younger," Dante said, circling back to the fundamentals. "If you're ready to get serious with someone, is it Tara? Can you imagine her as the mother of your children?"

Until he'd almost come inside her without a condom, he wouldn't have.

Now it was all he could think about.

Remy waved that off. "Hell, I got stuck on that for a while with Harper. Four kids later and here we are. And you might think my wife is hands-off because she's running the show with the Rebels, but no. She's all over it. Couldn't meet a better mom." He rubbed the lip of his coffee mug, looking thoughtful. "But Harper had some hang-ups about that herself. Thought it had to be one or the other, career or family. Sometimes it takes a woman meeting the right man, who can support her all the way, that makes the difference."

Something turned on in Hale's chest, like a winking flame that had finally been fueled with enough oxygen to make it viable.

The right man.

Could he be that for Tara? Because he sure as hell knew it wasn't O'Malley.

"You didn't think Harper was what you wanted?"

Remy shook his head. "Hell, no. Besides the boss-player thing, there were other obstacles. Sometimes we get caught up in preconceptions about who will work and why when really we should be paying attention to what's working right now and what we can see with our own eyes or feel with our own hearts and dicks. You say you can't imagine being with anyone else?"

"Neither can he imagine her for his future," Dante said, the voice of reason. As the former Rebels GM, he operated more on facts than instinct, just like Fitz. But that cautious approach had gone out the window when he risked his job and career for love with a player.

Fitz swallowed. Love? No, not love. That wasn't what was happening with Tara. Obsession was a better way to define it. Mixed up in there was care for her and the desire to knock this absurd idea of hers to marry for money on the head.

While he was pretty sure that Tara was not his future, neither did he want her selling her soul so she could take care of her sister.

Which meant he needed to do something to allay her concerns.

Time to make a bold move.

28

<hr>

Tara waved at Rosa as she walked by Misty Pines reception. "Hey, there!"

Rosa was on the phone and waved back.

Tara felt a touch guilty—it had been a couple of days since she'd made it in to see her sister as she'd had a number of Rebels player hair appointments. (Hockey flow grew so quickly!) To make up for her absence, she'd brought Chloe a new batch of princess stickers she had found at the dollar store. She also had her kit with her so she could give her hair a trim, along with special shampoo and Minnie Mouse barrettes.

Ready to call for her princess, she put her head around the door and got the shock of her life.

Hale.

More precisely, Hale with her sister. The two of them were playing with a doll that looked like Elsa from *Frozen*, definitely not part of Chloe's collection. Hale was showing Chloe how to brush the doll's hair while Nurse May looked on approvingly. Tara's heart went all squishy.

"Hello," she said, feeling like she was intruding, but

when Chloe heard her voice, her lips stretched in a toothy grin. "What's going on here?"

"Just having a nice time with Miss Chloe," Hale said with a doting smile.

"And a new friend." Tara meant the doll, but she could as easily be talking about Nurse May, who was gazing at Hale like the sun shone out of his penis!

Okay, put a stopper in it.

She had no claim over this man. Nurse May would probably be exactly what a guy like Hale would go for: cute, bubbly, educated, a nurturer, and clearly great with kids or kid-like people.

Yet yesterday morning as Hale slipped inside her—without a condom!—she had felt a rabid possessiveness that rocked her.

Mine.

Skin to skin, they had eliminated all the physical barriers, and maybe the rest, and Tara would have happily let him shoot his shot if she thought that was what he really wanted. But it wasn't. She had merely ensorcelled him for a spell and he had come to his senses about one second after she did.

Yet all day, a little voice chirped at her. *A baby. With Hale. Why not?*

May grinned at Tara. "Chloe was a bit down this morning, but as soon as Fitz showed up, she's done nothing but smile."

"Well, she's a natural flirt," Tara said.

"I think you've got competition." Hale's lips curved, a different kind of smile that felt personal to her, and Tara's heart stuttered, stopped, and died on the spot.

Don't do this to me, General. Don't make me fall for you. It's bad enough I have a ridiculous case of baby fever. Don't make me love you as well.

She wasn't the only one, it seemed. Every woman in the room—meaning Tara, Chloe, and May—was gazing in adoration at his handsome, bruiser face.

Tara needed to eliminate the immediate competition. Churlish, perhaps, but she wanted Hale to herself and Chloe.

"May, you must be busy. Don't let us stop you from whatever you need to do."

"You're right, I need to head out on my rounds." Serenely, she smiled and laid a hand on Hale's shoulder. "It was great to meet you, Fitz. Don't be a stranger."

Hale gave her that Georgia gent grin while Tara took a seat beside her sister.

"Hey Clo-Bear, I've missed you! I thought I might cut your hair today and I brought some new hair clips." Chloe was still playing with the Elsa doll with its long flowing dress and sheer sleeves, ignoring Tara because she had better things to look at. "This is really generous," Tara said to Hale.

"I figured it would be nice for Chloe to have something to remind her of her sister."

Her throat felt tight, the emotion of the moment overtaking her for a brief second.

"I also got somethin' for you." He reached into a shopping bag beside his chair and pulled out another box. "I think this was once your favorite."

An Ariel doll, complete with sea-shell bandeau and a glittery, green tail fin. The hits, they kept on coming.

"You okay?" Hale asked.

She managed to find a few words. "Fine. Absolutely fine. This is so nice of you."

Unable to meet his searching gaze, she fixed her own on Ariel. Hale had remembered Sad Sack Tara whining about having to give her doll away on her birthday. Not only remembered but thought about her and Chloe when he wasn't actually with Tara.

No one thought of her when she wasn't in their eyeballs making them think of her. Yet here was Hale being more considerate than any man or boy in her past.

She felt as frozen as that Elsa doll's heart. (Metaphorically. She knew it had no internal organs.) Was this what love did? Turned you into a Chucky doll? Because she was not enjoying this. Not at all.

Tara liked herself, for the most part. So she wasn't the smartest tool in the box and definitely wasn't everyone's cup of tea. But she would make a good girlfriend for someone who didn't expect too much.

Like Dex. All he wanted was someone to listen to him and give him a boost on game days.

But Hale's expectations were as high as Tara's heels. A smarty-pants nurturer who was ready to birth his superchildren, a woman who he'd be proud to have on his arm instead of sneaking around with under the radar.

Not a chatterbox airhead who hauled a trunk load of baggage behind her.

She shut her eyes. *Chloe's not baggage.* That attitude was what started this whole mess in the first place and got Tara sent away to the Cliff. Well, she was here now. And while she loved seeing Hale with her sister, it wouldn't last.

Because they wouldn't last.

A part of her combed through the options, searching for the one that gave her the most pleasure: *Enjoy it! A hot, sexy, intelligent guy wants to buy you gifts. He wants to make you omelets and ply you with popcorn and orgasms. He's so enthralled by your magic vagina he forgets to roll on a rubber. You deserve this.*

But the endorphins couldn't smooth this ride. Emotional hiccups kept returning for renewed assaults because Hale would not stop.

Playing with the Elsa doll.

Talking to Chloe like the sweet girl she was.

Making Tara fall in love with him with every honeyed word out of his mouth.

He looked up at her, likely startled at Tara abruptly standing on wobbly legs.

"Tara?"

"I just need to get some air. Back in a sec!"

Outside, Tara leaned against the wall, trying to catch her breath and fend off her panic.

Kindness shouldn't feel so oppressive.

A minute later, Hale came out to the lobby to find that Tara hadn't even made it as far as the building's entrance. So much for her smooth exit.

Her first instinct was her sister. "Is Chloe alone?"

"No, May's with her." Hale's first instinct, too, it seemed. "What's going on?"

She snatched a breath and gestured to the lobby chairs. Placing her hands in her lap, she struggled for calm. "Why are you here?"

He looked like he'd been caught doing something naughty. "This wasn't really planned. I only meant to drop off a gift for Chloe and maybe have a chat with the people in charge. I know it's kind of presumptuous to visit behind your back."

"Yes, it's—it's that but more to the point, it's confusing. For Chloe."

Not just for Chloe. Hale was here because he was a

decent man, but his presence gave Tara reasons to be hopeful and hope was something she really couldn't indulge in.

"I understand and that wasn't my intention, but Caroline said I should give Chloe the gift in person and—"

"Caroline? As in Mrs. Cheney?"

"Yes, I wasn't sure it was appropriate but Chloe seemed to recognize me."

Hale had made an impression at the hospital. The man was remarkable in every way and apparently on a first-name basis with Misty Pines' director.

"That's all well and good, but you won't always be in her life. I have to protect her." *And myself.* "And I don't want you to feel obligated to me or my sister because of what's happening between us."

He stared at her for an extra-charged beat, that muscle in his jaw working overtime. Was he angry because she'd implied his kindness was some sort of payment for the fabulous turns in the sheets? Was that what she meant?

She didn't even know anymore.

"Let me tell you about why I really stopped by Misty Pines today. I had a chat with the director about your bills. Chloe's care is covered for the next year, so you can stop worrying about that."

Her heart thudded as she parsed the words out of his mouth.

Covered. The next year. Stop worrying.

It should feel like a great weight had been lifted, yet it didn't.

"I can't accept that."

"Yes, you can," he said, his tone one of great patience. "I want to help."

"But I can't pay you back, at least not for ages."

"I'm not expecting anything in return. Why does this have to be a quid pro quo?"

"Because that's what relationships are."

He scoffed. "All of them?"

"Most of them. Most of the ones I've been in."

"Is it a quid pro quo with Chloe?"

Needing to burn off the negative energy, she stood and paced a few steps. "Of course not."

"Is it that way with Mia? She's an heiress. She could pay for your sister's care for life and it wouldn't make a dent in her wealth."

"I would never ask her to do that. That's not why we're friends. It would change everything and now you've gone and done this, and it-it-it changes everything!" They were supposed to be equals, each contributing pleasure and good company. Only Hale had changed the rules and upended the balance she'd so carefully strived to maintain. "I didn't ask for that."

"Damn it, Tara. You need the help and I can do that for you. I wanted to do that for you."

"And I don't want that between us. That shadow. That cloud. It's supposed to be just fun and games."

"We're long past fun and games. Sometimes it's about other stuff. Like friends helping each other out."

Friends. She didn't want to be his friend. She wanted to be his world.

A wisp of hope curled inside her chest. He had done this for her. Yes, as her friend, but maybe it was ...

Don't go all fucking Disney.

"So you did this ..."—*for me*—"For Chloe. It's a truly wonderful gesture, and I'm sorry I sound ungrateful. We can't take it."

He stood and grasped her hands. "Why not?"

"I haven't earned it."

His mouth straightened into a grim slash and he released her. "Is that what you would be doing with a pro-athlete husband? Earning it?"

Her mother had told her numerous times that her worth was measurable only in ways that could be exchanged. Smiles, flirtation, even sex were a currency she could use, *had* to use to guarantee Chloe's future. She had never pretended otherwise.

And now Hale stood before her, his disapproval like a heavy fog of disdain. He had no right to throw shade.

"Yes, I'd be earning it if I was married."

"Right, because that's what relationships are to you—an opportunity. No such thing as a strings-free gift in your world."

She rubbed her forehead. "This isn't a gift. It's an obligation you've created. If I was to accept it, I'd never be able to appreciate a single moment in your presence without wondering what I need to do to make up for it."

His expression was sheer exasperation. "That's why it's a gift. You don't have to pay it back in any way that fits into the paradigm you have for how relationships are supposed to work. Not everything is about who owes who."

"It just doesn't feel right."

"But if O'Malley gave it to you, it would? Do you even hear yourself?"

He sounded furious and maybe he was right to be. But she couldn't back out now. She was doing it this way to protect Chloe and her own fragile heart.

"I'm trying to keep these pieces of me ... separate. A relationship with someone like Dex is different. Everyone goes in with their eyes open. No one's promising more than they can give. But this thing with you, that's over here."

She gestured to a spot outside herself because it was easier than pointing to where Hale truly existed—inside her, a part of her.

This fling was for her and her alone.

With Hale, she didn't have to worry about how she looked—much—or whether her laugh sounded weird or if she wasn't 100% on. That Tara didn't have to worry about money or the future or the crushing weight of a lifetime's mistakes. That Tara was free of obligation.

But now Hale had forced a collision between these different versions of herself. And they were duking it out for supremacy.

Hale wasn't buying it. "I don't care where this thing with us is, if it's over here or halfway to the Arctic Circle. I just know that I feel it every time I'm with you."

"Well, you should care! What could you possibly be getting out of this?"

"Goddamn it, Tara, this burden you're carrying is crushing you. I am offering to take on some of that weight, but all you can see is a ledger with credits and debits." He gripped her arms and pulled her close. "You want to know what I get out of this thing with you? I get fun and pleasure and laughs. But I also get a feeling of contentment, of something innate and unexplainable, deep down in here." He held her hand against his chest, against the thrum of his beating heart. "I threw a few dollars your way. So what? It's just money."

"Only ever said by someone *with* money."

He shook his head. "Forget that for a moment. Think about the rest, what's important. We're not that different, you and I. Both looking to belong, to connect, to create something that lasts. I think we could do that for each other. I think we already do."

"Hale," she gasped. "You can't be serious."

"Why? Is it so crazy to want to build on this chemistry? To do what feels right?"

When had *that* ever helped anyone? She'd acted out as a kid, followed those "feelings" to her and Chloe's detriment. Her sister ended up in a crappy home because Tara had put herself first. These days she kept her emotions in check and her heart in glass because anything else would threaten the life she was trying to build for this one special being.

"Tell me this. What did you think of me before you knew about Chloe?"

He looked taken aback, just for a second, which was her answer. Before he could respond, she spoke the words his Southern gentility couldn't verbalize.

"You thought I was silly and ridiculous, but sexy enough for a fling."

"Tara—"

She held up a hand. "Only when you heard about Chloe did you start looking at me differently. I'm still all those things but my motives make me a bit more worthy. A bit more suitable. Am I right?"

His expression turned grave. "I can't pretend that my opinion of you didn't change when I found out about your sister. Sure, before that you were hot as fuck and fun to be with. After, I saw what was going on in here." He touched her breastbone. "I saw the heart of you."

Just as she suspected. But for Chloe, Hale wouldn't have thought twice about a future with Tara. That other girl, the silly, flirty, gold-digging chatterbox, the woman Hale seduced on an airplane, didn't deserve anything more and no way in hell would she use her sister to unlock this achievement.

"Chloe's the reason I'm doing this but I won't use her to make myself look better."

He leaned in, his forehead against hers. "You're overcomplicatin' it, honey. I want you and I think you want me. I know O'Malley earns a helluva lot more than I do, but my money spends just the same. With all things being equal then why can't you—" His hold on her arms loosened. The spark in those beautiful blue eyes dimmed, dulled. Died. "Unless he's what you want. For real."

For real? She wasn't sure she knew the difference anymore. Dex met all her pre-specified criteria, but most important, he didn't have the capacity to hurt her. She would never feel for him what she felt for Hale and that made him the safe option.

She had no words, mostly because she was stuck, thinking what it might be like to go all in with this wonderful man. As real as it could get. It thrilled her some. Terrified her more. And when it came down to it, the fear would always win.

It wasn't even the money.

It was the fucking doll.

So thoughtful, so Hale. Why had he gone and ruined it by showing her a hint of what perfection could look like? And why was it all tangled up with the money to cover Chloe's fees?

"I didn't ask for this." For love or a single iota of kindness.

For you.

"Yet you'd ask this imaginary husband of your fucked-up dreams to do it."

"And that person will know what they're getting."

"A piece of arm candy? A woman with dollar signs in her

eyes? Something as fake as cardboard? That's not you. That's not right."

But wasn't it? Hale was looking for something real. He would demand it, and when she fell short—because inevitably she would—he would realize the mistake he had made. How much he had compromised.

He would get bored with her and Chloe and then her heart would break into tiny fragments as she watched him drift further and further away from her.

It would crush her.

At least, with a jock, it would be on her terms. She controlled the playing field and wouldn't be stupid enough to fall in love.

It would never feel like this.

"It's all very well to say 'do what feels right,' but not when it goes against all the wishes and hopes you've ever had." Surely, he had to see that.

Something changed in his expression, a shadow over the sun, a gathering storm. His hands fell away.

It appeared he might have figured it out after all.

"I'd never want to get in the way of your wishes and hopes, Tara."

"That's not what—"

"It's okay," he cut in. "I misread the situation."

She meant *his* wishes, *his* hopes. Hers were all Hale. Every dream and desire centered around the man before her. But she could see he had taken it the wrong way. That he thought she was still determined to stay on this path to a hockey superstar husband and that accepting anything else contradicted her grand scheme.

Better not to disabuse him of that notion. Because he wasn't all wrong. It might not be her deepest hope and it might not make her ultimately happy, but at least Chloe would be safe and Tara would know she had done her best to fix it without screwing up this man's life.

Hale had shown her how amazing it was to be with someone smart and funny and sexy, who understood your weird and accepted you with all your flaws and foibles. And boy did she have a boatload.

But that wouldn't last. Because Tara was much too extra for anyone, even a man as patient and kind as Hale.

"I'm sorry for the ... misunderstanding. I'll talk to the director about returning your payment." His silence ripped her open. She just about managed to eke out, "It was really kind of you."

Curt nod. Then: "Could you tell Chloe I had to leave?"

"Course."

He turned his fist and rubbed his knuckles against her arm, giving her a final blast of warmth, taking any she had remaining with him.

"Good luck with the plan, Tara."

She could only nod as he walked away, leaving her chilled to the heart and frozen to the bone.

29

———————

"HEY, where have you been? I've been trying to get ahold of you."

Broom in hand to clean up stray hair, Tara looked up at Dex who had just walked into the Rebels' yoga room after morning skate.

"Sorry, I've had some stuff going on."

Dex sat in her chair. "Hair stuff?"

"Sure, hair stuff." She wouldn't be confiding in Dex, even if she needed someone to listen so badly it hurt. She dialed up her peppiest smile. "How was morning skate? Ready for the game later?"

"It was good. I missed you in the stands."

"Yeah, PR Sophie heard about my stylist talents and decided to stop by for a trim. She said things are going well —so well that it might be time for this grand romance to call it a day."

Dex's eyebrows drew together in a V. "But we've barely started. And how does that look to the fans?"

It had surprised Tara as well. She suspected Hale was

behind it, forcing the break-up so she wouldn't have any good reason to remain on Rebels property.

Fair enough.

It would be easiest if she didn't see him either, though maybe she could talk to Harper about continuing as the team's unofficial stylist in some capacity.

"It's not a big deal. People break up all the time." She placed her hands on the top of the broom's stick. "This was always a short-term thing, Dex."

"But you bring me luck. And when you're out there, skating with my jacket on—that does great things for my ego! Plus, you look hot in pink."

She lay the broom against the wall and took a seat on a nearby floor mat. "The purpose of us dating"—she added finger quotes around that word—"was to keep you out of trouble before the playoffs."

"There are still six weeks left to the regular season!"

"And you are now an established part of this team, healthy, fit, and not likely to backslide to some of your whorish ways. You've started to make a real impact and play better. You're not going to risk that with all-nighters at the club and getting your dick sucked on camera, are you?" Did she have to spell it out to him? "This way you can meet someone nice, for real. And have sex, but not in public."

Though she suspected Dex had not truly gone without for the last month. None of her business.

He looked so forlorn. "But what about you and me? Everyone thinks we're dating. Not just the fans, but all the guys."

"Right, I heard you've been telling people that. But be honest, if we had been dating in real life you would have dumped me by now because you're not interested in a relationship."

He shrugged. "I could be with the right girl. I see all the guys here and they seem so happy. Kids and dogs and wives that adore them."

That wives came last in that laundry list was no surprise. So he still had some growing up to do, and the right woman could mold him into something special.

She could be that woman.

She should be reeling him in right now, telling him how they could transition to actual dating that led to actual marriage that led to the culmination of her grand plan. The guy was here, ripe for the taking.

Yet she couldn't go the extra step.

Good luck with the plan, Tara. That's what Hale had said. And for once, he hadn't been snide about it.

"And when you find the right girl, you can have all that as well," she said.

"Not sure I believe in it." He placed his hands behind his neck. "Not sure you believe in it, either."

She squinted at him, surprised at the source of such an astute observation. "How would you know what I believe?"

"Some of the guys said you're looking to bag a player. That you only date pro-athletes. It sounds like you have a certain type and you have a plan to get what you want."

Reciting those bare facts, Dex didn't sound judgmental, not like Kaz who thought she was a gold digger. Or Mia who thought she was cutting herself off from possibly finding *the one.* Or Hale who thought she was selling her soul for security.

Maybe she was. But she had to use the gifts she was given.

"I'm not expecting to fall in love," she said. Been there and look how that turned out. "If I like a guy and he treats me well, it'll be enough."

"What if you think he's hot?"

She looked around. "Hot? I guess I'd have to see him to make that call."

He smiled, and she smiled back, and it was nice to talk to someone and not feel any pressure whatsoever. No sparks. No challenge.

No chance to get hurt.

"You want to go get lunch?" he asked.

"Sure, let's do that."

FITZ TWIDDLED his pen between his thumb and forefinger and looked at Sophie sitting across from him. "Where the hell is he?"

As if summoned by Fitz's bad humor, O'Malley loped in and sat down. "Sorry I'm late. Morning skate went a little longer than usual."

"No problem, thanks for coming by." O'Malley wasn't usually one to apologize, so that was a surprise.

"We wanted to talk to you about the campaign to rehabilitate your rep," Sophie started.

"Yeah, I heard our fake dating ruse is over." O'Malley shrugged. "Fun while it lasted."

Sophie smiled. "You did a great job, Dex. Everyone in the front office is very happy with how it all turned out. Social media metrics are increased across the board, in a good way. Even merchandise rev is up since we started creating the bomber jackets, with a cut to the original creator, Theo's grandmother, of course."

Dex folded his arms and sat back. "And I'm playing better, too. Don't forget that."

"We haven't," Fitz said. "That's what happens when you treat your body well and get some sleep."

"Sure. Or maybe it's because I have Tara in my corner. She's the MVP here."

Fitz fisted a hand against his thigh under the desk. This fucker didn't deserve to be within twenty feet of her, never mind have her in his corner.

Of course, what did Fitz know about what anyone deserved? He had thought Tara deserved him, but apparently Fitz would never check any of her boxes. He would never figure in her dreams—and he sure as shit refused to pay her to figure in someone else's, even if it was a set-up.

All he'd wanted was to take off some of the pressure, but she saw it for what it really was—a land grab. If he could get in there first with a donation to Tara's grand cause, then maybe she would see Fitz as a contender.

Instead, she'd rejected him and his money, making it clear that any offer from him would never make the grade.

A couple of days later he made his feelings obvious by putting a halt to this absurd fake relationship malarkey. Childish, perhaps, but he wasn't feeling very adult right now. Tara Becker was no longer needed on the Rebels payroll.

Sophie nodded. "There'll be a bonus in it for Ms. Becker, for sure."

"Good. And I'll take care of her as well."

"Meaning?" Fitz said far too quickly.

"Tara and I are—uh, I'm not sure if we need to report it to management. Maybe we should, given how it all started."

"Report what?" Fitz's voice didn't sound like his own.

O'Malley grinned—that drop-your-panties grin he doled out to all the nameless women in those videos and photos. "That we're officially dating now. Knowing Tara, she'll keep up with the Instagram stuff and all that. Which you should pay her for because she's awesome at it."

That rushing sound in Fitz's ears meant he didn't hear what O'Malley said next. Or whatever he said after that.

He had to backtrack to ensure he wasn't going mad. "Let me get this straight. You and Ms. Becker are a couple? Officially?"

O'Malley was looking at him strangely, probably wondering how Fitz had missed the details in the moments before when Fitz's brain went offline. "That's what I said. Having her around makes me play better and I don't want to mess with that."

"Does *she* know about this?"

O'Malley made a face. "Of course she knows about it! You think I'd make up a girlfriend? That's the kind of shit *you* pull, not me. We've gone out a couple of times—sure, we always clicked, but now without the added pressure of doing it as a job, we can see if we're a good fit." He leaned in and whispered, "Spoiler: we are."

Did that mean they were already ... sleeping together?

"Now if there's nothing else, I have a woman to woo."

It was a good thing Sophie was here because Fitz had lost the ability to form words. In ending this fake relationship, Fitz had forced them into making a call on moving forward with the real thing.

Tara had made her choice.

"No, Dex, you're free to go," Sophie said cheerfully because Fitz had yet to speak. "Thanks for stopping by."

Thankfully the man left before Fitz could skirt the desk and roundhouse kick one of his star players into the middle of the playoffs.

~

A DAY LATER, Fitz was not feeling any better when he answered Bode's call. "Yep?"

"Sounding a little grumpy there, bro. Trouble in Rebels paradise?"

Seated in the stands, he cast his gloomy gaze over the practice rink. "Nope, doin' just fine. The boys are lookin' good today. Should do well tonight."

"Uh, don't care." Next came a muffled voice, what sounded like a dropped phone, and Bode's return. "Ava said I'm to ask after Tara."

"And you can't think of that for yourself?"

"If I asked, you'd think I was being nosy."

Since meeting Tara in Atlanta, his family, but particularly Ava, had been pumping him for intel on the "sparks" they claimed to have witnessed in the visitors' box at the Rockets arena. He'd told them they were imagining things.

Fitz was beginning to think that wasn't so far from the truth.

"You can tell Ava that Tara's just fine as far as I know."

"As far as you know?"

He rubbed his forehead. Tara had made it very clear that he wasn't in the running for her future. Maybe his bank account wasn't big enough or his brain wasn't small enough. He had thought he was doing the right thing paying for Chloe's fees, and perhaps he should have run it by Tara first. But all he wanted was to make it better for her. To lighten her load.

She had so much on her shoulders. Now she had made up her mind and moved on.

But to O'Malley? Fitz shouldn't have been surprised yet he couldn't wrap his head around it.

"She's just an employee of the organization. Or was."

"Who you couldn't take your eyes off of. And who you went to a whole lot of trouble to assist in her time of need."

"Tara's a lot of fun, Bode, but that's where it ends."

"Why?" Ava's voice came on.

"Am I on speaker?"

Ava scoffed. "He would just tell me anyway. I like Tara. So does your momma."

"She's never even met her!" Christ, these people.

"You have our approval to take things to the next level."

Fitz inhaled deeply. "I appreciate that, but Tara and I don't think of each other that way. And her plans do not involve me. She's with O'Malley. Officially."

What the hell was the difference between his money and O'Malley's? So the guy had a multi-million dollar contract, but Hale did okay. He could provide for any woman in his life.

Which meant the difference was *him*. He wasn't enough. And Tara had been trying to let him down in her inimitable Tara way. He just needed to take the hint.

"She might be with O'Malley for the press," Ava went on. "But I saw the chemistry between you."

"I've had that with women before."

She sighed. "Really? Not with anyone I've met, not even Peyton. I took some photos of you two in the box."

"What?"

Not two seconds later, he was looking at pics of Tara holding Gracie, smiling at him over his niece's head. A couple of the photos had those live buttons, so he pressed, eager to relive the precious moments. The photo rewound a second, capturing the two of them drinking each other in, caught mid-joy. Chemistry in bits and bytes.

"You two look great together," Ava murmured.

"Tara makes any guy look good."

Including O'Malley who was currently hamming it up on the ice, waving at …

She's here.

Tara was seated a few rows up in the stands. He'd missed her entrance and now he wished he could miss this public support of her boyfriend, or whatever the hell he was.

Target? Mark? The future Mr. Tara Becker?

"Listen, I gotta go," he muttered to his brother.

"Say hi to your 'friend'," Ava chimed in while Bode could be heard laughing evilly in the background.

While it depressed the hell out of him, he needed to put it, and her, behind him. He'd made a mistake with the offer to cover Chloe's fees—it had clearly thrown her—but it had also brought things to a head. Tara wasn't comfortable with Fitz in her sister's life and she definitely wasn't comfortable with any financial assistance. As it seemed likely those two things would need to happen with anyone she decided to date or marry, then the only logical conclusion was that Fitz didn't meet Tara's specs.

He'd lost out to O'Malley.

That stung. But not half as much as the gaping wound that had opened up without this woman in his life. He missed her. In his bed, on his sofa, sitting at his kitchen island in his sweats while she gave her very decided opinions on whether Ben and Jen were going to work out the second time around. Even Goober looked more dejected these days.

They'd get over it. Over her.

Fitz would assign what he'd had with this woman to the trash heap of fling history. Chemistry, after all, was fleeting. He'd played his hand and come up wanting.

Literally.

He checked his email, noting that the Perfect Match

people were emailing him—again—to complete his profile and activate it. A couple of weeks ago, Tara had created an account for him and took a photo. She'd loved a candid shot of Fitz, Goober, and Pickle and thought it would strike the right vibe.

He opened the dating app and read the profile blurb again: *"I'm a driven guy who loves hockey, family, travel, and my dog. My life is crazy, noisy, and busy, but I'm hoping to find someone to enjoy coffee and the quiet times with me."*

He probably should mention Pickle, who would be a little pissant if he was left out. And maybe that last line could be more definitive. Or maybe it was fine as it was because Tara had written it and she seemed to have a finger on the pulse of him.

Because he wasn't in enough pain, he snuck a glance Tara's way.

She raised her hand in greeting.

He nodded back.

Looked away and hit "Activate" on the app.

There, done. Now he needed coffee and to not breathe the same air as Tara Becker.

ON HIS WAY into the coffee shop, he ran into Kennedy, Reid Durand's girlfriend. The pink-streaked pixie blonde was on her way out and gave him a blast of her infectious smile.

"Hey, just the woman I want to see."

"Sounds promising."

"So I need a dog-walker." Tara had been helping out, but he wouldn't be asking her now. "I've been using my neighbor's kid, but she's kind of young. Would rather have a pro and I hear you're getting your business off the ground."

She smiled. "You heard right."

"I also have something else I want to run by you. Can I buy you a pastry to go with that coffee?"

Five minutes later, he was seated with Kennedy, figuring out how to work Goober into her schedule. She was currently running background checks for staff she could rely on for home check-ins and had a guy in mind. Until then she could fit Fitz's puppy in on her regular rounds.

"So I wanted to chat about Bastian Durand."

Her eyebrows rose. "I know you're courting him, but he's being kind of coy about it."

"That's the usual negotiation gamesmanship. But really I'm more concerned about how the dynamic might change with both Durand brothers on the team. When I've asked either of them about it—"

"Reid squints into the middle distance and Bast says everything's fine, amazing, couldn't be better?"

"Yeah. Pretty much."

She took a moment before replying. "So things were tough for them just before the holidays, the finale to a multi-season production of 'Papa Henri is a Dick.' Dad of the Year had been setting them against each other all their lives, and it all blew up at that crosstown classic game."

Hockey was known for its fair share of hard asses, but Henri Durand, a former enforcer with a bad attitude, took the puck. It didn't surprise Fitz that he was responsible in some way.

"Bastian with a broken wrist and Reid with a two-game suspension," he said. "That's one way of letting off steam. But how are they now?"

"Closer than ever. It clarified things for them both."

"Enough to work together on the same team?"

Kennedy smiled. "I think it would make them play even

better. They grew up, pushing each other to be the best. Just think what having that level of competitiveness on your crew would be like. As long as they stay at different positions."

Reid played center while Bastian was a right-winger. That worked and Fitz saw no reason why it should be changed.

"And they won't kill each other on the ice?"

"More likely, anyone who strikes against one Durand, strikes against both." She raised her fist in a victory gesture. "You'll have some top-notch ice fights! Is that what they call them?"

He chuckled. He liked the idea of the Durands passionately defending each other during a game. That closeness might be the intangible the Rebels needed.

"One other thing. Do you know Pepper Calhoun?"

"Coach's daughter? The mascot?"

"Yeah, she's filling in while we find someone suitable. But it seems she and Bastian have some history, and whatever happened, didn't end well. You know anything about that?"

Kennedy shook her head. "I do not. But I can do a little digging on the down low and see if I come up with anything."

He wasn't sure it would affect any decision to acquire Durand, but he'd prefer to know all the potential complications up front. He tapped the table. "I should have talked to you sooner. Tara said you'd know what's what."

"Tara?" Her eyes gleamed. "I didn't realize you were on such friendly terms."

"We're not."

"Oh, I see." Something like pity shone back at him. Wonderful.

His phone pinged and he took a quick look at it, unreasonably hopeful that it might be Tara wanting to talk.

It was a notification from the dating app, informing him he had matches.

Several matches.

That was that. He had taken the plunge and started dating. It gave him no pleasure.

"Hot date?"

"Not yet ..." He waved a hand. "I've been putting it off, using a bunch of excuses. Dating in general."

She pushed a strand of pink-streaked hair behind her ear. "Because?"

Because the woman I crave doesn't want me the way I want her.

"The usual distractions."

"Tara?" At his dark look, she added, "And Dex? All that PR stuff probably took up a lot of your time."

"It did. We have people to handle it, but I needed to see it through for myself."

"And now you have?"

Tara had made it clear he wasn't what she had in mind for the future. He wasn't some pretty boy she could place an Instagram filter over to make it to her liking. She wasn't looking for anything real—and goddamn it, if she was with him, it'd be as real as it could get.

Raw, dirty, sweet, all the parts that made up Tara.

All the parts she couldn't see but were as clear to him as a blue Spring sky above Lake Michigan.

"Now, I have."

30

Tara sat on the plush velvet sofa in Sadie's studio, housed in the coach house on the Chase estate. Sadie had lived here for a few months before she and her sister Lauren moved in with Gunnar. Now she used it for her dress design business, which had taken off like gangbusters in the last few months.

Sadie had offered to design Mia's wedding dress. As Kennedy and Tara were to be her bridesmaids, along with Isobel, they had stopped by to look at designs and help Mia come up with something amazing.

"We should have talked about this *weeks* ago." A slightly frazzled Sadie pulled out one of several bridal magazines and flipped through the pages. "Like the minute you got engaged."

"Sorry," Mia said with a quick glance of oh shit at Tara, who smiled back at her. Sadie had a waiting list a mile long so this was really pushing the boundaries of friendship. "I know I'm a pain in the ass. Isobel and I have been running around trying to get the Athenas organized. But we're here now and ready for whatever you can manage."

Sadie smiled her forgiveness. She was such a sweetie

and these days was so happy now that she and Gunnar were expecting their first child. "Okay, I have a few ideas based on the brief chat we had a few days ago. You want something off the shoulder and on the simple side, but maybe a fuller skirt? We could do knee-length and show off those great calves. All that muscle tone should be on display. Something like this, perhaps?" She showed Mia a photo of a bride with a fifties-style rockabilly number. "Or tea-length?" That version was a bit more Twenties Flapper.

Mia worried her lip. "Maybe I should go with more traditional? I dunno. Tara, what do you think? You're the fashionista."

Tara was half-listening, her eye on her phone. Dex had texted to ask if she could meet for a drink tonight and yesterday, they'd had a pleasant enough lunch. (Bonus: he barely looked at the server's ass.) A part of her recognized that this might be her best chance at the brass ring: a hot, rich pro-athlete who was interested in what she had to offer.

Because she didn't have the goods to hold Hale's interest for long.

Is it so crazy to want to build on this chemistry? To do what feels right?

Maybe not. She wanted Hale, more than anything. She wanted to spend lazy Sundays in bed and make his coffee the way he liked it and cuddle up with their fur babies while they talked "politics" and more. Such as a real future, one with equal partners and someone who had your back in all things, not just the financial.

So he had paid—or tried to pay—for Chloe's fees, but that didn't mean he was buying Tara's body or time or soul, did it? It meant he cared. Mrs. Cheney couldn't believe Tara was turning down this funding source. Neither could Tara, but she had to. Even without Hale in her life, she couldn't have that between them.

As for being with Hale, could they return to that split second before the money entered the equation? He hadn't ignored her at the practice yesterday morning. He had just nodded sternly and carried on, like he was hurting.

Oh, God, what had she done?

"Tara?"

Tara blinked at Mia and tried to fake her way into the conversation. "I think anything you wear will be gorgeous."

"Okay. What's up?"

"Nothing. Just ignore me."

Kennedy leaned in. "You look like you've been crying and are about to go on another crying jag that will beat the first one into submission. What's happened?"

So much for using 'roid cream on her bags. "I-I had an argument with someone. No big deal."

"Who? Dex?" Sadie asked.

"No." She took a breath. "Hale."

"Fitzpatrick?" Mia practically yelled. "What the hell did he say to you? He's always been such a snob about you and Dex. If he's been getting all up in your grill about anything, I will ..." She narrowed her eyes, then widened them as cold, stinkin' realization kicked in. "Oh."

"Yep," Tara said. "Oh."

All eyes met hers, filled with compassion, which made her heart swell in appreciation. She loved these girls, truly.

Kennedy went first. "So you and the General have been going to war on each other's privates?"

"It was a one-time thing. Well, a multiple-time thing. Orgasms and times." Too much information. "And now it's done."

"Because you had a fight?" Mia prompted.

"Yeah, he did me a favor and I felt weird about it."

Sadie frowned. "Did he want something from you for this favor?"

Just her heart. Which should have been for sale but which she couldn't seem to gift-wrap for Hale. Why the hell not?

Because she wanted him, not as part of a plan, not for some great sacrifice. She wanted Hale for herself and that was a little too selfish.

"No. Well, yes, but not what you think. I think he wants to go out with me. To, uh, date."

"And you don't want to because he's ... older? Judgmental? Disapproving? Too hot?" Mia sounded as confused as Tara. "Has he been a jerk or not?"

"No. He's been an absolute gentleman. In the streets, that is." She gifted her friends a sly look to let them know they should have no concerns for Tara's sexual health. "But I don't want him giving me anything. Because then I feel like our relationship is based on something transactional."

"But if you hook up with a hockey player," Mia said carefully, "you'd take his money?"

"Right. But I'd have earned it by being an amazing partner. That was always the goal." She didn't want to earn anything to win Hale, and therefore, she wasn't sure how to separate his gift to her from the obviously fucked-up view she had of relationships. Dr. Bill would have a field day. "He needs someone more appropriate."

Mia looked stormy again. "He said that?"

"Not in so many words. But I met his brother and sister-in-law and their cute little girls. So adorable. And Hale needs someone like Ava—that's his SIL—a Super Mom type. You know, yummy mummies who can make wheat-germ pancake breakfasts, drop off the kids at three different schools, hit Pilates and yoga classes, run their pyramid scheme businesses, bake muffins for the PTA meeting, learn ukulele, and keep the house looking pin-neat. They have Masters' degrees in childhood education and were high-school gymnasts before they got model-tall. They're willowy but still have great child-bearing hips because no way in hell are they having a C-section. They are perfect and I could never be like that. Never."

Mia took her hand and spoke slowly, like she was talking to a very dim or very drunk version of Tara. "But did he say he wanted all that?"

"He didn't have to. When we started sleeping together, we both made it clear that sex was all either of us had to offer the other or wanted. We'd go our separate ways, but then he fucking ruined it by being nice and funny and smart and—" The tears were threatening, mini-storms behind her eyelids. "Kind. He was so kind."

Tara might have slept with the Ariel doll on her pillow last night.

She would take that information to her grave.

"And he wants to date you?" The confusion was catching if Sadie's tone was anything to go by. "Why don't you go out with him if you like him?"

"Because that's not what's supposed to happen. You know he's divorced? Well, with his first wife, they figured out they had nothing in common during the off season and it all fell apart. I'd probably drive him crazy after a while. Besides, I have plans, and I know you all think I'm ridiculous to be so one-track about it all, but it has to happen this way."

They all stared, no one questioning why it had to happen this way. After all, Tara Becker had been clear about her goals from Day One. She could tell them about Chloe, but now she wondered if Chloe was just an excuse. Sure,

Tara needed the money to ensure her sister's security, but perhaps she needed the plan because it meant she didn't have to think of the alternative:

That her fast-fading beauty was her only weapon and she had to snare her prey before time ran out.

Hale hadn't acted like he was trapped. He'd acted like Tara might be worth the effort.

"I might have made a mistake."

Sadie brightened. "Really?"

"Maybe I could be what he wanted. After all, we have chemistry and attraction and I could probably learn to make pancakes, be some sort of Barefoot Contessa clone. He'd be away so much with the travel that he wouldn't really have a chance to get bored with me. I'd just sex the hell out of him when he's at home so he'd be worn out and looking forward to those away trips just to get some rest."

She looked around at her friends. "What do you think? Could I make it work with Hale?"

"I have no idea!" Mia threw up her hands. "This is the first I'm hearing about it. About any of it." She sounded so miffed, and Tara realized she might have miscalculated the bounds of their friendship.

She'd already lost Hale. She couldn't lose Mia, too.

"I didn't think you'd approve."

Mia's eyebrow shot up. "Like I approve of the marry-a-hunk-you-hardly-know plan?"

"I know you don't like that. Maybe that's why I kept Hale to myself. In case you judged."

"Tara." Mia's tone was more hurt than aggrieved now. "I'm sorry if I came off as judgmental. I just want you to be happy, to find a guy who deserves you and treats you like the truly awesome person you are. And if that's Fitz—which is still blowing my mind, by the way, and not because I don't think you should be with him, but because you've dropped it on us like a two-ton Zamboni—then you should go for it. Get that geriatric ass!"

She reached out and gripped Tara's hand, and Tara's heart filled with joy because if Mia didn't think she and Hale were so out there, maybe it wasn't such a bad idea after all.

"What do you guys think?" She valued Sadie's and Kennedy's opinion, too, but theirs would be a bonus. Mia's was the one she craved.

Sadie smiled, all approving. Kennedy not so much. The pink-haired dynamo was frowning.

"Not a good idea?"

"He's dating," Kennedy muttered, as if speaking it under her breath would make it less horrific.

It did not.

Tara's heart contracted. "What?"

Kennedy winced. "I ran into him at the coffee shop yesterday, and we were talking about hiring me to walk his dog and some other stuff, and he got one of those pings on his phone. A dating app. And then he said he was starting to date after putting it off for a while."

Tara, you fucking idiot.

Of course he was dating. She had told him to do it, had even set up his profile, and the man—a proven unicorn— had listened!

This was why she shouldn't let hope get in the way of goals. It was far too painful.

"Oh, well, that's that, then. Phew! Lucky escape. Sure, I could have bedazzled him with my wiles and kept him in thrall for a few weeks, but it could never have lasted. And if he's in that much of a hurry to get out there, then he's not so heartbroken by a rejection from me!"

Mia scooted her chair closer. "Tara—"

"No, not a second of pity, Wallace." She smiled at her friend, urging her not to push it. Because if she did, Sadie's hardwood would soon be warped by a Tara Becker teary flood of biblical proportions.

Deep breath, smile pinned on, back to business.

She grasped the first magazine to hand. "Now, let's take a look at the design contenders. You have the best collarbones of any girl I know so that has to get some love with a little low-cut action. Sadie, make it so."

"ANY REASON why you're in such a foul mood? We're two goals up."

"Not that I have anything to do with it."

Harper looked at Fitz, who had uttered that last statement with so much self-pity even he cringed.

"Well, maybe not directly," she said with plenty of side eye. "But the attitude from top down reflects in the locker room and on the ice. You've also done a great job of reining in Dex. He seems to be a changed man."

Was he? He was definitely less of an asshole—objectively. Playing better, too, so that was something.

"It's Tara. She seems to have the magic touch."

They all loved her, the Rebels very own Disney princess.

"Yeah, she's managed to surprise just about everyone. Mia adores her, of course, and she's always been a pretty good judge of character. But I thought we were going to play this strategy to the start of the playoffs?"

"They're officially dating now, so I don't see why the org should fund their couple lifestyle."

Harper managed to look down her nose at him, a mighty feat considering she was a foot and a half shorter than him.

"Tara and Dex are official, as in the real thing?"

As real as Tara was capable of. "So I'm told."

"Yet, this seems to not sit well with my general manager." She touched a finger to her lips. "I told you she was one of a kind. She got under your skin, didn't she?"

He growled. "I know that this org seems to think everyone has a God-given right to everyone else's business, but I'd rather not talk about my personal life." He coughed and added mutinously, "Boss."

The door to the suite opened and in walked Mia, alone. Usually, Tara would be with her in the box for the final period, and he was torn between a painful need to see her and an irrational relief that she was staying away.

Mia took a seat on the other side of her sister-in-law, Harper. "Hey, sis!"

"Hey, my favorite hockey player."

"Even more than Remy and Isobel?"

"Definitely. You're much nicer than those divas." Harper stood, saying, "I need to take a walk and stretch. Tell them not to score while I'm peeing and maybe see if you can cheer this guy up. We're winning, but to look at him, you wouldn't know it."

"Will do," Mia said with a chuckle as Harper headed out. "So how are things, fearless leader?"

"Fine."

"Heard you've started dating."

He turned to her. "How did you hear that?"

"Oh, word gets around. Hard to keep a secret in Rebelandia."

Tell me about it.

"Though Tara's pretty good at it," she added.

Now she definitely had his attention. "Is she okay?"

"Define 'okay.' Is she still acting like everything is peachy and there's no problem that can't be fixed with a hockey hunk on her arm? Then yeah, she's okay." She leaned forward just as Foreman made a break for the blue zone. "Come on, Cal! Oh, hell, that sucks."

"Mia."

She frowned at him.

"What's going on?"

"She came clean to me about you two. She even seemed a little sad that you weren't going to work out."

His heart lifted, cheered by the prospect of Tara's misery, which was mighty mean-spirited of him.

"What did she say exactly?"

Mia ignored his question. "Fitz, why does Tara want to marry a hockey player?"

"You're her friend. Hasn't she told you?"

"She says it's because she wants a hot guy and security and all the trappings that come with being a hockey WAG. I just accepted that at face value because who knows, it's Tara, right? And now I realize that I haven't probed as much as I should have. That maybe I haven't been that good a friend. The last few months have been kind of crazy, and every time I try to dig deeper with Tara, she blows me off. But I get the impression that maybe you know more about her motives."

Fitz could spill, but it wasn't his place. Tara had chosen to keep her counsel for a reason.

"It's not my story to tell."

"So there is something?"

"Just ask her."

The clock ticked down on the final period with the Rebels still two goals ahead. At the final buzzer, the crowd erupted and the box crowd cheered and patted him on the back as if he was the winner here.

Hard to feel like a winner when everything was falling apart.

Loving Tara Becker wasn't easy.

And Fitz knew that he was jaw-deep, close-to-drowning, can-barely-breathe in love with this woman.

Getting matched on that dating app should have given him some glimmer of hope for a life post-Tara, but no. All he'd felt was dread and a bone-deep sense that anyone else was wrong. He needed to talk to her, make her see the light. Tell her she was the one he wanted and that he would do whatever it took to make it work.

"Where's Tara tonight?"

Mia looked a little troubled. "She said she didn't want to watch the game in the box, which I assumed was because you were here."

He would find her and fix this. He stood and shot his cuffs. "You headin' down to the locker room?"

"Sure, I'll walk with you."

The players were still on the ice along with Rowdy Rebel, the team mascot who had just skated on. Rowdy, it had to be said, didn't look quite as smooth as usual.

"Rowdy been knockin' 'em back, has she?"

"She's been known to like a shot or two. But never on the job."

Rowdy didn't skate around for long but headed straight for Dex O'Malley and grasped his arms. Dex stopped and stared while the mascot took off the headpiece ... to reveal Tara.

Fitz's skin seethed. So she was on the ice, goofing around after the game, doing the kind of PR junk the team had once paid her for.

Except all that was supposed to be over.

"You knew about this?" he managed to gut out to Mia.

"No." She was frowning at what she was seeing. "I don't know what this is about."

Just some harmless fun, the PR wonks would say—if fun equated to Fitz getting his fingers slammed in a car door. He wasn't one for premonitions, but he had a bad feeling about this.

An instinct that was proven correct when O'Malley fell to the ice.

Not because he was injured.

He was on bended fucking knee.

Half the crowd was still on site and had stopped in their tracks as they realized there was more to see, and now the entire shit show was on the Jumbotron.

"Oh my God," Mia murmured. "He's going for it."

Tara dropped the Rowdy headpiece and clasped her hands to her mouth. All this was happening close enough to the tunnel that someone was able to get a mic out there and shove it under O'Malley's nose.

Of course, the asshole waited until he was sure everyone could hear him.

"Tara Becker, would you do me the honor of becoming my wife?"

"Oh ... Dex. Wow!"

Don't do it, honey. Don't fucking do it.

She held a hand to her chest and breathed in deeply.

You're making a huge mistake.

The mic was now under her nose, and Fitz's heart had climbed into his throat. What was he supposed to do here? Pound the window like Dustin Hoffman in *The Graduate*?

Accompanying the mic, a camera had materialized and was in front of her face. Hers. Because she was the star of the show, always had been.

Fitz saw the moment she made the decision.

The security of her sister.

A future without want.

The heart she was terrified of giving to anyone else.

To Fitz.

He was already turning away before she responded.

Was out the door of the box as the crowd went wild.

Was halfway to the nearest bar before the ring was slipped on her finger.

31

Tara walked into the tunnel in a daze.

She was engaged. To be married. To a hockey player.

And nothing had ever felt more wrong.

She might have preferred not to be wearing the Rowdy Rebel mascot costume when she accepted a marriage proposal, but Sophie had said it would be fun to go out there with it on, that the crowd would love it. So technically Tara was no longer under contract for PR work, but she wanted to be a team player.

And Sophie was right: the crowd had loved it.

But they'd loved what came after even more.

"That was amazing!" Sophie took the Rowdy Rebel costume head from Tara's hands and passed it to a minion. "You were just the perfect amount of stunned."

"I said yes."

"Of course you did!"

Dex had already gone into the locker room and the noise from inside was something else. Drumming on the benches, cheers that rivaled the crowd in the arena, yet Tara's heart beat them all for volume.

This was it. Everything she had ever wished for was hers all because she had said a three-letter word to a question she hadn't seen coming. Sure, she and Dex had become friendly in the last couple of weeks, but friendly enough to get to this level?

What are you looking for? A years-long courtship? Someone just Willy Wonka'ed your ass and handed you the golden ticket.

They hadn't even slept together. Had barely kissed except for that sneaky smooch he laid on her at Erik Jorgenson's party and the quick post-proposal one before all those people.

And each time had felt like her stomach was about to turn inside out.

She didn't know what his favorite movies were or if he liked animals or wanted kids.

She knew all these things about Hale.

Miracle (of course), *yes*, and *yes*.

A shiver coursed through her, and not one of sensuous anticipation. She wasn't attracted to Dex, not the way she was to Hale. If anything, she'd been so indifferent to him she wondered if maybe that was the source of *his* attraction to her.

She blinked at Sophie. "Did you know this was going to happen?"

She gave a cheeky grin, evidently thrilled at what must be a PR coup. The Rebels social media accounts must be blowing up. "I might have. Dex came to me and said he wanted to do something special."

And the woman thought Tara in the Rowdy Rebel costume was how this moment should be immortalized? Fine, whatever.

"I need to change."

Mostly, she needed to think. Her eye caught the

diamond on her finger. At least two carats, flawless, the perfect topper to a perfect evening.

The team had won and so had Tara.

Yet, she didn't feel like a winner. She felt like she was … compromising. Exactly what she had accused Hale of when he said they should build on their chemistry.

Do what felt right.

"I left your stuff in the yoga room." Sophie shook her keys and moved across the corridor to open the door. "Don't take too long because I have a photographer ready for when you're back in civvies."

Tara nodded dumbly and headed into the yoga room, shutting the door behind her.

She would have to tell Dex about Chloe. It wouldn't be fair to proceed without giving him all the details. It would be the ultimate test. Was he still interested in her with all she was bringing to the table?

Like Hale had been. Of course, Hale knew the score, understood the scared, ridiculous girl she was beneath, and somehow still wanted her.

Or had for a brief, flickering moment.

But as soon as she pushed back and became difficult, unsure of herself, he figured out she wasn't worth the trouble. Better to hit those dating apps and find himself the right kind of woman.

Had he seen what happened? Was he watching from the box, his gaze disapproving, his heart hardening with every passing second? Had she hurt him, even a little?

Not that she wanted to, but if there was a chance he might care …

The door pushed against her back. Someone was coming in and Tara braced for a rollicking from Hale.

Mia entered and closed the door behind her, her expression saying it all: *You've only gone and done it now, Tara Becker.*

Tara immediately went on the defensive. "I didn't know that was going to happen, I promise."

Mia's eyes went wide. "I figured as much. You looked like someone had lodged a puck in your gullet."

"It came out of nowhere. Sophie told me to put on the costume and skate a couple of circuits, so she knew it was happening."

Mia rubbed a hand along the furry duck-cat arm. "Is this what you want, Tara? Really?"

"I've always said so." She blew out a breath, grasping for an anchor amidst the hurricane of change. "It has to happen."

"Why?"

"I need the security."

"Because?"

Mia had this determined look on her face, and Tara was suddenly fearful.

"Do we really need to talk about this now?"

"As good a time as any." Mia folded her arms. "I have to admit I've always thought it was kind of a joke. That you liked hanging with me and the hot hockey hunks were a bonus, not that you were truly gunning for one. I feel like there's something you're not telling me and Fitz said—"

"What did he say?"

"That I should ask you about your motives. About what's going on with you."

So he had kept her confidences to himself. He still had her back.

"Did Hale see what happened?"

"Yeah, but he didn't really react, unless you count leaving the box a reaction." Mia frowned. "I don't understand why you're doing this. I thought you wanted Fitz, so how can you just turn around and say yes to Dex? And don't tell me that it's for security or whatever. Because if you like Fitz—if you love him—but you're willing to choose some guy with more millions over him, then that's kind of fucked up, Tara."

"It's not that simple."

Mia threw up her hands. "Isn't it? Because I saw how upset you got when Kennedy said Fitz might be dating. And this is your next move? Which makes me think you care only about Dex's money. But really the worst of it is, I'm not sure I understand this person who I thought was my friend."

Tara blinked. "No, that's not it at all. I mean, yes, I need the money—"

"And you're willing to marry the first guy with fat pockets who asks you."

Tara reached for her friend, but Mia flinched.

Oh.

"Fitz made it sound like you had some good reason, but all I see is a woman who acts like we're besties but doesn't let me in. I love hanging with you, yet you're constantly hiding things. What happened with Fitz, the fact you're far enough along in a relationship with Dex to get a proposal, your motives for all of it. I don't really know you, and all these surprises kind of prove it."

That would have been a conversation-stopper in any situation, but Mia remained, her gaze fixed on Tara, waiting for her to ... fix it.

She didn't know how.

The storm was battering her senses and she had no idea how to keep it at bay.

"I know you think I'm some sort of user. I've certainly

made no secret of my ambitions, and while you and everyone else we know has laughed about it, I've let you think it was just me being silly because it was easier than admitting I'm a basic bitch who wants someone to take care of me."

Mia grimaced. "So that's all there is to it. You want a rich husband. Nothing else?"

Nothing else. No deeper motivations. Or none that she could explain without sounding like a two-faced hypocrite. She had lied to her friend for months, and now it seemed easiest to maintain the facade.

Gold-digger Tara had finally scored the big prize.

For the second time in a week, Tara's heart broke.

Her friend looked so disappointed, but she quickly regrouped. "Okay! If this is what you want, then congratulations?"

Mia hugged her but there was a hesitancy to it.

Everything had changed, and not for the better.

AT 11:15 A.M., Fitz answered the door and immediately got an earful from a barking dog that set off his barking dog. Remy stood on his doorstep with a bundle of fur that should not be capable of decibel levels like this. Behind him stood Bren with his own dog, a friendly beast called Gretzy, and behind him was Dante with a stroller.

No text, no call, no warning.

This team was going to be the death of him. And this lot weren't even on the team!

"Merde, mon ami, you look like hell," Remy said.

Looking wasn't even half of it. Two thirds of a bottle of bourbon was never going to be good for his beauty regimen, and now his head pounded, insisting that he was too old for this shit.

"Like I said in the text, I wasn't feelin' so great. Sorry I missed breakfast."

"Which is why we brought it to you." Bren held up a box of Ann Sather cinnamon rolls, which meant he'd gone into the city to get them. At least a ten-mile drive there, so now Fitz was obligated to be polite.

"Fuckers," he muttered, which made Remy laugh knowingly.

Fitz blocked Goober with his foot so he wasn't tempted to make a waddle for it. "Are your dogs gonna be trouble?"

"Nah, this puppy is so well-behaved." The little terrier mix sniffed Goober's butt and headed into the house, soon to be followed by Gretzy, rocking an air of elder statesman.

Bren helped Dante with the stroller, and then the proud papa took the baby into his arms.

"You okay, tesora?" Dante asked little Rosie, who was dressed in a little dress that made her look like a ladybug. All of seven months and commanding rooms.

Rosie gurgled her assent and gave a big gummy smile that lifted Fitz's heart.

"Come on through."

The troupe followed Fitz into the kitchen.

"So, O'Malley gettin' hitched?" Remy started because Fitz's hangover wasn't bad enough. "Didn't see that coming."

Fitz grabbed the coffee filters and started measuring out the grounds. "It's certainly good for the team's image." Sophie had sent him updates last night on the social media metrics. *Through the roof* was the term used.

He might have spent a little too long examining the photo of Tara accepting O'Malley's ring, searching for clues to her state of mind. She had looked stunned, and stunningly beautiful, even in that absurd mascot costume. There was video, but he couldn't bring himself to watch. Something too damn real about it.

"Yeah, amazing," Bren muttered.

Fitz daggered a look his way. "Something to say, St. James?"

"Just that I admire your dedication to the team above your own needs."

"Might be the first time someone in this org has actually thought of the team first," Dante said as he claimed a seat at the kitchen table and settled his daughter into his lap.

"Now, hold on," Remy said. "If you recall, I had a chance to trade out of this loser team my first season, but I stayed—for the team."

"You stayed for Harper." Bren started rooting around in cupboards until he found plates for the cinnamon rolls. "It so happened the team's needs corresponded with your own."

"Oui, oui," the Cajun conceded. "The question is whether O'Malley and Tara gettin' married is good for the team—"

"Certainly good for PR," Dante commented.

"At the expense of a broken heart, though?" Remy added, like Fitz wasn't even here.

Four sets of eyes—even Rosie was getting in on the act—turned to Fitz.

He stopped mid-scoop. "Broken heart? Bruised ego, perhaps. Very different animal."

"You missed breakfast," Bren said. "You couldn't even muddle through a few eggs and a cup of coffee in public."

"Christ—"

"Uh, do you mind?" Dante gestured to his smiling daughter. "Impressionable ears."

"Yeah, Gretzy hates that sort of language, too," Bren said as he sliced into and separated one gooey roll from the grid of gooey rolls and deposited it on a plate.

Fitz shoved the filter basket into the maker and pressed the ON switch. "Let me explain it to you knuckleheads in language you might understand. I don't have any say over what Tara does. She's a free agent."

"Though I'm guessing you wish she wasn't," Dante said as he rose from the chair. "Could you hold her a second? I need to wash my hands."

"Sure." Fitz took the baby into his arms, enjoying the weight and warmth and sheer vitality. With her perfect blue eyes, she watched him carefully. "You're gonna break so many hearts, Rosie."

He sighed and switched the baby to his shoulder, patting her on the back. "I can't go into the exact details, but the bottom line is that Tara has good reasons—or what she thinks are good reasons—for hitching her star to O'Malley."

"Yeah, he's young and good lookin' and about to have his contract extended," Remy muttered as he grabbed cups. "Hard to compete. But hell, you've got to take your shot, man."

Fitz met their searching gazes, his heart beating in time with the drip-drip-drip of the coffee maker. Bren moved to the counter to grab a cup but ended up squeezing Fitz's shoulder instead.

"She turned you down?"

"She turned me down."

Dante was drying his hands. "Fuck, no."

"Uh, impressionable ears." Fitz rubbed Rosie's back. "So that's that. I'm ridin' the pine. Hell, I'm not even on the roster. I don't think he can make her happy, but this is her choice." Fitz inhaled the baby's scent, seeking the magic bullet of calm, then switched her to the crook of his arm so he could see her beautiful face. "And we have to respect women's choices, don't we, button?"

"If one of my girls said she wanted to marry a dickhead like O'Malley, I'd have something to say," Bren said around his cinnamon roll chewing. "It's not always as simple as choice. If you love her ..." Bren sniffed. "You do love her, don't you?"

"I do."

Dante asked, "And you told her that?"

"Not in so many words."

Remy shook his head. "What did you tell her?"

"That this—us—felt right and I wanted to explore it. I knew I loved her, but there was all this other stuff in the way, and it seemed like I was treading through mud just trying to get her to accept the possibility of us as a real couple. She didn't trust the emotion, the connection. She thinks it can't last, that I'd be compromising when nothing could be further from the truth. But I was so mad at her that I couldn't get any of that out. And by the time I'd calmed down, she was accepting O'Malley's ring in front of thousands of people and millions online. This is what she wants ..."

"What she thinks she wants," Remy said definitively.

"I'm not going to second-guess her choice here. She's an adult. I could talk to her, but this is something she needs to work out for herself. I just have to hope she'll get there in the end."

"And if she doesn't?" Dante asked.

I may never recover. "Then the team has just scored another PR coup with the wedding of the century."

~

TARA STEPPED into the lobby of Misty Pines and got the shock of her life.

"Mom! What are you doing here?"

"Can't a mother come see her daughter?" Monica added quickly, "Daughters?"

Tara blew out a breath as awareness hit her with a two by four. "You heard I got engaged."

"Heard? I saw! I always knew you'd come up trumps, baby." She held Tara's chin, her eyes sparkling with the glitter of misplaced pride. "That pretty face of yours can't have been for nothing."

Monica Becker, now Galliano, looked good, if a little weathered by the Florida sun. She'd always gone to substantial lengths to maintain a youthful appearance. Botox, lip plumpers, the odd tuck here and there—you name it, her mother had done it. All tools to maintain her edge in the fight against time, poverty, and irrelevance.

"Mom, I'm here to see Chloe. She's expecting me."

"I know, I know. I'm here for Chloe, too. For both of my girls."

Tara didn't like this one bit. Monica hadn't seen Chloe in a couple of years, hadn't even answered her texts about her recent illness.

Her mom waved at the reception. "They wouldn't let me in. I thought I was on the list of approved visitors, though why I'd need to be on some list, I don't know. I'm her mother."

"They have to be careful. It's for Chloe's protection."

"She doesn't need protection from me."

Tara didn't comment on that, or rather let silence be her response. She sat in the lobby seat, the same seat where a week ago she'd had that blow-up with Hale. When she refused his help because his kindness had scared the living daylights out of her.

Scared away all common sense, too.

Here she was with a ring on her finger and a hot hunk for a fiancé. Every hope, wish, and dream was coming true, all that work paying off. Yet she had never felt more unlike herself than she did at this moment.

"Let's talk first before we go in."

Monica grimaced and checked her manicure. "If you like." She took a seat beside Tara and grasped for her hand. "Let's see the rock, then! Oh, that's very nice. Two carats?"

"Two and a half."

Monica maneuvered Tara's hand so the diamond caught a shaft of light from the lobby's window. "You've done well for yourself, baby. Chip off the old block."

Tara drew back her hand. Disgust shuddered through her, and not just with her mother. "How is Rocky? Is he with you?"

"No, he's off fishing with his buddies. Every weekend he's off somewhere. But it suits us! Just like you and Dex. All those away trips will do wonders for your marriage. No need to be in each other's pockets, getting on each other's nerves, opening up cracks. That's never good for a relationship."

"How would you know?" Her mother was on Husband No. 4. She'd yet to perfect the formula.

Monica glossed over that. "Once you're settled, you're bound to be lonely with Dex on the road so much. I can come stay, maybe even help with a baby. You really should get working on that, the sooner the better. That way, if anything goes wrong, you still have an—"

"Anchor?"

Her mother smirked. "If that's what you want to call it. Maybe don't use that terminology around Dex. Men are very sensitive about that kind of thing. A baby will be the clincher for your security."

Yesterday, Tara had told Dex about Chloe. He'd been surprised but supportive, even said he wanted to meet her.

It was the best possible outcome. Another check in the column.

Her life reduced to ticks in a ledger.

She could have brought Dex today, but something had felt off about it. Introducing him to her sister seemed like the last link in a chain that tied her to the wrong person forever.

"I'm not sure I'm ready for a child." An image of Hale holding little Rosie at Erik's party popped into her head. He'd be so good at it—and now that his work woes were under control, he could focus on his personal life. Find someone suitable to settle down with, knock her up with a perfect bundle of joy, live happily ever after ...

"Well, you'd better get ready for one! There are no guarantees. Look at me—I thought your father would stick around after that one night, but I chose a loser and he bailed. The thing with you and Dex is he can't bail, and even if he does, he has to support you or the court of public opinion will crush him. You've made a great score here. You're set for life!"

Tara's heart was beating too fast, her skin itching with panic. She fisted both hands to minimize the shakes.

"I left a message with you a few weeks ago about Chloe. She had bronchitis and had to be hospitalized."

Her mother blinked at the abrupt change in conversation. "I know that. I called here and the staff said she was fine."

If Tara asked the staff to check the call logs, would she

find a confirmation? "You didn't return my call, though. You didn't ask me if she was okay."

"I was in Atlantic City with the girls for Anthea's divorce party. God, the settlement was a mess—he fought her tooth and nail for the house in Cabo. Things got a bit crazy and I meant to call back, but you had it under control, right? This is why you became her guardian, baby. So you could be in charge!"

Tara placed both hands in her lap. "You could have visited your oldest daughter at any time in the last few weeks. But as soon as you hear I'm engaged, you show your face?"

Monica's expression flickered between cunning and blankness. Was that what Tara looked like when she spoke about her grand plans to score a pro-athlete? Hard and grasping.

I'm not her. I won't be her.

Yet, she was following the blueprint this woman had outlined. Marry well, and if it didn't work out, move on to the next sucker. Tara might claim she had her sister's best interests at heart, but did the end justify the means? If she continued with this strategy, she would never be happy.

She wanted that. Or at the very least, she wanted a shot at it.

"I'd like you to leave."

Monica blinked in surprise. "Leave? I just got here."

"Go back to Florida, Mom, and don't come to visit unless you clear it with me first. I won't be adding you to any approved list for Chloe, and I won't be inviting you to the wedding."

Because there likely wouldn't be one.

"Tara! What has gotten into you?"

Tara hauled in a breath. "I don't want you here. If you

truly want to see Chloe, I'll allow it. But then you have to leave."

The mask fell away, revealing her mother's true self. Rapacious and greedy.

"Are you suddenly too good for your momma now that you're floating about with the rich and famous? You were always trouble, always ungrateful, after everything I did to make sure you had the best life." She stood, smoothed her skirt. "This is the thanks I get?"

"Like I said, you can see Chloe as long as you run it by me first. But you and I don't have a relationship, Mom. You let me down when I was a kid. The opinion of your latest husband mattered more than the welfare of your children. Sure I acted out and gave you a fair share of heartache, but I was suffering. Mostly because of how you treated me.

"But really I can't forgive what you did to Chloe. How you abandoned your flesh and blood. I know it was hard for you—I've spent time in your shoes and it's back-breaking work sometimes—but you haven't been a mom to either of us for some time and you can't start now. Not that I think you truly want that because your timing in showing up here as soon as I have a rock the size of a planet on my finger is suspicious, to say the least."

"You little bitch," Monica spat.

"One with more maternal instincts than you." She picked up her purse and stood, ready to head in to see her sister. "This bitch wants you gone, but I'll let you see your daughter, if you still want that."

Her mother merely stared, and before Tara could walk away, she headed out the door.

32

———

MAKING amends and atoning for her sins was something Tara Becker thought she had a handle on. After all, she'd spent much of the previous two years working her butt off to put herself in a position to be everything that Chloe needed.

Only in doing so, she'd hurt other people.

She'd hurt herself.

Now she had to put some of that right.

Hudson exited the locker room after practice and leaned in for a hug. She held him tight, glad to have comfort from someone whose life she had yet to screw up.

"You recovered from Sunday?" she asked. A few days ago, he'd done the Polar Plunge, a jump into a frigid Lake Michigan for charity, with a few of the Rebels.

"Barely." He blew out a breath. "I ran into someone I know and as you can guess, not the best timing."

"Shrinkage? Hard to come back from that."

He chuckled, but it was nervy. Before she could probe more, Dex appeared behind him.

"Hey, beautiful!" He leaned in to kiss her, and she turned

so he could buss her cheek. Anything else felt like she was cheating on Hale.

Hale who had jumped into online dating quicker than a quick swipe right.

Yet letting Dex put that ring on her finger was worse. How had she allowed her hurting heart to make that decision for her? So Hale was dating—good for him! More important, at one time he had thought Tara was worth considering for his arm candy. So they wouldn't have gone the distance, but she'd never forget that for a moment in time, he'd wanted her enough to think it might be a good idea.

Maybe she wasn't so undeserving after all.

She and Hale didn't have a future, but she might find someone nice, who liked her for ... well, her.

Before she could take those next steps, she needed to talk to Dex.

"Hud, let's connect later. I want to hear about what happened." She gave him a knowing eyebrow. "Maybe at Cal and Mia's party?"

"Sure." He headed off as Tara turned to Dex. "Could I bend your ear for a second?"

"Sure."

She led him to the yoga room and closed the door behind them.

He rubbed a hand over his chin. "This isn't good news, is it?"

She took off the engagement ring and placed it in his palm. "It's a lovely ring. And you're a great guy. But I don't love you, Dex. I'm sorry."

He frowned. "I thought you didn't believe in all that."

"I thought so, too. But it seems I do. I want that."

A range of emotions danced over his handsome features.

He clasped her hand to his chest. "How about we have a long engagement? Get to know each other and see if it could work out? We're good together, Tara."

"How are we good together?"

Surprise at being put on the spot crossed his brow. "You're gorgeous and you know hockey. You know tons of stuff, like how the world works. And you're great with people. You know how they tick and how to make them feel good about themselves. All the guys like you. When I was with you, I felt like I could do anything."

"You *can* do anything, Dex. You have so much talent, more than I have in my little fingernail. You just need to listen to people around you who have been doing this for a while. The veteran players and the management who know their shit. You'll learn so much if you just open your ears. And you'll find someone who wants to listen to what you had for lunch yesterday."

He blew out a breath. "Knew you were tuning me out."

"Only because I can't eat that many carbs, and hearing someone else detail all that delicious pasta is tough on me!"

Chuckling, he grasped both her hands. "You sure about this? I think we'd be great in—" He checked himself. He had been about to say "in the sack," the little rascal. "Great in general. I didn't even get a chance to show you just how great." Cheeky wink.

"I'll survive, Dex. Let's keep some mystery." She put her arms around him and gave him a hug. "Thanks for thinking enough of me to pop the question. It was so nice to be the center of someone's world for a moment."

He gave a glum nod, but she suspected his ill humor wouldn't last. Dex and his bruised ego would be at the club before the night was through, reveling in relief at being let off the leash. She'd have to call Sophie and give her a heads up.

First, she needed to get some coffee.

MIA WAS ALREADY SEATED at their usual spot when Tara arrived. She raised a cup, indicating that she'd already ordered on Tara's behalf.

That gave her a spark of hope.

"Hey, thanks for this."

"No problem. I was so glad you called."

Tara gusted a sigh. "Really? Because I know things have been weird between us. I also know that it's my fault."

Mia looked miserable. "No, it's not. Well, maybe a little. I think I reacted badly to you and Dex because I felt so out of the loop. I expect to be informed at all times! Really, you're not obliged to tell me anything. I wasn't the chattiest when I was going through my stuff last year."

"But if I was a real friend to you, I would have told you everything." She sipped her coffee, using the moment to center herself. "If you have a minute, I'd like to spill."

Her friend looked like she was bracing herself for Tara's tale of woe. "I'm ready."

Deep breath. "Okay. First, you should know that there will not be a double wedding in July. You're heading down that aisle alone, friend."

Mia's mouth dropped open. "You mean—"

"I called it off with Dex."

"Oh, Tara!" Mia grasped Tara's arm and leaned across the table for an awkward half-hug that Tara sank into as best she could. "Are you okay?"

"Nope. But breaking it off was the right thing to do. It

was a knee-jerk reaction to hearing Hale was dating. So stupid and short-sighted." She sighed. "And I'm sorry about our weird argument that wasn't an argument but felt like one. You're right. I have been hiding things. I haven't been truthful, with you or with myself."

"Okay." Mia was staring at her, her eyes filled with such love and compassion that words Tara intended to speak calmly came out in a gush.

"I have a sister! Her name's Chloe and she has some developmental and physical disabilities and she's the love of my life. She's in a residential home and it's round-the-clock and she loves it, so this is the place for her. But it's not cheap. There's some aid, but to make sure she has the best care, I needed money. And I wanted to tell you, but I didn't want you to think we were friends because of the money thing." Tears spilled down her cheeks. "When I became friends with you, it was because I liked talking to you. You didn't think I was out of my tree after the whole bouquet thing—or at least you didn't show it. And you wanted to get Tommy Gordon and I wanted to help. Maybe a part of me thought I could win back Cal, but that didn't last long, not when I saw how good you guys were together. And then you and I were friends, and I had this secret, and revealing it would mean I looked like a mercenary. Which apparently I can be when it comes to husbands, but not when it comes to friends. The longer I left it, the harder it was to tell you. Hale said I should trust that you're my friend. He was right. He was right about a lot of things and I think I really hurt him. Or maybe not, because he jumped right onto dating, the dick! So much for a broken heart."

And so much for Tara taking the high road and accepting Hale's decision to move on.

"Uh huh," Mia said, and that was about the wisest *uh huh* Tara had ever heard.

She swallowed, thought on it for a second, then came up with some wisdom of her own. "Do you think he did that because I told him I wasn't interested?"

"She's getting warmer. Also, Dex might have dropped some knowledge about you two dating officially after the fake thing ended. Sophie filled me in there and she said that Fitz was pissed, which she could tell because he was sending Dex to an early grave with death squinting during a meeting. I guess our fearless leader is not the only one who responds to news like that with a spot of revenge-dating. Dummies, both of you."

Tara sniffed. "But this isn't about Hale and me. It's about you and me, and how much I love you. Mia, please forgive me."

Her lovely, amazing friend swiped away a silvery tear. "There's nothing to forgive! I should have asked more questions, tried to get to the bottom of it. Hell, I didn't find out you cut hair until we had been friends for months and you kept making those passive-aggressive comments about my split ends. You are quite the cagey chick, but it's your business. You don't have to tell me anything." She smiled. "But I'm glad you did. I'm so glad to hear about Chloe, and it sounds like she's the luckiest girl in the world to have you as her sister. Now how can I help?"

Tara's heart exploded. What had she done to deserve this sweet person in her life? "Just by being my friend. I don't want your money, I swear. I'll figure something out. I always do."

"So, you needed a rich husband to foot the bill."

"I can't believe I thought this was a good idea. I had convinced myself that I was living in an episode of *Real*

Housewives and that this was a valid strategy to get ahead. I thought that ensuring Chloe's security would lift the weight off, and that once I felt lighter, I'd feel happier. Instead I made a mess of it. I hurt Dex, though I'm hopeful that we weren't together long enough to do much damage."

Mia cocked her head. "And Fitz?"

Tara let out a low groan then face-planted on the table.

Mia patted Tara's head affectionately. It felt so nice. "He knew your drink. The martini."

Tara peeked up. "I know."

"Your coffee one, too. I think he told Dex what it was that day we all met here for your first fake date."

She had suspected as much but she didn't dare put any stock into it. "He's thoughtful like that. He tried to help with Chloe. Pay for her fees. That's what we fought about."

Mia's eyes lit up. "Wow."

"Uh huh. And I told him I didn't want his help. Not only that, but that his introduction of filthy money to the situation had tainted everything between us. I was so awful to him."

"Oh, Tara."

"Right. Oh, Tara." She lifted her head from what was likely a germ-riddled surface. "I thought he was interfering —okay, so he was—but he was doing it with good intentions. Yet all I could see was that I would owe him. That this sweet, precious, amazing thing we'd created now had a price on it. As you've probably figured out now, I have some hang-ups about my self-worth. And I know you tried to tell me to wait for the one. It's just I never thought I deserved that."

"Everyone deserves that. In fact, assume that as read, my wooly-headed friend." Mia squeezed her hand. "More to the point, do you think Fitz deserves you? Because you are such a great catch and he would be so lucky to have you."

Tara shut her eyes, wishing she could open them and find herself back in Hale's arms before she'd screwed everything up. Why didn't they have time travel yet? Probably because she had to sink this low, make all the mistakes, before she could realize how foolish she had been.

"I do. I want him so much, but I'm not sure he could forgive me. I've spent the last month dating one guy and falling in love with another. That's pretty messed up."

"You never slept with Dex, though?" Mia scrunched up her face, ready for bad news.

"No, I'm not total trash, thank God. Barely kissed him, which was kind of like kissing a brother. So weird. But it doesn't matter because Hale has moved on."

Mia bit her lip. "Ken said he was dating. Which app?"

Tara hadn't dared to look.

"I don't think I want to know. Seeing him out there looking for someone who's not me might destroy what little sanity I have left. If I was to talk to him, I wouldn't even know where to start. How to convince him that he's, well, my world?" She held her friend's compassionate gaze. "How could Hale trust a word out of my mouth when I've been lying to everyone, including myself, for so long?"

Tonight the Empty Net was closed for a special event: a celebration of Mia and Cal's engagement. Fitz expected that would be a joint celebration now that Tara had landed her big fish.

All he needed to do was show his face and wish the couple well.

Maybe both couples well.

That would be tough. But he was an adult and the better

man had won … and if he believed that then he needed to have his head examined.

The first person he met on the way in was Tara. Because, of course.

"Hale! Hi!"

He fisted a hand so as not to touch her. "Tara. Congratulations."

She looked gorgeous and perky and bright-eyed and had she been crying and he was this close to killing O'Malley and fuck, this would not do.

"Are you okay?"

"Could we talk?" She placed her hand over his curled up one. So soft. The things her hand could do. Had done. Holding it was the best thing to happen to him since the last time she touched him.

He tore his hand away. "Might be better if we didn't. I'm really not good company right now, and I kind of need to keep my cool for Mia and Cal so I don't look like a sore loser. I realize you made the choice that made the most sense to you. I get it. I just can't pretend to like it."

Her eyes welled. "Okay. So, are-are you dating someone?"

Christ, did he have to run this by her? "I can't get into this with you. I really should just say my piece to the happy couple."

She blocked his path, a nice check that wouldn't have looked out of place on the rink. "My mom showed up at Misty Pines."

"What?"

"Yeah, just appeared out of nowhere. I've left messages for her about my sister's illness and nothing. But once I get engaged on national TV, she comes crawling out of the woodwork."

"Christ, Tara, that's harsh. I'm sorry you had to go through that."

"Um, I'm not. Because it made me realize a few things. About bad precedents and patterns and how tunnel-visioned it's possible to be. How absurdly dangerous that is." She stared up at him with those big green eyes. "I told my mother not to bother visiting again. It was quite … liberating. But as I was listening to her, I started to realize how I was treading in her dark shadow. How I wanted to escape that and go into the light. Which sounds like I want to pass through to the other side like in *Poltergeist* or something. That's not what I mean." She inhaled with effort. "What I'm trying to say—very inadequately—is that with you I felt bathed in light and sun. I felt both free and safe, and I'm so grateful to know you. To have known you."

She moved in closer and he almost buckled at her proximity. In heels, she came up to his chin and she kissed him on the cheek. "Thanks for looking out for me."

His heart softened.

No, it melted into glue.

"Always." No point in hiding it. He was a fool for this woman.

She wiped away a tear and it took all his strength not to kiss it better.

"I don't think I got that before, or even understood it was possible for someone as real and smart and amazing as you to care about someone like me. You're one in a million, Hale, and I think you're going to get snatched up very quickly on that dating app."

Good to hear. Fantastic.

"By the way, I'm no longer engaged to Dex."

His heart jumped out of his chest. "Tara, did you just say—"

"I broke it off with him. It was all wrong and I don't even know why I said yes. Well, that's not true. I'd pushed you away and thought you were moving on, dating and carpe-ing the fucking diem and all that. You were actually taking my advice to get out there. Listening to something I said for once!" She sniffled and pinned on a smile that made her look like she was about to kill someone on the cheerleader clown squad.

"Are you telling me you and O'Malley are finished?" He looked down at her left hand.

No ring.

No fucking ring.

"I'm telling you we never started. Except for the engage-ment, but that was it." *That was it?* She looked around. "Lis-ten, I need to do a host thing. And while I'm doing that, maybe you can check the Perfect Match dating app. See what your options are."

"My options?"

She smiled. "Yeah, and we can run through them after. I promised I'd help you find someone, remember?"

Stunned, he could only nod.

With a watery smile, Tara moved to the center of the bar and stood on a chair. "Hey, everyone, can I have your attention?"

Raised off the ground, wobbly on heels, Fitz had an amazing view of her legs, barely covered by a short skirt. As usual his eyes were magnetized to her, and not just because she was beautiful and sexy. Sure, she was all that, but his soul recognized another seeking to connect.

He prayed he was still in with a chance to make her his.

She waved her hands, asking for quiet.

"Thanks so much to you all for coming tonight to cele-brate Mia's gold medal—woo hoo!—and her engagement to

Cal. I only wish I could have been in Beijing in person to see all of it go down, but I know lots of you were there and made the proposal so, so special." Foreman and Mia stood off to the side, grinning like lovesick fools. "These two are made for each other, and I'm so happy to have had a teensy-weensy part in bringing them together. Now, if only I had a bouquet to throw."

Everyone laughed with her. But then that was Tara, the funniest, kindest, sweetest, most irritating woman he knew.

"To the best people in the world, Mia and Cal!"

The crowd echoed the toast. Somehow a flute of champagne had made it to his hand and Fitz raised his arm in a daze, muscle memory kicking in when a celebration was happening.

She's no longer engaged to O'Malley.

A crowd of admirers had gathered around her and several (male) hands were thrusting forward, eager to guide her from chair to floor. No sign of O'Malley, and Fitz had to say he couldn't blame him. He wouldn't want to watch Tara as she fluttered her eyelashes at other men and smiled at the idiots who thought they had a shot with her.

Well, he wouldn't if he had a single doubt about her intentions.

Over here, Tarabell. Look this way.

She blinked at one of her many admirers and turned her head enough to meet his gaze. Those green eyes gleamed, her luscious lips curved, and the slightest shoulder hitch let him know she had this.

A modern Disney princess with her own plan. The million dollar question: did it include him?

His phone pinged with another notification from Perfect Match. Usually he would ignore it, but something about what Tara had said nagged at him.

He checked, and Christ, it was worth it.

"*I'm a girl who loves hockey, family, travel, and a hearty beef stew. I like my coffee with oat milk, my martinis with extra Chambord, and my pillow talk with a side of current affairs. Full disclosure: I've been told I'm kind of extra and hard to handle. But if you're up for the challenge, so am I.*"

"She's something else, isn't she?"

Fitz didn't want to miss a second of Tara, and not even Bastian Durand could sway him. Without sliding a glance his way, Fitz declared, "She's taken."

"Last I heard, she's a free agent."

"You heard wrong."

Durand let out a soft chuckle. "Okay, got it. Speaking of free agency, if you have a second, we should talk about next season."

"Later, Durand. I have something I need to take care of."

He stepped forward just as Tara did, discarding her multiple hangers-on like dirty laundry.

"Do you have time to talk, Ms. Becker?"

"For you, General, always."

She took his hand and led him away.

Everyone noticed.

Good. Let them see that the digger had struck gold and her shovel was back in the toolshed. All eyes watched their progression through the crowd as they traveled down the corridor heading to the restrooms, then into a back office.

With the door closed, she stepped back, her expression one of worry. "I-I need to ask you something."

"Okay."

"Why did you want to pay for Chloe's fees? Really?"

He rubbed his mouth. "Really? Well, I told myself I wanted to remove the ticking time bomb from the equation. If you didn't have that obligation like a monkey on your back, then maybe it would clear your mind and give you some breathing space. Help you make a decision that didn't have money as a crucial component." He took a breath. "Now for the truth, which isn't nearly so noble. I wanted to eliminate O'Malley and any other guy from competition. I wanted to slay your dragons and show you that I could provide. Then you might view me as a viable candidate."

Her mouth formed an O. "Viable candidate for—"

"Mr. Tara Becker."

"Oh my God."

He nodded. "Honey, I wanted to fix it. All of it. But now I realize that it came off as no better than me trying to buy my way into your life. Not the classiest move."

"I didn't think you were doing that, but I did think that introducing it into our relationship would ruin what we had. The friendship we had. And I couldn't allow myself to see further than that because if I did, it would break my heart."

"Tarabell—"

She waved in front of her face. "Please, let me get this out before I lose it. I was already so in love with you, which was the worst possible outcome because I didn't think you could want me like that. I didn't think this chemistry between us could last, and in the meantime, you would be wasting your time with someone like me."

She loved him? He ran his hands over her upper arms, noting her chill. Off came his jacket, which he caped over those beautiful shoulders, an original itch scratched at last. In the only chair available, he sat and brought her onto his lap.

"You were saying? Something about me wasting my time with someone like you."

She snuggled into him. "I didn't think I was good enough for you. Classic self-esteem issues, y'know."

"And now?"

She raised her head. "I'm always going to have doubts. And if I was to disappoint you …"

"Can we be honest with each other, Tara? Let's talk about what we both want. I'll start."

She nodded, her eyes soft with tears.

"I want to wake up next to someone who thinks I'm the center of her world. Who cares about people, is kind at heart, who has opinions and knows what she wants, whether that's a half oat milk-half skim caramel macchiato or a guy who can give her multiple orgasms. I want a family and I think you want that, too, but you've been so focused on atoning for Chloe that you thought you didn't deserve it. That you didn't deserve happiness for yourself. Well, you do. And I'm best placed to give you that. I get you. I know what's happening inside that pretty little head of yours. I know your game and I'm here to tell you that you've won. So have you checked that app yet?"

"I-I haven't had a chance to because every moment since you walked in here has been spent with you or looking at you or thinking about you. I've barely had a chance to breathe. You make it hard for me to fill my lungs." Her lips curled. "Did we match?"

"We did. We so fucking did. Now tell me if you want your prize."

She placed her hands on his shoulders and drew back. For a moment he worried she might scramble off his lap, hand off his jacket, and tell him no deal.

"Remind me of the prize again?"

"This old heart of mine."

She swallowed audibly, sniffed a little, and swiped at her welling eyes. "It might be too valuable."

"Ain't worth a damn without the woman who owns it."

"Really?"

He nodded. "Really. But I need to know what you want, Tara."

"What I want." She drew a shallow breath. "It's been so long since I've thought about that, I mean, the fundamentals of it instead of the surface stuff. But with you, it's all I think about. Mostly in the context of wishing and hoping and dreaming—you know like the song—because I didn't think it could ever happen. But the minute I said yes to Dex, I knew that was all wrong. I knew you were the one I wanted, the one I dreamed of and hoped for, before I even met you. This dream guy who would understand me and what I had to offer. My Disney prince. I'd closed off that part of myself for so long, and it took all those precious moments with you to unlock my heart and take it out of that box I'd placed it in all those years ago. I'm only sorry I had to cause you any pain. The whole Dex thing, please forgive me." She let out a little sob that cracked his heart. "I thought you'd given up on me. Kennedy said you were dating."

As if he could hold that against her. "Honey, you were hurtin', too. Sure, I got as far as clicking a button in an app. Not quite the same as accepting a proposal—"

"Hale!" She buried her face in his neck, horrified by his teasing, while he chuckled evilly. "I said I was sorry. I love you so much, you've got to believe me."

"I believe you."

She drew back, her eyes wide and filled with love.

"Really?"

"Really."

She let out a breath of relief. "Now I'm not expecting a ring just yet. I know we need to do some work here first, but I want to do that work. I want to earn that heart you say belongs to me, not just get it as a gift."

That same heart was filling up, ready to burst. "You earn it with every look, every smile, every time you walk into the room or skate onto the rink or arrive late for a plane ride, Tarabell. All I need to know is that I'm the guy you want. That you want to create a good life with me. That you love me as much as I love you."

"I do, Hale. I so do."

"Then everything else will fall into place."

She frowned. "I know you'd like to think so, but we really should discuss the future. The nitty gritty. Can you see me as a mom? As the mother to your kids? I know that's important to you."

"Hell yeah, I can see it. I've seen you with Chloe, with my nieces, with Rebels spawn. You're going to make a great mom, and if that's what you want, I would be so proud if you bore my children."

She grinned. "Okay, then we'd better get cracking on that soon because while I've no doubt my eggs are ova-prime, sperm deteriorates with age ..." He gave her ass a light swat for her insolence. "Oh, don't get mad, babe, get bangin'. Let's make a little Hale or Tara."

The thought of filling this woman with his babies was turning him on big time. "Right now?"

A knock sounded and the door cracked a smidge. Tina, the Empty Net's owner, called out, "Tara? Someone said you're the only one who knows how the karaoke machine works. Can you help?"

"Be right out!" Tara kissed Hale sweetly, but he wasn't letting her get away with that. He cupped behind her head and held her in place for a thorough exploration with his tongue, his hands, and his heart.

A couple of minutes later, she blinked, her beautiful lips kiss-swollen, looking completely owned by his mouth.

By him.

"Foiled by karaoke. Guess that baby-making is going to have to wait." She clambered off him and held out her hand. "Come on, I think there's an ABBA tune with your name on it."

He doubted that, but who knew?

Tara Becker could probably convince him that anything was possible.

EPILOGUE

Tara loved a wedding.

She especially loved a wedding that featured two of her favorite people showing the world how perfect they were for each other.

"That's the twenty-somethingth time you've given that pretty little sigh." Hale pressed a strong hand to the small of her back and tightened her body against his as they took a turn on the dance floor. "Either you're satisfied with how this all turned out, or you're feelin' wistful."

She peered up at his far too handsome face. "I'm very satisfied. And wistful. All the hair looks great, so it's nice to see my influence. And these two crazy kids made it! How could I not love that?"

A year ago, she had thought she might be scooting toward the altar herself with the groom of this very wedding. What a messed up, wrong-headed, all-up-in-her-feelings woman she was! These past few months she had figured out a few things about herself, one of which was:

She wasn't just a nice body and great hair (though all those things were definite pluses in her favor). Tara actually had more to offer the world, and recognizing that was key to opening her heart to her closest friends and the man holding her so tight she knew he'd never let her go.

As the official hair stylist to the team, Tara had found a niche, even setting up her own mini-salon in the Rebels compound. She still had her trusty magic cape for on-the-spot trims, but Hale said she needed something a little more permanent and had made it happen. Having the ear of the players and the general manager meant she was uniquely placed to advise while she trimmed and sculpted. Of course she treated the client-stylist relationship as a priest would the confessional (*your penance is three Hail Marys and a deep conditioning mask, lol*). Creating that safe space was important to her.

As for her own safe space, it was here in Hale's arms. Chloe felt it too, instantly recognizing that he was one of the good 'uns. (It helped that her sister now had the best Disney princess collection in the Midwest, courtesy of the man himself.) What lucky girls they were to be sheltered by this man.

"Hey, looks like the bride is doing one of her bridal things," Hale murmured.

Sure enough, Mia was standing at one end of the dance floor in a Sadie Yates original with her bouquet in hand while a number of female guests clumped in readiness for this particular (and outdated?) tradition. As maid of honor, Tara had already held the bouquet during the ceremony—with a joking aside of "Finally!" when she took charge of it —and no way on God's green earth would she be reaching out to grasp this one. Those desperate days were long behind her.

Hale kissed her on the forehead. "Better get up there."

"I'm fine right here." She traced a finger along one of his

lapels. "I know I'll eventually lock you down. Good luck escaping my clutches."

She felt a tap on her shoulder, and when she turned, Mia was standing there with a big smile and glossy eyes.

"I don't think there's much point in throwing this, T."

Tara blinked at her friend, then at the bouquet she was holding like an offering. "What? Why not?"

"Because you're the person who deserves it most. And I was under strict instructions to make sure you, and only you, got it." A couple of women with stormy expressions stood off to the side, throwing daggered looks their way.

"Wait—what? Oh!"

Hale was on one knee with a raised eyebrow, an open ring box, and an awfully flashy diamond.

At someone else's wedding! Ooh, they'd be having words about this, for sure.

"Before you say he should not be upstaging the happy couple," Mia said, reading Tara's mind, "let me assure you that this is exactly what Cal and I want for you both."

Cal was there, too, with a huge smile on his face. "Take it, Tara. With our blessing."

Mia handed off the bouquet and squeezed her tight, then stood back to give Hale the space to make Tara's dreams come true.

Hale looked up at her. "Tarabell Becker, are you ready to be my princess?"

"Uh, hell, yeah."

Mia squealed and Hale stood, muttering something about his knee, and slid that ring on her finger, the perfect fit. Tara hugged Mia, then Cal, then what seemed like every player and player's better half, until finally Hale had to intervene and pull her away.

"I'd like to kiss my fiancée, please."

She giggled. "You have a lifetime of me all to yourself."

"Not enough," he said as his lips found hers. "Never enough." And when more people insisted on congratulating them—how dare they?—her fiancé—oh, she liked the sound of that—pulled her away to outside the marquee set up in the grounds of Chase Manor.

On the way, they ran into Dex with his plus one, a very buxom redhead.

He kissed Tara on the cheek. "Congrats. I'm really happy for you. You too, boss."

It could have been awkward, but Tara still gave Dex what he needed—a once-a-month trim and a sympathetic ear for his griping. The guy did not need an actual fiancée, though Red here looked a little moon-eyed and overly optimistic.

Not Tara's problem!

They murmured their thanks and headed through the tent flaps to the July afternoon sun.

Hale wrapped a strong arm around her. "Okay, aside from the peer pressure to say yes to a public proposal, how about you tell me how you really feel?"

"How I really feel? That this day couldn't get any more perfect. My friends tied the knot, my gorgeous man proposed, and the sun is shining. But ..."

"But?"

"I think I can improve on it. Maybe even bedazzle it. Can you keep a secret?"

Her guy eyed her with suspicion. "Probably not."

She took his hand and placed it on her stomach. "You sure?"

Hale had made her dream come true today, and in approximately seven and a half months, Tara would give him the one thing he wanted more than anything.

"Honey ..." He drew a sharp breath while his expression ran the gamut, from no-shit to absolute joy. Eyes misting over, he asked in an emotion-rusted voice, "Really?"

"Oh, yes. Looks like that powerful sperm of yours hit the target, and there I was, thinking it would *struggggle* ..."

He spun her around, kissing away her insolence and lifting her into a cloud of ecstasy. "You've made me so happy, Tara, more than I ever imagined possible."

"Right back at ya, General."

ACKNOWLEDGMENTS

Thank you to my editor, Kristi Yanta - this one was a doozy! As usual you steered the ship away from the rocks to a safe harbor. I couldn't do this without you.

Thanks also to copyeditor Kim Cannon and proofreader Julia Griffis. Your attention to detail saves my blushes every time.

To my cover designer Michele Catalano Creative, my gratitude knows no bounds. So this one wasn't as chesty as our usual but it's still as hot :)

Thanks to the kittens for all your support. Here we are on the thirteenth Rebels book - can you believe it? Your excitement about this band of brothers keeps me going. I have more stories to tell, so I hope you stick with me.

To my agent, Nicole Resciniti, thanks for another great year.

And finally, to Jimmie — we did it! We're on the grand adventure and I'm so happy to be traveling this road with you. Onward to the next port!

ABOUT THE AUTHOR

Originally from Ireland, *USA Today* bestselling author Kate Meader cut her romance reader teeth on Maeve Binchy and Jilly Cooper novels, with some Harlequins thrown in for variety. Give her tales about brooding mill owners, over-sexed equestrians, and men who can rock an apron, a fire hose, or a hockey stick, and she's there. Now based in Chicago, she writes sexy contemporary featuring strong heroes and amazing women and men who can match their guys quip for quip.

ALSO BY KATE MEADER

Rookie Rebels

GOOD GUY

INSTACRUSH

MAN DOWN

FOREPLAYER

DEAR ROOMIE

REBEL YULE

JOCK WANTED

SUPERSTAR

WILD RIDE

Chicago Rebels

IN SKATES TROUBLE

IRRESISTIBLE YOU

SO OVER YOU

UNDONE BY YOU

HOOKED ON YOU

WRAPPED UP IN YOU

Hot in Chicago Rookies

COMING IN HOT

UP IN SMOKE

DOWN IN FLAMES

HOT TO THE TOUCH

Laws of Attraction

DOWN WITH LOVE

ILLEGALLY YOURS

THEN CAME YOU

Hot in Chicago

REKINDLE THE FLAME

FLIRTING WITH FIRE

MELTING POINT

PLAYING WITH FIRE

SPARKING THE FIRE

FOREVER IN FIRE

Tall, Dark, and Texan

EVEN THE SCORE

TAKING THE SCORE

ONE WEEK TO SCORE

For updates, giveaways, and new release information,
sign up for Kate's newsletter at katemeader.com

www.ingramcontent.com/pod-product-compliance
Lightning Source LLC
Chambersburg PA
CBHW030708190726
48286CB00001B/230